I0565200

BANTAN INCREDIBLE

By

MAURICE B. GARDNER

With jacket and six full-page illustrations
by DAVID PROSSER

WILDSIDE PRESS

Dedicated to

STANLEIGH B. VINSON

and

JOHN HARWOOD

CONTENTS

LIST OF ILLUSTRATIONS

BANTAN INCREDIBLE

BANTAN INCREDIBLE

CHAPTER I

A STRANGE ISLAND

A nearly naked bronzed giant knelt in a canoe which he propelled with a sturdy paddle across the undulating surface of the mighty Pacific Ocean on this late afternoon. He was handsome with muscles rippling his smooth skin. His shock of dark hair was pushed back in a crude pompadour fashion, revealing a broad, unseamed forehead above dark eyes that now smouldered because of his seething thoughts. This individual was Bantan—upon a new adventure in his quest for Amar, who was indirectly responsible for the death of Nao, his Amo Island sweetheart. In addition, certain insults to himself had been perpetrated, and these must be avenged. This injustice coursed through his mind—his score to settle with the Amo Island prince—if he were to be found.

While he cogitated thusly the young giant's seemingly blazing eyes did not notice the changing atmosphere. There was something eerie and ominous about the pall that settled upon the ocean surface. Suddenly, without warning, about a hundred yards ahead, there was to be heard an awesome, whining sound. A curious facial expression supplanted the other as Bantan saw a dark, cone-shaped object that seemingly appeared from nowhere. It was connected to a large, purplish cloud and stretched from the heaven to the very surface of the water. Where the mouth of the cone

11

touched, there was a mighty effervescence. He instantly ceased paddling and braked the canoe to a stop. Momentarily he wondered if some monster of the deep was about to surface. He watched the water boil and foam madly for fully a minute and then his eyes followed the cone-shaped object to the upper end above which an ominous cloud hovered.

The churning water rose upward quickly in a column fully ten feet in diameter to a distance of fifty feet in height. It was directly in line with the setting sun. The young giant could only stare at it in silent wonder. He had heard tales from the Beneiro warriors of such a phenomenon occurring at intervals, but this was the first time he had witnessed such an unexplained occurrence of this nature.

For ten minutes the geyser-like column of water spouted unabatedly, accompanied by the whining sound. And then the watcher noticed the suction in the heaven must apparently be lessening. Gradually, as the minutes passed, the awesome sound subsided and the dark, cone-shaped object faded. The column of water lowered at last, and the surface, except for myriads of sparkling bubbles, was as serene as before the unexpected phenomenon had occurred.

Shaking his head as though in disbelief at what he had witnessed, Bantan once again resumed paddling the canoe. He was careful to skirt the particular place where the waterspout had been seen, as though to avoid a possible recurrence. In a vague way he wondered what his reaction would have been had his canoe been passing and the waterspout occurred directly beneath him. He shrugged his shoulders noncommittally.

In these last minutes of daylight following the sun's setting, the bronzed giant's paddle strokes seemingly increased despite his tiring arms. His dark eyes intently searched the western horizon for possible sight of an island. Multicolored clouds of varying shape and description in the heaven above where the sun had sunk beneath the waterline were beautiful beyond compare. No bird winged lazily in the stillness of the early evening.

As the shadow of night swiftly advanced over the immensity of the mighty Pacific Ocean just below the equator, the paddler's keen eyes never left the horizon. The thought that he would be compelled to pass the evening in the canoe did not cause him any alarm, for in the past he had passed many nights under similar circumstances. But it would have been more comforting to know that an island might be seen before darkness obliterated all possible hope. It was evident that such good fortune was not to be his, thus the passing minutes brought the quick, enveloping darkness for which the tropics are so well known. As well, a noticeable chill swept over the water as is common when the sun no longer shines upon the earth beneath.

Stars began to appear in the heaven—those of greatest magnitude were first. Venus, the evening planet, naturally, was the first to make an appearance. Bantan remembered his hope that Nao's departed spirit might have found sanctuary upon it. Sadness appeared in his eyes with the recollection. His lips parted and a soft sigh was emitted.

"Poor Nao!" he murmured at length. "We could have been so happy together."

Now, other stars of lesser magnitude were beginning to appear in the darkened canopy. As though in a trance Bantan continued paddling the canoe, his eyes constantly upon the planet Venus. Miles were covered across the trackless ocean's undulating surface in the time that passed before the evening star gradually neared the horizon, and with passing minutes began to sink beneath it.

All the while the paddler's thoughts had seemingly been reliving his happy hours with Nao. Her comely features and smiling dark eyes were filled with devotion for him. When, at length, the bright, yellow evening star was no longer to be seen, then did he realize how very wearied he was after the day's constant paddling. He lay his paddle aside, and with groping hands sought some of the fruit in the bottom of the canoe with which to appease his now conscious hunger.

When he had eaten sufficiently of his allotted stores, he rearranged the grasses in the bottom of the canoe and in another moment was curled thereupon. He had hardly closed his eyes when the lapping of gentle wavelets against the side of the canoe lulled him into deep, refreshing slumber—from which he hardly stirred as the hours passed and the pilotless canoe was borne in the arms of a favoring current. Many miles were thus covered without any effort on the sleeper's part.

The sun had just cleared the horizon when Bantan's eyelids twitched for a few moments before opening. Presently he had arisen to a seated position and breathed deeply of the crisp, morning air. His searching dark eyes were aware that not a cloud dotted the heaven, but there was a sea gull to be seen in the distance lazily winging its way toward the west. This was indeed heartening to the bronzed giant, for he was positive an island could not be too far distant.

While he partook of his morning meal his watchful eyes kept track of the sea gull until it vanished from sight. Then did he take up his paddle, and once again with steady, rhythmic strokes, first upon one side and then the other, propelled the canoe faster over the undulating water. A gentle breeze stirred favorably, and the paddler was assisted to some extent in this manner, adding to the miles to be covered that he would not be compelled to wield his paddle.

With the passing minutes Bantan saw flying fish flit through the air. In the distance to his left were porpoises seemingly at play with one another as they fed upon the smaller marine life. Soon a turtle was seen to his right ahead of him, leaving in its wake ripples as it swam along, and shortly the paddler passed it. Unconcerned, the turtle resumed its way.

As an automaton the bronzed giant wielded his paddle, pausing only when he wished to partake of his dwindling provisions, and by so doing, managed to assuage his craving for food and water and maintaining his strength.

Time and again thoughts of Wanya and Lori would occur to him, and he would shake his head, remembering as he did, how very devoted both were to him. Sometimes he wondered if he were being fair, especially, to his long-devoted foster sister. Only too well did he recollect her expressed wish to him that he return soon—to her.

His scores to settle with Amar—if he had escaped the cataclysm that had obliterated the Aoona Islands from the sight of human eye—was the reason he had left Marja Island, his foster parents, and his many other friends. Now that he knew the Aoona Islands were no more, it was quite possible that Amar, or any of the other villagers, had not survived.

The coming evening, at sundown, would be the time for decision. If no islands were sighted at that time, then would he turn the canoe about, and proceed toward distant Marja to resume his life among the natives he had lived with.

Vaguely as his thoughts rested upon Wanya, he shook his head sadly. Too well did he know of her long devotion for him. But, having always considered her as a sister, he had been unable to feel that his love for her might be realized in the true fashion love of a man for a maid should be. A tingling flush momentarily mantled his cheeks as he recalled to mind a vivid dream he had once had wherein he and Wanya were about to be mated.

Then, his thoughts turned to the self-renounced princess of Ono Island. Bantan knew he owed his very life to her, and he would not soon forget his debt of obligation to her. Already she had confessed her love for him. But, in the depths of his heart, could he feel that he might one day love her? And so the trend of his mind as he unwaveringly wielded his paddle, and the canoe was propelled over the undulating water until noonday came.

Following his noonday repast, while the canoe drifted aimlessly—sometimes becoming almost stationary—Bantan decided it was time to view the western horizon for possible sight of a landfall. He knelt near the center of the canoe, and a hand was braced against each side of the gunwale preparatory to arising. Then it happened with such suddenness that momentarily he was paralyzed—but for a brief instant only—not knowing whether it was some gigantic monster of the deep that sought to upset the canoe, or some phenomenon of Nature that could not be accounted for, was making itself known.

He was first aware of an awesome, whining sound such as he had heard upon the late afternoon of the previous day. Looking upward quickly, he saw a dark-coned object forming directly above him. It was connected on the further end to a large, purplish cloud. Bantan seemed enveloped in a vacuum as the yawning cone descended upon him.

There was a momentary effervescence of water directly beneath the canoe's bottom that spread outward in all directions until its base was some ten feet in diameter. Then, strangely, the boiling water beneath seemingly centered itself upon the underside of the canoe.

It was fortunate for Bantan that he was kneeling with a hand on each side of the gunwale, for in that way he maintained his equilibrium. To his astonishment he felt the canoe rising up from the water. Ten, twenty, thirty, forty, and now he reached a point of fifty feet above the surface as the waterspout drew the canoe upward above its surging effervescence.

Upon the late afternoon before the young giant had witnessed such a disturbance from a respectable distance, but today he was in the center of it. He realized he was helpless to avert his present plight, though he did have presence of mind to keep his balance. When he would feel the canoe dip one way or another, he would quickly ease his weight in the opposite direction, and in this way he could manage to keep the water craft from overturning or sliding down the column of erupting water.

While at this elevation, facing the west as he was, he cast quick glances in the direction of the horizon. In the first, brief glimpse he thought that he sighted a landfall; but he could not be sure, for the sun could play unusual pranks upon the shimmering ocean surface.

Bantan had no idea just how long the waterspout would keep him aloft in his precarious position. A minute passed, and then another. Still he managed to keep the canoe balanced, though at times he would have to act quickly by leaning his weight one way or another. Were either bow or stern to pass that certain point in balance he would be unable to retain the present position he was in.

Another minute passed—and then another—each following one seemed longer than the preceding one. But with steady nerves and every sense alert, the slightest incline at either end of the canoe was almost anticipated, and in this way Bantan felt no alarm. Another minute passed, and then more of them.

For fully fifteen minutes the canoe rode the crest of the waterspout, and then without warning, the whining sound abated and the surging force above it lessened. He felt the canoe being returned to the surface. The bronzed giant still maintained his vigil, hoping that he would not be capsized should the waterspout spend its energies too quickly. But the surging water gently subsided, and in a few minutes the canoe was deposited lightly upon the surface without a splash.

Bantan shook his head, and a smile now touched the corners of his lips as he realized more fully what had happened. With a shrug of his shoulders he picked up his paddle, and without further delay proceeded to propel the canoe westward. With the thought of the possible landfall that he had sighted was an added incentive to cover as many miles as was possible before nightfall.

With the passing of another hour the paddler's vision was now becoming hampered because of the sun's bright rays having passed from directly above him to his front. By shading his eyes he could still look toward the western horizon without too much difficulty at first, though the fruitless reward that awaited him was always the same. Still no landfall was to be sighted. However, as the time passed, and the sun was sinking lower in front of him, with more difficulty did he try to scan the horizon.

No further sight of bird life had he obtained since early morning. As the late afternoon sun neared the waterline, it was then that Bantan was aware of a number of sea gulls flying in his direction. This was encouraging—would have been more so—had it been the previous afternoon that bird life was to be seen. A glance at his dwindled provisions made the paddler only too well aware that he could not afford to continue paddling much longer without sight of a landfall before he must consider returning from whence he had come.

Pausing now in his paddling, and giving his weary arms the opportunity to rest, for the time being he watched with shaded, keen eyes the possible goal of the birds while they passed overhead. Turning, as they did so, he uncovered his eyes and watched them in silence. They were cawing dismally as they flitted by. For a short distance they continued in a straight line, then the watcher was aware they were circling about. Sure enough, they completed a half circle, and once again were in full flight, returning from whence they had come—due west.

Again shading his eyes, Bantan did not remove them from the sea gulls until they had vanished in the distance. As he strained his eyes to catch the last fleeting glimpse of them, it was then that he noticed the broken line on the horizon. Could it be a miracle? He strained his eyes again. A sudden hope welled within him. It must be a landfall! He hoped if such were the case that the object of his quest would be found there.

With increased strokes of his paddle now, the bronzed giant exerted himself to his greatest effort hoping, meanwhile, before the sun's setting, that the landfall would have increased in size for assurance that it had been no mirage, as at first he was inclined to believe. But the fact the sea gulls had vanished in that direction was ample proof that an island *must* be present, even though a number of miles must still be paddled over the trackless ocean from where he was at present.

Though his muscles protested at the added strain placed upon them, because of the urgency to cover as many miles as was possible before the darkness of night enveloped the surface, the canoe's progress increased considerably. Meanwhile, so, too, did the landfall gradually begin to take shape in the form of a fairly large island.

The lower edge of the flaming red ball now touched the horizon, and though the sun's rays were still strong, Bantan would look intermittently toward the west. Each glance that he gave revealed more of the setting sun slipping beneath the waterline until, when over half of the blood-red disc was concealed, then he permitted his eyes to linger longer upon the island which was now clearly revealed. But he was well aware he would not reach it for many long hours to come, and that meant a considerable distance must still be paddled by his wearied arms.

As soon as the sun had completely set, for long moments Bantan peered toward the island, and he was aware, even at the great distance that intervened, that it was a most unusual one. From a low point at the end on his left it stretched to the right with gradual elevation until the extreme end was considerably higher, and seemingly barren of foliage.

With methodical strokes of his paddle in the quick-setting darkness, the bronzed giant now observed Venus, the evening star, high in the sky directly over the island. Though he was wearied from the day's toil, he paused and partook of more food to bolster his flagging spirits. Afterwards, refreshed, with the brilliant yellow planet as his guide, he resumed paddling.

With the complete setting of darkness myriads of other stars in the form of constellations appeared in the dark canopy, but always the paddler kept his eyes riveted upon Venus. Remembering his hope that Nao's spirit had found peaceful rest there, his lips parted.

"Guide me to my goal in safety, dear Nao," he murmured.

As the weary hours passed, and the canoe continued on its way without the slightest deviation, Bantan was also aware his guiding star was at length nearing the western waterline. By this time the large island was clearly outlined upon the horizon.

The paddler had long since decided to continue his way despite his tired arms. With his objective near at hand now, he could not consider sleeping even for a few hours for fear a whimsical current might carry the canoe astray. Then, indeed, his would be a pitiful dilemma. Fortunate for him that his decision was thus made.

A partly eaten moon cleared the horizon in due time, but her effulgence did little toward illuminating the watery expanse below. With the passing of minutes, however, her dull rays did ascertain the paddler's surmise that the higher, northern end of the island was barren of foliage. And, too, the silvery rays lighted upon what seemed to be a large, stone building of some sort, the like of which the young man had never seen before. Wonderingly would his eyes look at it from the distance, and natural curiosity was roused within him as to its purpose.

The paddler was aware now that a strong current was encountered, and it was bearing him away from a true course. Had it not been for that reason he should, in due time, beach his canoe upon the east shore of the island. As it was, his wearied muscles did not feel equal to the task of forcing the canoe against the strong current merely to maintain a true course. As a result, he was longer covering the intervening distance, but less effort was required. When within a half-mile from the south shore, the strong current lessened; thereafter, he maintained a more direct course.

Presently Bantan heard the tumultuous surf breaking upon the beach. With a long-drawn sigh he realized he was near the end of his weary trip. His keen nostrils were also aware of a slight, acrid odor which he identified as smoke from cook fires, but his sharp eyes could detect no sight of a village at the point on the south shore where his canoe approached.

In due time the stout little water craft was being guided through the breaking water, and moments later, the prow scraped on the beach. Quickly the occupant lay down his paddle and stepped out. He gripped the bow with tired hands. The moment the force of the retreating wave lessened, he drew the canoe to the very edge of the foliage. Straightening, he breathed deeply of the fragrant air and with seeming reluctance exhaled.

In the east, above the horizon, the first fingers of dawn were stabbing the heaven. Looking toward the partly eaten moon now hovering overhead, Bantan knew he would have no difficulty falling asleep, for his eyelids were exceedingly heavy, and it had been with difficulty that he had been able to keep them from closing during the past hour or so.

Without further delay he drew the canoe within the screening foliage, then stepped within. Kneeling, in the almost pitch darkness he rearranged the grasses in the bottom and curled upon them, heaving a deep sigh. Almost instantly he was fast asleep.

CHAPTER II

A RESCUE IN THE SURF

It seemed the sleeper had hardly closed his eyes when they opened quickly, his every sense of perception fully alerted. It was daylight, and the sun was several hours high. Bantan quickly arose to an erect position with ears strained. Once again that shrill, terrifying cry—a similar one had interrupted his deep sleep—was to be heard from the direction of the beach. Through a break in the foliage he saw the reason for the scream.

About a hundred yards from shore, just beyond the breaking waves, a native boy was in evident distress. His arms were frantically beating the water about him in his efforts to frighten off his attacker. Intermittently his brown arms would make a few strokes toward the shore, but then he would again pause, and beat the water about him with the palms of his hands.

The bronzed young giant admired bravery. Though the native boy was a total stranger to him it did not matter. The fact he would expose himself as an alien on this strange island to one of its inhabitants did not cause him to hesitate a moment. Instinctively his right hand touched the handle of the keen dagger sheathed at his hip, and at the next instant he had leaped out of the canoe, forged through the screening foliage, and dashed down the sandy beach to leap into the foaming surf. His strong arms were mightily cleaving the

turbulent water even before his head bobbed above
the surface. His keen eyes at once located the still
struggling native boy, and with his object in sight, his
flashing arms and kicking legs speedily propelled him
in that direction.

The young native boy was too intent upon the
preservation of his life to observe succor coming
toward him. The shark had nipped his left leg just
above the knee, from which blood copiously flowed;
but since that first nip had been unsuccessful in furthering the gratification of the luscious meal the young
boy's tender flesh offered. The shark was not without
hope, however, as it continued to harass further its
would-be-victim. Again it circled about and turned
just before an attack with wide-gaping mouth expos-
ing its vicious inverted teeth.

The youth's agility was all that had spared him
thus far; but now he was tiring, and it was a question
of just how long he could manage to keep his attacker
at bay. Frantically he would look shoreward in the
vain hope some one in the distant village might have
heard his terror-stricken cries and would come to his
rescue.

Then it was the native boy saw a movement in the
water near him just within the breaking water. In despair, he realized all was lost, for he could not hope to
battle two vicious creatures of the deep. A shrill cry
was emitted from his lips in a last, desperate hope that
the distant villagers might hear; then, with a final surge
of strength, he struck out for shore with short, overhand strokes, but away from the movement of water
that he had just noticed. To his somewhat bewildered
mind the native boy seemingly forgot his first attacker
while seeking to elude this new menace.

The shark, however, had not relinquished the hope of partaking of the youth's tender flesh, for it quickly veered, and in moments was approaching the young boy. Overly anxious, the shark's yawning mouth just missed one of the boy's kicking legs, and as its cold, rough skin brushed his would-be-victim, the latter thought for sure he would expire in fright from mere contact with the sea monster.

More frantically he splashed his arms, and as his mouth opened to give vent to his distress, water entered, almost gagging him, so that he sputtered and coughed, and finally spewed that which had nearly strangled him. Remembering the presence of the new menace, the youth looked quickly toward the edge of the breaking water. Whatever it was seemed closer to him—not more than twenty yards intervened.

With a gasping sob he desperately struck out away from this new menace. At the same time he was thinking of his first attacker. At that very moment he felt a swirling of water close by, and with renewed strength beat upon the water with the palms of both hands before striking out again in earnest for the shore.

For a few moments all went well—the youth covered a number of yards, though in truth at any second he had expected to feel the shark's inverted teeth fasten upon one of his kicking legs. A quick glance over a shoulder revealed the second menace was much closer than before—now scarcely ten yards separated them. While he looked, the creature submerged. Horror gripped the youth, and whatever deity he worshipped was now the recipient of numerous prayers that he voiced from the depths of his heart in that brief period.

Again he was headed for the shore with glistening arms flashing in the brilliant morning sunshine. Then it seemed his end had come, for a swift-moving body lunged at him from beneath the surface. He felt himself helplessly and rudely shoved aside. At the next moment there was a violent thrashing of water close at hand.

Bantan engaged the shark at an opportune moment. Had he not shoved the youth to one side, the creature would surely have seized one of the boy's kicking legs. With unbelievable agility, he quickly avoided the shark's thrust, and as the monster was turning over, thwarted in its designs, the young giant's arms and legs encircled the course gray form. At the next moment his right hand had withdrawn the keen-edged dagger from its sheath, and he repeatedly plunged the blade to the hilt in various portions of the whitish belly, hoping to pierce a vital spot.

Enraged because of the man thing clinging and administering excruciating pain to it, the shark swam forward with lightning-like speed, and then came to an abrupt halt. It veered suddenly and plunged to the depths below. Almost nearing the bottom—at this point some thirty feet down—the sea monster swerved about quickly, hoping to dislodge the tenaciously clinging man thing. Again and again Bantan's dagger was buried into the shark's belly. Already blood was copiously flowing from the numerous wounds inflicted.

Meanwhile, the youth, believing the two sharks were battling over him as a prize, was not too bewildered to take advantage of his unexpected good fortune. Breathing easier, he started swimming once more toward the outer breaking waves, and as soon as he reached them, he felt he was as good as saved. A smile of relief came upon his wearied features.

Now, at last, Bantan's plunging dagger found a vital

spot in the maddened shark. The moment he felt the cold form appear paralyzed, he knew he had no further fear from the sea monster. Sheathing his dagger, he released his hold and with feet braced against the inert creature, he thrust himself upward toward the surface. His lungs were aching from holding his breath so long, for nearly four minutes had elapsed since first engaging the shark. The moment his head bobbed above the surface he expelled the foul air from his lungs and gulped fresh air through his opened mouth.

His eyes quickly sought the native boy. Looking shoreward, he saw that he was battling the tumultuous surf rather feebly now, for the loss of blood from his wound had sapped his strength, and he realized that courage alone could not sustain him for long.

Quickly Bantan's bronzed arms cleaved the water with powerful overhand strokes as he forged into the breaking water in the direction of the struggling youth who was not aware of his approach. So intent he was in his efforts to merely keep afloat and let the breaking waves carry him shoreward, the native boy entertained thoughts of nothing else.

Time and again chopping waves washed over the youth's head, much of which he inhaled through his nostrils, causing him to cough. While doing so, much more water entered his mouth so that he was choking and gasping at the same time. He felt his strength ebbing fast. His arms and legs were like dead weights over which he had no control, and his senses were reeling. It seemed he had about reached the end of his physical endurance, for now he felt himself sinking, and the breaking waves washed over his head.

Then, as though by a miracle, a strong hand fastened

about his chin and drew his head above water. The youth was positive his end had come, and his fleeting senses offered a final prayer to his deity before unconsciousness enveloped him completely.

Bantan experienced no difficulty bearing the native youth to the shore. When solid footing was attained, he swept the limp form into his arms, and carried him to the very edge of the shading foliage where he gently placed him upon the sand. Without a moment's delay he proceeded to apply artificial respiration.

He also noticed the wound upon the youth's left leg. It was still bleeding quite freely. From the foliage he gathered leaves and fastened them to the wound with pieces of wiry grass. By the time he had completed this, the youth drew a deep breath. A paroxysm of coughing overtook him at once so that he finally expelled what water was left in his lungs. His eyes presently opened. Realizing that he was on land, he looked up in silent wonder at his concerned savior.

Bantan had been wondering if they would be able to converse when the youth regained consciousness. He estimated him to be about thirteen years of age. He was built along rugged lines, having broad shoulders and sturdy legs. His features were round and well molded, being topped by short, curly dark hair. Now, as the native boy stared up at him, a friendly smile touched the lips of the squatting man at his side.

"You saved me?" the boy asked presently in a tongue the bronzed giant could easily understand, for it closely resembled that of the Beneiro and the Marja.

"I saved you from the shark," Bantan answered simply.

The boy shuddered momentarily.

"It was you who was swimming toward me?" he asked then.

The bronzed giant nodded.

"You seemed afraid of me," he commented. "Did you think I was another shark?"

A sheepish smile now touched the youth's lips and he admitted that he did.

"That was why I started swimming away from you," he explained. "Did you kill the shark?"

"I killed the shark," was the reply, accompanied by a nod.

The youth's dark eyes now regarded the young giant with seeming awe.

"You are very brave," he remarked. And then he added: "Who are you, and why did you risk your life to spare mine?"

"My name is Bantan," was the reply. "I am a stranger to your island. The reason I saved you was because I admire bravery, and you were very brave out there. I couldn't let you be killed by the shark. When I was many moons older than you a very good friend of mine by name of Ramo was killed by one. Since that time I have never hesitated to attack and slay one of the sea monsters, for where there is hate in one's heart, there can be no fear."

The native boy nodded thoughtfully.

"That is true," he admitted.

A moment's silence intervened before Bantan spoke.

"What is your name?"

"Tamur," was the reply.

"Tell me, Tamur," Bantan said then, "have other strangers come to this island recently?"

The youth nodded.

"Several suns ago a lone canoe came hither," he answered. He then indicated four fingers of one hand to designate the number of warriors occupying the canoe. "They said they were from an island called Amo."

Bantan experienced a wave of vengeance surging through him and his eyes narrowed momentarily.

"Can you describe them to me, Tamur? he then asked quietly.

The native boy described them as best he could, adding that one of them had stated he was a chief from his island which had sunk beneath the water, and that his son was with him.

Bantan's hands clenched involuntarily. Amar was alive! That single thought dominated above all else.

"Tell me, Tamur," he asked, "were they received as friends—or enemies?"

The native boy's face seemed to change expression.

"They were taken prisoners," he declared. "Our village receive no strangers as friends."

Bantan nodded in understanding, then a friendly smile touched his lips. He looked directly at the native youth.

"You do not consider me an enemy?" he asked.

"No, Bantan," was Tamur's reply, accompanied by a shake of his head. "I shall forever be grateful to you for having saved my life. If I thought my uncle, the chief, would accept you as a friend because of my debt of gratitude to you, I would gladly lead you to the village." The native boy again shook his head sadly. "I fear for your safety should you remain upon this island."

"I have been paddling for four suns, Tamur," the bronzed giant then said. "I came hither in pursuit of the son of the Amo Island chief. He has harmed me in the past, and indirectly through him, my sweetheart was killed. Knowing he is here makes it difficult for me to leave without settling my scores with him."

The native boy remained silent.

"Does this island have a name, Tamur?" Bantan asked after a short silence.

"It is called The Great One's island," the youth answered.

A perplexed expression overcame the bronzed giant's features.

" 'The Great One's Island?' " he questioned.

"That is so," the native boy said with a nod. "We of the village are known as Mandoes. We have a chief—he is my uncle. But we are governed by The Great One."

"What is he like?" was the next question.

The youth shrugged his shoulders.

"I have never seen him," he answered. "No one in the village has ever seen him. Talking to The Great One is done by a drum on a platform at the side of the chief's hut. When this was done, some of the villagers, both warriors and girls, would be selected by emissaries from The Great One. They would be taken to the huge stone hut upon the high end of the island. They were never known to return. They just vanished, as though they died and were buried."

Now indeed was Bantan's curiosity aroused. He must investigate the matter of the huge stone hut and The Great One who occupied it. Tamur did not know of his immediate plans. But first, there was the matter of settling scores with Amar, for only then, in his way of thinking, would Nao's dearly departed spirit rest at ease.

"Do you feel well enough to return to the village, Tamur?" he then asked the boy.

The native youth smiled with assurance as he arose to his feet, as did Bantan.

"I feel very well," he answered. Then a cloud overcame his smiling eyes, and concern for his savior was revealed. "But you will be careful and keep concealed until you are ready to leave the island?"

Bantan smiled confidently.

"I'll keep concealed for a few suns, Tamur," he promised. "By that time I should have been sufficiently rested, then I'll be on my way."

The youth appeared very solemn.

"Have no fear that I will reveal your presence on our island, Bantan," he said. "Owing you my life as I do, my greatest regret is that I cannot ask you to come with me to the village and be acclaimed the hero you are in my eyes."

The bronzed giant smiled and nodded.

"I'll trust you, Tamur," was all he said.

"Are you going to remain here during your short stay?" the youth added.

The young giant nodded.

"My canoe is concealed within the foliage," he answered.

"Perhaps I may visit you later in the day," Tamur suggested hopefully.

"If you wish," Bantan agreed.

The native boy left his savior with some reluctance, but a smile in parting radiated his features.

Realizing that he was hungry since he had eaten nothing as yet, the bronzed giant then gathered some fruit and nuts in the nearby vicinity, and returned to where his canoe was concealed. There he satisfied his hunger. He was in deep thought as to just how he was going about the business of settling his scores with Amar. Since the Amo chief's son was a prisoner, Bantan realized the difficulties which lay ahead if the objective of his quest was to be successfully concluded.

CHAPTER III

THE NATIVE GIRL—MAURIA

Although Tamur had warned him of the hostility
to be expected of the village warriors, Bantan decided
to seek the village, and reconnoitre in the hope he
might catch a glimpse of his enemy, if that were possible. Perhaps there would be a way that he might
effect Amar's "rescue," and when he had settled scores
with him—if all went well—he could return to Marja
Island with the feeling his mission had been completed.

Remembering the direction the native boy had
taken, the bronzed giant presently was following along
a well marked trail. With eyes constantly on watch and
ears fully alerted, he went his way with caution. His
keen nostrils were aware of any alien odor. Noting the
slightly acrid smell of smoke from the distant village's
cook fires was another way of determining his proximity to his objective.

In due time he was nearing the village. Sounds of
voices and other noises could be heard. The young giant
deserted the well marked trail, and with extreme caution picked his way through the underbrush until he
observed a rather stout tree that would serve the
purpose he had in mind. It stood perhaps fifty feet from
the edge of the village.

Bantan scaled the stout bole with agility and presently was able to see above the smaller undergrowth.
He paused there to swiftly appraise the village. The
huts were almost identical in size and shape with the

exception of a larger one near the center. This un-
doubtedly was the chief's hut. At its side he noted a
platform all of ten feet high, and upon it set a large
tom-tom. A knobbed club rested nearby. This must be
the talking drum Tamur had mentioned.

At the side of each hut was to be seen garden plots.
In some of them men and women were weeding by
hand or hoeing with crude implements. Before other
huts women were cooking the noonday meal. Earthen
pots were suspended over the fires and vapor was
rising from their interior. Warriors were to be seen
squatting nearby engaged in conversation with others.
Numerous nearly naked children of both sexes were to
be seen dashing about while engaged in some favorite
game. Their raucous cries were clearly heard by the
silently watching man in the tree.

Looking upward, Bantan noted a convenient crotch
from which he might be more comfortable than his
present position. In a few minutes he attained this more
vantage position. He had become comfortably ensconced there when he heard excited voices from an
edge of the village farthest from him.

Two stalwart warriors clad only in loin cloths had
made an appearance. They were armed with long
spears, and at their hips were sheathed daggers. About
them village warriors were gathering. Toward the
most prominent hut the newcomers were moving up a
village lane, while the warriors trailed behind.

Watching the proceedings carefully, something
about the bearing of the newcomers assured the silent
watcher that they did not live in the village. Where
they had come from he could only guess—that being
the other end of the island. With keen interest he

noted their utter disdain for the warriors of the village.

Before the larger hut they now came to a halt. Almost simultaneously a middle-aged warrior of noble mien appeared upon the threshold of the doorway. He was nearly six feet in height and was raw boned. He was garbed in an open jacket and a loin cloth made of *tupa* from the bark of the mulberry tree. Sandals encased his rather large feet. A shell necklace encircled his large neck. No other ornaments did he wear. At his side a moment later a youth drew near. Even from the distance, Bantan recognized the young boy as Tamur, whom he had rescued from the surf.

One of the two warriors was apparently the spokesman. He engaged the chief in conversation, and after a few minutes an agreement in their controversy was reached. All then went to a nearby hut about which a guard was on patrol. The chief spoke to him. In another moment the door of the prison hut was unbarred and opened. Presently four prisoners marched out in the open in single file. Their hands were not bound. Bantan's eyes narrowed, and he was aware of a seething rage within him as he recognized Amar.

In the moments that passed, the silent watcher saw the wrists of the four prisoners bound with thongs. Lastly, a strong rope was fastened to the waist of each, allowing them several feet clearance in between.

Without further amenities the four prisoners, preceded by one of the stalwart warriors, with the other trailing, returned to the edge of the village where they had made their appearance. The chief and Tamur, also many warriors accompanied them, but they did not follow when the guards with their prisoners departed from the outskirts of the village.

Remembering what Tamur had told him about The Great One's emissaries coming to the village, Bantan believed they were taking the prisoners to that personage, and for what purpose he could not even guess.

Realizing there was nothing he could do to prevent the delivery of his enemy to The Great One, the bronzed giant shook his head as he now lowered himself from the tree. It was quite possible Tamur would shortly come to the other side of the island, and he was sure the native boy would tell him of the probable fate of the prisoners.

Without meeting any one upon his return to where his canoe was cached, gathering fruits and nuts for his noonday repast, Bantan was eating when he heard the native boy call softly to him from nearby. Answering, in a few moments the excited Tamur approached with a smile upon his dusky features.

"What is it, Tamur?" Bantan asked.

"The four prisoners have been taken to The Great One," was the excited reply.

"Yes, I know," the bronzed giant answered with a nod. "I watched from a tree near the edge of the village."

The native boy gasped.

"You mean, Bantan," he asked, "that you dared approach the village?"

The young giant nodded.

"There was no danger for me," he answered.

"You were very brave to do so," Tamur added.

Bantan smiled deprecatingly.

"Did your uncle, the chief, notify The Great One of the prisoners?" he then asked.

The native boy nodded.

"The same day they were taken prisoners," he replied, "my uncle, the chief, sent word to The Great One by the talking drum."

"What do you suppose The Great One intends to do with them?" Bantan asked then.

Tamur shrugged his shoulders.

"No one knows what The Great One does with those who are taken to him," he answered.

The bronzed giant appeared thoughtful following the native boy's answer. He was wondering in a vague way if there yet was some possible way that he might effect Amar's "rescue" from The Great One for his own purpose. Tamur stood silently watching his bronzed savior. Presently he spoke.

"You need not worry about settling scores with Amar now, Bantan," he said. "I'm sure The Great One will see to it that your enemy will meet death—in one way or another."

The bronzed giant nodded his head. What Tamur had said would, in all probability, take place. But since Amar had wronged him and his deceased sweetheart, he felt he was the rightful one to hasten his enemy's end. The Great One had no actual reason to slay Amar, whereas Bantan had every reason in the world. His reveries were interrupted as the native boy spoke further.

"Now that you don't have to worry about Amar's fate," he added, "I hope you are successful in not being captured by the village warriors until you leave."

"That is so," the young giant admitted. And then, to change the subject, he asked, "Your leg, Tamur, does it bother you much?"

The native boy shook his head.

"Did your parents ask how it happened?" was Bantan's next question.

"My mother did," the boy admitted. "I told her about it. I did not say that you spared me from the shark. I was loyal to you by not mentioning what really happened."

"That is good, Tamur," Bantan said approvingly.

The native boy then asked the bronzed giant about the island from which he had come, and details of his life there. The questions he asked were answered truthfully. Then at last Tamur decided it was time he returned to the village.

"Be careful, Bantan," he warned. "I wouldn't want any harm to befall you."

The young giant assured the native boy that he would heed his warning, adding that if he wished to come again on the next day that he would look for him. Tamur expressed delight and promised he would surely come.

After the native boy had taken his departure, Bantan's brow seamed as he tried to formulate some method of reaching the huge stone hut on the other end of the island without observation. Time and again he would shake his head and dismiss the various solutions that were offered. At last he felt drowsy as a result of his futile cogitations, and the fact he had only slept a few hours earlier in the morning. He stepped within the canoe and curled himself upon the grasses in its bottom, falling asleep almost at once.

Though Bantan slept soundly for an hour, a snapping twig aroused him to wakefulness with every sense alert. He peered cautiously over the gunwale of the canoe in the direction from which the sound had come. At first he thought that Tamur was returning. His

Bantan Sees a Native Girl

keen ears heard soft footsteps approaching, though as yet he could catch no glimpse of the intruder in his seeming Eden. Presently his watchful eyes saw a movement of foliage. Soon the fronds of a tall fern were pushed aside, and a young native girl appeared. She did not notice the canoe at once, for her attention seemed interested in a small bird which flitted above her in the foliage.

Bantan watched her in silence. Clearly to be seen, she seemed rather attractive. Her long, dark hair flowed over her smooth, brown shoulders, and he noted a white flower above her left ear in the glossy sheen. Her features were well formed. A shell necklace encircled her smooth neck. A strip of *tupa* cloth covered her bosom, and a short, skirted loin cloth girded her mid-section. Her well shaped arms and legs were sturdy. From the sound of the snapping twigs underfoot he assumed she wore sandals.

The watcher realized the awkward position that he was in. He did not wish to frighten the girl; and at the same time he realized he couldn't arise from the canoe, and hope to drag it away without such a sound attracting her attention. Numerous suggestions passed through his mind to relieve him of his dilemma; the only one that seemed plausible was to pretend he was asleep, but keep his ears alert. There was a possibility that the native girl might not even notice the canoe. In the event she discovered it and its occupant, whatever her reaction would be the cue for making a move in his own behalf.

Lying there in the canoe's bottom, breathing easily so as to better improve his already acute hearing, he now heard the girl moving about. And then he heard her muffled gasp. She must have sighted the canoe! For a few moments there was absolute silence. Presently he heard the girl stealthily approach in his direction.

She drew closer with hesitant footsteps until she must have reached a position from which she could observe the apparently sleeping young giant within the canoe. Now her soft footsteps halted, and the feigning sleeper could hear her swift, indrawn breath at sight of his recumbent form.

The passing moments seemed like an eternity to Bantan. Would the girl turn and stealthily leave the immediate vicinity, and thereafter, return in haste to the village and announce her discovery—or, what would she do, otherwise? His keen ears now detected her more even breathing. She took several more steps closer until she stood at the side of the canoe, and looked more fully down upon him.

The bronzed giant lay with a forearm over his eyes, as though to shield them from the sun's bright rays. He now wished that he had left them uncovered so that he might open them the merest trifle to read the expression upon the native girl's face. It might mean the difference between life and death to him.

For long moments the girl studied the apparently sleeping stranger. Where at first there had been amazement in her eyes at sight of him, this feeling soon left her. A smile touched her lips and a gentleness appeared in her dark eyes. Comparing the sleeping giant with the warriors of the Mandoes village she was well aware they suffered in comparison. With admiration apparent in her eyes now as she looked down upon the clean-limbed young man, a long-drawn sigh was emitted from her parted lips.

Mauria was unmated, and though she had had many suitors in the past, none seemed to possess all the qualities that she hoped a man would have with whom she desired to mate. Perhaps she was a trifle particular in her choice of a mate. Because of that, she had been scolded upon a number of occasions by her mother who, naturally, wished to see her daughter married —as most mothers do—and bearing children for the prosperity of the village's future. However, the girl felt that she wanted to be happily mated, and until she could find the man who possessed all the qualifications necessary to her happiness, she was resolved to endure the scoldings of her mother, as well as the scorn of the other village women.

For that reason she passed as little time as was necessary in the household of her parents, and she associated with few of the native girls, since those of her age had been mated many moons now, and had children to care for. After all, Mauria reflected upon a number of occasions, she was only eighteen years of age. Her method of estimating age was by moons, not years, as the other members of the Mandoes village. To make the telling simpler, however, I shall use years in reference to moons when considered feasible.

Under ordinary circumstances girls in the Mandoes village were mated within a few moons after coming to the age of womanhood. The fact that many children resulted from these early marriages did not overflow the population, for the mortality rate was high among infants. And, too, in the cases of deformed children being born, infanticide was practiced for the benefit of all concerned. In all instances the chief of the village passed judgment on the destruction of a new-born child. The simplest means was to smother it. When life was extinct, then the tiny corpse would be burned. For generations the villagers had handed down a decree against burying a deformed child for fear fruit trees and other growing things would absorb diseases from such flesh when putrified under the ground.

Many an ardent admirer had been discouraged by Mauria's indifference to their passionate avowals of love—some even going as far as attempting to force their unwelcome attentions upon her. As the moons passed, the village girl became known as taboo because of her indifference to the charms of the young males. But she did not care too greatly, since in her mind she had formulated an image of the perfect man with whom she desired to mate.

As she looked down upon the apparently sleeping young giant, the girl's heart had never before been affected as now. Her dark eyes lovingly traced the perfect lines of the Apollo-like body. She admired his dark hair ever so inclined to curl in front. And his features, that his bronzed arm did not fully cover, were perfect in her estimation. The native girl heaved a deep sigh. As though to ease her emotions somewhat, her right hand clasped her left breast tightly. She could feel her heart thumping loudly against the walls of her bosom.

From within her the silent cry went forth to the spirits of her dearly departed ancestors that they forgive her for spontaneous love for this alien to the island of her birth. So great the emotion that welled within her she felt herself trembling and her throat was becoming excessively dry so that she swallowed repeatedly and with difficulty. Her breathing became labored and her bosom rose and fell with apparent effort. Repeatedly she shook her head in an endeavor to relieve her of the giddy feeling that seemingly affected her.

The dilemma which faced the native girl now was what to do. She reasoned logically that were she to rudely waken the sleeping young man he would be angry for being disturbed, and that he would reject any overtures of friendship she might make in his behalf. That she did not wish for anything. And so Mauria decided what any coy female would under similar circumstances.

All the while Bantan, feigning sleep, wondered what the native girl would do. He had reached the point of exasperation when he heard her move stealthily away. Quickly he uncovered his eyes and raised his head cautiously and peered over the gunwale of the canoe. With amazement he saw the girl gathering soft grasses and ferns. As she turned with an armful, he quickly resumed his former position, still failing to understand just what she was about.

His alert ears were aware of her approach, and he almost wished that he might stop breathing as he heard her place the grass and ferns at the side of the canoe, and then repose upon them. So silent everything was, the feigning sleeper could even hear her breathing and each time that she swallowed. He even thought that he heard the loud thumping of her heart in response to the emotion that surged through her.

Acutely aware of the embarrassment of his position, Bantan was convinced of one thing that was paramount to all else. The native girl was not afraid of him—the stranger that he was to her. He had that in his favor. With this in mind he decided he must face the inevitable, whatever the consequences. He uncovered his eyes and drew a deep breath, then arose slowly to his feet. He pretended not to know the native girl was lying upon a pallet of grasses and ferns along-

side the canoe. His ears were alert, however, as he
stepped out upon the other side, but he heard no sound
from the girl, feigning sleep. Shaking his head, he
stepped around the end of the canoe, pausing beside
the girl's head. She reposed upon her right side with
her cheek pillowed upon her lustrous hair.

CHAPTER IV

MAURIA'S IDEAL

As though aroused from a deep sleep, the native girl slowly attained a seated position. Her hands were folded in her lap. Very deliberately she raised her head until her eyes met those of the bronzed giant. For long moments their eyes held with no expression being reflected by either. Gradually, then, the girl's eyes gave way to softness. A slight smile touched the corners of her lips.

"When I saw you lying in the canoe," she said, breaking the short silence, "I thought I would lie down and await your waking. I have heard that some warriors are very angry if they are aroused from sleep."

Bantan nodded, but no smile touched his lips.

"Can you understand me?" the girl then asked.

Again he nodded.

"Can't you speak?" she interrogated.

Once more he nodded.

"You are a stranger upon Mandoes Island," she said then. "Who are you and from where do you come?"

"I am a stranger," he answered. "My name is Bantan. I come from an island far in the direction where the sun rises over the horizon. What is your name?"

The native girl now smiled more openly, revealing her even white teeth.

"My name is Mauria," she replied. "I am glad that

we can understand each other. We can talk of many things."

"You aren't afraid of me, stranger that I am?" he asked anxiously.

Mauria slowly shook her head. With some coyness she turned her head but continued to look up at him with a tantalizing smile upon her lips.

"If I had been afraid of you, Bantan," she said, "when I first saw you I could have returned to the village and told of your presence here. You would have been captured then."

The bronzed giant nodded.

"That is so," he admitted. "Tell me, why are you so considerate toward me?"

Mauria sighed deeply, and woman-like, shrugged her shoulders, but she could not deny the friendliness in her dark eyes.

Bantan now squatted at her side. Her hair was scented with coconut oil, and a very pleasing perfume obtained from crushed flowers emanated from her. He noted that her smooth, dark features were unblemished. For some reason Mauria reminded him of Lorni, the Waneiro maiden, who had been infatuated with him when he had been a prisoner of Mazona, the village woman chieftain.* The native girl was aware of his appraisal, and she was pleased with his attention.

"Why do you look at me so closely, Bantan?" she asked, but with no reproach in her gentle voice.

"You remind me of a Waneiro maiden that I used to know," he answered.

"You loved her?" Mauria asked softly.

He shrugged his shoulders.

---

*Note: See *"Bantan Valiant."*

"At the time I was hoping to mate with another," he answered truthfully; "and for that reason I could not truly love Lorni. She was infatuated with me when I was a prisoner in her village. I owe her my life. Poor girl, I learned later her leader mutilated her horribly because of her good deed to me."

"That was too bad," Mauria agreed, shaking her head. "But the other you speak of—did you mate with her?"

Bantan shook his head.

"She and her father were destroyed indirectly by our enemies," he answered in a low voice. A gleaming light then entered his eyes as he added: "But I avenged their deaths. Even so, that did not bring my sweetheart back to life."

Mauria took new interest now. One of her hands covered one of his as it rested upon one of his knees.

"You have known sadness and disappointment, Bantan," she murmured with sympathy.

He nodded his head, then strangely looked down at the girl's hand upon his. Noticing, Mauria removed her hand with a shy smile.

"Are you mated now?" she then asked.

The bronzed giant shook his head.

The native girl held her breath while awaiting his reply. Now she exhaled with relief, and a coy smile touched her lips.

"I, too, am unmated," she confessed in a low voice. "For many moons I have been scolded by my parents, and I am scorned by the village women because I have not done so."

Bantan regarded her in silence for a moment before he spoke.

"You are very comely, Mauria," he remarked approvingly. "There should be no reason why you shouldn't find a mate to your liking."

The coy smile lingered upon the girl's lips.

"Perhaps I have been too particular," she murmured. "None of the unmated males in the village appealed to me. Perhaps I have expected too much of a mortal man."

An understanding smile touched the lips of the young giant.

"A girl naturally desires the best she can get," he said.

Mauria smiled broadly and closed her eyes tightly. She drew a deep breath.

"In my mind I know the kind of mate I want," she said. "Many times I have pictured him when I close my eyes. At night when I sleep he seems so real that when I wake in the morning and find that he isn't at my side, I am disappointed. My father has told me repeatedly that if I don't become mated soon that he shall have The Great One send for me." She shuddered visibly.

Bantan did not wish Mauria to know that he had heard of The Great One from Tamur. Where she was older, perhaps she had greater knowledge of that personage.

" 'The Great One'?" he asked innocently. "Who is he?"

The native girl shrugged her shoulders.

"No one seems to know who he is," she replied. "The emissaries who come to the village at intervals never speak of him."

"He must be very mysterious, Mauria," he remarked, somewhat disappointed that she could not enlighten him more than Tamur had.

"When children misbehave in the village," the native girl added, "all their mothers have to do is tell them that they will be sent to The Great One. Thereafter, they behave."

Bantan remained silent.

Mauria looked up at him curiously. She moved closer to him until her brown shoulder touched his. The contact seemed to arouse him from his reveries—as the girl intended that it should. He looked down at her without speaking. The girl's bosom rose and fell noticeably.

"You think I am comely, Bantan?" she murmured huskily. With her words she inclined her head closer to his, their cheeks almost touching. One of her hands again sought his where it rested upon his knee, and she clasped it with her small, warm one.

"You are very comely, Mauria," he declared, at a loss to think of anything else to say to her.

"Do you know," she said then, a dreamy expression coming into her dark eyes, "that you look very much like the man in my dreams?" As she spoke, she turned so that she faced him. Her left breast pressed against his arm, and beneath its voluptuous warmth and softness he could detect the rapid beating of her heart.

The bronzed giant did not speak. He realized at once that his position was becoming a very difficult one, and just how he was to extricate himself from his embarrassment without injuring the girl's vanity presented a dilemma of growing proportions.

As Mauria's dark eyes now glowingly looked up at his features, she caught sight of the birthmark upon his right temple. She softly caressed it with her fingers.

"I, too, have a mark like that," she murmured.

"When I was a young girl my playmates always teased me about it. When I was older and wore a breast covering it was seen no more. But it is still there—and much larger than when I was a small girl."

The bronzed giant maintained a silence, but his features were becoming perplexed. Inwardly he was vainly attempting to formulate some reasonable excuse to keep Mauria in hand. He realized the native girl was infatuated with him because he so resembled her dream man. As a matter of fact he wished that she would leave him so that he might further plan just how he was going to effect Amar's "rescue" from The Great One. He tried to avoid the girl's glowing eyes as she leaned still closer to him and rested a burning cheek against his. He heard her sigh deeply as her warm breath fanned his ear. Now her other hand went to the one that already covered one of his at his knee, and she clasped it gently but firmly in both of hers. She raised it unresistingly and pressed its back to her right breast. Now she was speaking in a husky voice.

"If you really think I am comely, Bantan," she was saying, "do you feel that you might learn one day to love me?"

Having spoken, she drew her cheek from his and looked directly into his eyes. Hers were glowing with increasing passion, and her breathing was deep, almost labored, because of the emotion that coursed through her.

The bronzed giant drew a deep breath and with some difficulty managed to maintain his composure. He was only mortal and Mauria presented an alluring proposition to him. The fact that she was comely and of pleasing disposition made it difficult not to injure her vanity which, he realized, were it wounded by him, could easily turn her into a veritable tigress of revenge. For that reason he must be extremely cautious in dealing with her.

"The fact that you and I are marked similarly, though in different places," she added in a husky voice, "makes me feel that we were meant for each other. Perhaps it is for that reason I have spurned the many suitors in the village—always hoping the day would come when the man of my dreams would appear in person. And now you have."

Releasing his hand at her right breast, she raised herself slightly, and with her fingers again caressed the birthmark upon his right temple. Then, before he could prevent, she inclined her face close to his, and at the next moment her warm lips pressed upon his right temple. As she drew away from him, she uttered a long sigh and her warm breath fanned his cheek. Her eyes were almost closed.

"I have shown my love for you," she murmured. "Won't you show me that you could care for me?"

Bantan could find no words to say. An involuntary smile touched the corners of his lips.

Encouraged, Mauria smiled sweetly.

"Look, Bantan," she said softly, "I want you to see what no man of the village has seen since I donned a breast covering."

At that precise moment, much to Bantan's relief, the attention of the two was alerted. The crackling of twigs was to be heard from nearby. At once the man arose to an erect position, his keen ears alerted to locate the exact direction of the sound.

"Some one comes, Mauria!" he exclaimed.

At the next moment the girl stood at his side, apparently disappointed by the interruption. She breathed deeply, but her eyes were alert as she looked hither and yon.

Bantan turned toward her.

"Perhaps it would be better that we separated," he suggested. "If the village warriors know you are friendly with me, you may be punished."

The girl appeared hurt by his words, but she understood that he meant well.

"You speak wisely, Bantan," she murmured. "Though I dislike leaving you, I will do as you wish. Later, I shall return—if all is well."

He nodded as Mauria gripped his hands for a moment then drew them to her bosom. Then, without further delay, she released his hands and left the bronzed giant standing there in the small clearing near his canoe.

The crackling of underbrush continued from a closer proximity, and before many minutes would elapse, Bantan knew that he would be discovered unless he acted at once. He regretted that he would be unable to conceal his canoe, but under the circumstances he could at least hope it would remain undiscovered. With stealth he crept through the screening foliage, making as little noise as possible. He concealed himself presently behind a dense fern, and parting its fronds, awaited the approach of the intruder.

It was apparent whoever had been heard was not aware of the presence of the stranger upon the island, for no effort was made to conceal his presence. Presently a lone warrior, tall and lithe, with a spear in hand and a dagger sheathed at his right hip appeared. He was looking here and there, mostly upward, apparently searching for something. By some miracle, the warrior overlooked the canoe. Watching him intently, Bantan at last heaved a deep sigh of relief.

Presently all sound of the village warrior had died away in the distance. The bronzed giant decided to hide his canoe behind the lush fern which had concealed him. When this was done he paused to consider what his next move should be. He hoped very much Mauria would not return immediately—or ever—for it had been with a sigh of relief that he had seen her depart.

Knowing Amar had been taken to The Great One, Bantan decided he should seek the well worn path that the guards had taken their prisoners to the other end of the island. He circled about in the foliage, being careful of every step so as to make as little noise as possible.

Meanwhile, the warrior from the village, by name of Doman, had also circled about. Once, when pausing to examine a certain tree, he thought he heard a not far-distant crackling sound. Listening more intently now, his eyes widened a trifle, and with a nod, decided to investigate.

Fifteen minutes later the village warrior was aware that he was gaining upon the one he followed. Presently he was able to obtain a fleeting glimpse of the bronzed young giant. At once Doman realized a stranger was upon Mandoes Island. Knowing he would be well rewarded should he take him prisoner, he increased his pace with narrowed eyes and grim face.

It was then that Bantan, pausing, heard the crackling underbrush to his rear. Turning about, he easily discerned the village warrior trailing him. At once he recognized him as the same who had appeared where his canoe had been cached. Though the Mandoes warrior was armed with a spear, the bronzed giant did not feel it would be helpful, since the underbrush was fairly thick, and a spear could not be used to good advantage.

Bantan might have escaped the stalker if he had been minded, but he realized the warrior would only return to the village and enlist the aid of others. Then, indeed, he would be at wit's end to elude his searchers. Upon the instant he decided he must silence his stalker.

Without further hesitation he quickly advanced toward the Mandoes warrior, who now stood still, awaiting the coming of the stranger. Doman realized his spear would be useless, so he stabbed the stone-tipped point into the soft earth. His right hand grasped the handle of his stone dagger and withdrew it. With grimness upon his dusky features he advanced toward the bronzed giant.

Bantan had not drawn his steel dagger, though his right hand hovered near its handle. When they were about ten feet apart, it was then that the bronzed giant came to a halt.

"I have no quarrel with you," he said.

Doman was surprised that the stranger could speak his tongue.

"You are a stranger upon Mandoes Island," he replied. "That is reason enough for me to take you a prisoner. If you surrender, it will go easier for you."

Bantan's dark eyes glinted. He shook his head emphatically.

"I'll never surrender," he declared.

Doman smiled grimly.

The two then continued to advance toward each other without further words. They pushed the underbrush to one side as they did so.

Bantan increased his pace a trifle. His dark eyes were resting upon a particular springing branch ahead of him. Seizing it, he stepped backward, but holding it firmly with one hand.

Doman thought the stranger was hesitating between advancing and retreating. He waved his stone dagger menacingly. Too late he realized the ruse that was being employed, for there was a sudden swishing of the branch, and though he tried to duck his head, too late, it caught him full in the face, dazing him momentarily.

As the warrior stood there, shaking his head with eyes closed, at the next moment Bantan forged toward him. He seized the wrist of the dagger hand and imprisoned it tightly. His right hand balled and in a flash he dealt his assailant a terrific blow in the face. The force sent Doman backward with his opponent following up with another powerful blow to the chest. Tripping, the Mandoes warrior went down.

Bantan's grip was loosened upon his opponent as he sprawled upon his back on the ground. He stood over the nearly prostrated warrior, alert for whatever move he might make.

Doman's reeling senses were restored in the following moments. Lying upon his back he glared up at the stranger with unmitigated hatred upon his face. He was aware that he still clutched his dagger. He made a feeble move to arise to a seated position, then feigned weakness. At the next moment his dagger slashed in a half circle toward his opponent's legs.

Bantan was alert, and he quickly stepped backward just enough to be out of reach of the dagger's path. At the next moment one foot descended upon the dagger hand's wrist, pinioning it helplessly. The warrior then reached with his other hand to clutch the foot, but as he half rose to do so, the young giant's other sandaled foot swung about. He caught Doman upon the chin, snapping his head back accompanied by a cracking sound—as of bones breaking. A shudder wracked the warrior's form as he lay still with grimaced features.

Bantan studied his opponent for a long moment. He removed his foot from the dagger hand which remained lifeless. Bending, he examined his foe. To his utter surprise, he was aware the warrior was lax. His vertebra had been broken by his sharp kick, and the spinal nerve had been severed. Death had been instantaneous. He placed a hand over the rib cage on the left side and could detect no sound of a beating heart.

Without further delay the bronzed giant scooped a trench with the warrior's stone dagger, and when it was of sufficient depth, he rolled the inert form into it and covered it over. Then he scattered underbrush over the newly made grave.

As he straightened, a subconscious sense warned him that he was being watched. Turning, he looked at three village warriors, each armed with ready spears, standing about twenty feet from him. Their features were grim, and their eyes were filled with bitterness.

CHAPTER V

CAPTIVE

Bantan at once realized the futility of engaging the three warriors in combat. Had they been unarmed would have been another matter. He was aware, too, there would have been nothing gained to attempt to escape them, for did he, in a short while the entire island would be swarming with searchers. He was not sure whether they had witnessed his brief battle with the village warrior, but that they had witnessed his burial he didn't doubt. He raised his hand in the universal sign of peace.

"I am a stranger upon your island," he said. "I come in peace. I have no quarrel with you."

One of the warriors, strongly built and with regular features by name of Bora, looked to his companions. Each nodded in agreement. The apparent leader then spoke to the bronzed giant.

"All strangers upon Mandoes Island are our enemies," he declared. "You are our prisoner."

The three warriors moved in accord toward the stranger, their spears poised to cast if necessary.

Instantly Bantan weighed his chances of a belated attempt to escape. While he disliked to surrender without a struggle, for some unknown reason he realized the hopelessness of making a break for freedom. He remained still while the three warriors neared him. No emotion registered upon his features, but his sharp eyes were alert.

The apparent leader of the three warriors now confronted Bantan. His two companions stepped to each side of the stranger and grasped an arm.

"What have you buried, stranger?" Bora asked.

"A village warrior attacked me," Bantan answered. "We fought. I killed him. I did not mean to do so."

"We shall see who he was," Bora stated.

With his words he stooped and brushed away the leaves and twigs that covered the newly made grave. In a few minutes he had uncovered the features of the corpse.

"Doman!" he exclaimed. The deceased warrior had been a good friend of his. His face became livid with rage as he arose and confronted the prisoner. "You killed him!" he shouted, spittle spraying Bantan's face.

The young giant remained calm, no emotion visible upon his face except for the slight narrowing of his eyes. He anticipated the warrior's move.

Bora was about to slap the stranger's face. It was not Bantan's intention of accepting such an insult from any one while the breath of life was his.

So quickly he acted, his two guards were befuddled. Bantan's arms snapped forward as would two springs, and before Bora's hand had travelled half the distance required, one of the bronzed giant's hands seized the wrist while the other reached for the leader's other hand. For a moment he held them in a steel-like grip, his glinting eyes never leaving Bora's.

The two guards, meanwhile, regained their wits. They placed their spears to one side. Once again they sought to imprison the stranger's arms. But this time Bantan was not to submit to capture without a struggle. As the two guards seized him, the bronzed giant forged ahead, forcing Bora, and dragging the two warriors with him.

As Bora tripped and fell backward, the bronzed giant was unable to check himself, and he fell upon him. At the next moment the two guards were upon him. For several minutes there was a free for all. Arms and legs thrashed, but the odds of three to one were too much for the young giant in his present setting. As a result, panting, with mighty chest heaving, he was pinioned helpless upon the ground.

Bora arose to his feet with livid features. Though he wanted to vent his rage upon the prisoner, he entertained a certain amount of respect for him. He had looked into his glinting eyes of defiance, and what he had seen therein had caused a chill to race the length of his spine. He shrugged as he spoke to his two companions.

"Rama and Stao, let him up. We'll take him to the village. Our chief will know what to do with him."

Bantan was dragged to his feet, and this time the two guards held each of his arms tightly. Stao, upon his right, appropriated the prisoner's dagger.

Bora gathered together their discarded spears, and with a nod, indicated they would take up their way.

There was nothing the bronzed giant could do now. Bora followed them, keeping a spear poised in his right hand while his left clutched the spears of his companions. Through the foliage they forged, and some fifteen minutes later had reached the edge of the village. As some of the inhabitants saw them, and noted the stranger who was their prisoner, their shouts attracted others with the result a number of men, women, and children quickly gathered about them, talking excitedly. They followed as the trio marched their prisoner in the direction of the chief's hut. A youth by name of Tulu hurried ahead to inform the chief of the prisoner.

Before they reached their destination the Chief, Muna, appeared upon the threshold of his doorway with Tulu alongside. With pensive eyes he watched Bora and his two companions march the prisoner in his direction until they presently confronted him.

"We have taken a prisoner, O chief," Bora spoke up. "He killed Doman. We apprehended him as he was completing the burial."

No expression was evident upon Muna's features as he looked closely at the prisoner with appraising eyes. He could easily discern that he was not a native despite the heavy coating of bronze upon his features and body.

"Who are you, stranger?" he asked in a deep voice.

"My name is Bantan," was the reply. "I was born in faraway America, but have lived the most of my life upon Beneiro Island. You would not know of that island?"

The chief shook his head.

"Bantan—that is a native name," he mused.

"It means child of the sea born of unknown parents," was the forthcoming explanation.

Muna remained silent for a few moments while he continued to appraise the stranger.

"You killed one of our warriors known as Doman?" he asked at length.

"It was a fair fight," Bantan answered. "I told Doman I was a stranger and that I came in peace."

The chief slowly shook his head.

"The fact that you are a stranger was reason enough that Doman fought with you," he said in answer. "All strangers are enemies of the Mandoes." He turned to Bora. "Put him in the prison hut," he directed. "The Great One shall be notified at once."

The bronzed giant desperately resisted his two guards, but in the end he was forced to the prison hut and thrust within. The door was closed and barred. He wondered then, in recollection, why Tamur had not made an appearance as he had earlier in the day. It was possible that he had gone to the other side of the island hoping to see him. And Mauria—she had not been seen either. It was possible that she, too, had gone to see him. Perhaps that was the explanation for their absence.

Meanwhile, the chief dispatched several warriors with Bora in the lead to disinter the body of Doman so that he might be given a more proper burial. Then he sent a messenger to summon Molo, the tom-tom beater, to his hut. When the giant warrior appeared, the chief informed him that he was to send a message to The Great One in the castle upon the other end of the island announcing that another prisoner had been taken, and that this one was of white heritage.

*   *   *

In the prison hut Bantan seated himself upon his haunches and tried not to think of what the future held in store for him. He was grateful, however, that his wrists and ankles had not been bound. Remembering that Amar had been imprisoned in this same hut earlier in the day now occurred to him. His hands clenched and unclenched. What wouldn't he have given if the Amo Island prince could only have been here at the present instead of being taken to The Great One in

the company of his father and the other two Amo
warriors. In a vague way he wondered if the opportunity would be his to meet once again the one who was
indirectly responsible for the death of his Amo Island
sweetheart.

Suddenly he was aroused from his reveries. He
heard a tom-tom beating. He immediately arose and
went to the barred window and peered through the
opening. Upon a dais, some ten feet above the ground
at the side of the chief's hut where a tom-tom set, he
saw a giant warrior swinging a mighty knobbed club.

He had never heard a drum beating in the manner
the tom-tom beater performed now. Had he knowledge
of the Morse code he would have understood the message that was being sent. Many years ago when The
Great One had come to Mandoes Island, and became
established in the castle upon the elevation at the other
end of the island, he had conceived the method of
sending and receiving messages from the village. That
first tom-tom beater was taught the Morse code with
instructions that he, in turn, would teach his successor,
and that he, in due time, would do likewise. From
father to eldest son this knowledge had been transmitted.

First, Molo dispatched a brief message, repeating
this at short intervals, while he listened intently for a
reply. Presently it came, and communication was thus
established. And now the message that was dispatched
from the village was:

"A white prisoner has been taken. Advise."

A full minute's silence prevailed. Bantan now saw
that Molo's attention was alerted. To his keen ears
he heard a similar coded message from the distant
drum.

"We shall come for the white prisoner at once. The Great One is anxious to see him."

Molo then sounded several coded beats to which was received a similar reply. Then he left the dais and reported to Chief Muna that his message had been delivered and acknowledged, and that guards would come at once for the white prisoner.

The chief was pleased. With the wave of a hand he dismissed the tom-tom beater.

Meanwhile, in the prison hut, Bantan conjectured at the message that had been sent and received concerning him.

In a little while Bora and his warriors arrived with the corpse of Doman. Since the deceased one was not mated, his father, mother, and two younger, teen-age sisters prepared the body for proper burial.

Zoma, the witch doctor, garbed in his ceremonial robes and with mask on, conducted the rites, while Chief Muna was a silent witness. When at last the final prayers were invoked to their deity, Doman was borne to the burial ground upon the outskirts of the village, and there was given proper interment.

These ceremonies were just completed when two giant warriors, identical in appearance, the same two who had come earlier, appeared from the trail which led from the castle on the higher end of the island. Their presence was immediately recognized. The two guards had come to take the white prisoner to The Great One.

Chief Muna, who had retired to his hut, was speedily informed of their coming. He lost no time greeting them.

"Come," he said, "the prisoner is awaiting you."

The chief instructed Bora, with several warriors, to

bring forth the stranger from the prison hut. As Bantan stepped outside, his wrists were bound in front of him with stout thongs, but not without resistance on his part, futile as it was. Meanwhile, some of the villagers vilified him because of his being instrumental in the death of Doman. The members of the deceased warrior's family, especially, were bitterly disposed toward the prisoner. The father of the deceased Doman restrained himself to merely glare in bitterness. His mate and their two teen-aged daughters sought to kick and scratch Bantan, and had to be forcibly dragged away from him, but still they shouted their rage.

"The prisoner is ready to be taken to The Great One," the chief at last announced.

The two guards nodded perfunctorily, then turned to Bantan.

"Come," one said, "let us be on our way."

Bantan looked at each warrior. They looked enough alike to be twins. Their height and physical construction was the same, and their features were of an identical mold. He estimated they were in their late twenties, but later, he had reason to wonder about this.

One of the guards stepped ahead of the prisoner while the other followed close upon his heels. They returned to the trail at the outskirts of the village. The chief and many warriors accompanied them to the edge of the village, but there they halted.

Chief Muna wished them the best of luck, to which the guard in the rear acknowledged with a grunt and a shrug of his broad shoulders. In a few moments the two guards and their prisoner were beyond view of the watching villagers.

While they traversed a well worn path, Bantan was aware he did not harbor any animosity toward his two guards. They had not harmed him in any way nor were they discourteous in their treatment of him. He wondered if they would converse with him. Without pausing, he spoke over a shoulder to the guard who followed him.

"You and the one ahead are twins, are you not?" he asked.

There was some hesitation before the warrior answered.

"It is true. I am Humo. He is Hulo. He is the eldest. That is why he leads and I follow."

Hulo turned about while still walking and looked seriously at the prisoner.

"You are not an islander," he remarked. "How is it that you speak our tongue?"

"When I was a small boy I was marooned upon Beneiro Island and adopted by the chief," Bantan answered. "I've been to different islands since then, and on only one was I received as a friend. Why must people of different islands be so unfriendly toward one another?"

Hulo shrugged his shoulders.

"It always has been," was the only answer.

For the first time Bantan looked squarely at the guard, and his interest was centered upon his features. He noticed the finely meshed wrinkles that covered his entire face, being more pronounced at the corners of his eyes and mouth. And as Hulo turned about, after speaking, he noticed a similar condition about his neck. His arms, too, were seamed similarly beneath their duskiness.

He then looked over a shoulder at Humo and noticed a similar condition. Though he had not spoken since revealing his name and that of his brother, he

seemed interested that Hulo had answered the prisoner's questions. As a general rule guards had little to
discuss with prisoners; but this young giant was much
different from the other prisoners that he had brought
to The Great One. He was white.

"I understand The Great One has sent for me,"
Bantan then vouched. "Does he come from a faraway
land—perhaps the same from which I came as a boy?"

Hulo paused, as did the prisoner. Naturally, Humo
came to a halt as well. The elder twin and his brother
exchanged a meaning glance, then with a shake of their
heads resumed their way. Over his shoulder Hulo
spoke.

"We are not permitted to discuss The Great One. In
due time you will meet him."

Bantan subsided into silence thereafter as they continued their way. The path was leading slightly upward, but no difficulty was experienced. Its surface was
fairly smooth. Numerous trees and thick foliage
bordered the trail at first, but as the trio proceeded,
the trees became scarcer and the foliage sparser. The
rich loam was giving way to rocky earth. To each side
in the distance a view of the broad ocean could be
glimpsed. A gentle breeze stirred. Insects of a flying
nature did not trouble them.

The fact that his wrists were bound did not trouble
the prisoner. The thongs were not too tight, and the
fact they were in front of him instead of in back did
not cause him any discomfort. He made no effort to
free his wrists of their bonds, feeling as he did he
would not be successful. The giant warrior following
him could observe any such attempt on his part, and
would doubtlessly discourage him.

Bantan's curiosity was roused at thought of The

Great One. He entertained the possibility that he might prove friendly to him—who could tell? He wondered somewhat why Hulo had said it was forbidden for the guards to discuss The Great One. He could only shrug his shoulders, but he knew very shortly he would understand all that he could only conjecture now.

The inclining path was becoming more steeper as the trio proceeded, and the trees were much scarcer and the foliage very sparse. Here and there rugged plants had taken root in the thin soil and they had managed to survive, though poorly. Sickly flowers grew there as well.

Bantan would look upward at intervals, and the stone hut where The Great One lived seemed to grow larger. Now he was aware that a great stone wall surrounded it, and he had reason to wonder why this precaution had been added.

The more he wondered the more puzzled he was. Most perplexing of all was the identity of The Great One and from where he had come to make his home upon this isolated island in the mighty Pacific Ocean. For what reason had he come hither? Again the young giant shrugged his shoulders as a result of his cogitations. Since he and the two guards had not spoken further, the young man's active mind would not remain still in his endeavor to seek answers to the riddles that confronted him.

Then, to still such burning curiosity, he wondered if he would have the opportunity of settling his scores with Amar. After all, the Amo Island prince was the reason he paddled over trackless miles of water. If there were a just god in the heaven he tried to convince

himself that he would not be denied the privilege of
meting to Amar the justly dues he was entitled to administer to him.

And so Bantan reasoned as they mounted the inclining trail with no stops. At intervals, Hulo would
stumble, but quickly regained his balance. His chest
seemed to heave to his labored breathing. A similar
exertion was apparent on Humo's part as well. The
bronzed giant, however, did not experience the evident exhaustion the twin brothers did. Fleeting glances
at their features also revealed the wrinkled mesh of
their skin appeared more pronounced, and he had
reason to wonder why this was so.

It seemed the two guards were anxious to reach the
castle before sundown. Perhaps they were hungry, but
more likely they were embarrassed at revealing fatigue
before the seemingly untired prisoner. This being the
second trip they had made this day from the castle to
the village and returning was reason enough for their
evident weariness.

In the west the sun was nearing the horizon, and
before much more time would elapse darkness would
sweep over the world beneath. The gentle breeze that
was noticeable for some time was slightly increasing.
Because of its coolness neither Bantan or the guards
perspired any as a result of their continued movement
ever upward. The prisoner breathed easily, his broad
chest moving rhythmically to his inhalations and ex-
halations, but the two guards seemed to gasp a trifle
with opened mouths for the slightly thinner air at this
higher elevation. It was evident their physical condition was not perfect as that of the prisoner.

Now at last the lower half of the sun had slipped
beneath the water horizon. The two guards and their

prisoner were nearing the great stone wall, which was all of ten feet in height. Bantan noticed the outlined portion, which was six feet in height and four in width, and he assumed it was a means of ingress. How the massive stone door would open puzzled him, but he was soon to learn.

As they presently confronted the outlined portion of the wall, both twin brothers heaved a sigh of relief. Hulo pressed a black button in line with his waist. A whining sound, barely audible, was to be heard.

Bantan watched in amazement as the stone door swung inward without effort. He noticed the wall was a foot in thickness. Before him he saw a smooth, stone walkway that led through a carefully cared lawn with various flower bushes growing in unique patterns to the very portal of the huge stone castle.

All three, Hulo leading, with Bantan and Humo following, stooped as they stepped within the doorway. Hulo pressed another black button on the inside of the wall, and as effortlessly as before, accompanied by the barely audible, whining sound, the massive stone door swung shut.

Chapter VI

PRISONER—OR GUEST?

Looking to either side of him, Bantan could see no living beings in the shade that now covered the entire walled area owing to the nearly set sun.

Hulo, the leader, started for the doorway. His twin brother spoke to the prisoner to follow. Without any comment the bronzed giant moved soundlessly along the walkway with the guard close behind him.

As they approached the castle, Bantan looked upon it, marvelling at its greatness. Then, noting that the windows on this side were all barred, a slight tremor raced the length of his spine, realizing as he did, that barred windows meant there was no escape through them.

Presently they mounted several stone steps and confronted another stone door. Hulo again pressed a button at its side, and as effortlessly as the wall door, this one swung inward with a barely audible, whining sound.

Hulo entered, followed by the prisoner, with Humo last. The leader then pressed a button on the inside, and the door silently closed with a similar sound.

Bantan looked in wonder at the large hall they had entered. The ceiling was ten feet high and the room all of twenty feet square. A peculiar fixture set in the center of the ceiling and suspended several feet below. A number of small glass bulbs were affixed to it in the form of a circle. Other than that the walls were bare. As the prisoner looked up at the chandelier, memory of seeing similar fixtures eluded him for the present, but that he had seen such in the past he was sure.

Hulo turned to his twin brother and nodded in the direction of an opened doorway at the far end of the hall. As he started toward it, Bantan was in the act of following, but Humo placed a restraining hand upon his shoulder. As the prisoner looked questionably at his captor, the warrior shook his head.

The young giant shrugged and just stood there with feet slightly apart. His eyes, however, looked up at the chandelier in the center of the ceiling. Now he remembered where he had seen similar fixtures. In the stateroom he had shared with Father Lasance aboard the ill-fated yacht, the *Comet*, which Mr. Roland Brown had chartered for his South Pacific cruise in his search for Bantan and his parents, was where he had seen the like. The glass bulbs furnished artificial light at night. He nodded as he realized The Great One had managed to generate that strange element known as electricity. At present the room was fairly light, and that he believed was the reason they had not been turned on.

Presently Hulo appeared at the doorway. Since his twin brother had been anticipating his presence there, there was no necessity for words. The leader merely indicated with a hand that they were to approach in his direction.

Humo did not need to nudge the prisoner, for Bantan had seen Hulo beckon to them. He merely looked at his guard and a nod was sufficient for understanding. Wordlessly they crossed the hall, Hulo drawing

aside as they passed through the doorway into a
smaller room.

The bronzed giant noticed that this room was not as
bare as the hall had been. Upon the walls were a number of framed paintings of strangely dressed men and
women in full length. From the ceiling a chandelier
suspended as in the hall. What interested him most of
all was directly across the room where a curtained
booth set upon a dais. At that moment the many lights
in the chandelier came on and the room was as bright
as day. The prisoner looked intently at the curtained
booth. The material was very much like silk. It was
pure white and of an exceptionally finely woven mesh.

Hulo and his twin brother each gently took one of
Bantan's arms and led him to about ten feet from
the curtained booth.

The leader bowed his head in due respect, then
raising it, spoke.

"This is the white prisoner, O Great One."

A short silence ensued before a reply from beyond
the curtain was to be heard. It was as though The
Great One was carefully appraising the prisoner before speaking. At last a voice that was clear and metallic spoke in the English tongue.

"First of all, what is your name?"

"Bantan."

"That is a native name. Yet, you look like a bronzed
white man."

"I was born in faraway America," Bantan added.
"When I was a small boy I was marooned upon
Beneiro Island. The chief adopted me and reared me
to manhood. I have since learned that my real name is
Arthur Delcourt."

A short silence ensued before the voice behind the curtain spoke again.

"Why did you come to this Island?"

"I came in search of an enemy—one by name of Amar," was the reply.

"Why was he your enemy?"

Bantan explained briefly.

Another short silence followed.

"You know that he is here in this castle now?"

"I do," was the answer.

"You would kill him were you given the chance to avenge your sweetheart's death?" The Great One asked then.

Bantan straightened his shoulders and lifted his head proudly.

"I would," he declared.

Again a short silence ensued before the personage behind the curtain spoke.

"Killing for mere revenge is not permitted upon this island. There are other more important means of sacrificing a life than for mere personal satisfaction. I am surprised that you, knowing you are a white man, would entertain such thoughts. Your religious training has been sadly neglected. Do you not know that it is against the laws of God that a man shall wantonly take the life of another?"

Bantan humbly bowed his head and closed his eyes for a long moment. The patrician features of Father Lasance were framed in his mind. Presently he raised his head and opened his eyes.

"A missionary of the church, with whom I was marooned upon an island taught me what you say," he answered. "But after we were rescued and went our individual ways, much misfortune befell me, and for that reason I forgot what he taught me."

A brief silence intervened.

"Tell me what happened," the clear, metallic voice stated.

Briefly, Bantan related his experiences with the Japanese, who had conquered and subjugated the inhabitants of Marja Island, and those of Beneiro as well. *

The prisoner was surprised at the changed tone of voice The Great One now spoke. It seemed saddened.

"In a time of war," he said, "the laws of God are strangely forgotten. It seems both sides are hoping and praying that their God will favor them in victory. War is a needless waste of money, materials, and human life. Even the Holy Bible predicts there has and always will be wars. Man alone is responsible. In the beginning man was given a free will to do as he pleased. That is why, I believe, God has allowed men to continue killing one another in warfare, hoping they will eventually learn from past experiences that war is useless. There are so many other more useful things that man might do. It is for that reason I abandoned the land of my birth and came here, hoping that I might continue my experiments in the ultimate hope I would succeed where all others have failed to the present day to solve the troubles of mankind."

"You speak with great wisdom, O Great One," Bantan declared. "I, too, would like peace to forever prevail. Never have I sought to foment trouble. But when it came my way, I did not step aside. I cannot feel that I would like being a coward."

*See *"Bantan Defiant"* and *"Bantan Valiant."*

The Great One did not answer at once. It was evident that he carefully studied the bronzed giant through the curtain, though he, himself, could not be seen. At last he spoke in a strangely solemn voice.

"Bantan, you interest me. Our interview for the present must come to an end. Tomorrow I shall speak with you further."

The young giant bowed his head, then lifting it presently, addressed the speaker concealed behind the curtain.

"Thank you, O Great One."

"Hulo, come closer," The Great One commanded, his tone metallic again.

The guard removed his hand from the prisoner's shoulder and advanced toward the curtained booth. He went down upon his knees.

The Great One spoke in a tone of voice audible only for Hulo to hear.

"Remove the bonds from Bantan's wrists. Lead him to the Guest room—and do *not lock the door.*"

"It shall be as you command, O Great One," Hulo murmured, lifting his head.

Arising, he returned to his twin brother and Bantan. Without a word he loosened the bonds encircling the prisoner's wrists, making no explanation.

"Follow me," the leader then said to Bantan.

Wonderingly, the bronzed giant did as he was bade. They returned to the hall, and Hulo went to an outlined door in the wall. He pressed a button, and the door silently swung open, revealing an elevator. All three stepped within, Humo last. Then Hulo pressed a lever. The door swung shut and the conveyance moved silently upward.

To say that Bantan was amazed would be putting it

mildly. Without a word he waited until the elevator at last came to a stop on the top floor of the castle. Hulo pressed a lever and the door opened into a corridor. He stepped from the elevator and motioned to the prisoner and his twin brother to follow. They passed several wooden doors to what appeared rooms, and then at last paused at the door of one at the extreme end of the corridor.

Hulo pushed the door open, then turned to Bantan.

"This is to be your room," he said. "Presently you will be brought food."

The twin brothers then departed.

The bronzed giant stepped within the well furnished room, leaving the door open. Strangely he was reminded of the stateroom aboard the ill-fated *Comet*. There even was a lavatory in one corner. Approaching the wash bowl, he turned each faucet and saw that both hot and cold water was available. He walked about the fairly large room with hands akimbo. He approached one of the two windows the room was equipped with and he was surprised that it was not barred. Quickly he stepped to the other and noted it, too, was unbarred. Looking down, he saw that this part of the castle overlooked the edge of a cliff. He could see and hear the giant waves smashing against the solid rock several hundred feet below him.

Now that the sun had set he noticed the quick setting darkness overcoming the broad expanse of water stretching to the horizon. Turning about, he looked for the button at the edge of the door frame which would illuminate the room. He found it, and pressing it, flooded the room with light from the many bulbs in the chandelier. He looked toward the half-size bed in a corner of the room, and approaching it, tried it for

comfort. He was assured he would sleep well after
the past several evenings sleeping in the cramped
quarters of his canoe.

Presently arising from the bed, he noticed the other
furnishings in the room. There was a small square
table and two chairs, and there also was a bureau. To
satisfy his curiosity, Bantan opened the drawers, but
nothing was to be seen in any of them.

It was then that he heard soft, shuffling footfalls
just outside the opened door. He turned to observe a
young-appearing native girl bearing a tray of food.
She wore a modest *tupa* dress that reached to her
knees, and sandals were on her feet. Her long, lustrous
hair was fastened at the nape of her neck to keep it
from tumbling over her shoulders in front. She appeared very comely; even though her features were
dusky, they were well molded. She was slimly built, but
of good proportions, and could not be over twenty
years of age.

As she entered the room she glanced apprehensively
at its occupant, their eyes meeting for a fleet moment.
Then hers lowered quickly as she went directly to the
table where she placed the tray of food. She looked up
at Bantan and spoke to him in her native tongue.

"Your evening meal," she said. "I will return later
for the tray and dishes."

He nodded and smiled, thanking her. He was aware
of a delicate fragrance from the perfume the girl
adorned herself permeating the room. It reminded him
of the aroma from crushed flowers.

A slight flush tinged the servant girl's cheeks, and
with a slight bow of her head, took her departure without further hesitation.

The bronzed giant approached the table. The aroma

of the food was pleasing to his nostrils, and just looking at it made him realize how hungry he was. There was a glass of fruit juice which he drank and found very tasty. There was baked fish, and some freshly cooked buns that tasted unlike anything he had eaten since he had been aboard the ill-fated *Comet*. There also was some fruit for dessert, bananas and figs. When he had consumed the last morsel he smacked his lips and sighed. Presently, while he contemplated his good fortune, the servant girl returned for the tray and the soiled dishes. She noted that he had eaten everything. The shadow of a smile touched her lips as her large dark eyes met his.

"Did you have enough to eat?" she asked in a soft-toned voice.

"Quite enough," he answered with a nod. "The food was very good. Thank you."

The servant girl's smile increased and her eyes lowered before his steady ones. She did not appear surprised that he spoke her tongue well; doubtless Hulo or Humo had informed her that he could. At the girl's smile it was then that Bantan noticed the wrinkles at the corners of her eyes and lips, and his keen eyes studied her features beneath the bright lights. He wondered now if she were as young as he had first assumed. A fine mesh of wrinkles seemed to cover her entire face, and her neck was similarly seamed. His eyes then noted her arms, and they, too, seemed unnaturally seamed.

Now the servant girl raised her head and once again her eyes met his for a brief moment before dropping again.

"I'm glad you liked the food," she said simply.

She started to pick up the tray.

"Who are you?" Bantan asked.

The girl hesitated, as though reluctant to speak.

"My name is Loula," she answered.

"You are from the Mandoes village?" he added.
She nodded.

"Do you like being here?" he questioned further.

He noted the sudden change in her eyes as she again
lowered her head.

"I must go now," was all she said.

Bantan regarded her in silence as she picked up the
tray with the soiled dishes and turned to depart. At the
doorway she paused momentarily to look back at the
occupant of the guest room. A secret smile touched the
corners of her lips as she left, leaving behind the faint,
pleasing aroma of the perfume obtained from crushed
flowers.

The young giant shrugged, then went to one of the
two windows and looked out at the darkened water
beneath. Presently he looked up at the star-dotted
canopy. For fully half an hour he remained there, al-
ternately looking upward and then down in the pitch
blackness below. He could dully hear the waves smashing against the cliff far beneath.

For no reason whatever did he feel inclined to leave
this luxurious room. Thus far his advent to the castle
of The Great One had not been displeasing in the least.
He seemed to feel now that he was more of a guest
than a prisoner. In recollection, his treatment by both
Hulo and Humo had been of the utmost respect. Having been served a most delectable meal had added to
his feeling of well being.

Later, feeling wearied, Bantan decided to retire.
First, he approached the opened door and peered into
the corridor. He could see no one, and all was silent.

He examined the door, noticing it had no contrivance for locking it upon the inside. He shrugged as he drew the door almost closed. He pressed the button that would turn off the lights. Then, unerringly, he walked across the darkened room and lay down with a deep sigh. So soft and comfortable the mattress was, before he was aware of the transition, he was fast asleep.

Much later, a seeming apparition approached the door of the "guest" room and listened carefully. The rhythmic breathing of the sleeper was easily to be heard. For long moments the listener remained immobile as a statue. Guided by the sleeper's breathing, the silent one approached to the very side of the bed.

Eyes becoming accustomed to the darkness, the apparition's soft breathing became a trifle labored. Standing there, undecided, the silent one hovered over the sleeping form, a hand outstretched which wanted above all else to caress the smooth brow and push back the tumbled curls.

And then the silent one seemed frozen. The sleeper's rhythmic breathing was broken. He swallowed several times and murmured something unintelligible beneath his breath. His arms and legs tensed for moments, then he turned over upon a side and became perfectly still.

The seeming apparition stifled a deep sigh, and hesitant, turned and left the room in absolute silence. In the corridor the silent one drew the door almost shut, as it had been when entering, and then was gone.

Belatedly alerted, Bantan's eyes opened wide, and he listened carefully. A pungent aroma came to his nostrils, and he was reminded of perfume obtained from crushed flowers. He remembered when Loula had left earlier in the evening with the tray and soiled dishes that a similar aroma had been noticed. She could have no reason to have returned thus late at night unless—

He heard no sound except the barely audible soughing of the wind through the unbarred windows and the dull sound of waves smashing against the cliff far below.

He turned over upon his back and remained perfectly still, hardly breathing. While sleeping, he had sensed the presence of some one in the room, and for that reason had waked—though belatedly. As his eyes became accustomed to the darkness of the room, he looked toward the door and saw that it was still slightly ajar as he had left it.

Perhaps ten minutes of tensed listening passed. Then, once again, aware of how very tired he was, he closed his eyes. With a sigh he thought of Wanya and Lori upon Marja Island, and he wondered if they had been thinking of him. And then once more he was fast asleep.

CHAPTER VII

DRUGGED

Bantan slept the entire night through thereafter without waking once. When he opened his eyes and saw that morning had come, he turned upon his back and looked up at the ceiling, orienting himself. Then, remembering that The Great One would interview him this morning, he quickly arose and performed his matutinal ablutions. He had just finished wetting his dark hair and was pushing it back in pompadour fashion when Loula entered, bearing a tray upon which his breakfast reposed. He smiled as he spoke to her.

"Pleasant morning, Loula."

The native girl's smile was shy.

"Pleasant morning, Bantan," she answered in a strangely trembling voice.

As the girl passed and set the tray upon the table, to Bantan's keen nostrils came the pleasant aroma of crushed flowers—the same pleasing scent he had noticed the evening before when Loula brought his evening meal, also later, when he had been belatedly awakened from his sleep. He made no comment as he walked to the table and seated himself.

Loula hesitated at the table and the bronzed giant could easily determine that she had a message for him.

"Bantan," she said.

"Yes, Loula?" he asked.

"The Great One regrets he will be unable to interview you today as he promised," she said. "He has other more urgent business at hand."

The young giant nodded as he looked up at the servant girl. She was gazing at him with admiring eyes; but as she noticed his attention, the spell was broken.

"A little later Hulo shall take you for a stroll about the castle grounds," Loula added.

Bantan again nodded.

"You are fortunate that you are a guest instead of a prisoner," she added. "The others that were taken to the castle are not faring as well as you."

The bronzed giant drank a glass of cold fruit juice and found it very refreshing. As he set the emptied glass upon the tray, he raised his eyes to the servant girl who was regarding him once again with gentleness.

"One of them is my enemy," he said. "I have vowed to kill him."

The girl shuddered momentarily because of the bitterness in his dark eyes.

"You must have a very good reason," she murmured.

He merely nodded.

"I'll return for the tray and dishes later," Loula then said, and turning, departed.

Bantan finished his breakfast in silence. Arising, he walked to one of the two windows and looked out at the sparkling ocean beyond, and then speculatingly at the waves dashing against the cliff below.

The servant girl returned in due time. Unknown to Bantan, she had paused at the opened door and looked at him with eyes of wistfulness. Then, shaking her head, she dispelled the thoughts which plagued her and entered the room. So silently she moved on sandaled

feet, else the bronzed giant's thoughts were far away,
he did not hear her only as she picked up the tray. He
turned about quickly.

"Loula," he said.

The girl looked up at him questionably.

"Can you tell me if Hulo and his twin brother have
been here long?" Bantan asked.

Loula hesitated a moment, as though undecided to
answer.

"Have they been here at the castle longer than
you?" he then asked.

She nodded.

"Do you remember them in the Mandoes village?"
he added.

The girl shook her head and without a further word
departed with the tray of dishes.

The bronzed giant in turn shook his head as though
vexed because of the lack of information Loula had
furnished him. What was the mystery of how long the
twin brothers had been here? Was there something
unusual about the length of time involved?

He returned to the window, and though he appeared
to be looking out at the sparkling water, a preoccupied
expression overcame his dark eyes. Numerous questions were presented before him, and for an answer,
he could only shake his head dubiously.

The Amo prisoners were not faring well, so Loula
had said. And yet, he had been taken a prisoner and
had been treated with courtesy by his two guards. His
first meeting—though he had not actually seen The
Great One—had resulted in his status as being unquestionably a guest rather than a prisoner. The inevitable question was—why? With a shake of his head
for an answer to his own question, he now wondered at

what work The Great One was engaged in, and what part he, possibly, was to play in the near future.

It was then that Hulo appeared at the doorway. His steady eyes rested upon the young giant standing at the window. No emotion whatever was revealed upon his features as he spoke to Bantan.

"Come," he said in a resonant voice.

Bantan turned about at the sound of the spoken word. A smile touched his lips.

"Pleasant morning to you, Hulo," he greeted him.

The trace of a smile touched the stalwart warrior's lips and he nodded.

"Pleasant morning to you, Bantan," he answered.

The bronzed giant advanced toward Hulo.

"Loula told me that The Great One would be unable to see me today," he vouched. "She added that you were to take me for a stroll about the grounds."

"That is true," the warrior replied.

In another moment they were walking along the corridor. As they passed the other doors, Bantan nodded toward one and spoke concerning it.

"They are rooms like the one I have?" he asked.

Hulo merely nodded.

Presently they reached the elevator, and in a few moments were descending to the ground level. No words were spoken by either. Bantan marvelled at this means of movement, and he had reason to compliment The Great One's ingenuity. He realized considerable time must have been consumed in building the castle and its surrounding wall. Time—that word again puzzled the young giant to the extent he questioned that such an element as time meant anything to The Great One.

Reaching the ground floor, there was to be heard

the barely audible whirring sound as the elevator door opened. Hulo stepped out to be followed by the young giant. The warrior nodded toward the door that led outside, and they walked side by side to it. Again the whining sound was heard as the stone door swung easily inward to the pressing of a button, and stepping outside, it swung closed as effortlessly.

Bantan filled his lungs to their utmost with the slightly cool, morning air and slowly exhaled. He felt good—the brightness of his dark eyes evidenced his physical state of well being. Looking about, he saw a male slave cutting the grass with a strange contraption. Nearby, another with a pair of hand clippers, was snipping grass from around a beautifully arranged flower bed.

As Hulo and Bantan passed the two slaves, they did not look up from their work. The bronzed giant's keen eyes noted the wrinkled mesh of their skin, and again he had reason to wonder why this was so.

Proceeding on their way without a word being spoken, they presently came to a swimming pool some thirty feet square. The young giant noted the door in the castle from which a walkway of smooth stone led to the swimming pool. He also saw a single chair beneath a canopy of thatched mats at the edge of the pool. He paused and looked with admiration into the translucent water to its sandy floor some ten feet beneath the surface. Hulo came to a halt as the "guest" did.

"Could I have a swim?" Bantan asked his companion. "The water looks very inviting."

The stalwart warrior shook his head.

"Only one swims in this pool, Bantan," he answered.

"Do not ask me who that one is, for I am forbidden to say.

The bronzed giant shrugged his shoulders as, with some reluctance, he left the swimming pool with Hulo at his side. In his mind he was wondering at the identity of the one who was so favored to bathe in the pool. There was no question that The Great One refreshed himself in the inviting water—that would be reason enough for its privacy, and that all others would be forbidden. The door beyond the walkway, he guessed, must lead to his quarters.

As they resumed their way, Bantan appeared thoughtful. Hulo walked alongside him in silence. Looking toward the warrior, and his eyes again noticing the finely meshed wrinkled skin, the young giant decided to ask him about his age.

"Have you been stationed in the castle very long, Hulo?" he asked.

A nod of the head was the warrior's answer.

Bantan laughed.

"That isn't much of an answer," he remarked. "Couldn't you tell me how many moons, for instance?"

"Many moons," was the reply.

A smile lingered upon the young giant's lips.

"How old are you, Hulo?" he then asked.

Had Bantan been looking directly at his companion, he would have been aware of a tightening of Hulo's lips and a saddened expression in his dark eyes. He dispelled the depressing thoughts from his mind as he answered in a low voice.

"I am many moons old. Does that satisfy your curious mind?"

Bantan merely shrugged as they resumed their way, but a moment later he again spoke to his companion.

"You are very evasive in regards to your age, Hulo," he said. "You may wonder why I asked you, and I'll tell you—if you are interested."

The stalwart warrior looked at Bantan questionably.

"Though you appear a young man," the bronzed giant said, "the fact that your skin is a mesh of fine wrinkles tells me you are of great age." He now came to a halt as did Hulo, and the latter was staring in wonder at his companion.

"Look closely at my face and you will see there is a great difference compared to yours," Bantan added.

The giant warrior merely nodded but uttered no words.

"Age is nothing to be ashamed of, Hulo," the young giant added. His tones became mollifying. "All of us grow old with passing moons. It cannot be otherwise. Even mighty trees grow from tiny seedlings, but when their time comes to die and wither away, they do so."

The stalwart warrior closed his eyes tightly for a moment to conceal whatever mental anguish that otherwise might have been revealed; then, with a resolute shake of his head, his eyes opened again. He turned about.

"Come, we have walked enough for this morning," he said. "I will return with you to your room."

Wordlessly they returned the way they had come, and when passing the swimming pool, Bantan sighed, thinking how delectable a swim in its inviting water would be.

Once again alone in his room, the bronzed giant returned to a window and looked out at the sparkling water beyond. He did not doubt that Hulo had been mentally disturbed because of the direct reference to his age, and what puzzled Bantan was the reason why.

He stood at the window for nearly an hour before
he was subconsciously warned that he was being
watched from the doorway. Turning about quickly, he
saw that Loula, the servant girl, was standing there,
staring at him wistfully. Then, with a shake of her
head, the expression of longing vanished from her eyes.
She swallowed nervously for a few moments, apparently embarrassed that the young giant had caught
her off guard. Now she seemed to have regained her
composure.

"I came to ask if you enjoyed your stroll about the
grounds," she said.

He nodded as he slowly walked toward her with a
quizzical expression upon his features.

"I can understand a girl would be offended by asking
her age," he said, "but I cannot understand why Hulo
would be offended."

A clouded look appeared in the girl's eyes. She shook
her head slowly.

"You would understand—if you knew the truth,"
she answered enigmatically.

A furrow appeared upon Bantan's brow.

"What I have been trying to understand," he said,
"is the reason for such mystery when the matter of age
is mentioned. Another thing puzzles me. We passed a
swimming pool. When I asked Hulo if I might swim
there, he told me swimming was forbidden to all but
one. Is that The Great One?"

Loula shook her head sadly.

"I cannot answer that question," she replied.

Bantan regarded the servant girl vexedly, undecided whether to question her further. Then he nodded,
knowing she would only refuse to answer any questions
that were forbidden.

"Tell me, Loula, is there anything that I might know about The Great One?" he asked.

The girl nodded and a slight smile touched her lips.

"Long ago The Great One had all his subjects understand clearly that anything that pertained to him was exceedingly private and not to be discussed with any one," she answered. "If there is anything he wants them to know he will be the one to tell them."

Bantan shrugged.

"Any question that I want to have answered concerning The Great One shall be asked when he sends for me," he said resignedly.

"That would be best," she agreed.

"There is nothing that you can tell me about The Great One, then?" he asked hopefully.

Loula shook her head in negation.

"And there is nothing that you can tell me about Hulo and Humo, and yourself?" he added.

Again the girl shook her head.

"There is nothing," she said with an absent expression in her dark eyes.

Bantan turned and walked to the window where he had been standing. He resumed his watch of the ocean surface. Since there was nothing to be discussed with the servant girl, he might as well be alone.

For long moments Loula watched him with wistfulness before at last leaving the room. So quietly she moved upon sandals the bronzed giant did not know just when she did leave.

Many were the questions that confronted him as he stood there, motionless as a statue. But at last he nodded, realizing as he did that The Great One must have his reasons for wishing absolute privacy.

In due time Loula appeared with a tray and dishes

of food for Bantan's noonday meal. Pausing at the opened doorway, she observed the bronzed giant still standing at the window where she had left him. She shook her head a trifle and the lids of her eyes tensed. A bead of moisture appeared at the corner of each eye. She quickly glided across the room and set the tray lightly upon the table. As yet the young man had not been aware of her coming. Quickly the servant girl rubbed the corners of her eyes with the knuckle of a forefinger.

"Your noonday meal," she announced with a forced smile.

Bantan seemed momentarily startled. He turned about with a smile touching the corners of his lips.

"I did not hear you enter, Loula," he said. "My thoughts must have been far away."

As he spoke the girl's eyes tensed, but she managed to maintain her smile. Bantan walked to the table and seated himself. He reached for the glass of fruit juice and raised it before him. What prompted him to say what he did there was no accounting.

"I drink this in the hope The Great One and I will soon meet," he said.

Loula closed her eyes tightly, and her hands pressed against her bosom. She muffled the sound that might have escaped her lips by compressing them with a mighty effort.

Bantan now set the emptied glass upon the tray. A puzzled look appeared in his eyes as he realized there had been a slightly different taste to the fruit juice— there had been a sweetness that was pleasing to the palate, instead of the slight acidity he had noted previously. Almost at once he became aware of the acceleration of his heart and there was a ringing noise in his ears which increased in tempo. His breathing became slower.

With difficulty he tried to focus his dimming vision on the servant girl, but she seemed to be fast fading before him. He was dimly conscious of hearing a sob escape her lips, and then she seemed to move away from him. He slumped in his chair, his chin resting upon his broad chest; then, as oblivion raced over him, he knew no more.

CHAPTER VIII

THE RETROVIDER

With tears in her eyes and sobs choking in her throat, Loula ran toward the door of the room. Hastily she dried her eyes and with superb will power quelled her sobs before emerging from the guest room.

Outside, in the corridor, Hulo and Humo were waiting patiently. The latter held a folded stretcher beneath one powerful arm. As the servant girl appeared, the attention of the twin brothers was alerted.

"He is unconscious," Loula announced in a trembling voice.

The brothers were aware of the girl's emotion and they looked at one another questionably in silent wonder. Then, with a shrug, Hulo leading, and Humo following, they entered the room.

Bantan was unconscious and had now slumped against the table, his face turned sideways. Placing the stretcher upon the floor, the twin brothers then proceeded to lift the inert man from the chair and place him upon the stretcher. When this was done they gripped the handles, and in unison lifted him and returned to the corridor.

Hulo nodded to the servant girl, and without a word she re-entered the room to attend to the dishes and the food which had been thereupon that had fallen to the floor when the drugged man's head had struck them, sending them in disarray.

Meanwhile, Hulo and Humo bore Bantan's uncon-

scious body to the elevator and placed the stretcher
upon the floor. In another moment the conveyance was
descending and in due time came to a stop at the level
below the ground floor.

As the door opened, the twin brothers picked up
the stretcher containing the bronzed giant and carried
it a short distance along an electric-lighted corridor to
an opened door on the left from which bright, artificial
light was streaming. This was The Great One's laboratory.

At one side of a white-sheeted table stood a tall,
straight, slim man clad in a white uniform and with
rubber, skin-tight gloves covering his hands. His head
and face was covered with a white, slip-on jacket, and
all that could be seen was a pair of sharp, blue eyes.
They glowed strangely under the many electric lights
suspended from the ceiling. At the other side of the
table stood a young woman, also clad in a white uniform, but her head and features were not covered as
was the man's. Her eyes were gray, and they were
softer and more gentle in contrast to those of the
man's.

Wordlessly The Great One looked at Hulo, and
though no words were spoken, the elder twin sensed
his wishes. Those blazing blue eyes were seemingly
riveted upon the inert form of Bantan lying flat on the
stretcher and they seemed to burn still brighter in the
passing moments. In contrast, those of the woman
seemed deeply concerned.

The Great One waited patiently while the unconscious body was transferred from the stretcher to the
table. Hulo and Humo at once fastened straps attached to one side of the table about the inert form—

one about his chest and the other about his thighs. They fastened them securely.

"You may go now." The Great Onee spoke in his metallic voice. "Close the door after you."

The twin brothers did as they were bade.

The Great One then turned to the nurse.

"My stethoscope, Luane," he said.

In another moment the nurse handed him the instrument. Affixing the tubes to his ears The Great One placed the cupped end upon various parts of Bantan's chest and listened intently. Presently he smiled beneath his mask and his piercing eyes reflected his pleasure. He placed the stethoscope to one side.

"He is in perfect physical condition," he said. "His heart is the most perfect I've ever listened to. Now, we must test his brain. That is very important for our experiment."

Alongside the end of the table upon which the subject reposed, there stood an aluminum box containing highly sensitive electronic equipment. It measured five feet square and was four feet in thickness. Within this one hundred square foot cube were a number of well insulated compartments. Years of thought and experiment with the usual trial and error procedures on the part of The Great One had gone into the manufacture of the retrovider, which was what it was called.

Upon its face were a number of dials and several charts with indicating needles, also variously colored small bulbs. A picture screen six inches in length and four in width was located at the top right-hand corner. Upon the top were removable panels in the event the contents of a certain compartment proved faulty and required certain adjustments or renewal.

In silence The Great One and the nurse went about

their respective duties. The former reached for a peculiar oval gadget attached to the retrovider. This he
fastened about the forehead of the unconscious man.
He pressed a master button and a barely percipible
humming sound was to be heard from within the machine. The Great One watched a small bulb slowly
light up until the maximum intensity was reached. He
looked at the nurse and nodded as he turned a dial
slowly while testing the subject's brain. He watched
the picture screen with studying eyes. Although slight
scars of past injuries were to be detected, he nodded,
positive that they would be immaterial to the contemplated experiment at hand. He looked toward the
silent nurse and spoke.

"He should be able to penetrate back to the beginning of time far more than any of our past subjects—
at the most five hundred thousand years. With the
strong heart he has, I'm hoping to record the entire
history of his earliest progenitors."

With his words he turned the dial in the opposite
direction until it was returned to its former position.
The band about Bantan's forehead was removed and
replaced with another, this one equipped with several
brass prongs. An electrical cord from the retrovider
with several clips upon one end were attached to the
prongs on the oval band, and in this way direct contact
was made. Another button was pressed. A small bulb
began to light up, and as the moments passed, its
luminance increased in intensity.

While this part of the retrovider was in motion, The
Great One pressed another button that was to give contact to another more delicate instrument, and a quick
look at the picture screen assured him it was working
perfectly. This particular device was at work on the

long-dormant brain cells of the subject, revivifying and
arranging them in chronological order.

This, naturally, had to be a reverse process. Upon
the picture screen could be seen the magnified brain
cell. It was a dark blob at first. As the electronic device
centered upon it, the darkness lightened, and the sub-
stance of which it was composed became clearly outlined. It appeared to be in numberless segments. Each
one of these represented a life span of a single individual through the generations past. Naturally, the
more recent segments became light first, and the delicately attuned electronic device automatically passed
from one segment to the next. When each of these
became light in color, a chart upon the face of the
retrovider enlightened The Great One of the centuries
being turned backward.

A small red bulb operated from this device was the
center of the scientist's attention as the minutes quickly
passed, for when it lit up, that would be the signal
that no further segments of the subject's brain cells
could be probed without injury to the delicate brain
system.

Time and again The Great One looked at his subject with appraising eyes. Not a tremor was to be
seen as the delicate electronic device probed Bantan's
long-dormant brain cells and gave them new life in
turn. Intermittently the scientist looked at the picture
screen, the warning bulb, and the chart indicator.

In absolute silence the nurse's gray eyes were fixed
upon the chart indicator and she saw the centuries being rolled backward. One—two—three—four—and
now five hundred thousand years was recorded. At
this phase, the last segment was charged to full capac-
ity, and the warning red bulb lighted.

The Great One nodded. His eyes caught those of the silent nurse. A sigh escaped his lips. He snapped the button that de-energized that particular portion of the retrovider so as not to injure the subject's brain.

"It is time," he murmured.

The nurse's eyes seemed blank, but as his words penetrated to her subconscious mind, she nodded.

The Great One slowly turned a dial with a needle recording the centuries which had rolled backward to correspond with the chart indicator. Intermittently he looked at the picture screen and could see that it was working properly.

The scientist was speaking in a mechanical tone of voice.

"Now we have revivified Bantan's brain cells to the period known as the Middle Pleistocene of the Old Stone Age. Man was then known as pithecanthropus about to graduate into *homo sapiens*. At that time his progenitors ranged the continent of Southern Asia, far below the great glacier's edge, and where tropical weather prevailed."

The Great One's eyes gleamed with satisfaction as he studied his subject for a long moment, then he pressed a small recorder lever, which operated a camera with an electronic eye so delicately attuned that it was capable of recording on highly sensitized film the events those long-dead eyes had witnessed but which had left their impressions upon brain cells. Now, through the scientist's retrovider, the revivified segment of that early progenitor was transmitted upon the film and to the picture screen simultaneously.

He watched the screen and the jumbled scenes that were presented kaleidoscopically at first. For only brief moments a picture would become clear. Both he and the nurse saw massive, ungainly beasts lumbering through strange foliage of a long-remote age. A strange bird winged through the heaven above the tops of the jungle's tallest trees. Then the picture became jumbled again—much as a television screen when sometimes turning on a set and the tubes had not become sufficiently warmed to present a clear picture, or perhaps some other minor defect might be present.

Presently the jumbled picture became normal again. Now the two watchers saw unkempt, naked men and women, sometimes in groups, and sometimes alone, stealthily traversing well worn jungle trails. Some of them walked on all fours, and again, others walked erect. Brief scenes these were and apparently made no sense.

The Great One's piercing eyes watched the picture screen sharply while the fingers of his right hand adjusted the dial on the panel of the retrovider. Intermittently he would glance at the silent form lying motionless upon the table, and his brief glances assured him the subject was in no danger whatsoever as a result of his experiment.

Now the picture screen revealed a mighty prehistoric man in a fierce battle with a saber-tooth tiger. The conflict was a savage one. The nearly naked man, armed only with a knobbed club, was hopelessly outclassed by the beast's sharp fangs and rending claws which were employed with incredible speed and accuracy. The end was inevitable; and as the troglodyte met his death at the tiger's merciless savagery, before the spotted beast had the chance to seize and drag his prey away and devour it, a number of the victim's friends and relatives appeared with waving knobbed clubs and angry shouts, and the carnivore was frightened away by such revengeful numbers.

The vision upon the picture screen faded, and then was followed by jumbled scenes again for a few moments. There now appeared a brief one that was clear —this time of a woman nursing an infant boy, while a naked young girl hovered nearby. Another scene showed the same infant, having grown somewhat, taking his first steps. Later ones revealed the same boy in various stages of childhood. Sometimes he was alone, sometimes in the company of his mother. Then, again, there was the older girl, a sister, perhaps, who appeared with the boy, she being several years older than he. But it was always the growing boy who seemed to dominate the picture screen.

The Great One's pleasure was reflected in his piercing blue eyes as he looked toward the nurse upon numerous occasions and nodded his head. The young woman's attention seemed mesmerized by the scenes upon the picture screen. She had not believed such things possible to behold, but through the ingenuity of The Great One's electronic machine the impossible was becoming reality.

The picture screen now was much clearer and it no longer became jumbled. Watching the developments thereupon, so shall we, as is unfolded a complete chapter of one of Bantan's earliest progenitors at that time of the Middle Pleistocene of the Old Stone Age, and he was known by the name of Bana.

Chapter IX

BANA—OF THE STONE AGE

Five hundred thousand years ago Bana, a Stone Age youth of sixteen, moved warily along a well marked trail through jungle growth which had been thrashed unmercifully by wild winds on the previous night. In his right hand he clutched a crude, knobbed club. He was naked save for an abbreviated loin cloth fashioned from grasses.

The youth was clean-limbed and already in some ways had reached man's estate. His shock of long, dark hair was unkempt, but for comfort and vision he had pushed it back out of his eyes into a crude pompadour style. His broad, though receding forehead denoted some intelligence, and his features were fairly well molded. Upon his right temple there was a blood-red circular blotch that had been his since birth. Though some hair grew upon a certain part of his body and beneath his arms, as yet his cheeks and chin were smooth and deeply bronzed. His dark eyes, though keen and ever alert, were filled with a peculiar gentleness, which might be construed as a sadness—because of the recent deaths of his widowed mother, Aman, and his only older sister, Anan.

Their tribe had been invaded by the males of a neighboring one, and before his very eyes he had seen his mother and sister resist the enemy to the very end rather than be subjugated by them and carried away as captives. Bana had fought savagely with his enemies as did the other males of the tribe. When at last the enemy had victoriously gone their way, taking with them the female captives for which they had come, the youth, dry-eyed, with the assistance of a couple of men, had buried his mother and sister under a pile of rocks a short distance from their cave dwellings. Afterwards, because of his grief, he had left the vicinity, and stopping only for food and drink, had traveled for seven full suns before at last coming upon a shallow cave. Numerous were the encounters with wild beasts and narrow had been the margin between life and death that he had experienced. But that is the way of the primitive—so long as he lived, that was all that mattered.

This morning as he walked along the well marked trail as he had upon other days, his thoughts were of his mother and his sister, and he tried to visualize how happy the three of them would have been in this new area so free of enemies and savage, grotesque beasts. They had gotten along so well together in their small cave, especially after their father, Naba, had been killed many moons ago by a saber-tooth tiger.

Bana had been twelve then, but his father had died a hero in his eyes—something for him to pattern after, if it were possible. He had made his mother and sister understand that there would be no need of another male taking his father's place, as was the case in most instances, for he would be the head man in their cave. They had humored and encouraged him; the youth knew he would not soon forget their love and kindness. And so they had lived thereafter, all three foraging for food together as occasioned in the primeval world. In the Stone Age food was the first requisite.

Now he paused, and his sharp ears were aware of a whimpering sound just beyond the edge of the trail ahead of him. With eyes alert and ears more intent, he brushed aside the foliage and went warily in the direction of the sound. He clutched his knobbed club more tightly. Ahead, he sighted an old tree, and as he came closer, he saw that a huge limb had been torn from the mother bole during the wild winds of the previous evening. Listening intently, he was aware that the whimpering sound had come from its direction.

Brushing aside some screening foliage, Bana was able to see the base of the tree. Nearby, with a leg pinioned beneath the heavy end of the limb, the Stone Age youth saw a bronzed young girl with dark, matted hair overflowing her shoulders. Her features, arms, body, and legs were streaked with dirt. A short grass skirt covered her midsection. With one hand she was endeavoring to lift the heavy limb enough to extricate her left leg on which it partly rested just above the knee.

As Bana looked at her, he tried to think of her as his sister, Anan. The resemblance was somewhat similar, though this strange girl was younger—even younger than he if he could be a fair judge of ages. He remembered that Anan was broad of shoulders and hips, and that her arms and legs were sturdy, and that she was full breasted, whereas this girl was smaller in proportions. The youth was positive were Anan alive and in a like situation, she would have been able to extricate herself from such a predicament, for she had been unusually strong for a female.

Not many moons before her untimely death, he had learned what had happened to one of Anan's most persistent suitors, a huge, ugly male by name of Mo. His

sister had repeatedly warned the male, who was no-
toriously known as a beater of women, about bothering her with his unwelcome attentions. One day she had
repulsed him with physical violence. To escape the
jeers of the tribesmen and their mates, Mo had deserted the cave dwellers and joined another group.
In revenge, it had been he who inflamed the males to
raid the tribe he had deserted for the purpose of pro-
curing more women. It was then Anan and her mother
were slain rather than submit to capture. Mo, however, was a victim of his own evil machinations, for a
blow upon his head by a knobbed club had deranged
his mentality, reducing him to the status of a gibbering idiot. The tribe he had joined managed to rid themselves of him by taking him far from the caves, binding
him helplessly, then deserting him.

Now, as Bana approached the helpless, unknown
girl pinioned beneath a heavy limb, whether she would
be frightened by his appearance did not matter. He
would free her from her present predicament, because
in his breast there was a humane spark that would
not permit him to see the girl suffer longer than necessary. He opened his mouth to speak. By that expression
I do not wish to convey the idea this Stone Age youth's
conversation was eloquent. Other than grunts and mur-
murs, a smile or a scowl, a nod or shaking of the head,
the speech of that long-remote age was extremely
limited. When Bana now spoke it was a mere: "Ah!"
But he nodded and smiled at the girl when he uttered
the word.

For a moment the strange girl was frightened at the
youth's appearance, but at his smile and the nod of his
head, she realized he was at least friendly. She smiled
in return, then indicated her trapped leg.

Bana Frees Zozo

In another minute Bana had reached the girl's side. She had been watching him with eyes of hope and awakening admiration, for the youth was handsome of features and possessed a nicely molded body.

The Stone Age youth dropped his knobbed club. He bent and gripped the heavy limb with his strong hands. His biceps bulged as he lifted it, but not without considerable strain, for the blood was sent rushing to his neck and cheeks.

The moment the girl felt the weight upon her left leg removed, with her two hands in back of her and her free leg, she dragged herself clear. She uttered a light gutteral sound to her savior and smiled sweetly. Aware that she was free, Bana let the heavy limb fall back to earth, then he straightened and breathed deeply.

Meanwhile, the girl surveyed her bruised and slightly swollen leg. She rubbed it with the palms of her hands. In a few moments she essayed to regain her feet, but the circulation had been restricted for many hours so that it seemed numb and would not bear her weight. She slumped back to the ground with a muffled sob of despair.

Bana drew near her with concern in his dark eyes and a smile upon his lips which revealed strong, even white teeth. He looked at the large black and blue blotch above her left knee where the skin had been bruised. He murmured softly beneath his breath and placed a hand upon it gently. Then, while the girl fairly held her breath and with her hands tightly pressing her naked breasts, his questing fingers kneaded the flesh, seeking the bone. Though the girl winced at times despite his gentleness, his probing fingers enlightened him that the bone in her leg was not broken.

He nodded and smiled, then with the palms of both hands he commenced to stroke her leg from above the bruised flesh to the calf; gently at first his hands moved over her flesh, but with slightly increasing pressure each time. Upon occasions the girl would grit her teeth, and several times she placed a restraining hand against his shoulder in an effort to push him away. However, Bana continued his treatment. The warmth of restored circulation was presently felt and the pain eased until the entire leg glowed deliriously from the effects of his massage.

While rubbing the softness and warmth of the girl's leg, the Stone Age youth was aware of a peculiar tingling sensation, completely unknown heretofore, pervading him, and with some difficulty he fought it into submission. He tried to think of this unknown girl as Anan; and thinking convincingly in this manner, he found there was less embarrassment while attending to her injury.

Zozo was the girl's name. It had been given to her by her mother. Her early life had been without incident until the last moon. Then her mother had made her understand an old man of their village wanted her for his mate. Zozo knew of whom her mother referred, and the girl, though terrified at the very thought of being mated to the toothless and smelly, wrinkled old man, was not so terrified that she had run away from the village and hoped never to return. She had foraged for food by day, and at night would lair where she felt she would be safest. Last night she had crouched at the foot of the old tree for shelter when the mighty wind had descended upon the world. She had been pinioned beneath the huge limb which was torn from the mother bole; and though she had been uncomfortable and in pain, she had been grateful it had not rained to add to her discomfort.

Now that this handsome youth had come to her rescue, Zozo was stirred to the full instincts of womanhood, and naturally, she wondered primarily if he had a woman of his own. If not, then she felt she would gladly be available, since she had nowhere in particular to go and no home whatsoever. She believed without question she would be as happy with him as any one else—most certainly preferring him to a toothless, odorous, wrinkled old man.

Bana was becoming wearied of massaging the girl's leg, which by now was becoming pink under the bronzed skin. With a smile and a low gutteral he conveyed the idea to Zozo that she try and see if her injured leg would now bear her weight.

The girl smiled and nodded in understanding. Though she held her breath while arising to her feet, her features became enwreathed with a happy smile as she realized, except for a tenderness of the bruised leg, she experienced no discomfort. She bore her weight of some hundred pounds first upon the uninjured leg, and then upon the other. She was radiant, revealing nice teeth. To show her appreciation for the service he had rendered her, stranger that she was to him, she approached with a little hesitation and a coyness in her dark eyes. Standing before him, she bowed her head.

Bana was acutely aware of the tingling sensation again pervading every fiber of his being with the girl's proximity; but remembering to consider her as a substitute for his deceased sister, he gently cupped her chin with one hand and raised her head. Zozo's dark eyes looked expectantly up into his, for he was a foot taller than she. Although she did not see the light in his eyes she anticipated, she was pleased that he was smiling gently.

The Stone Age youth indicated that they should sit upon the limb. When they were side by side, their shoulders and thighs touching, he then tried to converse with her through cumbersome signs, grunts, nods, and shaking of heads. When some little time had passed he learned the simple facts about her that he wished to know.

To impress upon her the name he was known by, Bana pointed at himself and uttered the word Bana—the accent upon the first syllable, and stressing the first a, but not the second one—uttering it as though it were spelled uh.

The girl seemed to understand and she smiled sweetly as she uttered his name several times in her musical voice. He nodded then looked at her questionably. Her lips parted sweetly and she indicated herself and uttered her name.

"Zozo." She accentuated the first syllable and stressed the first o, as well as the o in the second syllable.

He smiled and rested the palm of his right hand upon her left shoulder, and spoke her name several times, to which she smiled and nodded. Then she rested a hand upon his shoulder and spoke his name several times to which, in answer, he smiled and nodded.

At last some progress was reached. They knew the name by which each was known.

Now Zozo interrogated him about something that was bothering her, so the same process of communication was employed. First of all, she wanted to know if he had a woman of his own. In answer to this, he shook his head to the negative and a flush tinged his bronzed cheeks. Then she asked him where he lived. Pointing in the direction he had come, he told her through signs of the shallow cave that was his home. She expressed the wish to see it, to which he smiled and nodded. Then, as though remembering her hunger, she rubbed her bare stomach, moved her mouth, and appeared to swallow. He nodded in understanding that she was hungry. Together they arose from the limb, and with Bana in the lead with his knobbed club in hand, sought food. Fruit and edible tubers were gathered, and both ate of them while returning in the general direction of the cave.

As they passed a small pond Bana indicated it with a smile. He waded out to his waist and Zozo eagerly followed him. They splashed about awhile enjoying its wetness and cleanliness, and when they at last laughingly left it, both felt considerably refreshed. The girl was much cleaner in appearance.

Once again they resumed their way with Bana in the lead while Zozo followed close behind him. In due time they reached the cave, and the Stone Age youth indicated with a touch of pride that it was his home. She entered and looked about with quick, appraising eyes.

The cave was a small one. Its ceiling was the same height as the opening which was slightly under six feet. It extended into the rocky hill about eight feet and was some ten feet in width. In the farthest corner the girl noted the leaves and grasses the youth slept upon. They were quite old and smelled of staleness. There also were a few bones scattered about, remnants of a meal he had partaken of.

Zozo looked at Bana who stood in the doorway. She smiled and nodded, indicating that she was pleased. In her mind she knew there would be a few necessary changes; but for the present she contented herself with gathering up the bones and throwing them outside, indicating that first of all a worthy helpmate must needs be a tidy one.

For some unknown reason Bana felt a trifle uncomfortable with Zozo in the cave, and he was happy to step outside in the brilliant sunshine. He breathed deeply, his hairless chest expanding noticeably so that his ribs were clearly outlined beneath his bronzed skin. Now the girl came to his side and looked at the scenery as her companion was. Tall trees in full foliage were to be seen with gaily plumaged birds flitting about their tops.

Not far from the cave was a beautiful flower bush with large red flowers in full bloom. At once the girl left the youth and went to it. She smelled the flowers and sighed deeply. Then her slim fingers selected one of them and picked it. Feminine-like she affixed it in her hair above one ear. With a secretive smile she picked another and with it in hand approached the youth.

Confronting him, her smile now became shy as he wonderingly looked down at her, and was again aware of the peculiar tingling sensation because of her nearness. Zozo indicated the flower in her hair and she looked at the one she held and made him understand she wished to place it in his hair. He bowed his head while she reached up and threaded the stem through his long hair over an ear. Then, standing back, she looked at him and nodded, satisfied with her handiwork.

To relieve himself of the secret embarrassment he

suffered, Bana made Zozo understand they should gather more food. He added he might be successful in catching some fish in the pond where they had bathed. The girl expressed her happiness to accompany him, so off they went.

The youth managed to fashion a crude net, and after several hours of patient watching and waiting had elapsed, he suceeded in catching two good-sized fish. With some fruit and tubers, which were more easily procurable, they returned to the cave.

They had no knowledge of fire, so the fish were eaten raw. After eating to his fill, Bana stretched in the sun outside the cave, and before he was aware of the transition, was fast asleep.

Zozo smiled secretly as she noticed the Stone Age youth sleeping. She then entered the cave, gathering up the stale grass and carried it outside. She then searched the immediate vicinity and fortunately came upon a clump of sweet-smelling grass fully a foot long. She gathered as much as she could carry and returned to the cave, spreading it in a corner. Surveying it, she nodded and decided another armful would be required for more comfort. When this was done and noting that Bana still slept, she again went to the pool where she bathed. When convenient, if there was anything that Zozo enjoyed above all else, it was to bathe. After doing so, she returned to the soft grass outlining the pond and lay down, allowing the warm sun to dry her wet body.

Nearing late afternoon Bana awoke and looked about for the girl. At the very thought of her his nerves tingled again. Looking within the cave he saw that she had gathered fresh grasses to replace the other stale ones which had been his bed. The cave

smelled much sweeter as a result. Wondering where
Zozo had gone, he started to search for her, occasionally uttering a loud:

"Ah—Zozo!"

Meanwhile, he noticed the sky was becoming overcast, and that a faraway rumbling sound was to be
heard in the distant heaven. From past experience he
was sure a storm was brewing. That moaning sound
also meant bright flashes would be seen, and usually
heavy rain fell.

"Ah—Zozo!" he shouted again.

His footsteps were carrying him near the pond. As
well, he knew nearby was an excellent place to gather
edible tubers and fruit. Looking toward the scurrying
dark clouds, which as yet had not blotted out the sunlight, Bana almost tripped over the sleeping girl.

Waking quickly, Zozo looked up at the seemingly
agitated Stone Age youth. As she arose to her feet, he
pointed excitedly at the overcast heaven and shook his
head warningly. Looking upward, the girl seemed to
sense what he was trying to tell her, also, that they
should gather fruit and tubers before the storm broke
in all its untamed fury.

Little time was lost in doing so. Within a short
while, with arms laden, the two returned to the
cave and deposited the fruit and tubers upon the floor
at the far wall. It was then that the first drops of rain
started to fall, accompanied by a flash of lightning and
a deep roar of thunder which rolled and reverberated
seemingly just above the rocky hill in which the cave
was burrowed.

Bana returned to the mouth of the cave, standing
against the opening, and watched the scurrying dark
clouds in the sky with fascination as lightning played

among them in a game of seeming hide and seek. When an extremely sharp flash of lightning appeared from them, he merely blinked; but when the subsequent crash of thunder followed, he trembled slightly, but not in fear. It was more in wonder at what caused the phenomenon.

Presently he was aware that Zozo had drawn close to him. She brought him an apple, and murmuring to attract his attention, gave it to him. She was gnawing nervously upon one. That she was afraid of the storm there was no denying, for she remained close to him, seemingly trembling when the bright flashes of lightning ribboned through the dark clouds to be followed by a crash of rolling, booming thunder.

Whether by chance or design is not known for a certainty, but the Stone Age youth's left arm went about the girl's waist. Looking down at his arm, the girl breathed more contentedly now as she snuggled closer to him so that her entire right side from shoulder to the outside of her knee pressed against his left side. The instinctive sense of belonging to him appealed to her, and she felt while she was thus close to him she need have no fear of anything.

When a crash of thunder sounded, tremblingly Zozo would try to get still closer to her companion. Now that she had eaten her apple, she flung the core out into the rain. Then, timidly, her arm went about his waist and she clung tightly to him. Time and again she would steal a glance up at his handsome profile and a deep sigh would escape her lips. She allowed her head to rest upon his shoulder.

Now that Bana had finished eating his apple he, too, tossed the core into the deluging rain. For the first time he was aware of his arm about the girl's

supple waist, and that one of hers encircled him. It
was a nice feeling. He also was aware of the pleasing aroma of the flower in the girl's hair so near his
nostrils. He inclined his head to inhale more fully its
fragrance.

And then it was an almost blinding flash of lightning
seemingly leaped past the cave's opening to be followed by a mighty crash of thunder that fairly rocked
the ground they stood upon.

Zozo uttered a squeal of fright as she turned and
flung her free arm about Bana and hugged him tightly
in her terror. For a moment the Stone Age youth was
befuddled as the tight pressure of the girl's body
against his almost made him forget that he thought of
her as his sister, for strange, tingling sensations instantly were coursing through him madly.

In a voice that trembled not in fear he spoke to her
while he smiled and gently disengaged her arms from
about him. Zozo regarded him in a seemingly stunned
silence, feeling that he had been displeased with her
fright. With a sorrowful shake of her head she backed
away from him, going to the pallet of grasses and
lying down. She regarded the youth in silent, mystify-
ing wonder. She was aware of her strangely beating
heart, for she, too, reacted in an unusual manner as a
result of the pressure of her body against his.

Bana resumed watching the electrical storm with
fascination. For the time being he was grateful he was
alone again, for that strange feeling which had coursed
through him had now calmed, and he felt more like
himself again. He was thankful that the wild wind
was not blowing toward the cave's opening, since he
could stand there and not get wet. However, this good
fortune was not to last, for suddenly the wild wind

came from the opposite direction, and the pelting rain was blown before it toward the mouth of the cave.

As the rain smartly struck his almost naked skin, Bana stepped back quickly—in fact too quickly, for he tripped himself. Before he could regain his equilibrium, he fell upon the grass alongside the girl. In falling, one of his legs crossed the other, and he was aware of a sharp pain.

Arising to a seated position with grimacing features, he started to massage the sore spot. At once the girl was aware of his injury. Remembering how he had treated her injured leg that same morning, she murmured to him as she knelt at his side. With a gentle smile she pushed aside his hands and nodded eagerly.

Bana lay back with a sigh as Zozo massaged his sore leg just above the left knee in the same place the girl had been bruised. While her soft hands gently stroked his injured leg, she hummed in a monotone, pleased with herself that she was able to do something for her companion. And that he seemed contented she was sure, for she would steal an intermittent glance at him, and she noted the blissful expression encompassing his features.

As he lay there Bana could not remember when he had felt so utterly happy. He tried to assure himself that it was his sister Anan who was massaging his injured leg, but for some unknown reason he could not convince himself that Anan could be so gentle were it she. The monotone from the girl's lips was very pleasing and it had a lulling effect upon him. He opened his eyes and looked up at Zozo as she leaned forward, her long, dark hair tumbling over her shoulders and concealing her small breasts. Intermittently, as she moved, first one and then the other would be revealed briefly.

Looking fondly at her, the Stone Age youth's eyes seemed mesmerized, but he could not deny the strange, tingling sensation that again was coursing through him. While he manfully attempted to repulse this unnatural feeling—as he had done before—he would shake his head repeatedly, for some reason his will power became more feeble in his endeavors.

Zozo then paused to look at Bana, and for the first time she was aware of a subtle change in his dark eyes. He smiled and nodded, then indicated his leg. His smile did not change as he arose to a seated position. His hands went to his leg, feeling of the glowing flesh gently. In another moment he regained his feet, testing his weight upon the injured leg. He was aware he felt no sharpness of pain now. It only felt a little tender. The glowing effects of the girl's massage seemed to spread over his entire body. His heart was beating faster than he had ever known it. Now he nodded to the girl and his smile remained gentle. He indicated for her to rise to her feet.

Zozo swept the tumbled hair back over her shoulders, and somewhat in wonder arose to her feet confronting the Stone Age youth. To show his thanks for the service she had done him, Bana now bowed his head before her—as she had done earlier in the day. She understood that he was humbly thanking her. In return, to show that she had been happy to have been of service to him, she placed her hands gently upon the side of his face and drew it to rest between her breasts. Then her arms went about his naked back and she caressed the smooth bronzed skin lovingly. She drew deep breaths that were exhaled flutteringly.

Bana inhaled the sweetness of the girl's body, and then as his head moved to one side, his smooth cheek nestled against one of her firm, warm breasts. With its contact an electrifying impulse deliriously surged through the girl, almost causing her to swoon. She clutched at him for a moment and uttered a low moan. And now the Stone Age youth moved his head to the other side until that cheek pressed against the other warm breast. Again the girl seemed to swoon with a low moan escaping her lips as she clutched at him with nervous hands.

Aware of her agitation, and as well only too acutely aware of his own, Bana now raised his head to look inquiringly at Zozo. An almost anguished expression was present in her dark eyes—as though she were in torment—something he had never been occasioned to know before in his short life. Momentarily he wondered if the seeming anguish she suffered was akin to the tremendous unknown power that likewise surged through him with terrifying intensity.

Then the girl, seemingly overcome by her tormented emotions, slumped to the bed of grasses and lay inert flat upon her back. A barely audible whimpering escaped her lips, and she seemed to tremble from head to foot as with ague. The rapid rise and fall of her upthrust breasts gave evidence to her agitation.

Bana looked down upon Zozo in awed silence, while outside, temporarily forgotten these past minutes, the storm was rising in crescendo to its peak. The lightning was more blinding, the thunder more deafening, and the wind-driven rain much more intense.

The girl's agitation quelled temporarily, but her breath came in stertorous gasps. She appeared to swallow with difficulty, then heaving a deep sigh she

slowly opened her eyes, and saw that Bana was looking down at her with deep concern. It was then a slight
tremor coursed through her body, and her legs from
thigh to dainty feet began to quiver again. She uttered
a low moan, then as her eyes met the youth's unwaveringly, into hers came a longing that openly revealed all
her love for him. As he understood the glow in the
girl's eyes, he slowly bent toward her, his heart beating fast and his breath became labored almost choking
him.

Zozo's arms lifted feebly. Then, her strength seemingly spent, they dropped at her sides. As she saw Bana
kneeling at her side, she became electrified. Her arms
again reached for him, and murmuring in monotone,
she locked them about his neck and drew his face down
to her burning one.

Outside, the lightning was sharper still, the thunder
more deafening, and the rain was wind-blown in deluging torrents.

But within the cave the Stone Age youth and the
girl gave no further thought of the storm. The tempest
within them must needs be quieted first, and though
neither had experienced this physical contact as yet
which confronted them, their panting endeavors and
not unfutile gropings were at last rewarded with complete gratification of each other.

*   *   *

Rapturous days passed for the Stone Age couple
now that they were mated. In their slightly develop-
ing brains, however, they realized the other was a
necessity in the happiness they shared. Never in his
life before did Bana realize the joy that Zozo had

made possible for him, and so the girl felt toward the youth.

She remembered the youths of her tribe, and how they had tried to force their unwelcome attentions upon her; but always she had repulsed them. In her way of thinking, she was glad she had rejected them, for Bana was all that she now desired in life.

Slightly sentimental that he was, Bana could not compare his mate now with his dearly beloved sister Anan. Zozo was more to him in the short while he had known her than Anan had been in her whole life. His mate was now a part of him as he was to her. In the beginning of time had not man and woman been created, living alone would have been a dull existence, indeed.

This new flame that had been discovered by the young Stone Age couple they realized was something to always keep fanned; and while doing so, they knew their joy and happiness would always prevail.

For a glorious moon Bana and Zozo never neglected their new-found affection for one another; but it was shortly, thereafter, that the girl became aware of a change in her natural functions which sometimes made her moody. The morning nausea that she experienced was a new trial for her. Bana, trying to understand, was sympathetic—perhaps for the youth he was, too much so. As the day grew older and the girl felt better, her blithe spirits returned much to her young mate's joy.

Accepting the new change in her life, Zozo became aware as the moons passed that she was becoming plumper, and she seemed always to be hungry. Bana, too, became aware of the change in his mate, but he loved her none the less. And after more moons passed, the girl became aware of the movement of life within her. Then she began to experience sleepless nights, much to her dismay, and for some reason her groping mentality tried to fathom the cause of her discomfort.

By some mental process she knew such a physical change in her had never happened before she had known Bana, and so she came to feel he must be the cause of her discomfort. It seemed odd that he had brought her such joy and yet could be the cause of the discomfort she now suffered. In brief moments, especially when she was very sleepy, and the movement within her was quite vigorous, it was then that she felt she hated her mate as she had never hated any one in her whole life. Looking at him, sleeping peacefully at her side, would arouse her to ferocity in a savage way. She would clench her hands and beat him about the face and chest while she sobbed despairingly.

At first Bana was amazed at the unaccounted actions of the usually docile girl who was his mate. He would grip her hands in his stronger ones and hold them tightly. Then he murmured softly and placatingly to her with the result her seeming fury subsided into choking sobs with tears filling her eyes.

One night shortly upon such an occasion she indicated that he release her hands. When he had done this, she took one of his and placed it to her abdomen where a strange, fluttering movement was to be detected. In wonder his hand felt of the stirring within her and he came to understand why she was so troubled. He then placed his arms about her, drew her close to him, and crooned softly in her ear with such good effect that Zozo felt strangely calmed and thereafter fell asleep in his arms. Within her groping mentality she was confident that Bana would always be a source of comfort to her as a man should always be to his mate when the occasion rose.

One day while huddled in the cave and feeling miserable because of her ungainly condition, Zozo remembered other women of the tribe to which she had once belonged, had grown fat as she was, and how awkwardly they had moved about. And then it seemed a miracle had occurred. Those women had told of experiencing sharp pains, and after their child was born, they were thin again, and shortly thereafter were as vigorous as ever. Her groping mentality made her realize that she was experiencing what they had.

When Bana returned to the cave with fruit and edible tubers, she tried to make him understand what was the trouble with her. The Stone Age youth could not fully comprehend no matter how Zozo explained through cumbersome signs—but he was to learn in the near future.

One night soon thereafter when darkness had fallen and the Stone Age couple were asleep upon their mats of grass, it was then that Zozo experienced her first pangs of imminent child birth. She winced as a searing pain within her brought her to full wakefulness. Her sudden movement waked the sleeping Bana. He seemed concerned, but she presently murmured she was all right and again lay back to sleep, as he did.

But shortly, once again the searing pain wracked her, much more excruciating than the first occasion, and this time she could scarcely muffle a painful sob. Again Bana was waked, and as the labor pains came more often now, Zozo gripped his hands tightly as though to draw strength from him to aid her in her anguish.

It was a long night, a sleepless one for both. But as

the sun rose clear of the horizon, and the cave was
lighted, it was then that Zozo heaved a deep sigh of
relief, for her child had been born. An examination
revealed it was a man child, already sturdy and vigorous, as revealed when, more through chance than design, his seeking lips fastened upon the protruding
nipple of one of her breasts and suckled noisily.

Then did the young mother sigh more deeply with
contentment—her pain and anguish of the night before
already forgotten. She smiled up at her mate and murmured crooningly as the infant suckled to his heart's
content. When his hunger had been satisfied, the little
new-born child promptly fell asleep in her arms.

By signs Bana indicated he was hungry and that he
would fetch food for them both. Zozo nodded and
smiled as he left the cave. Then did she stroke the
infant's body with gentle hands, and many were the
sighs that she heaved as she looked lovingly upon the
little reincarnation of her mate.

It is ever the mother who examines her child for
defects, and Zozo was no exception to the rule. As she
looked upon his right temple and saw the circular
blood-red birthmark she sighed deeply. As the father
had been marked since birth, so was his son. When he
returned with fruits the young mother drew her mate's
attention to the birthmark, and she indicated their
son was marked as he was. Bana could never deny his
parentage.

Placing the sleeping infant upon the grass mat, Zozo
arose to a seated position and she and her young mate
ate to their fill. Afterwards, Bana examined the tiny
babe, being careful not to waken him. When he
straightened he felt proud, as was Zozo, of their first
born.

As the days passed they eagerly awaited the little boy's first utterances, for then they could name him.

One day when Bana returned to the cave with fruits and edible tubers, he was met by his excited mate. She was flushed of face and smiling happily.

"Bazo!" she murmured, pointing at the sleeping child. "Bazo!" she repeated excitedly.

"Bazo?" he questioned, almost as excited, as he nodded at the child. "Bazo?"

Zozo smiled and nodded.

And so the first-born son of Bana and Zozo was named, for that was the word he uttered to his surprised mother a short while since.

When they looked down at the three-month child as he slept peacefully and content with the world, Bana's eyes glowed proudly as he looked at his mate's again trim body. She looked very desirable. It had been some time before the baby had been born that he had been joined to her. Now one of his hands touched her shoulder, and she looked at him inquiringly. Then he placed his smooth cheek against one of her not quite so firm breasts as before. Zozo began to breathe deeply, and her hands closed upon his head and drew it closer to her heaving bosom. She did not realize how tight she was holding him, for he was having difficulty in breathing.

* * *

With the child to care for, Zozo joined her mate less often when he searched for fruits and nuts and fished in the pond. She remained at the cave, and home-making instinct that Nature endows in most women, induced her to keep clean their cave home, to replace the stale mats of grasses that was their bedding, also to prepare the meals.

Meanwhile, with the passing moons, Bazo continued to develop as all small children do, and soon he was able to recognize his parents, as would be natural. In particular, when his father returned after short absences, the child, were he awake, would greet him with vociferous shouts of welcome, and would stretch his arms and kick his legs vigorously. Only after Bana laughingly swept the little child into his arms would the boy become quiet and gurgle in seeming contentment, and amuse himself by touching his father here and there with his tiny fingers, while his dark brown eyes —just the same color as his father's—would look up at him in awe. His father would laugh and make little grunting noises which the child tried to imitate.

As the days passed, Bana was compelled to forage farther from the cave until late afternoon in search of fruits, nuts, and edible tubers for his family. Even the little pond near the cave no longer gave up fish, despite the weary hours that he passed with his crude net. It now seemed that all of his time was consumed in his search for sustenance, and many a night all three would go to sleep hungry. Since animals and birds scarcely frequented this area, the Stone Age youth realized that very soon he and Zozo, with their child, would be compelled to desert their little Eden in search of a more provident area.

Late one afternoon when he returned to the cave, all that he had found was a half-dozen nuts and a few dates. He had eaten sparingly during the day, for he was thinking of his mate and their ever ravenous son. Long since Zozo's breasts had ceased to yield sustenance for the little boy, and Bazo must eat whatever his father could provide.

And, too, about this time Zozo was again aware of a change in the normal functionings of her body, and her memory was refreshed to that other occasion before Bazo had been born. She knew she was again with child. This fact she communicated to her mate, and he was all the more determined that they must move before Zozo became too heavy and awkward to do so. He decided it best that he go alone first, and were he to find a more provident area he could then return for Zozo and Bazo.

One morning he tried to make his mate understand what he intended. Naturally she wished to accompany him; but thought of the baby enduring such possible hardships and dangers that might be encountered would not permit him to consent to his mate's entreaty. He assured her he would not be too long away, for he could move much faster alone.

And so he departed, taking with him a knobbed club for protection, for he knew not what dangers might beset him. He studied the sun before he left the cave and his sorrowful mate and hurried on his way. Remembering the trails he had trod fruitlessly during the past moon, he avoided those on this day and traveled in an entirely new direction—due south. Sometimes the going was comparatively easy, but upon other occasions as equally difficult. Always he searched for fruits, nuts, and edible tubers, and even small animals that, were they not too large or ferocious, he might attempt to slay.

On this new trail he managed to find some berries and these he ate. Also, certain tubers that he knew from past experience were edible, he chewed to allay the pangs of growing hunger within him. The hours passed and Bana was tiring, for he was only mortal and still very hungry.

Finally, somewhat discouraged, he paused in a grassy place and decided to rest a short while before continuing his seemingly aimless search. Everything was so peaceful in this seeming Garden of Eden that, before he was aware of the transition, he was fast asleep.

In his dreams, Bana, Zozo, and little Bazo dwelt in a perfect Eden. Luscious fruits of all sorts were bountifully hanging from numerous trees waiting to be picked and eaten. Small animals and birds were tethered nearby, awaiting their slaughter so that they might keep the trio contentedly fed. Never in his wildest fantasies did the youth feel so completely at peace with the world.

But it seems even in the Stone Age one's dreams, however happy, must come to an abrupt end. How long he had slept Bana had no means of computing, but he was aware at the instant of his waking, that he was as hungry, if not more so, than when he had lain down. But he had no time to reflect upon that at the moment, for the mighty roar that had rudely aroused him from his slumber took the shape of a monstrous beast towering above him.

A huge mastodon was glaring down at the nearly naked youth with burning eyes of savagery. It was in the act of lowering its fearsome head with its shovel-like jaws and its gleaming tusks when another mighty roar sounded near at hand.

With heart that almost stopped beating, Bana saw a mighty black bear leap upon the mastodon, uttering a ferocious bark that near frightened the Stone Age youth to death.

The two monsters snarled and roared at each other, and the ground trembled as they engaged in savage warfare—the law of the primitive that decreed death to the weaker of the two.

Bana was compelled to roll away quickly and scramble to his feet lest he be trod to death. Behind the bole of a mighty tree he hid and watched with wide-staring eyes as the savage monsters battled to the death. Huge and ungainly they were, but the bear's slashing teeth and sharp claws inflicted numerous wounds upon the mastodon, while the latter managed at times to catch the cave bear off guard as he thrust with his tusks, inflicting serious wounds as well, until both were covered with hot, sticky blood, and the ground about them became gory as the raging battle continued without let-up.

First, one of the monstrous beasts was down with the other atop, seeking to strike a death blow. Within a few minutes the tables would be turned. And so the death battle raged until it seemed impossible either could live because of the enormous amount of blood shed by each. But on they battled, neither asking or giving quarter as was their stubborn nature.

Behind the bole of the tree from where he watched, Bana stood entranced, his hunger forgotten for the time being. Now he was aware that both battling beasts were weakening, though still, dominant in their small brains, was the one desire to destroy the other.

Some half hour later both beasts were so exhausted and weakened from loss of blood that they could not gain an erect position. They lay where they had fallen, but still slashed and tore at each other with teeth, claw-like fangs, and tusks, rather feebly now. Each was still hopeful of besting the other and retaining the prestige of being the victor of the encounter.

The Stone Age youth now shook his head in an effort to orient himself. He realized he had escaped certain death, and he was also cognizant if he wished to preserve his life, he had better be on his way, for now the craving of food was even greater than before.

Looking toward the two dying monsters who had battled over him, he noticed they were quite still. Realizing they were near death, he could not resist the temptation to approach and lap the blood which was still flowing copiously from their numerous wounds. In a few moments he had neared the cave bear, and at one of the more serious wounds upon the beast's forearms, he drank his fill of the flowing hot blood. It was sickening but his starving stomach welcomed it.

Refreshed now, he looked for his knobbed club, and finding it, once more went his way after glancing momentarily at the sun to fix his bearings. He regretted that Zozo and Bazo had not been with him to feast upon the flowing blood from the dying beasts.

Presently he emerged into a large clearing. Almost at once a large shadow blotted out the sun's light for a moment. The Stone Age youth quickly looked upward to learn the reason why. He saw a savage archaeopteryx swooping down upon him, its keen eyes having discovered him as he emerged from the jungle. Its feathered, wide-spread, clawed wings wildly flapped as they beat the sultry air, and its wicked-looking beak was already gaping, revealing its sharp teeth. Its long bony tail seemed to be the rudder in its flight.

Bana quickly ducked back into the sanctuary of the

jungle with only moments to spare. With an enraged squeal the savage bird angrily veered in its course, disappointed to have missed its would-have-been victim, and not wishing to become entangled in the tops of the mighty jungle trees.

The Stone Age youth drew a deep breath and wiped his brow of the perspiration that had gathered there in these past moments. What kind of a savage area was this compared to the peaceful one he had left? He had never seen such fearful monsters, both on land and in the air in his short life. He did know that his father had been slain and horribly mutilated by a savage saber-tooth tiger, for the wounds upon his father's body had been terrible to behold. Upon the instant he decided to return to the cave where his mate and infant son awaited him, even though he would bring them no food.

It would be certain death were he to continue the way he had. Thinking of Zozo and Bazo, and the unborn child as well, he realized how alone and unprotected they would be in this savage land were he to be slain by some fearsome beast.

Gripping his knobbed club more firmly, the Stone Age youth with every sense alert against possible dangers retraced the way he had come. To the left, and then ahead, and to his right Bana looked as he stealthy advanced along the trail he had passed a short while since.

Presently he reached the place where the two fearful beasts had battled to the death. Upon their bloody bodies carrion birds and small carnivorous animals alike were feeding. The birds flapped their wings angrily and cawed viciously at the youth as he passed, while the animals snarled and bared their fangs. But

Bana had no quarrel with them; in a few moments he had left them alone to their grisly feeding.

Unsuspectingly ahead, a monstrous python all of fifty feet in length and nearly a foot in diameter slithered silently along a low-hung branch. Its beady eyes were aware of the approach of the bronzed youth. Hungry as it was, this choice tid-bit was not to pass unapprehended.

Bana still walked with extreme stealth, his ears alert and his sharp eyes ever watchful. He continued to glance to his left, then ahead, and in front of him before he looked to the right. Occasionally he cast fleeting glances overhead, but each brief glimpse at the interlaced foliage with numerous creepers was not careful enough to detect anything unusual.

The fact that the python's skin was the same color as the bark of the low-hung limb upon which it slithered would have required careful study to recognize it for what it was.

Nearer the Stone Age youth approached the low-hung limb of a giant tree, and now that the trail was becoming less dense, he heaved a sigh of relief. He paused momentarily, feeling certain that he had heard an unusual noise, but looking to his left and then to his right his keen eyes could not see anything out of the ordinary. With a shake of his head he resumed his way, and a few moments later was passing beneath a low-hung limb several feet above his head.

The weight of the heavy coiling body in motion descended upon him with such unexpectedness that Bana was knocked to the ground. Before he could collect his scattered wits several coils of the writhing, scaly body of the python were encircling him, pinioning his arms to his sides helplessly. Strive though he did to free his arms, to no avail were the Stone Age youth's mighty efforts. Large drops of perspiration beaded his brow as he vainfully strove to loosen the tight, seemingly steel-like bonds about him.

Agonizing groans escaped his close-pressed lips as those entwining tentacles closed ever tighter about him. Gradually Bana's breathing became more labored owing to the tremendous constriction of the imprisoning python. Within him there was an awful suffocation present.

Bana's thoughts wildly pictured Zozo and Bazo, and if there was sorrow in his heart for leaving them, there was no time for regret now. His last conscious recollection of life was as the powerful python's head came around to face him with its hateful, beady eyes, and then he saw the jaws gape wide.

At the next moment, so great the pressure the encircling coils exerted upon him, an agonizing moan escaped his lips. His bulging eyes closed as an excruciating pain surged throughout his body, and as his mouth unconsciously opened, blood copiously gushed forth. Oblivion raced over his roaring senses, and thus ended the young life of Bana, the Stone Age youth, who had lived such a short span of life nearly five hundred thousand years ago.

But he had left behind a mate, a son, and a still unborn child. What their fate was to be, who could tell?

CHAPTER X

BANTAN'S CONSENT

When Bantan opened his eyes he looked about curiously, and observed that he was lying in bed in the guest room that he had been assigned to in the castle of The Great One. At his side, seated upon a chair, watching him silently was Hulo, the elder of the twin brothers, who had escorted him from the Mandoes village. The bronzed giant felt wearied, or weakened, from the drug that had been administered to him.

The last recollection that he had was of the meal Loula had brought him. He remembered drinking the glass of fruit juice, but almost at the next moment he had felt unconsciousness overcoming him, but not before he had heard a choking sob escape the servant girl's lips.

Now he was aware of an unpleasant taste in his throat which he attributed to the drugged fruit juice he had drunk. He swallowed several times, making a wry face. With an effort he arose to a seated position, swinging his legs to the side of the bed, and rested his feet upon the floor. His senses swam and he shook his head violently for a moment; it was then that his head cleared somewhat, though it still felt light. He forced a smile to his lips as he looked at Hulo, who was regarding him curiously, but not hostilely.

"I don't suppose you will tell me why I was drugged, Hulo?" he said questionably.

The stalwart warrior only shook his head in answer;

then, strangely, a slow smile spread upon his face, making the fine mesh of wrinkles more noticeable.

"I can tell you this much, Bantan," he answered. "The Great One is very pleased."

"Thank you," the young giant said.

Bantan arose from the bed and shook his head a trifle. He walked unsteadily toward one of the windows overlooking the edge of the cliff. He looked up at the heaven and observed that the time of day was late afternoon. He realized he had been drugged since about midday. He turned about to face Hulo. The warrior had arisen to his feet and was watching him without expression upon his face.

"I'll see that Loula brings you something to make you feel better, Bantan," he said.

The bronzed giant merely nodded as Hulo departed. He remained at the window, looking out at the shimmering water, meanwhile, wondering for what reason The Great One had had him drugged. He hoped very much he would be granted an audience with that personage so that he might know what everything was about concerning him.

Presently his keen ears heard the slight shuffling of sandals in the corridor, He turned just as Loula paused upon the threshold of the doorway and looked apprehensively at him. Bantan could easily determine that the servant girl was inwardly disturbed, and he believed he knew the reason. A wry smile touched the corners of his lips as he spoke to her.

"Hello, Loula."

An affrighted smile was upon the girl's lips, but her dark eyes were serious when she realized that Bantan did not appear angry. She carried a tray of food. He noted a glass of sparkling fruit juice was also upon the tray. Loula set the tray upon the table. As she turned about, the bronzed giant had noiselessly come to her side, almost startling her.

"Drink the contents of the glass, Bantan," she urged. "It will make you feel much better."

A smile of amusement appeared upon his face.

"I have your word it is not drugged like the last I drank?" he asked.

The servant girl at once became humble and contrite.

"Please don't blame me," she begged. "I had to carry out orders. I'm so relieved that you are none the worse for your experience."

He nodded deprecatingly, but uttered no words.

Loula wrung her hands nervously and looked about the room, trying to avoid his attention. At last mustering her courage, she managed to face him.

"I don't want anything to happen to you, Bantan," she declared. "Please believe me."

The young giant reached for the glass of fruit juice. Looking at the girl intently, he raised it to his lips and drained it to the last drop. He was at once aware that his throat tasted different, and he then realized how very hungry he was. He seated himself and smiled up at Loula.

"I understand The Great One was very pleased," he remarked.

A strange expression appeared in the girl's eyes.

"He is very happy," she answered. "More than that I cannot say."

As he commenced to eat of the food upon the tray, Loula lingered near the table. It seemed there was more that she wished to speak of; but years of stern obedience to The Great One compelled her silence.

"I'll return for the dishes later," she said in a slightly trembling voice; and without waiting for him to speak, the servant girl departed.

Bantan watched her in silence, then shook his head as she left the room. He was sure she had wanted to speak further, but concerning what, puzzled him not a little. He shrugged his shoulders and resumed his meal. The food was delicious, and by the time he had finished eating, he was aware his head no longer felt light. Arising from the table and approaching the window again, he realized he felt more like himself.

In a short while Loula returned for the tray of dishes. Though Bantan heard her pause at the doorway before entering, he pretended not to know she was present. His keen nostrils were soon aware of the aroma of perfume, and as the scent became stronger he leisurely turned about to find the girl standing near him. A shyness had overcome her, but her dark eyes were warm as they appraised him. Now that the bronzed giant looked upon her, a gentle smile appeared upon her lips and an eagerness came into her eyes.

"I can tell you something now, Bantan," she whispered. "It has taken a lot of courage on my part to defy The Great One."

He shook his head warningly.

"Don't tell me anything, Loula," he said, "if the telling will get you in trouble."

"I can trust you," she murmured with a nod. "And I feel you should know."

A smile touched his lips as he shrugged.

"I don't want you to be punished," he demurred.

The girl's eyes were eager. She placed one of her hands upon his arm. She shook her head slightly and he noticed her eyes now appeared worried.

"I have never known The Great One to be so pleased," she confessed. "I think he is going to send for you later to talk of further experiments."

A slight furrow creased the young man's brow.

" 'Experiments'?" he repeated.

She nodded slowly, the worried expression still in her eyes.

"You were drugged so that The Great One could experiment upon you," she added. "He has stated you have been the best subject he has ever had."

Bantan became intensely interested.

"Do you know the nature of the experiments for which I was used?" he then asked.

The girl wet her lips nervously and she seemed a trifle agitated. She shrugged her shoulders.

"I am not too familiar with what happens in the laboratory," she admitted. "But I overheard him telling his—his nurse that never before had he probed into the past so far as he has through the memory cells of your brain."

Bantan shook his head, still not fully understanding.

"But for what reason does The Great One wish to probe into the past?" he asked.

"It's his life's work, Bantan," Loula admitted. "All of us, in one way or another, have served as subjects, but we were never told the results. Some of us were used many times, and others only once."

"Hulo and Humo were used as subjects?" he asked then.

The servant girl nodded.

"Many times."

He stared at her, noting the fine mesh of wrinkles upon her otherwise clear skin.

"And yourself?"

Again she nodded.

"Many times."

Bantan appeared in deep thought. It was the servant girl's voice that made him realize she was still there.

"I must go now," she murmured with some reluctance. "I know I can trust you not to mention what I have told you."

He smiled assuringly and nodded.

Loula's eyes acknowledged her gratefulness, and without a further word she went to the table and picked up the tray of dishes. As she passed the young giant she flashed him a silent smile, and then was gone.

Bantan returned to one of the windows and looked outside at the shimmering water, his thoughts somewhat in a jumble as to the enlightenment provided him by the servant girl. Thinking of The Great One's life's work brought a tolerant smile to his lips. In a vague way he found himself wondering what his memory cells had revealed. Was there a possibility that he might be told merely to satisfy his curiosity?

While thus engaged in mental speculation, the bronzed giant's much-discussed sixth sense failed to apprise him of the presence of another in the room. Only as that one spoke did he slightly react. Even before turning about he recognized the voice and he saw that Hulo had returned. A pleasing expression was upon the warrior's face.

"Come, Bantan," he said beckoningly. "The Great One wishes to talk with you."

With no comment, the bronzed giant left the window and approached the warrior.

"You are feeling all right?" Hulo asked with concern.

Bantan smiled assuringly and nodded.

Without further delay the two passed from the room through the corridor to the elevator, and in a few minutes disembarked upon the ground floor.

"He is waiting for you in the same room," Hulo said.

Presently Bantan was ushered into the room with the curtained booth. The warrior approached close and knelt.

"Here is your guest, O Great One," he announced.

The same metallic voice from behind the curtain bade Hulo to take his leave. When the stalwart warrior had left the room and closed the door, The Great One addressed Bantan in a pleased tone.

"You have proved an excellent subject for my experiments—far beyond my fondest hopes," he said.

A smile touched the young giant's lips.

"I am pleased to know that, O Great One," he replied with respect.

"Are you curious to know for what reason I used you for an experiment?" The Great One then asked.

Bantan shrugged.

"I would like to know," he answered.

"For many years I have been interested in the Stone Age," The Great One said in a gentle tone of voice. "I've read everything that eminent scholars have written; but I was still not satisfied. I have developed a machine with the proper attachments that probe the long-dormant memory cells of a subject's brain, and in this way I am able to go into the past of that individual. I have used the Mandoes men and women as subjects in the past, but for some reason the memory of their brain cells is extremely limited. Through them,

I could only probe into the past for several thousand years, but that was very unsatisfactory for me.

"Constant adjustments were made upon my machine, feeling I did not have it perfectly attuned for the purpose I created it. Repeatedly I used the same subjects, but the results were always the same. I was positive my machine was attuned to its utmost frequency, and I finally realized that my subjects were at fault, not the machine. Through you this fact has been established. Do you have any conscious conception of time, Bantan?"

The bronzed giant shrugged.

"I have an excellent memory of my past life," he answered. "Is that what you mean?"

"That may have something to do with it," The Great One answered. "You have been afflicted twice with amnesia caused by a blow upon the head. Am I not correct?"

"That is so," Bantan admitted with surprise.

"Each time that your memory was returned to you," The Great One added, "you were able to remember what had happened during those periods of amnesia. Am I not right?"

The young giant's surprise was still greater.

"That is so," he admitted.

A brief silence followed before the voice behind the curtained booth spoke again.

"Would you like to know how far back into time my machine was able to probe your memory cells, Bantan?" The Great One asked

"I would like to know," the young giant said with sincerity.

"Just stop and realize what I am going to tell you," was The Great One's statement. "Through you, I have probed five hundred thousand years into the past! That period was the Middle Pleistocene of the Old Stone Age. By reading their lips I learned their names. At that time your remote ancestor was known as Bana, and as the other inhabitants, went about nearly stark naked in a primeval world. His father was killed by a saber-tooth tiger when Bana was twelve years of age. Speech was exceptionally limited, other than grunts, the shaking of one's head, and cumbersome signs being employed for communication. Bana's widowed mother and only older sister were killed when a tribe of neighboring males raided the cave dwellings for the purpose of stealing women. For that reason, after burying them he left the tribe, and seven days later made his own home alone in another cave. He came upon a girl named Zozo and mated with her. In due time a son was born, marked as you are with a blood-red blotch upon his right temple. Another child was conceived, but unborn, when Bana met an untimely death. A giant python trapped him, crushing the life from him and then doubtless devoured him. Would you like to see a motion picture recording of your early ancestors, Bantan?"

The bronzed giant was amazed by The Great One's report of his experiment for which he had been the subject. He nodded.

"I would like very much to see the motion picture of that time, O Great One," he answered.

"Turn about and watch the wall above the doorway," he was directed. "There you will see what my machine recorded through your memory cells."

Bantan did as he was bade. From the curtained booth to his rear his sharp ears heard a slight whirring sound. A bright, rectangular light appeared upon the wall, covering an area of six feet in length and four in width. And then before his bewildered eyes he saw what The Great One had told him he would see. Within him rose a great wonder as he saw his prehistoric progenitor as a boy, and the following scenes increased his wonderment to a stage of incredulity. When he saw Bana trapped by a python and crushed to death, he could scarcely repress the shudder that raced the length of his spine.

The scenes upon the wall terminated and the rectangular light went out. The whirring sound behind him ceased. Bantan shook his head unbelievingly. As he turned to face the curtained booth, he heard a low chuckle issue from behind the curtain.

"It's difficult to believe possible, isn't it, Bantan?" The Great One questioned.

The bronzed giant again shook his head.

"It must be true," he answered.

"It *was* true," The Great One corrected him. "What you have seen was as true as the fact you are standing before this curtained booth at the present moment."

A visible shudder again raced the length of Bantan's spine.

"Poor Zozo, her little son Bazo, and the child that was unborn," he murmured. "I wonder how they managed to survive?"

"They must have survived else you would not be living today," The Great One declared. "We can't know exactly how Zozo and Bazo survived immediately after the death of Bana; but we can pick up the threads of existence through Bazo's brain when he reached the age of reason. In all probability that would be after he was twelve years of age."

Though a shudder raced the length of his spine, Bantan realized his curiosity must needs be satisfied.

"I would be a willing subject for a further experiment, O Great One," he declared.

"Fine!" was the reply. "Since you are willing, there will be no necessity to administer a drug. Hulo will go with you to your room, and later in the afternoon will return for you. Believe me, Bantan," he added, "I am pleased that you are a willing subject in furthering my experiments. It makes everything just that much more pleasant."

The bronzed giant merely shrugged his giant frame. In truth, he suspected he had no choice in the matter —and his suspicion need not be confirmed. For now that The Great One had experimented with his brain cells, and he had been rewarded beyond his fondest hope of success, there would be no limitation to his constant experiments in the future. Willing, or unwilling, subject that Bantan might be, there would be no stopping the scientist now that he had acquired what he considered the perfect subject.

"Hulo!" The metallic voice of The Great One echoed throughout the room.

In another moment the warrior appeared in the doorway.

"Yes, O Great One?" he answered.

"Return with Bantan to his room," Hulo was bade. The warrior bowed his head.

"It shall be as you wish, O Great One," he said.

Hulo nodded to the bronzed giant to join him. Without further delay they returned to the elevator.

"The Great One was very pleased with you, Bantan?" Hulo questioned, as the elevator commenced to move upward.

"Very pleased, Hulo," was the reply.

They did not speak further until the top floor was reached. Hulo pressed a lever which opened the door. He nodded toward the corridor.

"I will return later," he said.

The young giant stepped from the elevator and without a word proceeded to the room assigned to him. Once more he went to one of the windows overlooking the shimmering water below. He stood there in deep reflection as he reviewed within his mind the scenes from the Stone Age where had been depicted the life of one of his earliest progenitors. He thought of poor Zozo, Bazo, her infant son, and the still unborn child, and for that reason alone he was eager to submit to another experiment to learn how they had fared after Bana had met his untimely death.

Bantan's keen nostrils presently became aware of the aroma of perfume, and without turning, he knew that Loula had come to his room again. Only as she spoke to him did he turn and face her.

"You have talked with The Great One, Bantan?" she asked anxiously.

He nodded.

Her eyes remained upon him unwaveringly.

"You are going to be a subject to another experiment?"

Again he nodded.

"A little later in the afternoon."

The servant girl's dark eyes were filled with concern.

"I hope all goes well, Bantan," she murmured.

He smiled assuringly to allay her fears.

"I'm sure everything will be all right, Loula," he

said. "I survived the first experiment, didn't I? There's
no reason why I shouldn't survive another."

The girl drew a deep breath and pressed her hands
tightly against her heaving bosom.

"I hope everything will be all right," she murmured.

"Why are you so concerned about me, Loula?" he
asked then.

A flush mounted to the girl's cheeks and a shyness
crept into her dark eyes.

"I must go now," she said in a hushed voice that
trembled slightly.

Removing her eyes from the bronzed giant she
glided noiselessly out of the room. At the doorway she
paused to turn about, and aware that he was looking
in her direction, she flashed him a tremulous smile, then
turning, vanished from his sight.

Bantan heaved a sigh and resumed his attention
upon the shimmering water below. Time didn't seem
to exist as the minutes passed and he meditated deeply.
The sun was still some distance from the horizon when
Hulo returned to the guest room and announced that
The Great One was expecting him in the laboratory.

Without a word the bronzed giant joined the stalwart warrior. While they walked to the elevator, Hulo
watched his companion with curiosity.

"You are not nervous, Bantan?" he asked as the
conveyance started down the shaft.

The young giant smiled and shook his head.

"Not a bit," he answered.

Presently the elevator came to a stop at the level
below the ground floor. As Hulo opened the door, he
nodded to the bright, electrically lighted corridor.

"This is it," he said. "The laboratory is the first
door on the left through which the bright light shines."

The warrior accompanied Bantan to the doorway where he paused, allowing the young giant to enter alone. So bright the lights from within, he was compelled to blink his eyes momentarily. Behind him he heard the door of the laboratory close. He then looked about the room in silent wonder. Various machines and glass tubes and bulbs were to be seen, but what interested him most of all were the two figures dressed in white, the man with masked face and rubber gloves covering his hands.

The tall, straight, slim man's eyes glittered as he looked at the perfect figure of Bantan. He was standing at one side of a white, cloth-covered table. Upon the other side a young woman stood. Her gray eyes appeared sad.

"This way, Bantan," The Great One's voice spoke, indicatingly.

The bronzed giant walked toward the table. As he stood at its side, he was instructed to lie upon it and he did so.

The nurse then fastened the straps in silence. Meanwhile, The Great One went to a cabinet and withdrew a hypodermic and a bottle of amber fluid. He removed the stopper, and dipping the end of the needle into it, filled the tube. He replaced the stopper and placed the bottle back in the cabinet. Then with eyes glittering strangely he approached his subject. He nodded to the nurse who, meanwhile, had obtained a bottle of alcohol and had saturated some absorbent cotton with it. She now rubbed Bantan's left arm above the elbow. The Great One stood silently until the nurse had finished, then he spoke to Bantan.

"This is a sedative with no after effects," he explained. "It is necessary that your nerves be completely relaxed while the experiment takes place."

He then emptied the contents of the hypodermic into Bantan's arm, and it was then that the bronzed giant's eyes met those of the scientist for the first time. The glittering blue eyes that looked down upon the subject were not the eyes of a sane, normal man—but wild and unrestrained—the eyes of a mad scientist!

Bantan shuddered momentarily, and then oblivion swept over him, as the drug took immediate effect.

CHAPTER XI

AGAIN THE STONE AGE

Back into the mists of antiquity Bantan's memory cells carried him through the ingenuity of The Great One's retrovider, and our scene shifts to the Middle Pleistocene of the Old Stone Age. Again he has gone backward in time—nearly five hundred thousand years, and takes up living in the boy known as Bazo, now fifteen years of age, and looking very much like the father he could not remember.

He dwelt in a crude cave with his mother, Zozo, and a younger sister, Lozo. Only recently an old man by name of Tobo, who had been mated to Zozo when Bazo had been a small child and his sister a mere infant, had died, leaving the three to fare for themselves. Since then other unmated males had tried to take over Zozo's poor cave, but she would have none of them. The fact that Bazo was now becoming a good hunter and fisherman kept his mother and sister provided with food—and that was all that mattered in that long-remote age.

Speech had not improved any, and children were still named according to their first utterances as an infant.

Bazo had reached that awkward age where he was no longer a boy, nor yet a man. Sometimes, in exasperation, he wished that he might always remain a boy. And yet, he realized, had he, his mother would have been compelled to mate with another male, and a

second time such an adopted father might not be so
considerate as old Tobo had been to him and Lozo
while they had been young.

In Bazo's breast now there was beginning to be
felt the yearnings of a full-fledged man. He tried manfully to suppress thoughts of that nature, but there
were occasions when his will power could not completely blot from his mind those tenacious thoughts
that sometimes became an incessant craving.

This day as he plodded through a jungle trail, seeking fruits, nuts, and edible tubers, he realized no dis-
turbing thoughts had been his until the day, just recently, his mother had brought to the cave to live
with them a sad-looking girl who had been the only
daughter of a widow-friend of Zozo's who had just
died. The girl's name was Mono and she was Lozo's
age, fourteen, but more fully developed. The mother
made her son and daughter understand that Mono was
to live with them hereafter, and they were to treat her
with consideration.

From the very first Bazo had entertained a compassion for Mono because of her sadness, and the fact
she had no living relatives. Her dark eyes during those
first days always seemed ready to fill with tears. The
passing days, however, dispelled her sadness, and she
began to feel more at home in her new living quarters.

Realizing that her son was nearing manhood, Zozo
constantly kept a vigilant eye upon him whenever
Mono was around. Perhaps she didn't wish Bazo to
become too infatuated with the adopted girl, for were
such to become the case, he would naturally want to
mate with her. Were this to happen, she realized she
would have to look about for another mate to provide
the food that was always required in a cave household.

Zozo still retained much of her girlhood good looks, and she knew she would not have to look far for another mate.

From the time they were very young, Bazo and his sister Lozo would frequently wrestle with one another. Knowing of their sport, Zozo always wished to be present, especially now, since Mono had been taken in to live with them. She felt sure her son might feel different were he and the adopted girl to engage in such sport.

Mono would watch Bazo and Lozo wrestle with interest, and after a while into her dark eyes would dawn a curiosity to know how she and the youth might react were they to engage in such playfulness. One evening after Bazo and Lozo had wrestled, and as usual, the youth had won the contest, Mono expressed a desire to wrestle with Bazo. The Stone Age youth shook his head in negation, indicating that she and Lozo do so. Lozo was willing, and though Mono was disappointed, she engaged the girl. Not knowing of the many tricks Lozo was familiar with, in a short time she found that she was the loser of the contest.

Zozo had been present, and she was relieved when her son refused to wrestle with Mono. She was aware that he, too, must realize the difference in wrestling with her, whereas he thought nothing of doing so with his sister. But, watching Lozo and Mono wrestle did arouse strange feelings in the Stone Age youth, and he knew how different it would be were he to wrestle with Mono.

One day when Zozo and her daughter were absent from the cave, Bazo returned with fruits, nuts, and edible tubers to find that Mono was alone. As he entered and noticed her, he nodded and grunted, but other than that he paid her no further attention. He deposited the provisions in a corner, and squatting upon his haunches, proceeded to sort them.

Mono watched him with steady eyes into which a peculiar glow came. She admired Bazo from the first day she had come to the cave, and she felt somewhat hurt to know he didn't seem to particularly care for her, and would not wrestle with her as he did his sister. Even now, as an added insult, he squatted with his back toward her.

Bazo did not see Mono approach him silently with a spirit of deviltry in her eyes. She stood for a few moments at his side, appearing to take interest in what he was doing. Then she went down upon her knees and watched him more closely. She leaned toward him until her shoulder pressed against his.

The youth moved away a trifle, but Mono was again close to him. Bazo's shoulder seemingly burned where hers had come in contact with his and he felt uneasy. He shook his head and uttered a gutteral that was intended as a warning for the girl to keep a respectable distance from him.

But on this day Mono was not to be repulsed so easily. She laughed softly. And then without warning, one of her well formed arms went about Bazo's chest, and before he could retain his balance, she upset him easily. Falling backward as he did, the Stone Age youth felt foolish, and an unmitigated rage instantly possessed him. Quickly he rose to his feet, growling. Glaring down at the kneeling girl, who was convulsed with mocking laughter, he approached her. Placing a hand upon her shoulder, he rudely shoved her backward. Then, as he turned to leave, Mono's foot quickly lifted and she thrust it between his, tripping him, so that he fell forward.

This time as Bazo fell—his hands saving him from falling flat upon his face—he was unprepared for Mono's next move. Having watched the youth and his sister wrestle, she quickly arose and flung herself upon him as he momentarily rested upon his hands and knees. The weight of her body flattened the youth upon the dirt floor. Quickly the girl's arms went about him, pinioning his helplessly, and her outstretched legs closed about him so that he was unable to rise, strive though he did.

For long minutes Bazo tried to twist and turn and extricate himself from the girl's more advantageous position, but to no avail were his efforts, squirm and writhe as he did. At last he lay still, feeling that he had lost the unexpected match. Mono was laughing softly and her face rested near his, her long hair covering his features. He was acutely aware of the pressure of her large breasts against his back, and his skin seemingly burned. The animal warmth of her nearly naked body covering his was causing the blood to sear his veins. He had never felt that way at any time when he and Lozo had wrestled in the past, but this was entirely different.

And then he thought of his mother and sister, and the possibility they might return at any moment. To find him and Mono in this embarrasing position he was sure would anger them. Now he turned his head, blowing her hair from his mouth as he uttered their names.

"Zozo! Lozo! Zozo! Lozo!"

At first Mono paid no heed to what he said. She was immensely enjoying herself because of Bazo's discomfiture; but at last she began to realize of whom he was

trying to warn her. She released her arms and legs
from about him and rolled off his back. She did
not rise, but remained upon her side, looking up at
Bazo as he arose to his feet. In silent wonder with
heaving breasts, she watched him, knowing full well
that she deserved a kick as a punishment for what she
had unexpectedly done to him.

As he gained his feet, there was no denying Bazo
wanted to punish the presumptuous girl; but for some
reason when his raging eyes met her now docile ones,
he could not bring himself to do so.

Every inch of his body where Mono's had come in
contact with his burned with the intensity of fire. For a
long moment he stood above her cowering form, as
though undecided what to do; then with an angry
shake of his head, he turned and barged out of the
cave.

With his going, Mono arose to her knees slowly,
and then to her feet. She clasped her arms about her
heaving bosom, and a gentle smile touched her lips, but
the expression in her dark eyes was a forlorn one. She
could not understand why Bazo did not desire her as
she desired him. At that moment she envied Lozo for
being his sister, wishing that she might have been more
fortunate.

Later in the day when Bazo, having bathed in a pool
to soothe his burning body, returned to the cave, he
was relieved to find that his mother and sister were
present. He also saw that Mono was there, but he
hardly looked at her, though the girl was saddened at
his lack of interest in her. Time and again she would
cast sorrowful glances at him, but if he noticed, he paid
no attention.

Before it became dark, Lozo indicated she would

wrestle with her brother. Bazo looked balefully at Mono as he accepted his sister's challenge. In a few moments they were rolling about the floor, grunting and groaning in mock pain. Once, the youth gazed in the direction of the watching Mono, who crouched near his mother. That moment of distraction was all that Lozo required, for she quickly turned him over with a squeal of delight and was astride him, rendering him helpless as Mono had done earlier in the day.

Though the youth tried his utmost to upset his clinging sister, his efforts were in vain. In his prone position he glared at Mono, inwardly blaming her for his defeat; but instead of seeing a revengeful gleam in her eyes, he was mystified that she appeared to be sad and on the verge of tears.

Zozo appeared puzzled that Bazo had been overcome by his lighter sister, but she shrugged her shoulders, realizing as she did that Bazo could not win all the time.

Meanwhile, aware that she had won the contest, Lozo at length arose from her brother's prone form. She was laughing triumphantly as Bazo slowly arose to his feet. His sister stood, her small breasts heaving, anticipating that her brother would challenge her to another wrestling match; but when he did not, she turned to Mono with inviting eyes.

The girl accepted Lozo's challenge, and they wrestled while Zozo and Bazo watched, the latter with scant interest, but hoping that Lozo would defeat her. Mono, however, being the heavier by about ten pounds, and having learned quickly, soon had Lozo at her mercy with the result she was acclaimed the winner in a few minutes.

Arising from her defeated opponent, Mono looked

challengingly at Bazo. He refused to meet her eyes directly, while Zozo watched with a strange chill growing in her heart. Lozo teased her brother to add to his discomfort, but with a shrug of his shoulders, the youth arose and angrily left the cave.

Presently, when darkness was setting, the inmates of the cave prepared for bed. Since the nights were cool, all of them huddled upon grass mats, their bodies pressed close together for additional warmth. Mono slept nearest the wall with Lozo next to her. Zozo was next to her daughter, while Bazo always slept upon the outside.

But on this night the Stone Age youth, when he returned to the cave, still nursed his ill feeling toward Mono, and would not sleep at his mother's side. Instead, he gathered some grass and placed it near the mouth of the cave, farthest from the others. His mother was perturbed that this was so, but she thought nothing further as she placed her arms about her daughter and they were soon asleep.

Across the cave, Bazo did not soon fall asleep. For the first time in his life he found himself wide awake as he tried to convince himself how much he hated Mono for having made him feel so uncomfortable.

Mono, too, was unable to sleep. She was thinking of how unfair she had been to Bazo. If only he had kicked her she would have felt relieved for having received her just dues. Instead, she had remained unpunished, and that troubled her greatly.

Listening to the soft breathing of Zozo and Lozo, the girl felt miserable that they had fallen asleep so easily, while she lay there wrestling with mental problems that would not permit her to do so. At last, she could stand it no longer. She noiselessly arose to her feet, and in the darkness, softly groped her way across the cave to where she suspected Bazo was lying. When she felt she must be near him, she went down upon her hands and knees and crawled toward him.

"Bazo!" she whispered. "Bazo!"

A sudden joy came into the Stone Age youth's heart, and he immediately arose to a seated position with a smile upon his face. But at the next moment some perverse streak froze the joy in his heart, and he turned over upon the grasses with a gruff gutteral that was meant to repulse the repentant girl.

Mono crept to the youth's side heavyheartedly and with tears in her eyes. She reached out her hands in the dark. Her left hand touched his head, and she stroked his hair gently. But Bazo paid her no attention. He couldn't bring himself to strike her, though he well knew she deserved such punishment. Now the girl, in despair, proceeded to lay alongside him, but Bazo quickly arose to his feet with a low growl and left the cave. The last sound he heard was a choking sob escaping Mono's lips.

The girl remained where she was, disappointed to be sure; but presently she became aware of the warmth of the grass where Bazo had been lying. She filled her nostrils with the scent of his body that cloyingly clung to the grasses, and thereafter she felt less sorrow.

Meanwhile, the youth had gone outside in the darkness of the night. He did not go far, as no one who inhabited the caves strayed very far because of the savage carnivore that roamed about at night. Even now he could hear their distant roars and he shivered somewhat. For some little while Bazo tried to analyze his feelings toward Mono, and when at last he could not seem to find an answer, he growled. The chill of the evening was keenly felt by his nearly naked body, and soon he was trembling and his teeth chattered. At last he returned to the cave with the determination that if Mono had not left his bed of grasses, he would kick her until she did.

In the darkness his groping hands felt about and to his relief the girl was not there. With a sigh he lay down upon the grasses, immediately conscious of their warmth. He could not know that Mono had returned to her own place just a few moments before he returned.

Bazo's keen nostrils were aware of the animal warmth the girl's body had left upon the grasses, and though he tried to convince himself that he was displeased, the truth of the matter was that he was not. He listened carefully, thinking that she might return now that he had come back. Should she, he was half decided that he would let her remain; but Mono did not come to him.

Strange dreams were his after sleep claimed him. It seemed that he and Mono lived alone in the world, and they wanted nothing else but each other. In the morning when he awoke, a smile touched his lips. When he was fully aware that he was really awake and not dreaming, perhaps a twinge of disappointment was to be felt.

Later, when they ate, Bazo would steal quick glances at Mono, and he noticed her eyes were surrounded with dark circles, indicating she had been weeping and must have passed a miserable, sleepless night. The youth decided he would be nice to her from now on, for his heart filled with compassion for her. Later, he would ask her if she cared to go bathing with him at the pool, and thereafter, they might search for fruits, nuts, and edible tubers. He was sure she would be pleased in the new change in him.

Shortly afterward Mono unostentatiously left the cave, and when Bazo looked for her he found that she was gone. Without a word to his mother and sister, he left. He thought that perhaps the girl had gone to the pool to bathe. But when he arrived there, though other cave dwellers were bathing, he saw no sign of her.

Shrugging, he traversed the jungle growth, searching for fruits, nuts, and edible tubers as he customarily did. In a crude way he mentally upbraided himself for thinking of Mono as he did last night; if he could entertain regrets for not having been more considerate to her, then he was regretful.

For some unknown reason because of a scarcity of fruits, nuts, and edible tubers, Bazo ranged farther on this morning from the caves than ever before. He carried a knobbed club since leaving the pool, as that was the only form of weapon he knew of.

He tensed and gripped his club the tighter as he thought he heard an unusual sound just ahead. And then he heard a snarl. A girl's scream of terror subsequently filled the air. Bazo started suddenly. The voice sounded very much like Mono's. He broke into a run, and presently reached a small clearing.

He saw a wild dog with bared fangs advancing toward a cowering girl. One glance at her was sufficient for recognition. It was Mono! What she was doing so far from the caves puzzled him for a moment, but at the present he had no time for retrospection if he would spare her life. The snarling wild dog was about to spring upon her with slavering jaws. The advent

Bazo Battles a Wild Dog

of the Stone Age youth upon the tableau of grim life and death resulted in the savage beast hesitating a moment before claiming its helpless victim.

At the next instant Bazo leaped to the front of the cowering girl, and fearlessly faced the snarling beast. He swung his knobbed club with all the might at his command and brought it down upon the wild dog's skull with a resounding smash, cracking the bones as though they were match sticks. Without a sound the beast crumpled to the jungle floor, dead. Not a quiver wracked the body, so instantaneous death had been.

The triumphant youth turned to the girl. Now that the wild dog was dead, she arose to her feet, her hands pressed tightly to her heaving bosom, but a grateful smile possessed her features as she recognized her savior. He proudly straightened as he looked down upon the dead dog. He didn't seem to mind that Mono drew near him, pressing close to his side so that he could hear her rapid breathing, nor did he mind the contact of her shoulder against his.

Knowing the wild dog would be good eating, Bazo turned to the girl and pointed at the animal. He rubbed his stomach and moved his jaws, smacking his lips heartily, as though eating. Mono smiled and did likewise. Then the Stone Age youth shouldered the warm carcass, and with the girl following close behind him, they returned to their cave.

Zozo and Lozo were amazed at the youth's return with meat, and without hesitation, when it was deposited upon the floor of the cave, all four tore at the beast and devoured the raw flesh, spitting out the hair which tickled their throat and caused them to cough.

Bazo and Mono sat side by side during the feast, and while they ate he didn't seem to mind that occasionally his and the girl's arms came in contact and he was aware of a pleasant feeling, instead of the burning one, that previously had troubled him.

Zozo, meanwhile, was aware of the changed expression in her son toward the girl at his side. She sighed as she looked at his young manly body, and realized that soon he would want to mate with Mono, and perhaps move to another cave. She remembered that she had not been much older than the girl when she had mated with Bazo's father.

After eating to their heart's content all lay upon the cave floor as though in a stupor. Bazo and Mono were side by side. Occasionally one or the other would half arise and belch gas, and then contentedly lay back again. Once, when stirring, the girl moved about uneasily until she came to rest upon her side, facing the youth. Realizing as she did that he had spared her life from the wild dog's attack, she moved closer to him until she pressed against him. And then, as though in a half dream one of her arms went about him and she rested her face against his with a low sigh. He was too stupefied to take notice.

Across from them the youth's mother was fully awake and watchful. Lozo was too contented with a full belly to pay attention to anything. Zozo, however, was aware of the girl's unconscious act. A little sadly she turned away, fully realizing that Mono wanted to mate with her son. She knew the signs, and she was also aware there was little she could do to prevent the natural inclinations of a young couple.

It was late in the afternoon when the effects of the feast wore away. Bazo and Mono awoke simultaneously and, stretching, they arose to their feet. A short distance from them Zozo and Lozo were sleeping.

The youth remembered his wish in the morning to ask the girl to go bathing with him. Now he indicated by signs, and she readily agreed.

Both seemed happy as they wordlessly went their way side by side. No other cave dwellers were at the pool, so Bazo and Mono were alone to enjoy themselves. They stood in the water up to their waist. The girl smilingly dipped water and washed the blood of the feast from his face and body, also the dirt from his back from the cave floor where he had lain. Her hands felt soft and soothing, and he exulted in her nearness, feeling all the regret possible because he had not been more friendly with her in the past.

When she had bathed him, he then decided that he should do the same to her. He turned and dipped water and washed her face, neck, and back. As his hands passed over her breasts, she would close her eyes and hold her breath for a moment, as though the pleasure she experienced was more than she could possibly bear. He was aware of her delight, and he realized she must enjoy such attentions on his part. Aware of the strange thrill that possessed him as well while doing so, he proceeded to give more of his attention thusly much to the girl's joy, so that at last she could not stand the ecstasy any longer without a repercussion on her part. She begged him to desist. She pointed away from the pool, and he felt that she had bathed sufficiently, and that she wanted the sun to dry her wet body.

They left the pool, Mono in the lead. She seemed to be searching for something, and he wondered what it was, until at last they came to a grassy clearing. The girl slumped to her haunches and smiled at the Stone Age youth. In a moment he was at her side, their damp shoulders touching as did their thighs and the full length of their legs.

The girl looked at Bazo curiously. Presently a smile touched her lips. She reached for one of his hands. Unresistingly he permitted her to take it and she fondled it before placing it against her cheek, holding it there for some little while. Meanwhile, he reached for her hand and held it for a little while before he placed it against his cheek.

Though a contented smile touched Mono's lips, into her eyes now grew a spirit of deviltry. A sudden thought had come to her. She wondered if Bazo might wrestle with her now? She had long wanted him to and nothing would give her greater pleasure. She released his hand, as he did hers. He looked at her wonderingly.

With a smile Mono arose to her feet and indicated that he do likewise. In another moment the youth confronted her. She then motioned to him that she would wrestle with him; but he smilingly shook his head and lowered his eyes. The girl was not to be disappointed and repulsed this time. She approached closer with arms outstretched, and when he did not look up at her, she pressed against him almost aggressively, and her arms went about his shoulders, her face close to his with her warm breath fanning his lips.

Bazo suddenly trembled as his eyes lifted. Hers were filled with deviltry, but a sultry expression also lurked in their dark depths. He drew a deep breath then as she pressed closer still to him, and her breasts were mashed against his hairless chest. A surge of what he knew not instantly seared his veins.

His arms went about Mono, one about her shoulders, and other about her slim waist, and then the girl, strangely vibrant and challenging the moment before, suddenly went limp in his arms. He lowered her to the grass, and when he would have drawn away from her, she suddenly became very much alive and clasped him closer, so that he had no choice but to remain at her side. Her arms, meanwhile, moved down to his slim hips as she clung tighter to him, endeavoring to merge her body with his while soft moans issued from her opened mouth.

* * *

Shortly before sundown Bazo and Mono returned to the cave. The youth was strangely stern, but the girl seemed deliriously happy. Both Zozo and Lozo were present when the two entered. The mother of the youth glanced quickly at the happy girl and then toward her son. She immediately guessed what had happened.

Without a word or sign, Bazo gathered some of the grasses Mono had slept upon the previous evening, and with those he reposed upon, he arranged them in another place slightly away from the cave's mouth. Then it was that he looked toward his silent mother. He indicated Mono and himself and made her understand that they were now mated. His mother nodded wearily while Lozo stared at the strangely happy Mono, who had eyes for nothing but her mate and the happiness she knew he was capable of giving to her.

Presently darkness settled upon the world outside and in the cave all prepared to retire. Zozo wrapped her arms about her daughter and tried not to hear the movements from the other pallet of grasses scarcely twelve feet from her. Lozo was all ears and she did not miss the soft movements of the two bodies across the cave, nor the hushed sighs that were emitted at intervals until long in the wee hours of the morning, then all was silent save for the quiet breathing of the four sleepers in the cave.

With light filling the cave, Bazo woke first. At his side Mono was sleeping, pressed close to him, with a smile upon her lips, and one of her arms resting across her mate's chest. The Stone Age youth lifted her arm and he arose to a seated position. Looking across the cave he saw that his mother had already arisen and had taken her departure. Lozo, his sister, was awake and she was seated with her back against the wall. She was watching the newly mated couple with rapt interest.

Now Mono waked, and at once aware that her mate was seated beside her, she reached out a hand and touched his arm. As he looked down at her she smiled seductively. He shook his head and explained to her that he was going to the pool to drink and bathe, and then he must set forth to obtain food. He entertained the hope that he might slay another wild dog so that they might have another feast. Mono arose and indicated she would join him at the pool.

Across the cave the rapt expression upon Lozo's face faded as she saw Bazo and his mate leave. At the pool none of the other cave dwellers were present, for the water was a trifle chilly this early in the morning. But the newly mated couple did not mind as they bathed one another, and in a short while both were alert to their physical needs. Without loss of time they quit the pool and in haste sought the grassy clearing nearby where they had dallied the previous afternoon.

They were panting from the effects of their surging emotions when they slumped to the grass, and immediately became entwined in each other's arms.

At last, however, aware of his hunger, Bazo disengaged himself from his mate's arms and arose. He made Mono understand he must be on his way if they were to eat that day. She was reluctant to see him depart, and there was some hesitation on his part as well. Presently he had found a good-sized knobbed club for a weapon, and he was on his way while Mono returned to the cave alone and somewhat unhappy, scarcely giving a thought of food.

Bazo set his footsteps in the same direction as yesterday, hoping that he might be successful in slaying another wild dog. With ears alert and sharp eyes quickly scanning the undergrowth about him as he went his way, it was not long before he realized he had reached the little clearing where he had rescued Mono from the wild dog.

The Stone Age youth paused to sniff the warm air with his keen nostrils. He was almost sure the odor of a wild animal was to be obtained, and his sharp eyes darted furtively as he looked about. Meanwhile, he gripped the handle of his knobbed club the tighter. He could discern nothing unusual, so he crossed the little clearing, seeking always the easiest pathways so as to make unnecessary noise. He noticed fruits, nuts, and edible tubers, and his assailing hunger compelled him to pause and pick and eat some before continuing his way.

Birds twittered and scolded as they flitted through the tree tops, disturbed by the youth's passage. Bazo would cast apprehensive glances upward. There always was the thought of a python coiled about a low-hung limb lying in wait for an unwary victim.

On he went, ever alert, and then suddenly his attention was attracted by the flapping of powerful wings overhead. Through an opening in the tree tops he saw an archaeopteryx winging its way through the sultry air. He had no fear of the fierce flying bird in such dense jungle growth.

In the distance he heard two savage, carnivorous beasts engaged in a death battle; but they were so far away he entertained no immediate concern over them. Insects buzzed about him, and he was compelled to slap at them repeatedly.

He paused now, standing perfectly still, his ears alert. He was sure he had heard the sinuous passage of a body through the undergrowth to his right. His keen eyes fixed in that direction, watching carefully for the movement of a bush that would warn him of the presence of a wild animal.

Now his sharp ears detected the barely audible snarl which reminded him of the wild dog on the previous day. The tip of his tongue licked the edges of his lips with the thought of being fortunate to slay another and the feast which would follow.

The minutes passed, but no further sounds were heard, nor did his sharp, watchful eyes detect a movement in the foliage. Bazo now moved toward his right where he had previously heard the sound. He squeezed the handle of his knobbed club. His nostrils twitched as he identified the odor of a wild dog. He paused to examine the jungle floor and recognize the imprints of paws.

Directly behind him, the mate of the wild dog he had slain the previous day, was stalking him. In her savage brain she had recognized the scent of the hunter as the same one who had slain her mate. Silently she had crept upon him, and he was unaware of her changed position. And now, reaching a vantage spot, the she dog uttered no sound as her hind legs tensed for the spring. The hunter was stooped, examining her recently made imprints.

The first intimation the Stone Age youth had of the presence of his enemy was a slight movement at his rear. Before he could straighten upright and turn, the wild dog had leaped upon his back with her teeth slashing at his neck and cheeks, and ripping his back with her raking sharp nails, from which blood copiously flowed from the more deeper gashes. Bazo went down beneath the wild dog's weight, dropping his knobbed club. With his hands he tried to ward off the dog's slashing teeth, but to no avail as the backs of his hands were likewise torn. He was no match for the lightning-like attacks.

The odor of blood now enraged the wild dog so that she growled ferociously as she continued to rip at the youth's neck and cheeks with her sharp fangs. Saliva from her slavering jaws mingled with the blood flowing from his numerous wounds, and her fetid breath fairly nauseated him.

Bazo felt himself weakening from loss of blood, but he was no coward. Now he turned over upon his back and reached upward with clutching hands to grasp the shaggy throat in a last hope of turning the tide of battle in his favor.

So quickly the wild dog's slavering jaws moved, the Stone Age youth could not avoid the attack. The sharp teeth fastened upon his throat, shutting off his windpipe; and though Bazo's hands feebly beat at the growling beast's head, her sharp nails tore his hands away, leaving him defenseless.

More feebly now he struck at the wild dog's head with his clenched fists, but deeper those burning teeth sank into his throat. He felt his senses reeling because of his inability to draw a breath. Ringing noises were heard in his ears as his heart hammered against his rib cage in wild tumult. A fleeting vision of Mono passed across the screen of his recollection. Then at last a violent shudder wracked Bazo's body and oblivion swept over him, erasing all the excruciating pain that he felt.

CHAPTER XII

PLANS FOR ESCAPE

When Bantan opened his eyes, the bright lights in the room at once enlightened him that he was still in The Great One's laboratory. He was lying upon the table, and at that moment he noticed the nurse at his side was starting to unfasten the straps about him. Aware that the subject had regained consciousness, she paused and looked at him intently for a moment.

"Do you feel all right, Bantan?" she asked in a well modulated tone.

He looked up at the questioning gray eyes of the nurse, and strangely at that moment he wondered why she was so solicitous of his well being. A smile touched his lips.

"My head seems clear," he replied.

"That is fine," she said. Presently she had unfastened the straps from about him. "You may sit up now."

The bronzed giant arose to a seated position. His reasoning faculties were functioning normally, and he was aware he suffered no ill effects from the sedative that had been administered. He looked about curiously, then turned to the nurse.

"Where is The Great One?" he asked.

"He is in a dark room processing the data obtained from the experiment," she answered. "Hulo will see you to your room. He is outside in the corridor. You may go now."

Bantan slipped from the table. The nurse walked at his side to the door which she opened. She looked through the opening and called to Hulo. In an instant the warrior appeared. He studied the bronzed giant for a moment; then, as the nurse nodded to him, he indicated to Bantan that they could leave now. While they walked to the elevator, he spoke to his companion.

"You are feeling all right, Bantan?" he asked.

The young giant smiled and nodded.

"Much better than earlier today," he answered.

Thereafter a silence was maintained until Bantan was returned to his room. He noticed that the sun was still some time from setting, thus he realized he had not been too long in the laboratory.

"Loula will bring you some food, Bantan," were Hulo's parting words as he left.   .

The bronzed giant nodded as he walked to the window overlooking the water below, but he was unseeing, for he was thinking of the strangeness in The Great One's eyes before he had become unconscious. For the first time he began to feel some concern for his immediate future, for he was positive the eyes had not been of a sane man. He realized now that he must start planning how he was going to escape from the castle. He knew it would not be easy, but he also was aware that he must do so.

Though Bantan was not a learned man, he entertained the feeling that The Great One's experiments were contrary to human existence. His Stone Age progenitors had lived their lives, and they had long since turned to dust. He felt that they should be left that way, and no mad scientist should resurrect them through one's long-dormant memory cells. Of what good to mankind in general was such knowledge of the long-ago Stone Age?

The fact that both the nurse and Hulo had asked how he was led him to believe dire results must be anticipated, and for that reason the young giant began to question whether he should continue to be a willing subject for The Great One's experiments. He also realized, willing or unwilling, so long as he remained in the castle, the scientist would do as he pleased.

It was then that his cogitations were interrupted, for he heard the shuffling of sandals at the door, and turning from the window, he saw that Loula had come with a tray of food. An expression of anxiety possessed her features, and her dark eyes were grave as she studied him. Then, with a shake of her head to dispel her fears, she noticed that Bantan was watching her curiously. She smiled tremulously as she walked to the table.

"You are all right, Bantan?" she asked with concern. "You feel like eating?"

"Much better than earlier today," he answered with a smile, walking toward her.

The servant girl set the tray upon the table as the bronzed giant seated himself.

"I asked Hulo if you were feeling all right after the second experiment," she said. "Looking at you now I can see that he did not tell an untruth."

While Loula had been speaking, Bantan drank the glass of sparkling fruit juice. Setting the emptied glass down, he looked up at Loula with steady eyes.

"Did you *not* expect me to feel well?" he asked with emphasis.

A startled expression was to be observed in the

girl's eyes, but she composed herself at the next moment. A sorrowful look appeared then.

"I wouldn't want anything to happen to you, Bantan," she said in a low voice. "I know I've said that before—but I really mean it."

"Why?" he demanded. "Why does it matter to you what happens to me?"

A mistiness appeared in her dark eyes as she looked at him for a long moment, then drew a deep breath before speaking.

"I wouldn't want anything to happen to you. Must—must I say any more?"

His steady eyes held hers as he searched for the real reason, but a seeming veil had come over hers, and he did not find the answer he sought. Loula's eyes at length dropped from his steady ones and she turned to depart. Bantan watched her in silence. At the doorway she paused to look back at him, but he did not speak. She shook her head sadly.

"I'll return later for the tray and the dishes," she said, then was gone.

With a shrug Bantan ate, and when he finished, he again went to a window overlooking the cliff. He noticed that the sun would not set for some little while. Within a few minutes he heard a sound at the doorway, and he assumed Loula had returned for the dishes. He was surprised that Hulo's voice addressed him.

"The Great One wants you to see the pictures of your last experiment," he announced.

The bronzed giant shrugged and walked toward the warrior. As they were descending in the elevator, Hulo spoke to his companion.

"I've never known The Great One to be so pleased with his experiments," he declared.

Bantan did not answer. The warrior looked at him curiously, and noticing the set lines of his jaw, did not venture to speak further. Thus a strict silence was maintained until the young giant was ushered into the room with the curtained booth.

"Remain outside, Hulo," The Great One instructed.

The warrior stepped out into the corridor, closing the door softly after him.

Bantan confronted the curtained booth.

"I want you to see what happened to Bazo after his father was slain and devoured by the python," The Great One said in a pleasant voice. "You will see the pictures upon the wall as you did before."

The bronzed giant turned about as a whirring sound was heard from behind the curtain, and he watched the short existence of Bazo, another of his earlier progenitors, to the moment the wild she dog slayed him in revenge for the death of her mate at his hands. When the picture ended the whirring sound from behind the curtain ceased. Bantan turned about as The Great One spoke.

"My life-long achievement is to be realized through you," he said with eloquence. "Just think—I'll have a complete record on film how people lived in the Old Stone Age. Already you know from Bana and Bazo's brief existences that obtaining food was the prime factor in their lives. Next, came their mating and the reproduction of the species. But something has been proven of inestimable value—and that is emotion. Eminent scholars have tried to make it clear that very little emotion existed among the Stone Age people. Since they could not carry on a conversation in words,

those scholars did not believe those long-ago people
could be reasoning and emotional. How they have
erred!

"Gradually, through your remote ancestors, I shall
have a record of their progress—when they first conceived the idea of a stone axe and stone-tipped spears
as weapons to slay wild beasts. And we shall see how
they progressed beyond uttered mere names.

"My learned colleagues, if they lived now, would
have reason to envy me. They expressed much sadness
when I informed them of my intentions, and many
scoffed when I told them it was possible to create a machine capable of revivifying long-dormant brain cells
to reveal their secrets of past generations. At the same
time this machine I have named a retrovider is capable
of recording on film the events that the brain cells
reveal what long-dead eyes have witnessed. Most of
those scientists called themselves my friends, yet I
learned some of them expressed their opinion that I
was mad. If they were to know of my success at the
present time, I wonder what they would say? Don't
think I'm not tempted to send their successors a message! Instead, I'll wait until I have a complete recording on film, and then let them judge as they will.

"But enough of that. The immediate present is more
important. Now, this last experiment tells of Bazo
meeting death at the fangs of a wild she dog. There is
no question Mono was impregnated with Bazo's seed,
and another experiment tonight should reveal what
happened to the child just conceived. Go to your room
with Hulo and rest awhile. Later, I'll have him return
for you, and we shall undertake another experiment."

Wordlessly, Bantan left the room and was joined

by Hulo. He told the warrior what The Great One had said. Hulo merely grunted.

Escorted to his room and being left alone, now that darkness was fast setting, the bronzed giant lay down on his bed. He closed his eyes and heaved a deep sigh. Presently the room was enshrouded in complete darkness, and the stillness was like that of a tomb. He was not aware of the quick transition between wakefulness and sleep.

While Bantan slept, the forces of Nature were gathering in the eastern heaven. Black clouds were forming and scudding across the sky before savage gusts of wind. Greater was the blackness enshrouding that part of the heaven with the passing minutes. Dim flashes of lightning played hide and seek among the black clouds. Barely audible rumbles of thunder could be heard.

When less than an hour had elapsed the greater part of the sky was covered with rolling storm clouds. The lightning was more vivid, and the dull rumblings of thunder were increasingly louder. A steady wind had risen from the east, and was a means of pushing the forming storm more speedily westward.

Upon the Mandoes Island a light, intermittent rain commenced to fall, and with a few more passing minutes it came down heavier. A growing wind whipped it savagely. And now the lightning was becoming sharper and the thunder much louder.

An exceptionally bright flash of lightning stabbed the darkness above the castle on the cliff to be followed by a deafening crash of thunder. The stone building seemed to shudder as a lightning bolt had found a target.

Ordinarily a light sleeper, it was then that Bantan's

eyes opened and he immediately sat upright, tensed. In another moment he arose from the bed and stepped toward one of the windows. Since the wind was blowing away from that part of the castle he could stand there without being drenched by the deluging rain.

Another exceptionally bright flash of lightning almost blinded him, and the subsequent crash of thunder all but burst his ear drums. Again he felt the castle shudder as another bolt of lightning had found a target. Again a brilliant flash of lightning—again the thundering roar overhead. The castle trembled. Another flash and a subsequent crash of thunder rocked the castle again.

Bantan merely blinked his eyes with each sharp flash of lightning, but no quiver of his nerves resulted when the thunder boomed overhead. His perfect nerve system seemed to anticipate the crashing thunder, and so well co-ordinated he was, there was no reaction whatever.

The peak of the electrical storm was now passing Mandoes Island, though the rain still descended in deluging torrents before a shrieking wind. The young giant shrugged and returned to his bed. He had hardly lay down when a flickering light appeared in the doorway. Looking in that direction, Hulo was seen carrying a candle.

"Bantan!" he called out. "Are you awake?"

"I'm lying down," was the reply. "Is The Great One ready for another experiment?"

"The Great One told me to tell you that lightning has struck the castle, and a greater part of the electrical equipment in the laboratory is temporarily out of order. There shall be no more experiments until it can be restored. He bids you rest well tonight."

Bantan thanked the warrior who then turned and departed without a further word. Lying there with his hands beneath his head, the bronzed giant listened to the storm's dying refrain. He recalled to mind why he had come to Mandoes Island. Amar—where was he located in this castle? Would he have the opportunity of meeting him and settling scores before he made a determined attempt to escape and return to distant Marja Island? Had the Aoona Islands not been engulfed following the volcanic eruption, he was sure he would have settled his scores with the Amo Island prince, and by now would have returned to Marja where Wanya, his foster sister, and Lori, the renounced Ono Island princess, awaited his return. Thinking of them now made him wonder if they had worried about him, and hoped that he was safe from harm, and would hurry back as soon as his mission was fulfilled.

To his delicate nostrils now was wafted a faint perfume which was familiar. Looking toward the doorway he strained his eyes, but in the almost pitch darkness he could not distinguish anything. Presently, however, a flickering light was seen beyond the doorway which increased until someone bearing a lighted candle appeared upon the threshold.

He was somewhat surprised to discern the candle bearer as none other than Loula. He at once arose to a seated position, wondering why the servant girl would come to his room at this time since she could have no reason.

As Loula approached, holding the candle slightly above her head so that she could see better, she presently recognized Bantan seated upon the edge of his bed. She placed the candle upon the table and looked toward him with a faint smile.

"What is it, Loula?" he asked.

She remained standing beside the table with her hands hanging limply at her side.

"I learned that the storm has put the laboratory electrical equipment out of order, and that there would be no further experiments until it is repaired," she said. "I felt happy—for your sake."

"But why, Loula?" he insisted.

She wrung her hands for a moment in evident distress.

"Please don't make me answer questions I shouldn't and by so doing disobey The Great One's wishes," she begged.

Bantan arose to his feet and approached the servant girl. Confronting her, he looked down at her humbled features. She seemed to tremble. One hand tightly pressed her bosom as though to quiet the pounding of her heart.

"Loula, you know you have no right to be here now," he said a trifle sternly. "Why have you come?"

The girl did not answer. She shook her head and merely looked up at him with eyes that tried bravely to meet his, but failed. She hung her head, seemingly ashamed. She was in the act of reaching for the candle when he spoke again.

"Wait, Loula," he said peremptorily. "You have not answered me."

The servant girl uttered a forlorn sigh as she looked up at him with a wistful expression upon her face while her eyes mirrored a wondering light.

"Bantan, I know I have no reason to be here," she said in a low voice that trembled a little. "The reason

I came was to tell you I was very glad there was to be no further experiment for you tonight." Now her features became grave, as she added: "You don't want me to be concerned about you, do you?"

"No, Loula," he answered in gentle tones, now realizing her state of feeling for him. "Please don't concern yourself about me."

For a long moment she looked up at him as though unable to believe what he had said. Her eyes became misty as she picked up the candle.

· "Good night, Bantan," she said tonelessly.

"Good night, Loula," he answered. "Please don't think unkindly of me."

The servant girl did not reply as she turned and departed. Watching her, Bantan was aware of her dejection. Upon the threshold of the doorway she paused momentarily and shook her head sadly before resuming her way.

When Loula had left and the room was again in total darkness, Bantan returned to the bed and again reposed upon it. He shook his head several times as his thoughts were of the servant girl's dejection, but he realized he had other matters more important to claim his attention.

Once again he tried to formulate plans for a possible escape from the castle. The thought of leaving without settling his scores with Amar made him realize his quest would have been futile. Even now Nao's features, enwreathed with a sorrowful smile, appeared before his inner vision. With the memory that she was buried upon the atoll, the resolution within him was strengthened that he would never rest content knowing Amar had not been punished by him for the wrongs he had perpetrated against Nao and himself.

The numerous occasions he had looked out either window in his room down at the surging water below had enlightened him that if no other avenue of escape could be devised, there was always the knowledge he could negotiate a dive from one of the windows, and trust to luck the surging water would not dash him against the face of the cliff below. He had studied the waves many times as they swept in, and he could almost determine how much of a lapse there was between each one. The time never seemed to vary, though some of the waves were larger than others. Naturally, those particularly larger ones smashed against the cliff with greater force.

Having calculated the possibility of being compelled to make such a high dive, Bantan had noticed at various stages of the tide that no rocks below had been exposed, so he was quite certain there was sufficient depth for a diver to feel reasonably safe.

Though the windows in the castle facing away from the cliff and the water below were barred, when assigning him to the room overlooking the cliff, it was assumed Bantan would not be so foolhardy as to attempt escape. But then, perhaps The Great One had no knowledge of the desperation that can be imbued in some men to make them risk anything so long as there was a possible hope of freedom being attained.

Bantan conceded that he had been treated more as a guest than a prisoner. Had Loula not informed him that others had not fared as well as he? With this thought in mind he had reason to wonder if she referred to Amar, his father, and the other two Amo Island prisoners. Was there not the possibility they were no longer alive?

He was determined on the morrow that he would make inquiries regarding them from either Loula or Hulo. Surely there would be no harm that they gave him such information. Would they suspect what motives he might entertain?

Thinking and planning thusly, Bantan fell asleep; but even in his dreams his mind was filled with countless possibilities for settling his scores with Amar, and making his eventual escape from the castle on Mandoes Island.

Chapter XIII

A RESCUE IN THE POOL

Bantan was awake the following morning at sunrise. Without delay he arose and performed his customary ablutions. While waiting for his breakfast, he went to one of the two windows and looked out at the water as far as his vision would permit, then at last he allowed his eyes to rest speculatingly upon the swirling depths below.

An hour passed while he remained there before his alert ears heard the soft shuffling of sandaled feet in the corridor beyond the slightly opened door. He hoped it was Loula bringing his morning meal, for he was hungry. Turning about, he waited patiently. In a few moments the servant girl appeared at the doorway. Her features were stoic, but her dark eyes looked hauntingly toward the bronzed giant.

"Good morning, Loula," he greeted her.

The girl merely nodded. Removing her eyes from Bantan she wordlessly walked to the table with the tray of food and set it down. He swiftly moved toward her upon noiseless feet. Just as the girl straightened and turned she was confronted by the bronzed giant. She would have stepped aside, but he quickly placed his hands upon her shoulders restrainingly.

"Loula," he said in a soft tone. "You are acting strangely this morning. It is very unlike you to not at least say good morning to me."

As he spoke, a gentle smile appeared upon the young giant's lips.

The servant girl avoided his eyes, and she seemed unwilling to face him.

"Loula," he said in that same soft tone a trifle more insistently. "Won't you even look at me this morning?"

A shudder seemed to pass through the girl's body. She drew a deep breath and her head lowered.

"Please don't be angry with me," he said softly. "I am not angry with you. It is not my fault that I do not have the same feeling for you that you have had for me. Upon the Marja Island, from which I came, there are two lovely girls who are very much in love with me. One is my foster sister, who has always loved me. She is not angry with me because I do not feel I can love her. I owe my life to the other girl, but I still do not feel I love her enough to wish her to be my mate. But she does not hate me because I cannot bring myself to love her.

"Can't you understand, Loula, that being a man of white birth, I cannot permit myself to mate with a native girl? It is not my fault that I am of white origin. On the other hand, were I of native birth, in all probability I would have mated long before now. Were that the case, I wouldn't have reason to be here now. I want you to be my friend. Won't you at least be mine? Captive or guest that I am, I need a friend."

The servant girl's reserve melted before Bantan's plea. She turned to him with moisture in her dark eyes, and her lips were trembling.

"Listen to me, Bantan," she murmured. "It is very difficult for a girl who loves a man to be asked to accept him only as a friend. My whole heart and body longs to be yours." She shook her head momentarily, but a slight smile now touched her lips as she looked up at him. "I find it very difficult to resist you—no matter what."

Bantan smiled and upon an impulse leaned forward, and pressed his lips to the center of her forehead. The girl sighed deeply.

"If only you had kissed my lips," she murmured.

The bronzed giant smiled and shook his head. In answer, Loula shrugged her shapely shoulders.

"What is it you wish of me?" she asked then. "I know you wish knowledge of something that I am not permitted to speak." She shook her head with ineffable sadness.

"Tell me, Loula," he said, "has any harm befallen the Amo warrior known as Amar?"

"He was used for an experiment," the girl answered; "but he suffered no ill effects. The Great One was not impressed with him as a subject, nor any of his companions." Now the girl's hands rested palmwise upon his mighty chest and she became agitated. "You must not continue as a subject to The Great One's experiments. Harm will befall you. His machine will rob you of your reasoning powers. You will become like a dead man in thought and feeling. It has happened to others. I wouldn't want it to happen to you."

Bantan nodded in understanding.

"That is why I was asked after each experiment if I was feeling all right?" he questioned.

"That is why," the servant girl answered. "And, Bantan, you are too good to have anything happen to you. It was of that horrible thought that I fear for you."

The bronzed giant gently patted one of the girl's shoulders.

"Have you learned this morning how The Great One is progressing on repairs to the machine in the laboratory?" he then asked.

"He worked all night," was the girl's reply. "He hopes to complete the necessary repairs before this day has come to pass. He is very anxious to continue his experiments. Hulo and Humo have been working with him all night. When I was preparing your breakfast they returned to the kitchen and told me they were to get some rest. Humo would return later to the laboratory. Hulo told me he had orders to take you for a stroll about the grounds later in the morning. Oh, Bantan!" It was a desperate plea that the girl uttered. "If it were possible to escape from here, I would want to go with you. I am weary of life here and could be no worse elsewhere."

Bantan smiled gently, and once again lightly patted the girl's shoulder.

"If I should decide to attempt to escape from the castle, Loula," he said, "would you be willing to go with me—only as a friend?"

The servant girl swallowed with difficulty for a moment, but a brave light came into her eyes.

"Yes, Bantan," she murmured, "I would go anywhere with you—even though I was to be your slave. You need never doubt my loyalty, for I would serve you faithfully so long as I lived."

A smile touched the bronzed giant's lips. Once again upon an impulse he pressed his lips to the center of the girl's forehead. Loula breathed deeply and her hands clutched at his shoulders. She lifted her head, and her moist dark eyes filled with adoration, met his.

She shook her head a trifle sadly.

"How could any girl resist you, Bantan!" she declared. "You are so handsome and reserved."

The young giant now became aware of his hunger, and also felt that Loula should leave—having been here much longer than she should have.

"You should go now," he said gently.

The girl smiled bravely through the moisture in her dark eyes.

"Yes, Bantan," she replied. "There are others who are awaiting their morning meal. But before I go, slave that I am to you, forgive me for my impulsiveness."

Before he could prevent, Loula had flung her arms about his neck, and her moist lips found his for a long moment as she clung tightly to him. As suddenly as she had acted, she drew away from him with lowered head, but her eyes shyly looked up at him repentingly.

"You won't be angry with me?" she asked.

A smile touched his lips as he shook his head, uttering no word.

Then, wordlessly, the servant girl glided out of the room.

Shrugging, Bantan seated himself at the table and proceeded to partake of his morning meal. While doing so, time and again he would shake his head. Though a gentle smile would touch his lips upon these occasions, he tried not to think what the future might hold for the servant girl.

Completing his breakfast, Bantan returned to the window. He was unmindful of the time that passed as he looked out upon the undulating water, as he had done a number of times in the past few days. The scene was the same and yet there always was that difference to arrest his attention. At intervals sea gulls were to be seen winging their way through the still, morning air. He watched as they glided effortlessly, and marvelled at their keen eyesight that from many feet above the surface a choice tid-bit could be spotted beneath, then plummet-like the bird would descend, and invariably arise at the next moment with its victim already swallowed.

In due time the bronzed giant heard sandaled feet outside in the corridor, and turning about he saw that Hulo had made an appearance. Bantan spoke pleasantly to the sleepy looking warrior, and in return was likewise spoken to.

"The Great One suggested that you and I take another stroll about the grounds surrounding the castle," Hulo then said.

The young giant nodded agreeably.

In a few moments they were descending in the elevator and presently stepped outside into the brilliant sunshine. Bantan filled his lungs to their utmost with the clear fresh air and exhaled slowly.

"It's a very nice morning after the storm of last night," he remarked. "The air after a storm always seems more refreshing."

Hulo merely nodded as he yawned, revealing a perfect set of teeth.

"Didn't you sleep well last night, Hulo?" Bantan asked.

The stalwart warrior slowly shook his head.

"My brother and I were with The Great One in his laboratory all night," he replied. "He hopes to have repairs completed later in the day so as to resume experiments."

The bronzed giant pursed his lips and nodded.

"Yes, I suppose he is anxious to continue," he agreed.

"And you, Bantan," he said, "are agreeable to continue as his subject?"

The young giant paused, as did his companion. He shrugged.

"Should I be agreeable, Hulo?" he asked.

Now it was the warrior's turn to shrug his shoulders noncommittally.

"The Great One's wishes must be obeyed," was all he said in answer.

"Then it wouldn't matter whether I were agreeable or not, would it?" Bantan added.

Again the warrior shrugged.

"You wouldn't have any other choice," he agreed.

Looking ahead, Bantan noted they were nearing the swimming pool which had aroused his curiosity on that previous occasion. How he would have liked to plunge into it and luxuriously indulge in a refreshing swim. He wondered if his companion would permit him do so today. He turned to Hulo.

"Do you suppose The Great One would mind if I were to have a swim in the pool?" he asked.

The warrior regretfully shook his head.

"The swimming pool is not for any of us," he replied.

At the next moment the bronzed giant's alert ears were aware of a cry for help in an unquestionable feminine voice which came from the direction of the swimming pool. Without a moment's hesitation, he broke into a run, and Hulo was quickly left behind despite his efforts to keep up with the fleet young giant.

Reaching the edge of the swimming pool, Bantan's

sharp eyes took in the situation at once. Near the center he saw a girl feebly struggling. A cap covered her hair, and her bronzed arms glistened in the brilliant morning sunshine. At that moment she uttered a wail of distress and sank beneath the surface. Her moving hands marked the place of her disappearance.

Without an instant's delay, the bronzed giant dived into the water, and as his head emerged above the surface, with strong, overhand strokes he drew himself rapidly near the spot marked with ripples where the girl had disappeared. He drew himself half out of the water and plunged beneath, opening his eyes as his strong arms and kicking legs drew him downward through the translucence. There, near the sandy bottom of the pool, he saw the girl writhing in evident distress.

Quickly he covered the intervening distance. One of his strong arms went under one of her armpits. Bracing his feet against the bottom, he thrust upward, bearing the unconscious form with him. As his head bobbed above the surface, he turned upon his back, and drew the girl's head upon his broad chest. With his free hand and his kicking legs he swam to the edge of the pool.

Hulo had reached the edge and was watching the swimmer with amazement because of the ease and efficiency Bantan seemed to employ in his rescue of the girl. The bronzed giant drew himself over the edge of the pool, with one hand keeping the girl's head above water, and at the next moment he reached over and lifted her in his arms and deposited her upon the soft grass. Quickly he turned her over upon her stomach and administered artificial respiration. Water oozed from the girl's lax mouth and nostrils, and then at times she would cough, and much more was expelled from her lungs. Her breathing was stertorous, but the more water that was expelled the more even her breathing became, and she had less reason to cough.

Presently the near victim of drowning was sufficiently restored to her senses so that Bantan desisted in his efforts. She turned over, as the bronzed giant arose and remained upon his knees at her side. Then the girl sat up. Her gray eyes looked upon her rescuer with gratefulness.

For the first time Bantan took notice of the rare beauty that the girl was gifted with. She was clad in a silvery bathing suit which set off to perfection the well developed lines Nature had endowed her with. Her features were delicate and well molded. She was unquestionable of white origin since no native strain marked her. Looking into her eyes, the bronzed giant realized he had seen those gray eyes before—eyes that had been somewhat worried. And then he knew that the girl was The Great One's nurse.

In a brief moment the girl looked toward the silent Hulo, acknowledging his presence, and then her eyes came to rest upon her rescuer again. A slight flush tinged her cheeks.

"I was suddenly taken with cramps, Bantan," she said in a gentle voice. "The fact that you were nearby and heard me, and came to my rescue makes me realize I owe you my life. Thank you."

"I am happy to have saved your life," the bronzed giant said, bowing his head a trifle. Then, quickly looking at her and up at the sun, "It is not good for you to remain under the warm sun in your weakened condition. May I help you to your quarters?"

The girl smiled sweetly, revealing nice teeth, and she nodded.

At the next moment Bantan slipped an arm under her knees, the other went about her shoulders. Straightening, and with apparently no effort, he attained an upright position. One of the girl's arms went about his neck.

"You picked me up with no seeming effort, Bantan," she remarked, marvelling at his strength.

He smiled deprecatingly and looked ahead, and started toward the walkway which he believed led to her quarters. Hulo accompanied them in silence, awed at the friendliness that had sprung up so speedily between them.

While carrying her, Bantan presently looked down at the radiant features of the girl. He instantly was aware that she had been studying him, for she quickly averted her eyes, but he could not fail to glimpse the flush that had mounted to her cheeks. A pleasing aroma emanated from her and filled his nostrils.

The bronzed giant remained silent and removed his eyes from the girl's features to look ahead toward the door which he now confronted. Hulo stepped forward and quickly opened it, and as the door swung open, Bantan entered a luxuriously furnished room. Directly across from the doorway he saw a couch. Toward it he carried the girl and gently deposited her upon it. Then, as he released her, his eyes met hers again.

"Thank you again, Bantan," she said with a gentle smile.

Straightening, the young giant smiled and bowed in deference.

"You will be all right now?" he asked with a trace of concern in his tones.

"Yes, thank you kindly," she assured him.

Hulo then nudged Bantan, and they returned outside, the warrior closing the door softly behind him.

The bronzed giant looked at Hulo then.

"She is The Great One's nurse," he said.

The warrior appeared confused for a moment as to answering, then he slowly nodded.

"The Great One should be grateful that I spared his nurse from drowning," Bantan added.

Hulo merely nodded, but made no verbal reply.

They resumed their way, not speaking for several minutes. Presently the young giant turned to his companion, who at that moment was smothering a yawn.

"Although others are forbidden to swim in the pool, Hulo," he said, "the emergency which compelled me to should not make my offense punishable. Don't you think so?"

The warrior's eyes held the bronzed giant's for a moment, then his head lowered slightly.

"I hardly think The Great One would punish you for such a needy offense," he replied in a low voice. "Luane did thank—" He caught himself and looked guilty for the moment.

" 'Luane,' " Bantan repeated. "It's a very becoming name for The Great One's pretty nurse. Yes," he added in mollifying tones in an effort to lessen the warrior's seeming guilt, "she thanked me very nicely. Would I be asking something The Great One would forbid by inquiring how long Luane has been his nurse?"

Hulo shrugged.

"I think, Bantan," he said, changing the subject, "that we have walked enough. Let us return to the

castle. I must return to the laboratory to further help
The Great One."

The bronzed giant's lips were touched with a faint
smile as he came to a halt, as his companion did.

"As you say, Hulo," he said without protest.

Wordlessly for the most part they returned the
way they had come. As they passed the swimming pool,
Bantan looked down at the inviting water and he
sighed deeply.

"Do you ever swim, Hulo?" he asked of his companion.

The warrior nodded and indicated the ocean beyond
the wall.

"Not so often as I used to," he answered. "But
when I go swimming I do so in the ocean."

"Before coming to Mandoes Island," Bantan then
said, "hardly a sun passed but I would swim in the
ocean. I've missed swimming these past few suns."

Hulo remained silent as he took a step, then turned
to his companion, indicating they would resume their
way.

As the two passed the swimming pool, from the
draperies of a window facing them, Luane watched.
As her gray eyes followed the Apollo-like figure of
Bantan, she heaved a deep sigh. Her left hand pressed
the vicinity of her heart and a shy smile radiated her
features. She remained there until no further sight
of the handsome, bronzed giant was to be obtained.

Chapter XIV

LUANE'S REQUEST

When Bantan returned to his room he noticed that Loula must have come during his absence, for the tray and breakfast dishes had been removed from the table. In a vague way he wondered what she would think of his timely rescue of Luane.

Once again he returned to one of the windows overlooking the cliff, and remained there for some time, his eyes fondly resting upon the sparkling ocean surface. He never seemed to tire of watching the scene that was presented before him.

Presently he heard shuffling sandaled feet in the corridor beyond the half-opened door, and turning about he saw the servant girl entering with his noonday meal upon a tray. There was a curious expression in her eyes as she looked at the bronzed giant.

"Hello, Loula," he greeted her.

The girl returned the greeting, then went to the table where she set the tray. She turned about as Bantan approached.

"I've learned that you have been a hero today," she said.

He nodded as he seated himself at the table and looked up at Loula. Inwardly he wondered if she were jealous.

"The Great One would have lost his nurse had Hulo and I not been passing the swimming pool when we did," he added.

The servant girl regarded him in silence. He felt she was deciding whether to reveal something that was forbidden her, and then he noticed that she was remindful of her obedience to The Great One. He observed the slight tightening of her lips.

"She told me she owed her life to you, Bantan," she said.

He nodded as he reached for the glass of fruit juice.

"Had you been in distress, Loula," he added, "I would have done likewise. Luane need not feel obligated to me."

The servant girl's brows lifted a trifle.

"You know her name?" she asked in surprise.

"Hulo did not mean to speak as he did," Bantan replied, and then he drained the glass of its contents.

Loula regarded the bronzed giant with passive eyes. Presently she shrugged and stepped to his side with a quick, indrawn breath. She inclined her head near his and her dark eyes looked into his for a long moment.

"I would have been very happy to have been saved from death by you," she murmured. She softly pressed her lips to his cheek, then drew back in apparent shyness. "I'll return for the tray and dishes later," she added. "I have others to serve, you know."

In another moment the servant girl left the room, and Bantan ate his noonday meal in silence.

An hour later Loula returned for the tray and the dishes. One glance at her from the window where he stood was sufficient for the bronzed giant to realize her agitation. The girl was breathing fast and her eyes were worried. She quickly came to him with outstretched hands.

"The machine has been repaired, Bantan," she announced; her hands rested upon his shoulders as she confronted him. "Hulo and Humo have just returned from the laboratory and told me. The Great One is anxious to resume his experiments with you as his subject. Oh, Bantan, I am so afraid for you."

The bronzed giant smiled assuringly as he took the girl's hands in his.

"You have nothing to fear, Loula," he said in quiet tones in an effort to calm the girl's fears. "Already I have undergone two experiments and I am none the worse."

Loula tried to smile bravely. Tears had formed in the corners of her eyes. She shook her head sadly.

"Perhaps you do not realize how dangerous it is to be experimented upon repeatedly," she murmured. "I wish that I might show you some of the victims who have no reasoning and feelings because of The Great One's experiments upon them. Then, perhaps, you would realize the danger."

"But, Loula," he protested, "I have no choice in the matter. Willing, or unwilling, The Great One is bound to have his way."

The girl now withdrew her hands from his gently imprisoning ones, and she wrung them piteously.

"Yes, I know," she murmured. "If only there was some way that I could help you to escape."

Loula went to the table and picked up the tray and the dishes. She paused to smile tremulously at him, then left the room. As she stepped into the corridor, Bantan heard a gasp escape the servant girl's lips. He heard a low voice speaking to Loula. As he was about to step in the direction of the doorway, he paused, amazement clearly writ upon his features, for upon the threshold appeared none other than Luane, dressed in a nurse's uniform. In one hand she carried a small bag. She was regarding the bronzed giant with a quizzical expression in her gray eyes, and then with a slight shake of her head, she entered the room.

Bantan wondered if Luane had overheard the conversation between him and Loula. He smiled now.

"This is unexpected," he said. "I hope very much you are none the worse for your experience of this morning."

The nurse flushed a trifle.

"I'm fine now," she replied.

She walked toward the square table. She placed the small bag upon it and in another moment opened it. She looked toward the bronzed giant with a peculiar expression in her eyes that for some reason did not wish to meet his.

"This is a professional visit," she said. "My—The Great One requested that I check you before you undergo another experiment later in the afternoon. Come —lie down on the bed while I do so."

The bronzed giant did as he was bade without a demur.

Luane brought forth a banded contraption from the interior of the bag and wrapped it about Bantan's left arm above the elbow. She pumped air into it by means of a small plunger until it was quite tight. Then she studied her wristwatch while he could distinctly feel the beating of his heart. When the allotted time was up, the nurse nodded. She removed the band from about his arm and placed it upon the table.

"Your blood pressure is perfect," she declared.

Bantan said nothing as she reached into the bag and produced a stethoscope. She affixed the hearing tubes to her ears then placed the rubber cup over the vicinity of his heart, and listened carefully while she studied her wristwatch. Presently she again nodded.

"Perfect," was all she said.

She placed the stethoscope upon the table, and reaching within the bag, produced a hypodermic and a small bottle of greenish fluid. Uncorking the bottle, she inserted the needle into it and filled the tube. Then she turned to the silent young man who had been wordlessly watching her. A peculiar smile touched the nurse's lips as she now turned to him.

"Hold this a moment, please," she said.

As the hypodermic exchanged hands, Luane then brought forth a small wad of absorbent cotton. She uncorked a small bottle of alcohol and turned it upon the wad of cotton. She then applied it to Bantan's left arm. He shivered momentarily because of its coldness.

"Now, let me have the hypodermic, Bantan," she said, "and you may hold this." She handed him the wad of slightly damp cotton.

In another moment she placed the point of the needle upon the chilled spot on his arm and injected the contents of the hypodermic into his veins. Placing the instrument upon the table, the wad of cotton exchanged hands and she applied it to his arm where she had punctured the skin. A tightening of her lips was to be noticed and a slight grimness to be detected in her eyes. She looked at her wristwatch and seated herself at the bedside.

"Are you aware of anything unusual, Bantan?" she asked then. "Do you feel a numbness in your arm spreading through you?"

The bronzed giant nodded, and in a voice that sounded strange to his ears, he heard himself admit-

ting that the feeling she had described was being experienced. And, strangely, though he was perfectly
aware where he was, he experienced an extremely light
sensation in his head. A swirling mist seemed to blank
his opened eyes. He was aware of his strongly beating
heart and that he breathed slowly. A peculiar buzzing
was to be heard in his ear drums. Now, as from far
away, he heard Luane's voice speaking to him, but his
glazed eyes saw nothing but a gray mist.

"Do you hear me, Bantan?" she asked.

"I hear you," he answered.

"Answer me truthfully," the voice said. "What were
you and Loula speaking about before I entered the
room?"

"We were talking about my possible escape from the
castle," he answered.

"You really wish to escape?" the voice added.

"I do," he answered, "but only after I have settled
my scores with Amar, the Amo Island prince, who is
a prisoner in the castle. It was for that purpose I followed him here."

"Why do you wish to settle scores with Amar?" was
the next question.

Without reserve, the drugged man told Luane of the
part Amar had played in his life prior to coming to
Mandoes Island.

"Nao, my former sweetheart, would never rest contented in her grave were he permitted to live," he concluded.

"Do you feel love for Loula?" the voice added
then.

"No," he answered truthfully.

"You are sure?" the voice persisted.

"I am sure," he said.

"Are you in love with any other girl?" the voice then asked.

"There are two girls upon Marja Island who are very much in love with me," he answered. "One is Wanya, my foster sister. The other is known as Lori. She is a self-renounced princess from Ono Island, which exists no more. I owe her my life. In my heart, however, I cannot truthfully say I could love either of them to the state of wishing to mate with one. Since I am of white birth, a missionary, by name of Father Lasance, advised me not to mate with a native girl."

"Has there been any white girls in your life, Bantan?" was the next question.

"Only one," he replied. "Her name was Leona Brown."

"Tell me about her," the voice requested.

Without reserve in his drugged condition, Bantan told of his experiences with the white girl he had known who came from faraway America in search of him with her father, and why she had sent him back to Kalma, the Marja Island goddess.

"Tell me about Kalma," the voice instructed.

And then Bantan told of his experiences with the daughter of an American doctor and a Marja Island princess, adding how she had self-inflicted death rather than be defiled by the leader of their enemy who had taken her and her father captives.

There was a short silence before the voice spoke again. The nurse moved a hand before his unseeing eyes.

"What about Luane, the girl you rescued from the swimming pool?" was the next question. "She is, as you must know, of white origin. Do you think you might learn to love her?"

Bantan drew a deep breath.

"I do not know her well enough to answer that now," he answered. "She is very beautiful, and I'm sure she would be worthy of the love of some fine man."

The nurse heaved a sigh, and one hand pressed against her heart. She closed her eyes for the moment, and when they opened, they were filled with gentleness. She shook her head momentarily, and then glanced at her wristwatch. She leaned forward again.

"Are you in favor of my—The Great One's experiments with you as the subject?" she asked then.

"At first I didn't mind," he answered. "After seeing how my remote ancestors lived and died, somehow I entertained the feeling it was not right to probe into their lives of so long ago. It would be better that they remain unknown."

Luane wet her lips with the tip of her moist tongue, and there was a slight agitation within her that her features could not conceal.

"You know, of course, that my—The Great One would not listen to any plea from you that was contrary to his wishes?" she stated.

He shook his head.

"I have the feeling that he is not sane," he answered. "He lives only for his work in the laboratory."

Studying Bantan's eyes, the nurse now noted a changing light from the glazed one which had possessed them. The full effect of the drug she had administered to him was wearing off, and very shortly he would be in full possession of his reasoning faculties.

"Do you know who I am, Bantan?" she asked then.

He shook his head.

"Luane injected something into my arm and told me a numbness would overcome me," he said. "Are you Luane?"

"Do you remember anything that you have been asked?" she then questioned him.

"I remember nothing," was his reply. "Now, I am beginning to feel the numbness leaving me."

As he spoke his eyelids fluttered several times. Watching him intently, the girl was aware normalcy was beginning to appear in his heretofore glazed eyes.

She remained silent, watching him with gentle eyes. Presently he seemed perfectly normal. He looked up at the white-frocked nurse. A smile of recognition appeared in his eyes.

"Luane," he uttered her name softly.

She smiled, a warmness now being detected in her gray eyes.

Bantan arose to a seated position, swinging his feet around and resting them upon the floor. He drew a hand wonderingly across his forehead. He then looked up at Luane, who was watching him silently. A quizzical expression now clouded his eyes.

"What has happened?" he asked.

The nurse smiled.

"I checked you as my—The Great One requested," she answered. "You are in perfect condition to undergo another experiment later in the day."

Bantan remembered his left arm where she had punctured the skin with the hypodermic needle. There was a faint tenderness to be felt, but otherwise he suffered no ill effects.

The nurse arose from the chair she occupied, and turning, replaced the articles upon the table in the bag.

She remained silent, and for some unknown reason the bronzed giant found that he had nothing to say. He arose from the bed and slowly walked toward one of the windows overlooking the cliff, and looking outside, stared unseeingly at the sparkling ocean surface. As though in a trance he heard Luane speaking to him.

"Hulo will presently come for you, Bantan."

He nodded perfunctorily, but offered no speech in return.

Luane stared at his turned back for a long moment, then with a slight shake of her head, she walked toward him. One hand reached into the pocket of her uniform and she withdrew a small envelope. Now standing beside him, her hand containing the envelope reached for one of his.

"Take this, Bantan," she said softly. "Don't ask me why, but when you hear Hulo in the corridor, open this envelope and swallow the pill that is inside."

Bantan accepted the envelope with a wondering expression in his eyes and he looked at it for a long moment, then lifted his eyes questionably to meet hers.

"Don't ask any questions," she murmured. "And please do as I request. You will understand—later."

Then, pressing his hand warmly for a moment, Luane turned and departed.

The bronzed giant watched the nurse as she left the room in silent wonder, then with a quizzical expression in his eyes he looked at the small envelope. He tore the end and tossed the strip of ragged paper out the window. He pressed upon the edges and held the opening above the palm of his other hand. A small, black pellet about the size of a pea dropped into it. He looked at it speculatingly for a long moment, his brow furrowed, and then he replaced the pill within the envelope. Folding the top edge which he had torn, he slipped it within the band of his loin cloth.

With some concern he thought of Luane's request as his eyes looked unseeingly at the sparkling ocean surface. He endeavored in vain to understand why the nurse had given it to him, but in the end he had to console himself that he would understand—later.

Keeping an alert ear for the sound of Hulo's expected footsteps, Bantan patiently waited, and at last, after what seemed a long while, he heard the warrior's footsteps in the corridor. He withdrew the small envelope from his waist band and in another moment was looking at the small, black pellet. He tossed the envelope out the window as he swallowed the pill and experienced no difficulty as he did so. It seemed tasteless. Hulo then appeared at the doorway.

"The Great One awaits you in the laboratory, Bantan," he announced. "Come, let us be on our way."

The bronzed giant turned about and joined the warrior, and presently they were descending in the elevator to the level where the laboratory was located. As Bantan entered the brilliantly lighted room, he saw that The Great One and Luane were awaiting him. Hulo closed the door behind him.

Bantan looked first at the scientist. The gleam in his maniacal eyes almost caused a shudder to course through him. Then he turned to look at the anxious eyes of the nurse He read the questioning look therein, and he nodded his head a trifle He noted that Luane seemed to heave a sigh of relief.

"Are you ready to go back into the Stone Age again, Bantan?" The Great One asked then.

The bronzed giant merely nodded. He approached the table and drew himself upon it, lying upon his back.

The nurse affixed the straps about him. The Great One waited with a hypodermic in hand, and when the subject was ready, he injected the contents into his arm.

Bantan looked up at Luane, and a slight smile touched the corners of his lips as their eyes met for a long moment. Then she nodded. He closed his eyes with the wonder of what the outcome of this third experiment would be. And with the thought in mind, he felt his senses leaving him; he seemed to be in a world of vacuum in which not even his mind seemed to function, and his body remained lifeless except for his slow breathing and the rhythmic beating of his heart.

Without loss of time The Great One attended to the attachments upon the subject connected with the retrovider. A button was pressed and a low humming sound was to be heard. Watching the gauges upon the panel, the scientist was pleased with his work of the previous night and the better part of the day, for the time machine was functioning perfectly. Now, all that remained was to have the subject's long-dormant brain cells recall the further adventures of his remote ancestors of the Stone Age.

CHAPTER XV

MORE EXPERIMENTS

When Bantan opened his eyes, for a few moments he merely stared up at the ceiling. As consciousness was more fully restored to him, he realized that he was not in the brilliantly lighted laboratory, but in the room he had been assigned in the castle. It was still daylight. Surprise was apparent in his eyes as he now sat up in bed. At the next moment he felt a cool hand rest upon his arm, and turning quickly, he saw that Luane, the nurse, was sitting at his bedside. A gentle smile was upon her lips, and her gray eyes were a trifle misty.

"Everything is all right for now, Bantan," she said softly.

"How did I get here?" he asked.

"Hulo and Humo carried you upon a stretcher," she replied. "The experiment was a failure and my— The Great One believes the retrovider is at fault. He was greatly upset, and is now working furiously in an effort to discover what had gone wrong."

As she spoke, Bantan was aware that a slight flush tinted her cheeks and that her eyes were somewhat evasive.

"The pill that you gave me, Luane," he said, trying to catch her eyes with his, "would that have been the reason for the experiment's failure today?"

The nurse's eyes revealed their guilt.

"Please don't mention that to any one, Bantan,"

she begged. "Were my—The Great One to know of my deception, I might be severely punished."

"No one shall ever know, Luane," he assured her.

The nurse thanked him with her eyes, then arose to her feet.

"Now that you are yourself again," she said, "I must go."

His hand reached out, resting upon her arm and detained her for a moment.

"You wouldn't want to tell me why you spared me from an experiment today?" he asked.

She shook her head.

"I can't tell you now," she replied in a low voice. "Perhaps—later."

He nodded, his eyes holding hers for another long moment.

Without a further word Luane left the room.

The bronzed giant arose from the bed and again went to one of the two windows overlooking the cliff. He was there only a short while when he heard the shuffling of sandaled feet in the corridor beyond the half-opened door, and turning, he saw that Loula was bringing his evening meal. A happy smile was upon her lips and her dark eyes radiated with happiness.

"I was very happy to learn that the experiment failed today, Bantan," she murmured, as she went to the table and set the tray upon it.

He walked toward the servant girl with a smile.

"No happier than I, Loula," he said, as he seated himself and looked up at the smiling girl.

She drew near him with flushed features, but her eyes were wide.

"The Great One is furious," she added. "Hulo and Humo are with him. They are testing the machine in an effort to locate the trouble. Humo told me he had never known The Great One to be so upset."

A faint smile touched the corners of Bantan's lips as he thought of the pill Luane had given him which had been instrumental in the experiment's failure.

Loula caught his attention and he at once was aware something was troubling her.

"Do you like Luane, Bantan?" she asked naively.

He shook his head slowly.

"What did she say to you earlier in the day outside in the corridor?" he asked then.

"She heard us talking," the servant girl answered. "She looked at me strangely. I'm sure she suspects something between us. She told me servants shouldn't have anything to say to a guest."

Bantan smiled good-naturedly, and reaching out, patted one of Loula's hands.

"I don't believe she would cause you any trouble," he assured her. "Tell me, how long has she been with The Great One as his nurse?"

The girl wrung her hands nervously.

"Please don't make me answer questions which The Great One would forbid," she begged.

"All right, Loula," he said, nodding, "I don't wish you to answer questions that would make trouble for you."

"I must go now, Bantan," the girl said. Quickly she brushed his cheek with her lips, then left, leaving in her wake the faint aroma of the perfume she used.

Eating his meal in silence, Bantan had ample opportunity to reflect upon recent incidents. Time and again he would shake his head at his failure to understand certain matters. Thinking of Luane, the nurse, even though he had spared her life from drowning earlier in the day, he had hardly expected her to act in his favor. Her years of loyal service to The Great One wouldn't permit disloyalty in his favor on her part unless she had an ulterior motive. Whatever it might be, the bronzed giant had not the slightest inkling.

At last, rising from the table, his evening meal completed, Bantan again went to one of the windows overlooking the water below. He remained there until dusk, watching the various cloud formations take on vivid hues as the sun neared the horizon. So intent he was, he failed to hear the hurried footsteps in the corridor approaching the door of his room, and was aware only as Luane entered. He at once noted the agitation that was present upon her face, and that her eyes appeared distressed.

"What is the trouble Luane?" he asked.

"My—The Great One thinks he has located the trouble with the retrovider, Bantan," she said, approaching him and pausing to draw a deep breath. "He had Humo submit to an experiment and it was successful. In my haste coming to you, I didn't obtain a pill which would render you safe from another experiment. In a very short while my—The Great One will send Hulo for you, for he is very anxious to resume his experiments with you as his subject. He is now taking a short nap. I do hope that you will suffer no ill effects from the new experiment." As she uttered the concluding words her worried eyes appeared misty.

The bronzed giant impulsively reached for her hands and clasped them gently in his large, brown ones. A wistful smile touched his lips.

"Thank you for your concern, Luane," he said in a low voice. "I am strong and healthy. I'm sure I'll survive another experiment without ill effects. It is heartening to know you feel concern for my welfare. I feel as though I might consider you as a—friend."

"You saved my life this morning," she reminded him. "I shall ever be grateful to you for that."

His smile became tender.

"You have thanked me for that," he said. "I would have as readily saved the life of any other whoever he or she might have been."

A flush tinted the nurse's cheeks. She withdrew her hands from his, but appeared ill at ease.

"I must go now," she murmured. "And please believe me—I regret that you must be a subject for my—The Great One's experiments again. I'll hope for your well being afterward."

"Thank you," he said in a low voice. "It already makes me feel better to know the nurse will be concerned over me."

Luane's eyes were misty as she looked at him for a long moment, then with a slight shake of her head, she turned and departed.

Bantan shrugged and turned to look out the window in the quick-setting darkness. For a few minutes he stood there, then with a shake of his head turned away and sought the bed. Lying upon his back, he clasped his hands beneath his head and seemingly stared at the ceiling above.

Discerning as he was, he was acutely aware of the fact that Luane thought of him since that same morning in a much deeper manner than mere gratefulness for having spared her life. Human beings might masquerade their voices and actions, but one's eyes revealed much more. Believing what he had seen in the nurse's eyes, he had reason to shake his head almost despairingly, and half-wishing that she had not looked at him in the manner she had. Thinking thusly, he fell into a doze.

Bantan became alert shortly afterwards, however, as his ears detected footsteps in the corridor beyond the door of his room. He sat up, swinging his feet to the floor. Looking toward the partly opened door he saw a faint light in the near darkness. The sound of footsteps ascertained that Hulo was coming for him. Presently the warrior stood upon the threshold, holding a candle above his head.

"The Great One is ready for another experiment, Bantan," he announced.

The bronzed giant arose and walked toward the warrior.

"I'm ready, Hulo," was all he said.

They traversed the corridor in silence, and remained so while the elevator descended to the level where the laboratory was. Both blinked their eyes when stepping from the conveyance into the brilliantly lighted corridor. The door to the laboratory was open, and as Bantan paused upon the threshold of the doorway, he looked at the familiar surroundings.

The Great One stood at one side of the table, his face and head masked as customary, while Luane, the nurse, stood upon the other side. But her eyes were worried, and she seemed to tremble slightly. The Great One's blue eyes were blazing pools that seemed to pierce the subject.

"Right this way, Bantan," the metallic voice spoke, seemingly causing an involuntary shiver to race the length of the bronzed giant's spine.

Bantan walked slowly toward the table, and without looking at either scientist or nurse, drew himself upon

it and lay upon his back. He closed his eyes and heaved
a deep sigh. He could feel the slight trembling of Luane's hands as she fastened the straps about him.
When the final adjustment was made, one of her
hands covered one of his for a long moment, and she
pressed it gently in assurance that he was not without
a friend.

The bronzed giant now sensed the presence of The
Great One. He felt his arm daubed with alcohol, then
a needle penetrated the chilled spot, and the contents of the hypodermic were emptied into his veins.
Before losing consciousness, he was aware of The
Great One placing the familiar oval band about his
forehead.

"Now, Bantan," the metallic voice was saying, "you
will back track through eons of time to the Stone Age
again. We must know the life of the unborn child of
Bazo and Mono—and, perhaps, other generations as
well."

As unconsciousness was overcoming Bantan, he
dimly heard Luane protesting with The Great One,
for he was positive he heard her utter a single word
distressfully several times as though from a great
distance.

"No! No! No!"

What further ensued, the bronzed giant had no
knowledge, for it was then that the swirling mists overcame his reasoning faculties, and he knew no more.

It seemed that time stood still for the silent form
lying upon the table in The Great One's laboratory.
But through the ingenuity of a brilliant scientist, his
long-dormant brain cells were revivified, separated in
chronological order, and eons of time were back-
tracked to the Stone Age.

To an unconscious person time's passage has no significance. Eventually Bantan's reeling senses began to dispel the haze that enveloped them. When he opened his eyes he was surprised to know he was still in the laboratory, for the bright lights overhead made him blink several times before becoming accustomed to them.

He looked to his left and the haunting eyes of Luane were watching him intently for his reaction. A smile touched his lips and his eyes assured her that he was all right. Then his eyes shifted to meet the blazing ones of The Great One, and he knew beyond a doubt that the burning eyes were those of an insane man.

"You are in full possession of your faculties, Bantan?" the metallic voice asked in an effort to be pleasant.

The bronzed giant nodded.

"Good!" was the reply. "For your information we have the life of Ba-an, who was the son of Bazo and Mono, recorded on film through your memory cells. Ba-an, too, was marked upon the right temple as you are, and as were your other male progenitors. Now, we must make up for lost time, so you must again go back to the Stone Age so that we may know of the son Ba-an conceived, lived, and died."

Bantan merely stared up at The Great One. The question in his eyes need not be asked.

"You have no choice, you know," the metallic voice spoke mockingly to him.

The bronzed giant heard a gasp from the lips of Luane, then once again he felt his left arm daubed with alcohol, the chill racing through the entire member down to his finger tips. He did not feel the sharp needle probe the flesh, but within moments after the drug entered his veins he was aware of his reeling senses, and it seemed a gray wall was closing in upon him. He could hear disagreeing voices which could be none other than Luane's and The Great One's. The former was protesting, "Not so soon!" But then unconsciousness welled through him and everything became blank.

Under the guidance of The Great One the retrovider faithfully reproduced on film the life and love of Abna, the son of Ba-an who, fortunately, in that savage era lived much longer than any of his ancestors, and begot a number of children of both sexes through his mate, Lala. The first child had been a son, and he, too, had been marked similarly as his father. This first son was named Ba-ab. The other sons—there had been three more—had been born with a daughter between each, but none of the younger sons had the birthmark upon their right temple.

Wordlessly The Great One watched the life of Ba-ab upon the picture screen, but his bright eyes gleamed with the maniacal light of a demented person. He would have liked to follow the life and love of Ba-ab's first-born son, who was named Bala, but he realized his subject must have some rest, for the energy having been extracted from his brain cells had been tremendous. Demented though he was, he was also aware he must not overstrain this subject who had thus far proven the most valuable of any who had preceded him.

With some reluctance The Great One pressed a button, and the retrovider became de-energized. He looked down at the subject's silent features, then he unfastened the attachments from the oval band about his forehead. This was then removed. He drew back

the lid of each eye and examined the eyeball. He nodded, looking up at Luane, who was watching him intently.

"He will be all right," he murmured.

The nurse heaved a deep sigh.

"Summon Hulo, and tell him to get Humo. They
can carry Bantan back to his room upon a stretcher. I
have finished my experiments for tonight."

The nurse did as she was bid.

As the twin brothers were carrying the unconscious
bronzed giant to his room upon a stretcher, Luane
looked at The Great One, masquerading the misery
she felt.

"May I follow and see that Bantan recovers consciousness all right?" she asked.

The scientist stared at the nurse for a long moment.
His blue eyes merely blinked his permission.

"Thank you," the girl murmured, and she hurried in
the wake of the twin brothers bearing the stretcher.

As from a great distance to the unconscious man's
faculties he was dimly aware, at first, of a soft voice
constantly repeating his name. He was slowly feeling
life course through his body. Cold hands clasped one
of his, and at times one of the cold hands stroked his
brow.

"Bantan! Bantan!" he heard his name repeated insistently, and then crooningly. "Bantan! Bantan!
Please come back out of the long-ago past and open
your eyes to the present. Please, Bantan."

The haze in his mind was slowly clearing, and he
became aware first of his regular heartbeat, and then
his breathing. Several times his eyelids flickered, and
then at last they opened. The multitude of lights in
the chandelier seemingly danced up and down crazily,

and they seemed to mesmerize him as he stared at them unseeingly. Presently he shook his head a trifle to clear it of the wisps of haze which still clung tenaciously to his faculties. He again closed his eyes and turned over on his side, so that the lights wouldn't shine directly upon his closed lids.

Once again his eyes slowly opened and he was aware of the white uniform the nurse wore. Her haunting eyes were filled with mist as they seemingly riveted upon the young man's handsome features.

"Bantan, do you hear and see me?" Her voice trembled with the great concern she felt for him.

The bronzed giant recognized Luane's voice. His eyes slowly lifted until he could visualize her worried features. A smile of recognition touched his lips.

"I hear and recognize you, Luane," he answered. With some effort he raised himself to a seated position. He drew a bronzed hand across his brow, then shook his head to dispel the last of the clinging mist from his faculties. "It seems so long," he murmured wearily. "I seem so tired."

"Of course you are tired," the nurse murmured. "You were subjected to two experiments instead of just one. I protested with my—The Great One that one was enough at a time, but he wouldn't listen to me." She shrugged her shoulders helplessly. "There was nothing I could do. My—The Great One is a very determined man. Sometimes I hate him very much."

The bronzed giant closed his eyes and drew a deep breath.

"I am so tired I think I could sleep for a long time," he murmured.

The nurse arose from her chair and stood over him.

"Your mind is clear?" she asked. "That is all I wish to know before I leave you."

"Yes, Luane, my mind is clear," he replied. "But it is very tired."

"I'll leave you now," she said softly. "Later, I'll return to make sure you are sleeping normally. Good night, Bantan."

"Good night, Luane," he murmured. His eyes opened and he smiled briefly, but at the next moment his eyes again closed and his breathing appeared even and normal.

Luane's eyes were misty as she bent above the sleeping giant. Then she restrained the impulse which surged through her. Straightening, she dried the corners of her eyes with the knuckle of a forefinger. Going to the wall she snapped off the light switch and the room was enshrouded in total darkness. Unerringly she found the doorway leading to the corridor.

* * *

Later in the evening a silent figure entered Bantan's room. The seeming apparition carried a lighted candle in a holder and held it above her head so as to see better. Loula had heard of the trial the bronzed giant had been subjected to, and this was the earliest opportunity she had had to go to him and see how he was faring.

Approaching the soundly sleeping young man, she placed the candle holder upon the table and seated herself upon a chair at his bedside. Clasping her hands together, she anxiously looked upon the composed features of the sleeper. The flickering light from the candle illuminated them with sufficient clearness.

Now the servant girl's hands unclasped and her right

one slowly neared his unseamed brow. With ineffable
tenderness she softly touched the skin, and then her
fingers smoothed back the rather long hair that tumbled in profusion thereupon. The softness of her dark
eyes clearly reflected her devotion for the bronzed
giant, and while she looked at his silent features mist
appeared in them. It was with magnificent control that
she did not suit to action what her heart longed most
to do, for above all else she wanted to cuddle his face
upon her bosom, and, as a mother would, lavish her
affection upon him.

And while Loula was thus engaged with her innate
feeling for Bantan, she was not aware of the silent
form that peered wonderingly within the opened doorway for a long moment. Recognizing the presence of
the servant girl, the newcomer shook her head momentarily, and tried to understand the devotion she
entertained for the bronzed giant without any jealousy
on her own part. Knowing as she did that Bantan did
not love Loula, Luane wondered just how to tell the
girl of her hopeless infatuation.

Upon silent feet she approached the table where
the flickering candle was burning, and only when the
nurse placed a hand upon the servant girl's shoulder—
startling her momentarily so that she uttered a slight
gasping cry—was she aware that she was not alone
in the room.

Luane pressed her lips with a forefinger, indicating
silence was to be maintained. However, there was no
danger of the sleeper waking, for he was lost in the
mazes of deep slumber.

With an affrighted expression in her eyes, Loula removed her hand from Bantan's forehead and arose to
her feet.

"I know I have no right to be here, Luane," she murmured. "But—" She could not find further words to explain her presence.

"You are very much in love with Bantan," Luane divined, shaking her head sorrowfully. "But he could never love you, a native girl, as you must know."

An ineffable sadness appeared in the servant girl's misty eyes, and she nodded slowly.

"Yes, I know," she answered. "Bantan has already told me that he could never learn to love me. But that doesn't prevent me from caring for him, even though hopelessly expecting no reward in return."

An understanding smile now came upon Luane's features.

"As you know, Loula," she said, "Bantan is of white origin. He deserves the finest our sex can offer him. Even *I* do not feel that I would be worthy of such a magnificent man."

Loula looked silently upon the sleeper's face so utterly in peace.

"Now that I know he is all right, Luane," she said, "I had better be leaving. You aren't angry with me because I came to see him?"

The nurse shook her head slowly and an understanding smile came to her lips.

"No, Loula, I am not angry with you," she answered. "But if I were you, I would not feel so devoted to Bantan. You know it is hopeless, and you will be spared the grief that surely will be yours some day should you learn that he could care for some one else."

The servant girl bowed then and silently departed, leaving the candle she had brought, since Luane had brought none. When the soft, shuffling footfalls of the departing girl could no longer be heard in the corridor, Luane then seated herself and looked upon the handsome features of the sleeper. She drew a deep breath and her dark eyes welled with emotion. She reached out a tentative hand several times before at last mustering the courage to rest her cool fingers upon his unseamed brow. Her eyes became misty as she realized the part she had played in using him for a subject to The Great One's experiments. She knew now, if it were in her power, she would not have him used in that manner again, realizing as she did the danger that was involved to his future well being.

Thinking thusly, for the first time in her life Luane had reason to upbraid herself. Hot tears formed in her eyes and rolled unheedingly down her cheeks to drop into her lap. Knowing herself as she did, she shook her head distressfully, and covered her eyes with her hands in an effort to blot out all memory of herself. She realized how great her love for Bantan had become in a single day. Bereft of love in her entire lifetime, she also was aware how hopeless her love was for the bronzed giant. Intelligent as she was, she knew he would never return her love—if he were to know the real Luane.

In despair now, she arose to her feet. She looked sorrowfully down upon the sleeper's composed features, and all the spontaneous love she realized for him welled into her misty eyes at that moment. Awareness of herself, however, was the reason for a horrified expression to replace her love. With a hoarse sob, she reached for the candle holder. Once more she looked upon the composed features of the handsome young giant, and then, as convulsive sobs wracked her, she turned and departed from the room.

When Luane reached her own apartment and put the lights on, she then snuffed out the lighted candle, and seated herself at her dresser. Looking in the mirror, she studied the reflection of her features. Though her cheeks were tear-streaked, her haunting eyes searched the pale face framed with lustrous black hair in a most becoming coiffure. Minutes passed while she looked at her features minutely, all the while trying to avoid meeting the reflection of her gray eyes. No seams or wrinkles were detected upon the smooth skin of her forehead, corners of her eyes, her cheeks, or around her mouth and chin. The lines of her well formed neck were smooth. She opened her mouth and looked upon beautiful white teeth.

Trying to avoid meeting her eyes by such minute inspections, it was inevitable that they would at last meet in the mirror. For long moments they fastened upon the other, seemingly mesmerized with the contact. But her reasoning faculties could not stand the strain with the true knowledge of herself.

A choking sob again wracked her, and her eyes closed tightly. Her head lowered and her face was buried between her two hands. Her shoulders quivered and the tears came at last, giving surcease to the tautness that gripped her tortured mind.

At last, however, she calmed herself and prepared to retire. It was a seemingly tired old woman who extinguished the lights and crept into bed. But it was a long while that she lay there, staring unseeingly at the darkened ceiling, before at last exhausted nature overwhelmed her distressed mind, only in turn, to give way to a troubled dreamland from which she waked numerous times.

Each time that she waked an inner resolution was taking strength within her. She would forget what had harassed her on the previous evening. Her spontaneous love for Bantan could not be repulsed. Bereft of love in her entire lifetime, now its full awakening could not be rejected. Be it only a day, a week, a month, at the most a year, it would be worth while. After all, she was only a mortal woman with all the yearning such was capable of. Remembering Bantan's apparent exhaustion of the previous evening, she decided to go to his room, and as a nurse, see how he felt now that morning had come.

CHAPTER XVI

BANTAN PRIMEVAL

All through the night Bantan slept, but from the manner his muscles writhed and the nerves of his giant body twitched, it was apparent his dreams were uneasy. His subconscious mind was strangely experiencing events beyond normalcy for the present day and age. It seemed he dwelt in another time—a remote age; and though conditions should have been alien to him, for some unknown reason the constant dangers were natural—that he knew of none other.

Gigantic, savage beasts, hideous to behold, were always a menace to human existence. There the mastodon, mammoth, trilophodon, the cave bear, and the equally dangerous saber-tooth tiger were man's constant threat to life in that long-ago age. And one had to watch, when emerging from jungle depths into the open, for the ever alert archaeopteryx with sharp teeth, claws on its wings, and a long, bony tail. It could swoop, seemingly from nowhere with startling swiftness, and tear an unwary victim with its teeth and talons.

Even when swimming in the restless water of the mighty ocean, fearful creatures of the deep, especially the plesiosaur, would harass one so that existence was constantly fraught with peril in the age-old struggle of that savage, antediluvian period.

But there were eventful interludes, fortunately, for a time of romance, brief though they were. In this way

only could Nature provide posterity in a world that
was old in birth but comparatively young with human
habitation upon whom the fate of the planet must de-
pend if it is to be a prospering one for generations
unborn.

In this primeval world of long ago Bantan dreamed
of himself as a mighty hunter. He was armed with a
stone dagger sheathed at his right hip. His left hand
clutched a stout, knobbed club and in his right he carried a stone-tipped spear. He was sharp of eye, keen
of hearing, and his nostrils were always alert to changing scents that might be wafted by a whimsical change
of breeze.

As yet, though he was a man of twenty-one seasons
in age, and an only son, he was not mated, much to the
disappointment of his parents. Usually before his age
a successful hunter had taken unto himself a mate, and
they had taken up residence in one of the many unused
caves that honeycombed the mighty cliff in which the
troglodyte tribe of Erb dwelt.

For some unknown reason the females of the tribe
did not appeal to Bantan, though many were the hearts
that were heavy because he did not desire one of them
for his mate. Were he able to count, there was a female for each finger of his two hands and the toes on
both feet who looked upon the bronzed giant with
secret and open admiration. If they could have prayed
to their deity—had they one—long and earnest would
the prayers have been from each heart that she be the
fortunate one to be his mate. Very comely some were,
while others, who lacked comeliness, had other favoring attributes to make up for their deficiency of passing
good looks. But, strangely, the young hunter did not
desire any of them.

Perhaps the aggressiveness some of them employed

to attract his attention had disgusted him. Had they been more coy and subtle, there was not an impossibility that he might have desired one for his mate ere now, for he was only human and possessed of man's needs. Some males desired forwardness on the part of a female. Perhaps their egos might have reason to inflate.

But such was not so with Bantan. Even in that remote age when reasoning was supposed to be slowly awakening, the mighty hunter knew within himself that when he met the right female, he would have no reason to look further. And when he was sure that he had met her there would be no necessity of endless courting and then perhaps stand the chance of losing the prize that a good mate is to be considered, even from the primitive times to the present age.

Even at that time it was a known fact that a male, or, a female alone, could never amount to anything of importance. It was as though Nature had endowed within the individual souls of the human race the important urgency of finding one another's mate, for through the fruits of such unions posterity owed its very existence.

On this day Bantan was hunting alone far from the troglodyte tribe to which he belonged. Earlier in the morning he had come upon the spoor of a cave bear. His delicate nostrils had sniffed unerringly in identifying the animal, and his keen eyes had noted the deep depressions of paw prints on the jungle floor he traversed. His ears were constantly alert for the slightest sound that would apprise him of his prey's proximity.

Presently when the sunlight was blotted from view by storm clouds, the jungle floor beneath became darkened, and a slight chill pervaded the sultry atmosphere, it was then that the hunter realized a storm was making up. He hoped the jungle growth would soon give way to more open terrain, and that an unoccupied cave might be within easy reach, for he did not relish being caught in a storm, and if it should be a noisy one, there was always danger of firebolts from the heaven striking down trees. With this thought came recollection of Taman, a cave dweller, who had been caught thusly not many moons ago, and a falling limb had knocked him to the ground, rendering him senseless. Thereafter, though he recovered, his mind had never been the same.

Now, hastening on his way so that he had developed a trot, Bantan was aware that the jungle growth was thinning considerably. Through open patches in the tree tops he could glimpse the overcast sky. As yet, no wind stirred the lofty tops, and no rain fell; but the imminence of this was anticipated with each passing minute.

Soon the thinning jungle growth gave him ample opportunity to look farther ahead in his ceaseless search for his prey. As yet there had been no sight to be obtained of the cave bear, but so strong its scent, the hunter momentarily expected to do so.

Ahead, Bantan could see a promontory with scant vegetation clinging to its rocky side. He hoped very much an unoccupied cave might be found there. Now, with a start, ahead of him he caught a fleeting glimpse of a shaggy, black bear as it lumbered along upon all fours. The hunter quickened his pace, his left hand gripping the stout, knobbed club the tighter as did his other upon the handle of the stone-tipped spear. A gleam of satisfaction now possessed his dark eyes. Already he was anticipating the conflict near at hand. He broke into a sprint so as to lessen the distance between him and his unwary prey.

When he had completely emerged from the edge of the jungle growth he found the ground uneven and rock strewn. Because of this condition, he had to pick his way more carefully, for at this strategic part of the chase he did not wish to injure his calloused feet.

It was then that the cave bear paused, and turning about, caught sight of his pursuer. It stood there upon its haunches, still as a statue for a long moment. Then, with a loud bark, it advanced toward the hunter with leaps and bounds. This was precisely what Bantan had anticipated. He went more warily now, his left hand clutching the handle of his stout, knobbed club more firmly, while his right gripped the spear handle tightly, his fingers flexing repeatedly so as to be more nimble. At first over a hundred yards separated them, but this distance was lessening considerably as the two advanced toward each other.

In the distant heaven dim flashes of lightning were playing hide and seek with scudding storm clouds, and dull rumbles of thunder were to be heard. Light, tentative gusts of wind would spring up and then die into nothingness. But each time the gusts took new life they were stronger and slightly longer in duration.

When the hunter and the cave bear were twenty yards apart, each instinctively halted in their tracks, apparently sizing one another up, then proceeded forward slowly toward each other. Presently the man halted his advance. He jabbed the point of his stone-tipped spear into the rocky soil where it remained standing erect. The stout, knobbed club then was swiftly switched to his right hand. With eyes never leaving the glaring ones of the shaggy bear, Bantan started swinging the club over his head to gain momentum with each cycle, also to limber his muscles as well. The bear seemed puzzled by his actions, but presently its short patience was exhausted. With a fearsome bark it moved forward.

At that precise moment the hunter released the knobbed club, and lightning-like, it flew through the intervening distance of ten feet. Almost at the same moment the bear lowered its head just a fraction—whether by instinct or chance—who can guess? The hurtling knobbed club bounded off the top of its skull—just missing the intended target, which was its receding forehead, where the blow would have been more telling in effect. The cave bear uttered a ferocious bark, more surprised than hurt by the missile. Its fury was not to be suppressed, for at the next moment it was advancing formidably upon the puny man.

The instant he had released the knobbed club, Bantan had seized the handle of his spear as it stood upright at his side, and with it clutched in his right hand, was awaiting the advance of the infuriated cave bear. Feinting with the spear menacingly, perhaps the bear's small brain realized the hurt the slender, stone-tipped stick was capable of inflicting. It reared upon its haunches, and with its forepaws sought to deflect the jabbing point.

Time and again its paws just missed the tantalizing end, for upon each occasion the hunter was quick to withdraw the spearpoint, knowing as he did that one blow of those powerful paws would be sufficient to tear it from his grasp. Then he would have only his stone dagger for protection in defense of his life.

The contest continued with Bantan feinting and withdrawing, but his sharp eyes were alert for the opportunity to pierce the bear's savage heart. He realized that the timing had to be just right, else disaster would be his lot.

Meanwhile, the lightning flashes were much sharper, and the thunder was becoming much nearer, for its harsh reports would fairly cause the ground to tremble. And now gusts of wind were steadily increasing with no intermittent let-up. Drops of rain hesitantly fell. They pattered upon both man and beast. Within a minute or so, Bantan felt the handle of his spear becoming slippery. Time and again he moved his hand upon it, wiping away the moisture where the advantage lay to grip it.

How long the grim contest might have continued was any one's guess, but in an infinitesimal second the hunter saw the opening that he sought in the bear's defense. In a flash he lunged forward with both hands now grasping the handle of the spear near the end and his entire weight was behind the thrust. At the last moment one foot slightly slipped, throwing him a trifle off balance.

The stone-tipped point, however, penetrated the thick hide at the precise spot intended. A hoarse bark was emitted from the beast's slavering jaws at that same moment, as though its minute brain realized the death thrust had been made. Enraged, before it felt the strength in its body slip away into nothingness, the cave bear swung a mighty paw at the man thing as it was already falling backward, the spear being torn from the hunter's clutching hands.

Had Bantan's foot not fortuitously slipped at that last moment of his forward movement, he would have received the full force of the blow. As it was, the edge of the paw caught him a glancing blow upon the side of the head, rendering him unconscious, but not before he was cognizant of a blinding flash of lightning before him, a thunderous roar overhead, then it seemed the flood gates of the sky were opened and torrential rain descended upon the earth beneath.

The cave bear fell backward, its forepaws futilely trying to dislodge the spear from its burning, bleeding heart, while its powerful hind legs kicked convulsively. Weaker became its efforts as its gasping breaths became shorter. Then, a final shudder wracked its entire body, and it rolled over upon one side and became still, its jaws agape and its beady eyes staring unseeingly.

Meanwhile, Bantan lay flat upon his back ten feet away His arms were outstretched and his legs were spread apart. His massive, hairless chest rose and fell rhythmically to his even breathing. Not a drop of blood was to be seen anywhere upon him, and a casual observer might have guessed that he was merely sleeping. But any one would know no one would, or could, sleep that peacefully with deluging rain descending, as it now was, upon his nearly naked body.

*   *   *

The first intimation the young cave man had that he lived was when he opened his eyes to find himself in a strange cave. He was lying upon a pallet of grasses that to his delicate nostrils were fresh and sweet-smelling. Although his head felt somewhat heavy, he raised himself and looked about the interior with eyes of wonder, truly astonished at his unfamiliar surroundings.

Immediately the question paramount to all else was how he had come to his present position.

His last conscious moments were of his victorious death battle with the cave bear, and then it seemed something had bashed him upon the side of the head. He dimly remembered the blinding flash of lightning, the loud clap of thunder, also that rain descended upon him in torrents. Now, here he was, as dry as could be, and lying upon a comfortable pallet of sweet-smelling grasses. Looking toward the mouth of the cave he saw the brilliant sunshine outside. Strangely he gave no thought of arising and making an investigation. He was too comfortable, and closing his eyes he heaved a deep sigh.

It seemed that time in passing was of no account to him. But at last his alert ears were aware of soft footsteps just outside the cave's mouth. With his eyes fixed upon the opening, he presently saw a young cave girl dressed in the fashion of the females in that remote age pause at the cave's mouth. The crudely tanned skin of some animal girded her mid-section and extended almost to her knees, leaving the upper part of her body bare. Her long, dark hair tumbled about her shoulders both in front and back. That which tumbled forward extended to her firm breasts, almost concealing them. She wore no sandals. Pausing at the cave's opening, she looked in his direction.

Conscious that she must be the owner of the cave, Bantan now sat up, his eyes riveted upon her. The cave girl nodded, and a slight smile touched her lips as she stepped forward, pausing only when she had come near his feet. Her features were attractive and seemingly familiar, though he was positive he had never seen her before. She appeared quite earnest now, and a quizzical expression possessed her gray eyes as she now stared down upon him. Then she placed her left hand upon her left breast, looking questionably at him, while pointing at him with her right hand.

Though conversation was extremely limited in this later generation of a remote age, the cave man and the girl introduced themselves.

"Bantan," he said, touching his chest with his left hand, then pointing at her with his right, a questioning look was in his eyes.

"Luane," she said.

Both smiled in acknowledgment at knowing each other's name.

Bantan then went through the motions of engaging the cave bear in a death battle, then closing his eyes and lying back, indicated what he had remembered. When he presently opened his eyes and sat up, he looked at the girl. She smiled, revealing nice white teeth, and nodded her head eagerly.

Through the universal sign language he asked about herself and if she lived here alone. In answer, she made him understand that her father and mother had been outcasts from their tribe. Only recently they had died and she had buried them nearby. She had been living alone, since she had no brothers or sisters. From her cave she had seen him and the bear battling, and she had watched until the end. Even though it had been raining hard, she must be sure that the man lived. Upon examination, finding that he did, she had managed to drag him to her cave and tended him.

While she had been speaking in signs, Bantan had arisen to his feet and stood before her. Now that she had finished telling him of herself, he was aware that she was looking up at him with admiration. There was no mistaking the glow in her gray eyes.

Even in that remote age the bronzed giant realized his obligation to the girl for having saved his life. He made her understand that he was grateful. To this, with admiring eyes, the cave girl assured him that a mighty hunter deserved such consideration, stranger though he had been to her.

Bantan was cognizant of a peculiar tingling sensation pervading him, and as he looked down at the girl's steadily regarding eyes, he was aware that his heart beat faster and his breath was shorter. Now he pointed outside and walked to the mouth of the cave. There he paused as the girl drew near him. He looked at her questionably then pointed to the scene of conflict. He tried to make her understand he must get his weapons.

Knowing of what he mentioned, she placed a warm, sun-tanned hand upon his arm and pointed to the rear of the cave. With the contact of her hand seemingly electric thrills raced throughout his entire body. Wordlessly he permitted her to lead him to the rear of the cave. There he noted another pallet of grasses. At its side he saw she had placed his stone-tipped spear and his stout, knobbed club. He smiled gratefully as he stooped and picked them up and fondled them affectionately.

Luane smiled as she watched him. In a few moments he placed them at the side of the pallet of grasses he had been lying upon, and once more returned to the cave's mouth with the girl close behind him. Bantan looked at the edge of the jungle several hundred yards away, and into his eyes came a sadness

as he thought of his father and mother. He wondered
if they had missed him. Watching him closely, the
girl's features became forlorn.

The young cave man now heaved a deep sigh, then
he turned to the silent girl standing at his side with
slumped shoulders. He was immediately aware of her
seeming sorrow. She looked up at him, holding his
eyes for a long moment, then she touched him with a
hand and pointed toward the jungle, nodding meanwhile. It was as though she said:

"That is where you came from—and now you wish
to return?"

He nodded slowly and sighed.

And then, as though a woman's curiosity must be
satisfied, she made him understand that she surmised
his mate was waiting for him, and perhaps wondering why he had been so long absent.

Comprehending what she had said through cumbersome signs, he shook his head and told her that he
had no mate to return to—only a father and mother.

At this reply the girl's sorrowful eyes brightened,
her slumped shoulders straightened, and she heaved
a deep sigh of relief. Then, her innate curiosity must
be satisfied more conclusively, she asked him through
signs if he intended to mate with some female of his
tribe.

With a smile and a shake of his head he made her
understand that there was no female in his tribe whom
he desired for a mate.

Luane then smilingly shook her head with eyes
glowing as much as to ask banteringly:

"Why? As a mighty hunter, don't you have the feeling that you desire a mate?"

He did not reply to this,

The cave girl, with a winsome smile upon her face and with questioning eyes, merely looked up at him as much as to ask:

"Am I not desirable to you?"

For a long moment Bantan studied her, keenly aware of his fast-beating heart and the sudden shortness of his breath again. Without knowing that he did so, he raised a hand and gently placed it upon Luane's shoulder. Looking up into his steady eyes, the girl then raised a hand and rested it upon his opposite shoulder as though in acceptance of him. Her breasts heaved to the emotion that pulsed through her; then, as though in submission to him, she placed her forehead upon his broad chest while her other hand sought his. Theirs was a short, strange courtship, not unusual in the remote age in which they lived, but in his heart the bronzed giant realized he had at last found his mate.

*　　*　　*

Two suns later they returned to the troglodyte tribe of Erb. The glow in the young man's eyes clearly indicated how very proud he was of his mate. The softness in Luane's eyes whenever she looked up at the young hunter was conclusive proof that she was happier now than at any other time in her life.

Bantan's father and mother were happy for their son, and they welcomed him wholeheartedly upon his return. Perhaps his mother was a trifle disappointed that he had not selected a female from the tribe for his mate, but as she came to know Luane better during the passing suns, she realized her son could not have done better had he selected a mate from the tribe.

The newly mated couple took up their living quarters in an unoccupied cave, and they were as happy as could be expected in that remote age. His mate, meanwhile, was accepted as an equal among the other females of the tribe.

Happy moons passed for them. But even in that long-ago age happiness could not prevail forever, since each day was a constant battle for survival against the carnivorous beasts that roamed the land.

One day when Bantan was swimming far from shore in the restless water of the mighty ocean, in his happiness of knowing he was soon to be a proud father because Luane was growing big each day with their child, he did not realize how far he really had been swimming. Only as a reptilian monstrosity of the deep known as plesiosaur attacked him did he become aware of the distance which separated him from the fancied safety of the shore.

Instantly he drew the stone dagger sheathed at his right hip, and with it clutched in hand was prepared to battle with the monster. Meanwhile, at each opportunity, he would strike out for shore with mighty strokes. Whenever the scaly monster drew near him, he would slash at it with his pitifully inadequate weapon. Sometimes he had the satisfaction of knowing the point of his dagger penetrated between the scales of its body.

Hissing shrilly at the audacity of this puny swimmer who sought to escape it, the plesiosaur circled about its victim time and again, snapping repeatedly with its sharp teeth at the swimmer's arms and legs. Following each short skirmish Bantan would strike out for shore again with renewed energy. Looking in that direction, he could hardly believe he had covered so

Bantan Battles a Pleiosaur

great a distance in his happiness with the knowledge that soon he and Luane would be parents.

In his thoughts the vision of his mate was ever present. He repeated her name over and over. For some strange reason now he felt enormous weights dragging at his arms and legs so that he was hardly able to swim. It seemed he became paralyzed as he saw the monster of the deep bearing down upon him. He was hardly conscious of the sharp teeth that fastened about his mid-section and the jaws snapped shut. Even as unconsciousness claimed him, he was piteously uttering the name of Luane.

CHAPTER XVII

A CONSIDERATE NURSE

As Bantan opened his eyes, resurrected from his dream death, the thought of Luane was still with him. He was repeating her name aloud. A smile now touched his lips as he realized it was morning. Then, strangest of all when he had oriented himself, he was aware that he was not alone in the guest room he had been assigned in The Great One's castle.

A gentle voice at his side was speaking to him. Turning over, he looked into the worried eyes of Luane, the nurse, seated in a chair at his bedside.

"I am here, Bantan," she said in gentle tones. "You were calling my name before you woke."

The bronzed giant closed his eyes for a long moment as though unable to grasp that this was reality. He opened them again wonderingly. He looked up at the nurse earnestly.

"Luane, I had been dreaming that you and I lived in a long-ago age," he said. "You saved me after I had slain a cave bear, and somehow managed to drag me to a cave where you lived alone. It all seemed very strange." He shook his head as though to clear his faculties. "In real life, it was I who saved you. In my dreams, had it not been for you, I would surely have perished."

The nurse smiled through the mist in her eyes, and she reached for one of his hands and held it, her fingers resting upon his pulse to check it, nurse that she was.

"Dreams have a way of becoming confused with the events of everyday life, Bantan," she said in soft tones. "Don't be too concerned about them. Now, that you are awake, do you feel ready for your morning meal?"

He arose from bed as she released his hand. Luane remained seated, looking up at him with wondering eyes. She comprehended from her nurse's training that Bantan was still under the influence of his dream. Having admitted that he had been dreaming of her, she realized, was the indication that his feeling toward her was becoming different than heretofore.

Now, with an effort, she arose to her feet. She remembered that he had not answered her. He was standing before her, looking down at her wistfully. She tried to be indifferent as she now faced him.

"You haven't answered me, Bantan," she said chidingly. "Do you feel ready for your breakfast? Perhaps you'll feel different after you have eaten."

The bronzed giant shook his head a trifle as though to dismiss thoughts of his dream and became aware of the present.

"Yes, Luane," he said, "I am hungry and feel like eating."

Luane's indifference prevailed, though she knew her cheeks were flushed.

The reason I came here this morning," she explained, "was, as a nurse, to make sure my patient would be all right after the ordeal of last night's experiments."

"Yes, of course," he agreed. "I understand."

"I'll have Loula bring your breakfast without delay," she added, and turning, departed.

Bantan performed his morning ablutions and then walked slowly toward one of the windows overlooking the shimmering ocean beyond. He was acutely aware of a peculiar lightness within his head, and that his heart beat faster than it normally would. It made him realize only too well the exhilaration within him was because of Luane's recent presence, and the dawning fact that he was thinking of her in an entirely different light.

Presently he heard Loula's shuffling sandaled feet in the corridor and he turned about as the servant girl entered. She paused at the threshold of the doorway to look at him curiously.

"Good morning, Loula," he greeted her.

The girl wished him a similar good morning, then with a shake of her head as though something was bothering her, she went to the table and placed the tray containing his breakfast thereupon.

Bantan left the window, went to the table and seated himself.

Loula was watching him intently with a curious expression in her dark eyes.

"The nurse was here already, Bantan?" she asked.

"She came to see if I was all right after last night's experiments," he explained. "When I woke she was seated at my bedside."

"She came to me and told me you were ready for your morning meal," Loula admitted.

Bantan drained the glass of fruit juice. Then he looked at the servant girl, holding her eyes with his steady ones for a moment.

"Loula, it may seem unnatural of me to tell you

this," he said. "But, this morning when I woke, I had been dreaming that Luane and I lived in a past age—and that we were mated."

The servant girl muffled the gasp she might have uttered by clapping her hands upon her mouth. In her eyes was mirrored disappointment. Her shoulders slumped as she looked at him.

Unaware of Loula's misery, Bantan had looked away as he spoke. Then he went on, telling of his strange dream in greater detail, even stating the fact he had been calling Luane's name as he waked from his dream death. When he had completed the telling, he turned to find that Loula had left the room without his knowledge. He looked about, then quickly arose to his feet and went to the doorway. There was no sign of the servant girl in the corridor. With a shrug of his giant shoulders he returned to the table to resume his breakfast.

He had told Loula he could never care for her in the way a man might care for a girl, and now he realized the depths of her disappointment when he related his unusual dream to her. It was apparent that the servant girl assumed he was already in love with Luane, and unable to listen further, she had unostentatiously departed.

Completing his breakfast, Bantan returned to the window overlooking the shimmering water. He stood there unseeingly for what seemed a long time before he heard footsteps outside the door. He sighed, believing that Loula had returned for the breakfast dishes. Turning, he was surprised to see that Humo paused upon the threshold with a peculiar expression upon his features. The bronzed giant managed a smile and greeted the warrior.

Humo returned the greeting with unchanged features, then with a shake of his head, entered the room and went directly to the table where the tray and dishes reposed.

Bantan instantly sensed something was wrong. He quickly crossed the room.

"What is the matter, Humo?" he asked. "Where is Loula?"

The warrior shook his head and turned to the bronzed giant.

"I don't know," he answered. "Neither has Hulo seen her since early this morning."

Bantan appeared in deep thought. A furrow creased his brow. He wondered if he should inform Humo what he had been telling the servant girl a short while before, then decided not to.

Meanwhile, Humo picked up the tray of dishes and wordlessly left the room. The bronzed giant watched him in silence. When the warrior was gone, he again returned to the window, wondering at the whereabouts of Loula.

Much later, Luane came to the guest room. Her features were strangely troubled as she entered. At the window where he was standing, Bantan observed the nurse's perturbation.

"You have learned of Loula's disappearance?" she asked as she approached him.

The bronzed giant's features were sober as he moved toward her.

"I can't understand it," he said in a low voice. "I had told her previously I could never care for her in the manner a man would care for a girl. This morning I related to her part of the dream I had concerning you. I was not looking at her when I spoke, and when

I had finished and turned toward her, she was gone."

Luane reached for one of his hands. There was no denying her agitation.

"I know she cared a great deal for you, Bantan," she murmured. "But she seemed to understand that she could expect no reward in return. Oh, I hope she hasn't done anything foolish."

"I hope not," he fervently answered. "I would not like to feel that I was responsible in any way."

"My—The Great One asked about you this morning," Luane then said, changing the subject. "He would like to resume experiments with you as his subject, but I told him he must wait a few more days at least for you to recover from last night's ordeal. He was not pleased, though I'm sure he understands the wisdom of such delay."

Bantan remained silent.

A slight flush now mantled the nurse's cheeks.

"I suggested that you be placed under my direct care," she said. "As a nurse, I could more readily determine when you would be ready for another experiment." Her voice dropped to a mere whisper as she added: "Confidentially, I am hoping there will be no more."

The bronzed giant regarded Luane with a wondering expression upon his face.

"There would be real danger for my well being?" he questioned.

She nodded, unable to meet his intent eyes.

"If you wish," she then said, "we can walk about the grounds. You need more air and sunlight and should not be confined to your room as—as—though you were a prisoner."

"You would trust me not attempting to escape, Luane?" he asked curiously.

She nodded emphatically.

"I don't think you would forfeit the generosity that my—The Great One had intrusted in me, his nurse," she answered. Her eyes met his questionably. "Would you?"

"It would not be my nature to forfeit such a trust," he answered.

"Good!" she declared. "Come, let us go outside."

Bantan nodded. Without further delay they were on their way. Presently, outside in the bright sunlight, the bronzed giant filled his lungs to their utmost with the invigorating morning air and almost reluctantly exhaled. The girl at his side was aware of the glowing pleasure in his eyes.

"You dislike being confined to a room, don't you?" she murmured.

"Very much," he answered. "I have nearly always been free—except at various times when I was a prisoner. But always I managed to gain my freedom —one way or another."

Luane regarded him in silence.

"Tell me of some of those experiences, Bantan," she urged.

For the time being the bronzed giant dispelled worry of Loula's disappearance from his mind and related past experiences to the nurse. Almost unaware of their progress while he talked, in due time they reached the swimming pool. He had just finished telling of an early experience when he paused to look down at the inviting water of the pool. He sighed and his eyes seemed riveted upon it.

Luane instantly guessed at what he was thinking.

"You would like to swim, Bantan?" she asked.

He looked at her with hope unveiled in his eyes.

"If only The Great One wouldn't mind," he murmured.

She smiled understandingly.

"As your nurse," she said, "you may swim if you wish. It should be beneficial to you."

"Thank you, Luane," he breathed softly. "Would you care to join me?"

She shook her head, though a smile lingered upon her lips.

"I'd love to, Bantan," she said, "but not this morning—perhaps later in the day."

He nodded as he approached the edge of the pool. He smiled over a shoulder to the watching girl. Then he dived into the water, swimming beneath the surface nearly to the opposite end before smilingly appearing. He gave a flip of his head and his disarrayed hair seemed to go into place. He turned and with methodical overhand strokes cleaved the water with his glistening arms, exulting in its cool wetness laving his body. Intermittently he would flash a smile to the watching girl, then he would luxuriate more without ostentation, but merely revelling in the joy of swimming.

Back and forth Bantan swam for fifteen minutes, then he drew himself out of the pool where Luane was standing, smilingly watching him. Straightening before her, he smiled gratefully.

"Thank you for such kind permission," he said.

She nodded and the smile upon her lips lingered, but her eyes were filled with gentleness.

"Shall we continue walking?" she then asked.

He nodded, and without further hesitation they resumed their way exchanging pleasant conversation until they reached the end of the premises where the stone wall joined the castle at one edge of the cliff. Since they could go no farther, they turned about and returned the way they had come. When reaching the pool again, Bantan again fondly looked at the inviting water.

"If I may, Luane," he said, "I'll swim across and join you upon the other side."

The girl nodded.

The bronzed giant dived into the pool and swam leisurely beneath the surface, emerging at the other side. Drawing himself out of the water, he sat there until the nurse joined him.

"Feeling more refreshed?" she asked with a twinkle in her eyes.

"Very much," he answered, arising.

They resumed their way with more pleasant conversation. The bronzed giant seemed saddened now, realizing his outing was nearly over, and he was to return to his room and be prey to thoughts of what had happened to Loula. He also was aware that he should not feel so concerned over the servant girl, but in some unknown way he felt responsible for her.

Luane and Bantan parted after entering the front door. The young man again thanked the nurse for her consideration, and then he went to the elevator. The girl watched him in silence as he stepped aboard. She flashed a smile to which he responded in a like manner before the door closed and he operated the lever which would put the conveyance in action.

Once again in his room, Bantan went to one of the windows overlooking the shimmering water. Foremost in his mind was why Loula had left his room in the manner she did.

The time passed with noonday drawing near. And then to his alert ears he heard the soft shuffling of sandals in the corridor outside the door. Turning quickly, the bronzed giant's delicate nostrils twitched as a familiar pleasing aroma was wafted to him. Instantly he knew that Loula was all right. He felt very much relieved.

In another moment the servant girl appeared, and the inward suffering she had undergone was evident upon her features. Her eyes were deeply hollowed. She carried a tray of dishes heaped with food. Her sorrowful eyes met his surprised ones for a moment, but she did not smile as she then walked toward the table. By the time she had set the tray upon it, Bantan had quickly, but silently, crossed the room so that as she straightened, he confronted her. Though a smile was upon his lips a quizzical light was in his eyes.

"Loula, why did you leave so suddenly this morning?" he asked with gentleness.

The girl's mournful eyes looked up at him, and he noted moisture in their dark depths. She shook her head slowly and looked down at the floor.

Compassion for the girl's misery was apparent in Bantan's eyes. He reached out and placed a gentle hand upon her head.

"Come, Loula," he murmured, "please don't be angry with me because of the dream I told you about. I want so very much for you to be my friend."

"You have Luane for a friend now," she mumbled. "She is white. You have no need of me."

"It is true Luane is friendly to me," he admitted. "She doesn't wish to see me subjected to any more experiments than you do. She, too, is well aware of what might happen to me, even though she is The Great One's nurse, and her loyalty has never been questioned. Perhaps she realizes the experiments are wrong to the subject, especially when one's well being is concerned, and the fact I am a white man by birth. Please don't hate Luane because she is friendly to me. She has never been unfriendly toward you, has she?"

Loula's head remained lowered, but she shook her head in answer to his question.

The bronzed giant now removed his hand from the top of the girl's head and he cupped her chin gently. A little reluctantly she permitted him to tilt her head back so that her eyes met his. She tried to smile, but in her miserable state of mind she was unable to do so.

In compassion, Bantan kissed her upon the forehead, then he smiled fondly down upon her. He saw her lips puckered sensitively, hoping that his might touch hers. Instead, he placed his forefinger upon them for a moment. Then with a shrug, as though to dispel his sentimentality, he seated himself and reached for the glass of fruit juice. He drained it to the last drop.

A little hesitantly the servant girl drew near him, and though she stood at his side wordlessly, the bronzed giant was aware of her proximity. Presently she spoke in a low voice.

"When you started to tell me about your dream this morning, Bantan," she said, "what I had feared since you rescued Luane from the swimming pool had happened. You are realizing that you could care a great deal for her. I know I am a native girl whereas Luane is of white origin. I ran away and hid for a long time trying to decide what I should do. I even thought of taking my own life. But because I am afraid to die, I couldn't do so. I reasoned with myself that Luane was much more deserving of you than I, even—"

Bantan had been listening to Loula's recital while eating, and now at her hesitation, he looked questionably up at her.

"Even—what?" he asked.

The servant girl wet her lips nervously with the tip of her tongue.

"It is not for me to say," she said at last. "In due time she will tell you—at least, she should."

The bronzed giant shook his head while a whimsical smile came upon his features.

"Come, Loula," he chided her gently, "you are looking too far ahead. I admit I appreciate Luane's friendship very much, but there has been no talk of love between us."

Loula smiled secretively.

"That time will come, Bantan," she said, smiling understandingly. "As for me, I am going to try and take more interest in Hulo and Humo. They are more my kind."

"That would be best," he agreed. "I have wondered why you didn't do so before."

"Now I must go," the servant girl said. "I promise I won't act so foolish again. But for now, forgive me for being so impulsive—"

Loula inclined her head near his and pressed her lips to his cheek for a long moment, then with a happy little laugh left him. Bantan watched her as she passed from sight, and with a shake of his head resumed his meal.

Chapter XVIII

WHY?

Following his noonday meal, Bantan went to one of the windows overlooking the shimmering ocean, and remained there for nearly an hour when he heard the soft shuffling of sandals in the corridor. He was not wrong in surmising that Loula was returning for the tray and dishes. As the servant girl looked at him he wondered at the secretive smile possessing her features.

"Bantan, would you like to go swimming this afternoon?" she asked teasingly.

The bronzed giant regarded the servant girl tolerantly.

Loula smiled and nodded.

"I mean it," she insisted.

He approached her, shaking his head slightly.

"You've learned that I was permitted to swim in the pool," he said, as the servant girl was picking up the tray and dishes.

A smile of understanding came upon Loula's features.

"Luane told me to tell you she would be waiting for you at the swimming pool," she said.

Bantan's dark eyes glowed.

"You mean it, Loula?" he asked with eagerness.

The servant girl nodded.

"I'll go at once so as not to keep her waiting," he added, starting for the door.

"I'll go down the elevator with you, Bantan," the servant girl said, joining him.

At the ground floor the bronzed giant stepped from the elevator, and Loula followed him.

"Have a good time, Bantan," she bade him as they parted. There was a trace of moistness in her eyes as she spoke.

He smiled in reply and presently was hurrying across the short grass in the direction of the swimming pool. When he came nearer, he saw that Luane was swimming leisurely in the clear water. She noticed him at the same time. She smiled and waved a beckoning hand to him which was an invitation to join her.

With a nod and a smile the bronzed giant approached to the edge of the pool and dived into the clear water. He swam beneath the surface a short distance, calculating Luane's position, so that he rose at her side. A smile instantly possessed his features.

"How can I thank you for this opportunity, Luane?" he asked.

The girl's eyes were shining, and she was smiling.

"As your nurse, Bantan," she reminded him, "it is my duty to prescribe such exercise for your state of good health." Then, in a lower tone of voice, added: "But I don't wish you to get well too soon."

A warmness appeared in his eyes as her cheeks flushed a trifle.

"Of course," he agreed.

They swam about the pool for some little while, enjoying themselves immensely, then the girl suggested that he join her beneath the canopy at the edge of the pool. The bronzed giant had noticed that she wore the same bathing suit as before. When they were seated she took off her rubber bathing cap and allowed her

Bantan and Luane

lustrous hair to tumble about her smooth, sun-tanned shoulders. She noticed his admiring eyes and she smiled.

"Would you care to tell me *all* about your dream of last night?" she asked then. "As your nurse, I should know."

"You really would like me to tell you?" he questioned.

"Please do," she urged.

"As you wish," he acquiesced. "It will seem strange, Luane."

"As a nurse, nothing would seem strange," she answered.

He looked at her in wonderment. She smiled and nodded, and her now glowing eyes importuned him to tell her.

And so he related his dream, and while he spoke he noticed the reaction on her part. At first she clasped her hands together at her smooth knees. When he related his death battle with the cave bear, her clasped hands went to her bosom which was heaving tumultuously. His cheeks were flushed a trifle as he went on to tell her that the Luane of his dreams had instantly appealed to him because of his obligation to her. When he told of their return to his tribe as mates, he observed the sigh that escaped her lips.

At this juncture he paused, and looking more closely at Luane, saw that she was gazing at him as though spellbound. Now that he had ceased speaking, she shook her head a trifle and her dreamy eyes became normal.

"But that wasn't the end of the dream, Bantan?" she asked.

He shook his head.

"As time came to pass the Luane of my dream was to have a child," he added, a trifle embarrassed. "And then one day I went swimming in the ocean near our cave home, for even in my dream I enjoyed swimming very much. I swam far from shore in my happiness, and then I was attacked by a monster of the deep. Had I not been so far from shore I might have saved myself. As it was," he concluded, shaking his head, "I was too far away. The sea monster devoured me. My last conscious thoughts were of my mate. That was why I was uttering her name when I woke."

Luane was silent for a short while. Her chin now rested upon her clenched hands and her thoughts seemed far away. As he looked at her Bantan saw that her eyes were a trifle misty. Noticing his attention, the girl shook her head a trifle and a soft smile touched her lips.

"Many dreams have a way of ending in tragedy," she said musingly. "Thank goodness it was only a dream, for you are very much alive and we can be thankful for that."

A serious expression now came over the bronzed giant.

"Luane," he said.

She looked up at him with questioning eyes.

"You know a great deal about me," he said in a low voice.

"Yes, so very much," she agreed, nodding. She was smiling with a dreamy luminance in her gray eyes.

"But I don't know very much about you." His protest was mild, but inferring.

"Does it matter too much, Bantan?" she asked. "You know me as I am. Isn't that sufficient?"

"I would like to know all about you," he declared.

"You and I are the only two persons, outside of The Great One, who are of white origin upon this island. I would like to know where you came from, and how long you have been in his employ as a nurse; how you came to be with him; who he is. There are so many other things—"

Leona stared across the pool and her eyes now seemed vacuous.

"It seems," she answered in a low voice, "that I have always wanted to be a nurse. From the time I was a very young girl I wanted to tend to growing things like plants, small animals, and human beings. As time came to pass I became a nurse. Did you ever hear of a city known as Boston, which is in the eastern part of the United States of America?"

The bronzed giant shook his head.

"I was born in a city called New York, which is on the east coast of the United States of America," he said. Then a slow smile lighted his features. "That makes us both Americans," he added.

She nodded in agreement.

"Boston is where I was born and trained to be a nurse," she added. "Later, I joined my—The Great One. For some reason his early experiments appealed to me. I—I had no near relatives, so I lived and worked with him. Shortly afterwards I learned what The Great One's life goal really was, and though I became afraid, I could not bring myself to leave him. I became as fascinated as he in his discoveries. However, when matters became difficult with other members of his profession, we were compelled to move. How my—The Great One ever learned of the Mandoes Island I don't know; but we came here, and here we are today. Sometimes it seems like an eternity has come and gone." With her peroration the girl sighed deeply.

Bantan was silent. For some inexplicable reason he felt Luane had only told him a part of what he really wanted to know, but he was too considerate at the moment to press her for further details.

She seemed to be in deep meditation when she had finished speaking—as though she were reviewing in detail what she had related to him. Long moments of silence passed before at last the girl closed her eyes tightly, and then a slight shake of her head seemingly dispelled whatever weighed upon her thoughts. As her eyes again opened, she smiled as she turned to the silent man at her side. She put her bathing cap on, carefully tucking her hair beneath the band.

"Let's swim some more, Bantan," she suggested. "Thinking of the past is depressing—and upon a beautiful afternoon as this we mustn't feel depressed."

"Of course not, Luane," he agreed, arising to his feet.

In another moment the girl was standing alongside him. Nodding to him, she dived into the inviting pool. At the next instant he followed. Once again they swam leisurely in the refreshing water. Bantan was well aware the girl was an excellent swimmer, and the fact that she was bronzed was an indication that she must have passed many hours swimming and sunning herself.

When they returned to the edge of the pool and were seated again after some twenty minutes had passed, Bantan noticed how smooth Luane's suntanned skin was. There was no trace whatever of finely meshed wrinkles upon it. With the recollection of the difference in Loula's skin, upon a sudden impulse he spoke to her.

"Luane, may I ask you something?" he asked.

She looked up at him in surprise.

"Of course, Bantan," she answered.

"Can you tell me why Loula's skin is covered with finely meshed wrinkles?" he questioned. "Were certain experiments performed upon her the reason?"

The girl regarded him soberly for a moment and he was aware of the dulling luster in her eyes.

"Why,—er, yes, that explains it," she said with a short laugh. "Repeated experiments of a certain nature affects the skin that way."

He shook his head a trifle and hesitated to speak further. Noticing this reluctance on his part, Luane nodded, her eyes importuning him to say what he hesitated to.

"Something tells me, Luane," he said after a moment's hesitation, "that the twin brothers, and perhaps Loula as well, are of greater age than they appear."

The girl's brows lifted a trifle in surprise at this unusual statement.

"What makes you think that?" she asked curiously.

"Tell me," he added, "has The Great One managed through his machine to prolong life beyond what Nature intended?"

Watching her closely for a reaction to his question, Bantan noticed that her eyes appeared startled for a brief instant; but she quickly resumed her normal poise. She laughed lightly.

"Why do you ask that?" she questioned, again assuming curiosity.

"When Hulo and Humo escorted me to the castle

from the Mandoes village," he said, "both were almost exhausted from the climb, whereas I was hardly breathing faster. They do not appear to be much older than I."

Luane regarded him for a long moment, and Bantan noticed a certain tenseness about her. Then she laughed again, but he felt it lacked the true ring of sincerity.

"Both Hulo and Humo recently recovered from a touch of fever, and the day they brought you from the village was the second time they made the trip," she explained. "That accounts for their seeming exhaustion. As for you, you were, and are, a perfect specimen of health—physically and mentally."

The bronzed giant then smiled sheepishly and shook his head in apparent contrition.

"Forgive me, Luane," he begged. "Perhaps the experiments have affected me more than I realized."

The girl smiled and placed a hand upon the back of one of his resting upon his knee. She seemed more at ease now.

"As your nurse," she said, "I think you should return to your room and rest awhile. You have not completely recovered from the effects of the two experiments last night."

He smiled and upon an impulse covered her hand with his other for a moment.

"You know what is best," he agreed.

Both arose to their feet. Without asking her permission, Bantan walked with the girl to the door of her quarters and there bowed as she entered.

"When am I going to see you again, Luane?" he asked, as she turned about and regarded him with steady eyes.

She smiled warmly and appeared to debate.

"As your nurse," she answered, "perhaps I shall check on you before you retire."

"Thank you for a pleasant afternoon," he said. "And thank you for the privilege of sharing your swimming pool."

"You were welcome," was her reply.

He turned then and departed.

Before closing the door, the girl watched the bronzed giant with a quizzical look in her gray eyes, but she could not deny the deep admiration she felt for him.

Back in his room, Bantan lay upon the bed, and with hands clasped beneath his head, stared unseeingly at the ceiling. Whatever the thoughts that passed through his mind who might guess?

In due time he heard the soft shuffling of sandaled feet, and he knew Loula was bringing his evening meal. He arose to a seated position as the servant girl entered with a tray and dishes of food. She was smiling in a teasing manner.

"Enjoy your swim, Bantan?" she asked, going to the table and placing the tray upon it.

He smiled as he arose and seated himself. Then looking up at Loula, his steady eyes held hers for a long moment.

"Very much," he answered. "Luane is a very good swimmer and very interesting to talk with."

"Naturally, since you both are of white origin," the servant girl remarked, "you would have much in common."

He nodded agreeably, and reaching for the glass of fruit juice, drained it to the last drop.

"We had much to talk about, Loula," he said, placing the glass upon the table. He looked at the servant girl for a reaction to what he was going to say.

"She is so young and beautiful that I am afraid I am falling beneath the spell of her charms."

He saw the twinge of bitterness that instantly flashed in the servant girl's dark eyes for a brief second, and now he realized that she was envious of the nurse. At the next moment she was regarding Bantan with a mocking smile to masquerade her true feelings.

"It was a happy day for her when you came to this island," she declared. "At long last she may have reason to feel she will not remain unmated. Nothing troubles a girl as much as that," she added with an unusual smirk. "For that reason I am going to take much interest in Hulo and Humo from now on. Perhaps I do not wish to remain an old maid."

A tolerant smile touched the bronzed giant's lips.

"Did you tend them when they recently had a touch of fever?" he asked. "That would have been an excellent time to study them."

" 'A touch of fever'!" the servant girl scoffed. "As long as I have known Hulo and Humo they haven't had a sick day." She regarded him curiously now. "Perhaps it is you who has a touch of fever—love fever."

His smile remained tolerant.

"Perhaps I have," he agreed, and then he proceeded to partake of his evening meal.

Loula regarded Bantan in silence for a long moment, then a mischievous smile touched her lips. She drew near him and inclined her face near his.

"Halo and Humo may be wonderful," she sighed. "I suppose I'll have to content myself with one or the other. But how I wish I had been born of white parents, for then perhaps you might have learned to care for me."

Bantan paused in his eating to look up at her with the appearance of being flattered.

"Perhaps I would, Loula," he agreed. "You are attractive, and I'm sure you would make a man a fine mate."

"An unmated girl often hopes the man she loves will be the father of her unborn children, Bantan," she murmured. "If I had the choice, you would be their father."

As she spoke, a softness appeared in the servant girl's eyes, and before he could prevent she pressed her lips to his cheek for a moment, then quickly left him. At the doorway she paused to flash him a smile, which he returned, and then she was gone.

Then did Bantan's smile leave his lips and his features became sober. His eyes appeared to be staring unseeingly at the doorway. He slowly nodded in understanding at the knowledge Loula had unknowingly provided him; but the question that troubled him was why Luane had lied when she said Hulo and Humo had recently recovered from a touch of fever to explain their exhaustion.

When one has recently acquired a friend—and the bronzed giant wanted to feel that the nurse was a true friend—why should she deviate from the truth in reply to a question that he had asked in good faith? He was convinced there was a reason, but how to solve it satisfactorily was something else. He finished his meal in silence and then went to one of the windows, where he remained until the servant girl returned for the tray and the dishes.

Bantan noticed that she appeared quiet, though she did smile and greet him when she entered the room. He sought to engage her in conversation, but Loula explained that she could not remain even a few moments because she had much work to perform. When she departed, he resumed his attention upon the shimmering water beyond the window.

In deep reflection, the bronzed giant was aware the day had been a near perfect one except for the one baffling question:

Why had Luane deviated from the truth?

CHAPTER XIX

AMAR'S PUNISHMENT

The hours passed as Bantan remained at the window. Looking down at the waves slapping against the cliff, he noticed that the tide was coming in, and within an hour should be at its maximum height. As though hypnotized, he watched the undulating waves develop some distance beyond as they rose and fell. Sometimes he watched one from the time of its inception to its final annihilation in foam as it slapped against the cliff far below.

Tiring of this at length, he watched the late afternoon change to the quick-falling dusk, and presently, when darkness enveloped the world beneath, stars began to appear in the heaven. Constantly in his mind as he visualized Luane's lovely features the one question —WHY? was before him.

She had demonstrated unquestioned friendship in his behalf, and while the questions he had asked had no personal bearing, either to her or himself, he was somewhat dismayed that she had deviated in answering them. Since he was beginning to realize his feeling for her was deeper than mere friendship, he had hoped there would be no rift within the lute. The fact that she was of white origin, as he was, gave his conscience no reason to upbraid him.

In due reverence to Nao, his former Amo Island sweetheart, whom he had buried upon the atoll, he realized he could not mourn her indefinitely. He was sure if she could communicate with him from that world beyond the living that she would send her blessings, for though she had loved him dearly, as he had her in life, in death one could not wish the happiness of the living to go unfulfilled.

Darkness had settled upon the world beneath for several hours when Bantan aroused himself from his reveries. Crossing the room to where he knew the wall switch was located, he snapped it on. He stood looking at the many lights in the chandelier suspended from the ceiling as though in amazement at man's ingenuity of being able to provide artificial light upon such an isolated island as was Mandoes. He could not question that The Great One had been properly named, for indeed he seemed capable of performing miracles. Even now as he considered the scientist, mad though he might be, only a brilliant man was capable of creating a machine which could revivify long-dormant brain cells, and be able to record upon film what long-dead eyes had witnessed in reality.

While he stood there thinking thusly, to his keen ears came the sound of quick-moving sandaled feet in the corridor beyond the doorway. He knew at once they were not Loula's, for she walked with a shuffling gait. The footsteps that he heard could be of only one person, and that was Luane. He had nearly forgotten during his reveries that she had promised to check on him before he retired.

As he stood there by the wall switch, he was not surprised as the nurse presently entered, but he was somewhat concerned by the evident agitation which seemed to possess her lovely features. Though her eyes appeared troubled she managed to smile to him. Her bosom heaved tumultuously as she approached him,

and her hands were clasped, but her fingers could not
be still.

"What troubles you, Luane?" he was quick to ask
as he moved toward her.

"My—The Great One and I have been discussing
you, Bantan," she said, almost pantingly. "He wants
very much to use you as a subject again this very
evening for another experiment. I tried to reason with
him that you were not ready for another ordeal so
soon. He told me he watched us this afternoon as we
swam in the pool, and he said nothing seemed wrong
with you."

As they now confronted each other, her worried
eyes were misty, and in their depths he could read her
fear for his state of well being. Bantan clasped her two
cold hands in his large, warm ones and he pressed
them gently in the hope of calming her fears. He smiled
assuringly.

"Perhaps it will be all right if I am a subject for another experiment, Luane," he said calmly. "I am
strong—and have no fear."

Tears appeared in her eyes.

"No, Bantan," she moaned protestingly. "As a
nurse, I am much too familiar with past experiments of
such a nature." Her tearful eyes revealed her inner-
most concern for his welfare. "No, Bantan," she
whispered, "I don't want anything to happen to you
now—now—that—"

"But I am not afraid," he insisted. "Having survived the past experiments—"

"No, Bantan," she murmured with a deep sigh,
"you mustn't undergo another so soon. I know of what
I am speaking. I know the dangers that you are sub-

ject to. I can't—I—I won't have anything happen to you."

So great the emotional stress Luane was under, she felt the strength drain from her legs, and she would have collapsed to the floor in a swoon. But Bantan was alert to the weakness that overcame the girl. He instantly released her hands. One of his arms went about her waist, supporting her, while the other went about the back of her knees. Lifting the unconscious nurse in his strong arms, he carried her to the bed where he gently laid her down. He went down upon his knees at the bedside, and with one hand gently caressed her brow.

The girl's breathing was almost convulsive, so greatly her bosom heaved. Her lovely features twitched to the stress of the inner emotion that coursed through her. Her milk-white eyelids fringed with dark lashes remained closed. Now her lips parted a trifle and they moved though no sound was to be heard.

"Luane! Luane!" he softly called to her. "Everything will be all right. Open your eyes."

Unconscious though she was, physically, her subconscious mind was fully awake. Now her lips moved again, and though she spoke no words, he seemingly could read what she was trying to say. She appeared to gasp, then as though some horrible thought within her was before the screen of her recollection, he saw tears oozing from beneath her closed lids. Her mouth opened now and he noticed a tremor pulse through her.

"No! No!" she was muttering in a plaintive voice. "I won't have anything happen to Bantan! I love him more than life itself. If anything should happen to him I would want to die. For the first time in my life I am in love with a man. Please, God, I know I have not prayed to You for a long, long time; but, I beg of You, don't let anything happen to the man I love with my whole heart and soul. It seems all my life I have waited for such a man to come to me. Please, God, don't let anything happen to him now."

Hearing the girl's confession was somewhat sacrilegious of him; but the bronzed giant had no choice in the matter. He closed his eyes tightly as he realized what she was saying concerned him. Moments passed unheedingly.

Now the girl's breathing seemed to change and appeared more normal. Her eyes opened, her lids fluttering for a moment until she oriented herself to her surroundings. She looked upon Bantan's bowed head as she realized what had happened to her. She sat up quickly, so that for an instant she was dizzy. She shook her head, clearing it.

"Bantan," she said.

He lifted his head and a gentle smile touched his lips. "You are all right now, Luane?" he asked.

"I fainted," she admitted. She drew a hand across her forehead, then rubbed the moisture from the corners of her eyes. She laughed lightly. "It's been a long time since I fainted," she confessed.

"You are all right now?" he asked solicitously.

"Of course," she said assuringly. She swung her sandaled feet from the bed to the floor and faced him. Her eyes were warm and filled with deep feeling.

It was with some difficulty Bantan could look directly at her, having heard her confession while unconscious without revealing something of this knowledge. He arose from his knees, and reaching for a chair near the table, moved it so that as he seated himself he faced her. He maintained a sober expression.

Meanwhile, Luane had recollected what she had been saying before she had swooned. Once more her features became serious and her worried eyes misty.

"Bantan, I remember what I had been saying," she said in a low voice. "You mustn't undergo another experiment tonight—or, ever. You have been fortunate thus far, but each time increases the danger to your well being."

"But, if The Great One insists, Luane," he reminded her, "I have no choice in the matter, have I?"

Luane slowly shook her head, and her eyes closed for a long moment, as though she were striving to form a momentous decision.

The bronzed giant reached for one of her hands and pressed it gently in his, seemingly arousing the girl to the present. Her eyes opened then, and a determined expression came upon her face.

"Bantan, I could help you to escape," she whispered. "You would take me with you?"

He stared at her unbelievingly.

"You mean it?" he asked.

She nodded decisively.

He appeared in deep thought. This plan Luane had evolved was not as he would have it. First of all, there was his score with Amar to be settled. He did not forget that poor Nao deserved that much consideration.

"But, what of Amar?" he questioned. "He is the reason in the first place that I came to this island. If I left without settling my scores with him I would forever have that thought in my mind. I would be unhappy."

Luane's eyes were strange to look at. It was as

though she was daring to be disobedient to The Great One. Her lips drew in a thin line.

"Suppose I told you the one called Amar is no longer worthy of your consideration?" she asked. "The experiments that he underwent has made his mind like a child's. Your conscience would be at ease—as far as he was concerned."

"Would you lead me to where he is confined?" he said. "I would like once more to see him."

The girl arose to her feet and reached for one of his hands.

"Come, I will lead you to the cell where he is confined."

Bantan arose and followed the nurse into the corridor to the elevator. In a few moments they were descending. Luane had nothing to say, and the bronzed giant respected her silence. The elevator came to a stop at the same level as the laboratory. Opening the door, the girl stepped outside in the dimly lit corridor and the young man followed her.

As they approached the closed door of the laboratory, Luane touched the arm of her companion, bringing him to a halt She pressed a hand to her lips, cautioning him not to speak. She then lay hand upon the knob of the closed door, and turning it, pressed gently upon it. As the door opened a few inches, she was satisfied to know the laboratory was in total darkness. She closed the door softly, and with an assuring smile, indicated they would resume their way.

A short distance farther, Luane paused at the barred opening of a door upon the same side as the laboratory. A wall switch at the side of the door frame was pressed, and the interior was lighted by a number of bulbs in a chandelier suspended from the ceiling.

Glancing through the barred opening, she then turned to Bantan.

"Look," she said.

The bronzed giant drew near, as the girl stepped to one side, and he looked through the barred opening. He saw three crude bunks in the small cell some ten feet square, and upon them reposed three natives, sleeping. One of them lay facing the door while the other two were lying in an opposite direction.

As Bantan looked at the uncovered features of the sleeper facing him, he was aware of a surging anger within him. But the longer he studied the native's features, he was finally convinced that he was not Amar. He appeared much older than the Amo Island prince —perhaps twice his age. He realized then that perhaps the sleeper was Amar's father, for the features bore a marked resemblance except that this native's face and neck were wrinkled somewhat, and the lines of his body were of an older man.

He then peered at the other two sleepers, and as chance would have it, perhaps disturbed by the light of the many bulbs overhead, both turned over at that moment with low moans so that they faced the door of the cell. The watcher at the barred opening studied their features for a long moment, but at last he shook his head. Amar was not among these three sleepers. He turned to the girl at his side.

"There should be one more," he said. "Four came from Amo Island."

Luane snapped off the light switch, then she nodded and indicated another door at the opposite side of the corridor at the extreme end.

"That must be the cell," she said.

In a few moments they confronted the door; this,

too, had a barred opening. The interior of the cell was
in total darkness. The nurse pressed a wall switch and
the cell was illuminated. She looked meaningly at the
barred opening and indicated for Bantan to look
through.

The cell was the same size as the other. Opposite
and facing him was a crude bunk upon which reposed a
native, naked except for a loin cloth, apparently asleep.
For long moments the bronzed giant studied the recumbent form, trying to identify him as his hated enemy
and the one he had vowed to kill. Since the sleeper's
forearm was across his eyes, it was difficult to determine his identity. Now he was stirring, as though the
many lighted bulbs in the chandelier suspended from
the ceiling were penetrating his closed lids.

He removed his arm from his features and he
blinked a number of times. Aware of the strange lights
overhead, he finally opened his eyes and looked up at
them in abject wonder. Slowly he arose from the bunk,
and facing the barred opening in the door, resumed
his attention upon the amazing lights.

Studying him carefully, Bantan felt a surge of hatred course through him, almost chilling him to the mar-
row of his bones.

"Amar!" The single word, filled with virulence, escaped his lips.

At his side Luane fairly shuddered.

The unkempt figure seemingly started at hearing the
voice speak his name, though it is doubtful that he
recognized it. He lowered his head and his vacuous
eyes stared unseeingly at the barred opening of the
door. If he saw Bantan's seemingly frozen features
and blazing eyes he gave no indication that he recognized him.

"Amar!" Again the single word with virulence escaped the bronzed giant's lips.

The Amo Island prince merely stared with vacuous eyes at Bantan's framed features, and though he unquestionably saw him, there was no recognition in his eyes. His lower jaw became lax, and as his mouth opened, his tongue now protruded.

A shudder wracked the bronzed giant's frame, and his eyes closed for long moments. He knew at that moment that Amar had been reduced to the status of a mentally deficient creature. No greater punishment could possibly have been conceived in due payment for the wrongs he had perpetrated against Bantan and his deceased sweetheart. He realized also that death would be a blessing to that pitiful-looking, unknowing nonentity.

He turned from the opening, shaking his head.

Luane snapped off the lights, and spoke to her companion in a hushed voice.

"Now you can see what The Great One's machine can do to a subject," she said in low, trembling tones. "Do you wonder that I am worried about you? Do you think I would want to see you reduced to such a pitiful condition?"

From within the cell unintelligible ejaculations were now to be heard. It was Amar, apparently protesting because the shining lights in the chandelier had been snapped off. He had never seen the many bulbs lighted before, and in his demented condition he had been attracted by them.

His babbling voice raised to a falsetto and then his gibberishness fell to a whimpering. Long-drawn wails of disappointment were then emitted from his throat to be followed by low, choking sobs of despair. This continued without surcease.

Bantan again shuddered and shook his head. He felt Luane's hand rest upon his arm.

"Come," she said, "let's leave this cell of horror."

The wailing and moans seemingly followed them as, without protest, the bronzed giant followed the girl along the corridor back to the elevator. As the conveyance was moving upward, Luane whispered to her companion.

"Isn't that a pitiful case?" she asked.

He merely shook his head in answer. He was acutely aware of a hollow sensation within him after witnessing to what a pitiful state Amar had been reduced through horrible experiments in the laboratory. While Bantan knew death would have been a better fate for his enemy, he felt no compunction for having seen the Amo Island prince. It was the thought that he himself might have been similarly reduced to such a state that resulted in a cold chill racing the length of his spine. Without question he knew now that he must undergo no more experiments.

Presently the elevator came to a stop at the top floor, and Luane and the bronzed giant stepped from it. As they walked to the room Bantan had been assigned, the girl was looking at him sadly; but until they had entered the room which was lighted as they had left it, no further speech was exchanged.

CHAPTER XX

UNEXPECTED HAPPENINGS

Preoccupied with his thoughts, Bantan paused in the center of his room and looked at Luane in silent wonder. She moved around so that she faced him.

"Did you ever see such a horrible sight as Amar?" she asked. "And to think that he was as sane and normal as any one before being experimented upon."

The bronzed giant merely stared at the nurse, but he could find no words to utter. He merely shook his head slowly.

"Can you not understand now, Bantan," she said, "why I cannot see you subjected to another accursed experiment?"

The bronzed giant now slowly nodded in an effort to dispel the sight that he had witnessed from his memory.

"How many experiments did Amar undergo?" he asked then.

"Only two," was the reply. "Something must have gone wrong during the second experiment, for he was all right after the first."

Bantan knew he had undergone twice that many, and until now he felt perfectly normal. Last night, it was true, his mind had felt near to exhaustion. He wondered if the prehistoric dream he had experienced was the first indication of a breaking down of his sanity. He met the girl's eyes squarely, and she noticed how very bitter his were.

"The Great One has no mercy, Luane," he declared. "He is not sane to subject human beings to his wild experiments. He should not be permitted to continue."

Sudden fright appeared in the girl's eyes and her hands pressed her bosom tightly.

"You mustn't think of trying to kill him!" she moaned. "I'm sure if there is a just God He will attend to him in due time and mete to him the punishment he deserves."

The bronzed giant's hands clenched and unclenched and his features were strained. The girl noticed the bitterness in his dark eyes began to lessen.

"Before you showed me Amar," he said remindingly, "you were speaking of escaping—"

"Yes, Bantan—if that is possible," she agreed with wide eyes.

"I had been planning since the first day I was brought here," he mused, "that I must find a way to escape after I had settled my scores with Amar. Now, that doesn't matter. He is suffering enough for the wrongs he has committed."

"How—how had you been planning such a means of escape?" she asked.

"If necessary, I would dive from the window into the water far below," he answered. "I'm sure I could successfully do so."

"But I wouldn't be able to," she demurred.

"Yes, I know," he agreed. "I have been hoping my canoe is still where I hid it. If so, I could easily find it. Since it is four days distance to Marja Island, that would mean sufficient provisions must be stored in the canoe for such a trip, for one cannot paddle four days without food and water."

"Yes, I understand," Luane murmured.

The bronzed giant now recollected Loula's request to accompany him in the event he made his escape from the castle and Mandoes Island.

"Poor Loula wanted to escape with me," he said in a low voice. "I have felt pity for her. She would find happiness upon Marja."

The girl nodded her head.

"Even that might be arranged," she agreed. "I've known she has been unhappy here for a long while."

Bantan appeared to be in deep thought.

"Do you feel that tonight would be the time to make the attempt, Luane?" he asked at length.

"It would have to be tonight, Bantan," she declared. "I don't believe I can persuade my—The Great One to delay further experiments upon you much longer."

"Then perhaps it would be best that you went to Loula's quarters and inform her what we plan to do," he suggested. "I'll wait here for you." As a sudden thought came to him, he asked: "Where was The Great One when you last saw him?"

"At the evening meal we were in his quarters when we talked of you," the nurse explained. "He was not pleased, as I've told you, when I begged him to wait a few more days before making you undergo another experiment. Perhaps he is still there. When I go for Loula, I'll check on his whereabouts to make sure."

"That would be best," Bantan said with a nod. "If all goes well, by morning we should be far from Mandoes Island—and The Great One."

Luane paused before leaving. She reached for his hands and clasped them tightly in hers for long moments. Her intent eyes studied his, searching for an indication of his true feeling for her that she hoped to see.

"You must know why I am doing this for you, Bantan," she murmured.

He nodded slowly as an understanding smile touched his lips.

"And, Luane," he murmured, "know that I am beginning to feel the same way toward you."

The girl's breath came in muffled gasps. She released his hands and flung her arms about his neck, pressing close to him, as her lips sought his. Instantly his arms were about her as well, and their lips clung for long moments. As they drew apart, Luane's gray eyes mirrored the depths of her love for him.

"Thank you, my beloved," she murmured. "Know that you are the first man I have ever kissed. It was worth waiting for. That first night you were brought to the laboratory I looked upon you with awakening womanhood," she added in a low voice. "The second time you came I knew I was falling in love with you. And when you rescued me from the swimming pool my life was yours. Oh, Bantan, you'll never realize how much love I will have for you when we are safely away from this wicked island." She appeared to hesitate before resuming: "There is something I want you to know. I hope you will not be angry with me when I tell you."

"I could never be angry with you, Luane," he assured her.

"But you may think it strange of me for having done what I did," she demurred.

He regarded her in silence for a moment.

"If you do not wish to tell me—"

"I must tell you," she declared.

And then she told how she had administered a drug on that day she came to his room to check him, as a nurse, for the purpose of learning if he were in love with Loula, and of his past life as well. While she spoke in hesitating tones that revealed her contrition, he smiled with gentleness.

"But why, Luane?" he questioned. "In time I would have told you everything."

Her cheeks were flushed and her luminous eyes revealed her shame.

"I couldn't wait, Bantan," she replied in a low voice. "It seems that I had to know before I found myself hopelessly in love with you. You'll forgive me?"

The bronzed giant merely smiled and nodded.

Her shining eyes were filled with joy.

"You are the perfect man I have waited for all my life!" she exclaimed with rapture.

Once again her lips sought his and they clung together for what seemed an interminable time. When at last they drew apart their hearts were beating fast, with cheeks flushed, and eyes glowing warmly.

"I'll hurry on my way now," she said; "and I'll hope that everything goes well. It must! It must!"

With mist in her eyes and a sweet smile upon her lips, the girl turned and left him. Watching Luane leave the room, as though in a trance Bantan shook his head, hardly able to believe unexpected events had been happening so rapidly.

Knowing their love had been declared, he wondered in a vague way if she was the one Destiny had selected at last to be his mate. With the thought of Wanya, his foster sister, and Lori, the self-renounced Ono Island princess awaiting his return, he experienced a twinge of regret, knowing how disappointed they would be when he returned with Luane as his choice for a mate.

But, that was thinking of the future, when the immediate present was what concerned him most of all. Furthermore, the escape from the castle had not yet been made, and the thought of the four days and nights in a canoe must still be considered. Preoccupied as he was, Bantan heard the sound of sandaled feet in the vicinity of the doorway.

Turning about quickly, he saw Hulo and Humo entering the room. There was no smile of greeting upon their stoic faces. Grim and determined they were. At once the bronzed giant realized they were acting upon orders that had been given them, and they were here to execute them. He subsequently suspected that The Great One was determined upon further experiments that evening despite Luane's endeavors to dissuade him.

Without a word Bantan moved in the direction of the window he knew to be the most favorable in the event he was compelled to leap to safety. As he moved, the twin brothers increased their stride without uttering a word, but their very intention ascertained that the bronzed giant would have gotten nowhere were he to try and reason with them. He entertained no ill feeling toward them, knowing they were merely acting upon orders from The Great One. It was possible they suspected what he threatened, and they doubted he would be courageous enough to attempt such a foolhardy deed. But then, they did not know the bronzed giant's constitution as he knew himself, and what he was capable of attempting when the exigency demanded.

In a flash Bantan leaped to the unbarred window, grasping the frame upon each side. He smiled over a shoulder at Hulo and Humo. At the next moment they leaped for him, hoping to imprison his legs. It was then

Bantan filled his lungs with air and sprang, seemingly diving far outward into darkened space!

After the initial outward force of his leap was expended and he was dropping plummet-like, gathering speed, the swift rush of air whistled in Bantan's ears as he directed his body in its downward plunge. Even in the pitch darkness he had calculated almost with precision so that he struck the surface at a perfect slant. His outstretched arms, hands, and fingers were tensed and cleaved the water in a perfect dive. The shock was terrific, naturally, but cushioned as his skull was with a mop of thick hair, he did not lose consciousness, though the impact did result in a momentary flash of dizziness as his perfect body cut through the water with blinding speed. His sandals were torn from his feet.

Down, down, down he went into the cold depths. When at last he felt the time had come to curve his hands he instinctively did so and checked the downward plunge of his body. At once it commenced to level off. He had no means of knowing how far he had descended beneath the surface, for though his eyes were now opened, he could distinguish nothing in the inky darkness of the water at night. But it was well that he altered his course when he did, for his kicking feet gently scuffed against the sandy bottom. He was grateful there had been no rocks in this particular spot, otherwise he might have suffered serious injury.

Now his strong arms and powerful legs were pulling and thrusting as he sought to reach the surface. His lungs were in need of renewed air. Gradually he released the foul air through his nostrils while he surged upward, and at the moment his lungs were depleted, it was then that his head bobbed above the sur-

face and his body followed clear to the waist, so swiftly
he had been rising.

Shaking his head, so that the water pressing against
his ear drums was dislodged, and his hair was swept
out of his eyes, he paused to cast a glimpse high up at
the castle window from which he had negotiated his
aerial dive. He recognized the window from which he
had sprung because of the light in the room. There,
in silhouette, he could see two shadowed faces looking
down, but in the darkness they could expect to see
nothing. Since there was no moon and the surface of
the water was very dark, he entertained no fear of discovery.

The swimmer required only a few moments to orient
himself as to the direction he must swim to reach shore
in safety. To his left was the shortest distance, and
realizing he was unarmed recalled to memory a warrior of the village had relieved him of his trusty steel
dagger when he had been brought there as a captive.

While he swam with methodical strokes toward the
shore where he hoped it would be possible to clamber
up on dry land, at the present he was compelled to
keep a respectable distance for fear of a possible strong
undertow that might suck him helplessly toward the
cliff and dash him unmercifully against the rocky bar-
rier upon which the castle rested at its peak. While the
cliff extended perhaps a mile from where he was, he
experienced no difficulty maintaining a safe distance.

The passing minutes accustomed his eyes to the
darkened water surrounding him so that gradually he
could distinguish the dark mass of land upon his right,
also that the castle was silhouetted against the star-
shot sky above. The sound of the waves slapping

against the rocks also helped to ascertain his distance being of comparative safety.

Unarmed as he was, he realized he would be easy prey for a shark, were one about; but the passing minutes increased his confidence that they instinctively did not lurk this close to the rocky shore for fear of being caught in a powerful undertow and bashed to death.

While swimming on his prescribed course Bantan's ears were alert for the sound of possible voices from the castle grounds, but strain his auditory organs as he did, he heard nothing. There was the possibility that the twin brothers believed he had chosen certain death rather than undergo another accursed experiment; and this information they brought The Great One when they returned to relate how the prisoner had escaped them. What The Great One might think was a matter of conjecture.

Seemingly tireless, the swimmer's powerful arms drew him through the cool water while his sturdy legs thrust with regularity while swimming parallel with the shoreline. The sound of waves slapping against the rocks kept him informed of conditions ashore. His ears were keenly listening for the swishing sound of the surf laving a beach, however small, for then he might go ashore with reasonable safety without being dashed against rocks.

Ahead, that welcoming sound was presently heard, and easing his powerful strokes and kicking thrusts, he allowed the waves to carry him more gently while he rested. A gentle movement of his hands sufficed to keep his head above water. In the darkness to his rear he could see the walled castle silhouetted against the starry sky. It must be all of a mile distant from where he was presently drifting shoreward.

Strangely now, for the first time since his escape from the castle, Bantan gave thought of Luane and Loula. What had happened to them, meanwhile? Was there a possibility that The Great One might have reason to distrust his nurse, and as a result inflict upon her some diabolical punishment that only his maniacal brain might conceive? With this horrible thought he knew he must in some way again manage to gain access to the walled castle, and if at all possible, effect the rescue of the nurse and the servant girl.

First, however, he must ascertain that his cached canoe had been undisturbed and was still procurable, for there was always the possible detection of the water craft by roving village warriors. There also was the recollection that Mauria and Tamur knew of its location. He must move it nearer to the castle for convenience, and see that it was provisioned against the time it would be needed. It was his wish that there would be no violence, for he had no reason to dislike the twin brothers; and The Great One, though he deserved to die, Bantan did not wish to strike down an elderly man, however wicked he was.

These thoughts passed in review in his mind as the gentle waves at last deposited him upon the small, circular, sandy beach. Finding the bottom with his feet, the swimmer walked slowly from the water. His eyes were intent upon the ground that he trod, for he had no desire to strike his unprotected toes against possible rocks.

After covering about fifteen feet he presently was standing at the base of the declining cliff. Looking up at its summit, silhouetted by the starry heaven, he estimated the distance to its top was some forty to fifty feet. An investigation revealed the only way from this small beach was to mount the face of the cliff.

In the darkness it was no simple task finding hand and footholds, but nevertheless he started to climb the almost perpendicular wall. More through feel than his ability to see he drew himself slowly upward. He would pause every few minutes to rest his bruised finger tips and his tender toes, for the holds that he found were sometimes sharp.

When he had reached about halfway to the top he came upon a natural cavern, perhaps caused by wind and rain and naturally soft formation in the mass of rock. He drew himself carefully upon the ledge and with groping hands and straining his eyes to their utmost he determined the cavern was some four feet in height and about six in width. How far it extended into the cliff he must investigate, for already he was planning the possibility that this could be a safe place of refuge until the time he procured his canoe and provisioned it for readiness to coincide with his attempted rescue of Luane and Loula from the castle.

At the next moment with such suddenness it happened, Bantan almost lost his balance upon the cavern's ledge. There was a raucous chorus from frightened birds seeking shelter there and countless wings flapped crazily. Some of the birds in their mad flight brushed the intruder with their wing tips in their fright to make their getaway, and the claws of some scraped against his bowed head and shoulders, tearing the skin. Some, more savagely, attacked him viciously with their beaks, and the man was compelled to wave his arms wildly to ward off their attacks. One, in particular, was so persistent in its attacks, that Bantan finally struck it a savage blow more through chance than design, resulting in its retreat. The outraged cawing of the birds soon died away as they took up their roost elsewhere and none sought to return to their former retreat. The cavern was now emptied of the feathered occupants.

Upon his hands and knees despite the stench from the birds' occupancy, Bantan carefully groped his way within. With each short step that he took he would pause and feel with his hands above him in fear of protruding rocks. Within a few minutes a smile overcame his features. The cavern was of sufficient depth to enable him to encamp here for the night, and the floor was dry, though rocky. He cleared away a place on the floor so that he might be seated in reasonable comfort. Now for the first time he heaved a sigh of relief.

He was grateful the night was not cool, and the cavern was not too uncomfortable despite the stench from its recent occupants. Now he realized the weariness that was claiming him following his swim. Drawing himself nearer the further end of the cavern from the area where the stench was not so strong, he made himself as comfortable as possible, and almost immediately sleep claimed him.

CHAPTER XXI

TWO OBJECTIVES ATTAINED

In the morning when Bantan woke, the sound of dull, booming thuds were to be heard. Lame and stiffened, he at once arose and drew himself toward the mouth of the cavern to determine from which direction the sounds issued. Within moments he was aware the talking drum at the castle was sending a message to the Mandoes village. The code signal was repeated several times. Then, during a brief intermission, the more distant drum from the village replied. As the minutes passed there was an exchange of messages.

Since the bronzed giant had no knowledge of the Morse code, which was employed, he could not determine the nature of the messages. His intuition, however, made it clear his escape from the castle on the previous evening must have been transmitted to the villagers, and there was the probability that The Great One wished search parties organized for the purpose of locating the escaped prisoner, if he still lived.

Remembering that his canoe was cached behind a clump of ferns, Bantan realized it would be in danger of being found. Now that his escape unquestionably had been announced, he must attempt to reach his canoe and transfer it to some other place for safety until the time he was ready to leave the island.

Even while the drums were still sending messages to each other, without further delay he clambered up the face of the cliff. There was not too much difficulty in the daylight reaching its summit. As he drew himself over the edge, it was then that the drums ceased their exchange of messages.

During the nearly two-mile journey to his objective, he gathered fruit with which to appease his hunger. His keen eyes were ever watchful and his ears alert while he hurried down the sloping cliff through the scant foliage that stubbornly clung to the rocky soil for life. Reaching the bottom of the slope, he noticed was where the beach began. To facilitate his progress he quickly descended to it, carefully picking his way along the sloping rocks. Just beyond the edge where the surf washed, he ran at top speed. His footprints were thusly erased each time the rushing water laved the smooth sand.

Within a short while he had reached that part of the shore where he had landed, and without any difficulty found that his canoe had not been disturbed from behind the clump of ferns where he had cached it. He quickly drew it out of its hiding place, aware that a quantity of rain water from the deluging storm of several nights previous had collected in its bottom. He turned it over, emptying it. Ascertaining his paddle was in good condition, he then gripped the canoe's bow and drew it through the foliage to the short distance that intervened to the edge of the beach.

It was then that a voice called to him, and looking up, from nearby saw a youth approaching. He smiled with relief. It was Tamur, whom he had rescued from a shark beyond the surf that first morning he had come to the island. The youth was smiling as he approached the bronzed giant. That he had hurried from the village was evident, for his brown chest was heaving, and his mouth was opened so that he might gasp air in greater quantities.

"It's good to see you again, Tamur," Bantan declared. "I think I know why you have come here so fast. The talking drum from the big stone hut has told the villagers of my escape, has it not?"

The native boy nodded.

"As soon as I learned about the message," he said, "I hurried to where you had hidden your canoe. I knew you would come for it if you wanted to escape from the island. I was hoping I would find you—and now I have. Search parties are being organized and they are to comb the island for the purpose of capturing you."

"I'm sure you won't report seeing me," the bronzed giant said hopefully.

"I owe you my life, Bantan," the boy answered simply. "I shall never forget that. Tell me, is it true that Mauria is in love with you?"

The bronzed giant smiled indulgently.

"Has she told you that?" he asked.

The boy hesitated, but Bantan's steady eyes and a nod encouraged him to speak.

"The same day you were captured and taken to the big stone hut where The Great One lives," Tamur began, "I was away from the village after leaving you and did not learn until I returned—that was after you were taken away. Later, in my sorrow, I returned to where you had left your canoe. I saw Mauria, and she seemed to be waiting. I watched her for some time in silence, then at last made myself known. She was startled at first and a little angry afterward. Finally we talked, and I told her about the white stranger who had been captured and taken to the big stone hut. It was then that she confessed that she was in love with you. She cried for some time, but at last, she became quiet and was very sad."

Bantan could well believe the village girl had exaggerated their meeting.

"It is true that the girl called Mauria and I met after you left me that morning, Tamur," he said. "She told me that I was her dream man; but I am not in love with her, no matter what she has told you."

The native boy smiled shyly.

"I am too young as yet to know of the meaning of love, Bantan," he said in soft tones. "But Mauria talked of you so much I have the feeling that she is very much in love with you."

"That may be," he added, shaking his head. "But I cannot love her. Where I am of white birth such a love on my part would be impossible. Mauria and I talked only a short while. She is a lovely girl, I will admit, and should make some warrior very happy one day."

The native boy's smile was still shy with the innocence of youth.

"If I were older I think I could care a great deal for Mauria," he said. "Since you were taken away to the big stone hut we have come here each day to talk, mostly of you, and hoping very much you might escape."

"And now, Tamur," Bantan added, "if I am to do so, I shall have to hurry. I'll always remember you. Good-by."

"Good-by, Bantan," the boy said with moisture gathering in his eyes. "I'll never forget you."

"After I am in the water," the bronzed giant said, "take a branch and erase my footprints and the mark of the canoe from the sand."

The youth assured him that he would do as he requested.

Without further delay Bantan launched his canoe into the surf, and before he reached the calmer water beyond, Tamur was doing what he had promised. Beyond the surf, the bronzed giant turned and waved to the watching boy. Tamur waved in return, after which, with the knuckles of one hand he wiped the moisture from the corners of his eyes. In his soul he wished very much that the giant white stranger did not have to go away.

While Bantan paddled, he cast repeated glances to his left at the island and hoped that he would be unnoticed. He saw no sign of searchers, fortunately, while he maintained his course just beyond the breaking surf, and in due time reached the cove and beached the canoe. Looking about, he finally observed a weather-worn crevice between two huge rocks nearest the cliff where the canoe could be concealed from a possible observer. With a little difficulty he cached it there.

That much accomplished, he decided he should fashion some sort of weapon since he was unarmed. He looked about and found a small, flat piece of rock with an exceptionally sharp edge. This he sheathed at his waist, and without delay clambered up the face of the cliff to the top in the hope he might find a piece of growing wood suitable for his requirement.

With comparative ease in the daylight he scaled the cliff in record time, and presently was rewarded in his search. At all times his eyes were watchful and his sharp ears were alert for sounds of the searchers who by this time must surely be combing the island. A stunted tree nearby furnished him with a piece of hardwood branch, fairly straight, about a foot in length and

two inches in diameter, which he hacked from the
mother bole. With it Bantan returned to the cavern.
Before engaging upon his project, the first thing he
did was clear away the droppings from the recent
feathered occupants so that thereafter the cavern
would be that much more habitable. Then he busied
himself fashioning a wooden dagger.

When some little while had passed the bronzed
giant's patience was rewarded with his handiwork.
The dagger was about ten inches in length and he had
managed to whittle a sharp point upon one end which
he also flattened. Sheathing it at his right hip he had
the feeling that at least now he was not unarmed.
While it was a poor substitute for the steel one that
had been taken from him when he had been captured
by Bora and two accompanying warriors, it would serve
the purpose required should he have the occasion to
use it.

Seated now near the edge of the cavern, Bantan's
watchful eyes were presently rewarded by the sight of
two canoes coming into view from the northern end
of the island where the castle surmounted the cliff top.
Four paddlers were in each water craft. They maintained a course a short distance beyond the breaking
waves, and their attention was constantly upon the
shoreline, as though looking for the possible body of
the escaped prisoner.

As they drew more abreast of the cove above which
the cavern was located in the cliff, the bronzed giant
drew back from the entrance. Watchfully he remained
close to the wall as the canoes seemingly halted when
directly in line with the cove. One of the paddlers in
the first canoe paused and spoke to his companion in
back of him. He pointed toward the cavern.

Bantan noticed the second warrior stare in his direction for a long moment, then he appeared to shake his head at the suggestion that the escaped prisoner might have sought refuge therein. It was apparent the first warrior was not entirely convinced at his fellowman's logic, for as the canoes continued on their way, the watcher noticed this warrior repeatedly cast glances in his direction as though he had reason to doubt his companion's opinion.

The bronzed giant watched the canoes until they had at last disappeared around a bend in the shoreline. He heaved a sigh of relief then returned nearer the opening. By this time he was beginning to feel hungry, and he knew he must venture from his hiding place and search for fruit.

A few minutes later Bantan was clambering gingerly up the face of the cliff. When reaching the summit, before drawing himself upright, he scanned the sparse foliage nearby to ascertain none of the village search parties were close by. Presently assured that none were, in a crouched position he made his way along the edge of the cliff in the same direction he had taken earlier in the morning, for he knew where fruit was to be found.

As he went his way he would pause every few minutes to ascertain there was no sound of crackling underbrush that a search party was bound to make whereas were there only one searcher the chances are he would make much less noise. Always were his keen eyes scanning the now-thickening foliage growth until at last he came to a banana tree. Breaking off several hands of the ripest fruit he then turned to a nearby fig tree and helped himself to these. Feeling he had enough food to last the rest of the day in the event he was compelled through necessity to remain in the cavern, he stopped to gather some wiry vines that he had noticed when passing a short while before, and returned to that part of the cliff below which the cavern was located.

Tying the fruit together and fastening one end of the vine about his waist, Bantan lost no time descending to his place of refuge. Upon reaching the ledge, he instinctively looked to his left and then to his right. It was fortunate that he was thus cautious, for upon the latter side he saw a lone canoe rounding the shore-line, and it contained a single paddler.

Quickly he withdrew to the concealment of the cavern's interior. While he ate of the fruit, he watched the lone canoe approach beyond the breaking waves. His keen eyes were aware that the paddler continued to look in the direction of the cove, and when the canoe was abreast of it, a turn of the paddle headed the bow toward the small beach.

Now indeed did Bantan have reason to feel concern. If the warrior, upon landing, were to notice the imprints of his bare feet upon the sandy beach, he might investigate the cavern for a sign of occupancy. There would be trouble, but the bronzed giant was prepared to defend himself. Even now his right hand touched the handle of his crude wooden dagger.

The paddler now beached his canoe. In another moment he agilely leaped out and drew it a short distance from the washing waves. Instantly his eyes became aware of the imprints of naked feet in the sand. He studied them intently, then straightened and looked about at the rock walls surrounding the little cove. At last he looked up at the cavern. A slow smile came to his dusky face and he nodded. His right hand went to the handle of the dagger sheathed at his hip.

This warrior was none other than Bora, the one who had been in charge of two warriors when Bantan had been first captured. One of the warriors by name of Stao had appropriated the prisoner's dagger, but later Bora had requested it and it had changed ownership, perhaps with a little reluctance on the part of Stao.

Since Bantan had, in defense of his life, slain his good friend Doman, Bora had felt sorrow and a want of vengeance. Though he had inwardly resented the prisoner being taken to The Great One, he was unable to prevent that. Today, while passing the cove, he had noticed the small beach and the cavern in the face of the cliff, and it had been he who mentioned to a companion that it would be a likely hiding place for an escaped prisoner. His fellowmate did not think it possible, however.

When returning to the village and the other warriors had disembarked, Bora was determined to satisfy his curiosity. He had returned and now believed his suspicions were not unfounded. The naked footprints were sufficient evidence that the escaped prisoner was somewhere in the immediate vicinity.

But now, he realized the dilemma which confronted him. If the escaped prisoner were seeking refuge in the cavern, how was he, alone, going to ferret him out of his hiding place?

Bora was no coward, though sometimes an undaunted man can take risks that are not feasible. Because of his want of revenge toward the bronzed stranger whose meeting with Doman had resulted in the latter's death, the warrior cast caution to the winds. He also realized that there was a possibility the escaped prisoner might not be in hiding at the present time; if so, it would be to his advantage to conceal himself in the cavern and await his appearance. Then, again, he might be there, perhaps even aware of his presence at that very moment. There was only one way to find out.

The Mandoes warrior looked upward, his keen eyes noticing the hand and footholds to be obtained in order to negotiate one's way. Then with a nod, he approached the rock wall a short distance from a direct line with the cavern, and with little difficulty started to clamber upward.

Bantan, meanwhile, was aware of the warrior's intention. He also recognized him now for who he was, and his eyes gleamed brightly as they rested upon the familiar handle of his appropriated dagger. He noticed that the searcher was no fool by climbing directly under the cavern, for he could easily have dropped some rocks upon his unprotected head if he were minded. As it was, he would have to wait until he was within arms' reach before he could engage him.

Bora continued his ascent, and when he had reached a place in line with the cavern's opening, he inched his way in that direction. Slowly he neared his objective, and just as he was about to rest a tentative foot upon the ledge, it was then that the one he sought appeared with a grim smile upon his face, but with eyes that glared mercilessly.

"Come, Bora," the bronzed giant beckoned to the warrior. "You are searching for me. Here I am."

Surprised by Bantan's unheralded appearance, and only too well aware of his own precarious position, Bora could only snarl in his hatred. With haste he sought to place his foot again upon the ledge, and missing, he lost his balance. The sudden transfer of weight from one side of his body to the other resulted in the loss of his equilibrium. His slim handhold was loosened. With a mumbled curse he felt his finger tips losing their hold, and unable to check himself, he fell, sliding and scraping his body against the rough surface of the cliff—a distance of perhaps twenty-five feet. The contact of his body against the side of the cliff served to break his otherwise hard fall, but at the last moment he caught one foot on a projecting crag, so that his upright balance was upset.

When striking the sand below, he landed upon his side, and turned over on his back. Blood was flowing from numerous cuts upon his arms, body, and legs. The fall had quite knocked the wind from him, but otherwise unhurt, his first thought was of the escaped prisoner who had taunted him from the safety of the ledge at the cavern's mouth. As he looked upward a snarl issued from his lips, for Bantan was descending the face of the cliff with amazing agility that did not seem possible for a human being.

Bora managed to draw himself to his feet, and his first thought was to withdraw his appropriated dagger. But at the moment he did so and raised his hand to strike, the bronzed giant had confronted him. Disregarding the dagger hand, Bantan swung a mighty, clenched left hand and clouted Bora at the right side of the neck where his head joined the shoulders. Seemingly paralyzed, the warrior dropped the weapon from nerveless fingers.

The force of the blow sent him reeling toward the cliff where his temple came in sharp contact with the edge of a ragged rock, resulting in instant death. He collapsed upon the sand and lay still.

Bantan appropriated his dagger and substituted it at his right hip in place of the crude wooden one he had fashioned. Then he bent and examined his foe for an indication of life. Realizing that he was dead, he arose, wondering momentarily what to do with the corpse and the canoe in which the warrior had come hither.

Since he had his own canoe he had no requirement of another, but the disposal of the body was an immediate necessity. Presently he decided there was nothing else to do but dig a hole in the sandy beach and bury it. With the wooden dagger he proceeded to scoop a trench of sufficient proportions to accommodate the corpse. Intermittently while thus engaged he would pause to look to his left and then his right beyond the breaking waves, also to look up at the summit of the cliff.

When an hour had passed he surveyed the freshly overturned sand beneath which Bora's body had been interred. The surplus sand was scattered about the small beach. Now came the matter of the disposal of the unneeded canoe. He searched about the outlining rocky mass to each side of the cove, and fortunately found that he might conceal it upon the opposite side from where his own canoe was safely hidden. A huge, flat rock lay over another in such a way that there was ample space to conceal his vanquished foe's unwanted canoe. With a little effort he managed to drag it up the rocky surface at last and push it into the crevice out of sight.

He then clambered up the face of the cliff to gain the refuge of the cavern, and seating himself upon his haunches near the entrance, leaned his back against the wall and heaved a sigh of relief. Two things had been accomplished thus far in a relatively short period of time since his escape from the castle on the previous evening. He had brought his canoe from its original hiding place to another, and he had reappropriated his stolen dagger, though to do so had resulted in a warrior's death. He also was aware the matter of settling scores with Amar did not concern him now. Ordinarily, he should be content to return to Marja Island at the first available moment.

The fact that his and Luane's love had been acknowledged was the one thing which now mattered. He must in some way gain access to the castle and attempt to rescue the nurse, also the servant girl, whom he pitied for some inexplicable reason. When this was accomplished, then might he return from whence he had set out upon a revengeful mission that had been unnecessary. His adventure on Mandoes Island would be a past event in his until-now exciting existence.

CHAPTER XXII

MAURIA AGAIN

The afternoon was well along when Bantan, from the mouth of the cavern, observed two more canoes, each with four occupants plying paddles, appear around the northern shore where the castle was located. Quickly he withdrew to the sheltering inner recesses, but not so far that he could not observe the canoes and their occupants.

He was wondering if Bora's absence had already caused concern in the village and that his fellowmates were searching for him. It was a difficult question to answer since he had no means of knowing; but he now maintained his interest upon the paddlers, noticing that their attention was directed shoreward.

And then occurred an incident which spared him an investigation. A tern, in all probability one of the very birds Bantan had rudely ousted from its roost on the previous evening, approached the cavern with flapping wings. It flew past the mouth and then returned, this second time alighting upon the ledge. For a few moments it was fidgety, ruffling its wings and seemed apprehensive, but presently was content to remain there.

The bronzed giant breathed easier and remained perfectly motionless, while his eyes still remained riveted upon the two canoes which by this time were abreast the small cove beyond the breaking waves. He was aware that the paddlers were watching the bird at roost upon the cavern's ledge in a clear view. Talking among themselves, they were convinced no escaped prisoner could be hiding there, for if so, they were sure the bird wouldn't remain.

With a sigh of relief the silent watcher observed the paddlers as they continued their way without further hesitation from the immediate vicinity. He still remained motionless, however, not wishing to disturb the tern in the event one of the paddlers might look back and notice the bird in hasty flight leaving the cavern ledge.

The sun had long since passed over the cliff and the east side of the island shore was in shadow. In the event he was to remain in the cavern a few days, Bantan decided to gather some grass, for lying upon the floor was not conducive to complete rest. He waved an arm, and the tern, disturbed in its meditations, took immediate flight, but not without too much protest.

The bronzed giant approached the mouth of the cavern then and looked to his left and then his right, but there was no sign of other canoes upon the sparkling surface beyond the shadowline to be seen. Quickly he clambered up the face of the cliff to its summit, again pausing to scan the nearby terrain for sign of searchers. With a nod, he arose to an upright position. Recollecting having seen a clump of sweet-smelling grasses earlier in the day, he now set his footsteps in that direction.

Soon he had gathered sufficient and bound them together with strips of wiry vines. Without loss of time he returned to the top of the cliff. With more vines which he twisted together for greater strength, he tied one end about his waist and attached the other to the bundle of grasses. Before getting into position to descend the face of the cliff, he moved the bundle so that it trailed at his back. Because of its bulkiness, he was compelled to descend with extreme care but presently had attained his objective. Within the cavern he unfastened the bundle of grasses and spread them near the rear where he hoped this coming evening to sleep upon them in more comfort than the previous one.

Looking at his dwindled supply of provisions, he decided another trip would be necessary to ensure ample food through the morning at least. And so he returned to the cliff's summit, returning some half hour later well laden. He had seen no sign of searchers, though he had heard voices in the distance.

Once again safely ensconced within the cavern, Bantan ate to his fill, meanwhile, planning the preliminary steps when he felt the time was ready to rescue Luane and Loula. He remembered upon his advent to the castle in the company of the twin brothers how the pressing of a button was all that had been required for the massive door to swing open. Since he had seen how it was done, there was no reason why he couldn't duplicate the act. In this way he would be spared the time and effort of fashioning some sort of ladder by which to reach the top of the ten-foot wall. He had no means of knowing whether The Great One would take any precautions in the event the escaped prisoner elected to return to the castle.

Unknown factors weighed heavily upon the bronzed giant. What might have happened to Luane? Suppose, under questioning, that the nurse had admitted her love for Bantan? What then? And there was Loula to be considered. The pity he felt for her was inexplicable. For a reason that he could not answer, he knew he would help her escape from the castle if she so wished.

But whatever mattered, the bronzed giant was determined to re-enter the castle when he felt the time was right. Only when the search was no longer prosecuted he would have greater freedom in carrying out his plans without fear of detection. Meanwhile, he might as well compose himself and obtain what rest he might with thought of the long, four-day paddling stint that remained before him until at last he would reach Marja.

Thinking thusly, and lying in comfort upon his pallet of grasses, he entertained no fears for the time being; but he did find that he was wondering and conjecturing at the possible fate of Luane.

Nearing sundown Bantan was alerted by the sound of the talking drums again. Drawing near the mouth of the cavern he listened intently. The drum from the castle was signaling to the village. Presently that one answered. An exchange of messages ensued in the passing minutes. But at last the drums ceased and all was quiet once more.

Just before dark terns sought to land upon the cavern ledge but the bronzed giant did not relish their companionship. He tossed small rocks at them, driving them away; though some persisted in returning, their reception was always the same, so at last by the time darkness had enveloped the water and the island they sought places elsewhere to roost, leaving the cavern occupant to his solitude and meditation.

The next morning, finishing his provisions on hand at breakfast, Bantan ventured forth to gather more fruit for his noon, evening, and tomorrow's morning meal as well. At the top of the cliff before drawing himself over the edge in full view, he ascertained no searchers were nearby. Satisfied that there were none, he was on his way without further delay.

A mile from the cavern he had gathered an armful of various fruits, also some nuts, and was returning to the cliff, inwardly congratulating himself on his good fortune, when suddenly he paused in his tracks. His keen eyes darted here and there and his acute ears were centered upon the crackling underbrush that he had heard just ahead to his left. He remained immobile as a bronzed statue. Again he heard the crackling underbrush, and his keen eyes darted in the direction the sound was heard. He deduced there was only one person and his intent ears were positive of the fact.

Then, to his amazement, he saw a lone, unarmed native girl step from behind a luxuriant fern a short distance ahead of him, and upon the instant that she looked in his direction, recognition was apparent to each. With a glad smile upon her lips, and happiness radiating in her dark eyes, the girl uttered the single word:

"Bantan!"

Without a moment's hesitation, she ran toward him with arms outstretched in welcome.

The bronzed giant at once was aware of the embarrassment that he was placed in, for the girl was Mauria. He remembered too well the occasion of their previous meeting. He was wondering how he was to rid himself of her without endangering his own existence, and at the same time not injuring her vanity. He had been successful thus far eluding search parties, and now he had to be discovered by the one person from the Mandoes village that he wanted least of all to see. With a shake of his head he placed the fruit he carried upon the ground, and as he straightened, he forced

a smile of welcome upon his face as he waited for the
girl to reach him.

"Mauria," he said in a somewhat flat and uncon-
vincing tone.

The smiling girl now reached him, and so great
her joy at seeing him again, she reached for one
of his hands, and unresistingly on his part, she kissed
its back several times, meanwhile, crooning in a soft
monotone. She then pressed it to her heaving bosom
and looked up at him with dog-like devotion.

"Oh, Bantan, my dream man!" she murmured
tremulously. "You'll never know how I've missed you.
Night after night since you were captured and taken
to The Great One I would go to sleep with tears in my
eyes thinking of you, and wishing there was something I could have done. Now that I've found you
again, you must take me with you wherever you go.
I can't live without you."

With the utterance of her words she again kissed
the back of his hand, and then the palm, and each finger as well.

Meanwhile, the bronzed giant was nonplussed what
to do in the dilemma which confronted him.

"Mauria—" he said, and then hesitated, unable to
find any other words to utter.

"Yes, Bantan?" she questioned with a smile. She was
aware that he had hesitated in speaking further. She
drew close to him and looked up at him with devotion.
"Anything that you wish of me, do not hesitate to
speak. I would be your devoted slave forever. I love
you so much, my dream man come true, that my poor
heart is thumping so hard it makes me dizzy."

With her words she pressed the palm of his hand
against her left breast, and he did not deny that Mauria

exaggerated, for her heart was beating like a trip hammer.

"Yes, Mauria," he agreed, "your heart is beating very fast."

Now the native girl, with a recollection of what Tamur had told her on the previous morning, regarded him in wonder.

"Tamur told me you had left the island," she said with a curious expression upon her face. "You didn't go away, then?"

"No, Mauria," he replied. "I have some unfinished business in the big stone hut to attend before I leave Mandoes Island."

The native girl regarded him strangely.

"Is—is there some one that you—perhaps love?" she asked in a faint voice.

He nodded.

"She is white like myself," he explained.

The native girl seemed to wilt and her hopelessness was apparent. She drew back several steps and regarded him sorrowfully.

"She is very beautiful?" she then asked.

Again he nodded.

"You must love her very much," she murmured, lowering her head. With the back of a hand she wiped her tearful eyes.

Bantan could only nod.

Now the girl's shoulders trembled and choking sobs issued from her lips. She clasped her hands to her mouth in an effort to muffle them.

With compassion the bronzed giant approached the weeping girl and placed a hand lightly upon her bowed head.

"Please believe me, Mauria," he murmured, "I am

very sorry that it had to be. You are a very lovely girl, and if I were a native instead of a white man, my heart would surely be yours."

The girl's sobbing abated and she looked up at him with shining eyes through the tears. Impulsively she reached out a hand and rested it upon his shoulder. A smile touched her lips.

"You really mean that, Bantan?" she asked.

He nodded as he looked up at the blue heaven.

"I mean it the same as there is light by day and darkness at night, Mauria," he answered. "I can think of no other way to express myself to you."

"Thank you," she murmured. She drew close to him and rested her face upon his broad, hairless chest. He was aware that her lips pressed his flesh for a moment, then she drew back. She nodded then. "I had hoped if we were ever to meet again that we might avow our love for each other." She sighed deeply. "But I can understand what you have told me, and I know we cannot change it. I'll leave you now, for I know you want it that way. Have no fear that I shall reveal your presence upon the island. I still love you too much to have any harm befall you. Good-by, my dream man."

Waving a hand, and smiling through her tears, Mauria left him standing there. Bantan was acutely aware of the dryness in his throat. He could hardly believe the native girl could be so generous.

When all sounds of Mauria's footsteps were no longer to be heard, the bronzed giant then picked up the fruit he had gathered and returned to the cavern. All during the entire day, and into the evening when his thoughts were not otherwise engaged, he thought of Mauria's generosity. From the depths of his soul he earnestly wished the best things in life would come her way, and that she would soon find the happiness she sought.

CHAPTER XXIII

RECAPTURED

For two more days the search parties combed the island, but there was no sign of the escaped prisoner. Canoes with paddlers time and again would circumnavigate the island, but their reports were always the same. They also sought evidence of the disappearance of Bora, but no sign of him or his canoe was found. It was as though he had seemingly vanished, as had Bantan.

Each morning and night there was an exchange of messages by the talking drum of the castle and that of the village. On the night of the third day it was conceded that the escaped prisoner either was dead or must have returned from whence he had come; but the whereabouts of Bora's absence remained an unsolved mystery.

Upon the fourth morning Bantan heard no drums. Now he was satisfied that the search for him must have been discontinued. He decided the coming night would be the time to gain access to the castle. With this thought in mind, during the day he stealthily gathered various kinds of fruit and stored them in his canoe cached between rocks at one side of the cove. No sign of searchers had been seen on this day, nor had he noticed any canoes riding the shimmering water upon the eastern side of the island.

Late in the afternoon he drew the canoe from its hiding place and left it a short distance from the water's edge. Now he felt the time had come to seek entrance to the castle grounds. He clambered up the face of the cliff. Once more standing upon its summit, he stealthily went his way upward toward the ten-foot wall surrounding the castle.

Just before dusk descended upon the island the bronzed giant confronted the massive door. A little timidly he pressed the button, as he had seen Hulo do, and without surprise he heard a barely audible whining sound. Before him the heavy door swung slowly open. Quickly he stepped through the entrance, then looked for the button which would close the door. Finding and pressing it, it swung shut noiselessly.

Bantan crept along the base of the wall, casting intermittent glances at various darkened windows in the castle. Everything seemed so dark and quiet that one would have believed it was unoccupied. As he went his way with stealth in the darkness that had fallen, he looked for that part of the building near the swimming pool were Luane's quarters were.

Presently he was able to see a light in the window of the nurse's apartment. As he skirted the swimming pool he remembered only too well the event of saving Luane's life, but most of all he thought fondly of the recent pleasant afternoon they had passed here. It was that same afternoon that he ruefully recollected that the nurse had deviated from the truth when answering certain questions he had asked her.

Upon silent feet now Bantan drew near the lighted window of Luane's quarters. Looking within, he saw the girl lying upon a couch with her back turned toward him. His heart warmed at sight of her, and he felt immeasurable relief at knowing she was safe and unharmed. A wistful smile touched his lips as he gazed upon her.

But now he blinked his eyes in wonder. Whether it was the effect of the electric light bulbs in the chandelier shining down upon her he wasn't sure. For some reason the body that he looked at appeared different. For the first time he saw her with a dress instead of the nurse's uniform, and it seemed ill-fitting, or perhaps, it was the way she was lying that made the dress bunch about her so that it looked much too large. Now his eyes went to her lovely hair as he had known it. For some unknown reason its luster was gone, and her black hair seemed to have turned to white, and it lay flat upon top and sides. He blinked his eyes, knowing that the electric lights probably were the reason for the change.

Bantan was about to tap upon the window to apprise Luane of his presence, but it was at that moment Loula entered through a doorway just out of his vision. She bore a tray and dishes of food which she placed upon a table near the couch. The watcher at the window was aware of the saddened expression upon the servant girl's features as she stood looking down at the nurse. With a sorrowful shake of her head she approached and spoke to her mistress.

"Come, Luane, you must eat something," he heard her say.

The figure on the couch shook her head and muttered incoherent words.

Loula now came closer and gently placed a hand upon the nurse's head.

"Please, you haven't eaten for four days," she insisted.

Listening, Bantan realized four days had passed
since he had escaped from the castle. Could it be that
because of his disappearance she had fasted, feeling
that he had deserted her, and disconsolate, she had no
reason to live?

The servant girl now placed an arm about Luane,
and tried to lift her to a seated position; but the
nurse was reluctant that she have her way. Finally
Loula removed her arm and remained standing at her
side, shaking her head sorrowfully.

For a reason he could not explain, the watcher at
the window seemed paralyzed. He tried to make himself tap upon the window with his knuckles and attract the attention of the inmates, but some inexplicable
force held him in check. There was something strange
in the way Luane was acting, something utterly different about her—as though she were another person than the one to whom he had acknowledged his
love, and she for him.

Now looking at Loula's dark hair, as Bantan knew
it in its natural color, beneath the electric lights he
stared strangely. It was unchanged! Straining his eyes,
he again looked at the flat, lusterless hair of Luane's
head, and his eyes could not be deceiving him. It *was*
white! He tried to convince himself the electric lights
were playing tricks with his eyes, but what could account for the fact that Loula's hair was as he had
known it—dark and lustrous?

Recollecting that Loula had mentioned that Luane
had fasted for four days didn't make sense to him that
her hair should be thusly affected. Now the servant
girl moved so that she was near the nurse's head, and
her body prevented the watcher at the window from
seeing her snow-white hair. Once again Loula bent over

and placed an arm about the reclining figure. She spoke
in gentle tones so softly that Bantan could not hear
what she said, strain his ears though he did.

Luane now moved, turning over, but the bronzed
giant could not see her features. He did catch a glimpse
of one of her hands and it seemed strangely thin, almost gaunt. As she set her feet upon the floor he
noticed that her legs from the knees to ankles were
unusually thin, and so different from the well formed
calves and trim ankles he had seen when they had been
seated at the swimming pool.

Bantan stared with a strange chill fastening upon his
spine. Now Loula was helping Luane to her feet, and
though her face was still shielded by the servant girl,
as she stood up, Loula had an arm about her and
helped her to the table. The watcher could not understand this strange transformation in the nurse, for
four days' fasting should not render her that weak and
so seemingly feeble. As she was assisted, she appeared
hunchbacked.

Seated with her back to the window, the bronzed
giant sensed something was radically wrong with the
Luane he had known. Loula now seated herself opposite the nurse and spoke softly to her so that the
watcher failed to hear what she said, but it was evident she was coaxing her mistress to drink the glass
of fruit juice. Reluctantly Luane did so, but Bantan
wondered at the shaking of her right arm as she
drained the glass of its contents and set it upon the
table. She then earnestly looked at the servant girl.

"Tell me," she said in a harsh, croaking tone that
was so very much unlike the sweet, softened one Bantan had known, "have I changed much in these past
four days?"

Watching Loula's features, the bronzed giant saw her shake her head sadly as a sympathetic smile touched her lips. Before she could speak, Luane spoke again in grating tones.

"I haven't dared to look in a mirror, Loula; but he said a year for each hour that passed. Is it true? Oh, please tell me!"

It was at that moment Bantan's sixth sense apprised him of the presence of some one to his rear. Instantly the fingers of his right hand closed upon the handle of his dagger and it was quickly withdrawn from its sheath. As he was in the act of turning about, powerful hands seized each of his arms just above the elbows. The dagger was released from his nerveless hand and dropped to the short grass noiselessly.

With the aid of the diffused light that was emitted from the window of Luane's quarters, the bronzed giant was able to identify his captors. They were none other than Hulo and Humo, the twin brothers. The former gripped his right arm, and the latter his left.

"Don't give us any trouble, Bantan," the elder of the twins spoke in a low voice. "We respect you, but we have our orders."

Bantan realized the odds were against him, but he was determined not to submit without a struggle. With a sudden, backward movement, he almost freed his arms from the imprisoning hands of his two captors. Quickly he lurched to his right, striking heavily against Hulo, then to his left, and he heard Humo grunt. But their hands still gripped him tightly, and squeezed harder upon his arms.

Forward, and then backward, to the right and the left, the bronzed giant lurched, striving as a madman to break their seemingly steel-like grips upon his arms.

He was positive were he to free one of his arms he might have a chance. He happened to look toward the lighted window and he saw Loula looking outside, having been attracted by the sounds of the scuffle. He saw no sign of Luane, however.

Time and again he surged in all directions possible in the hope of breaking free. Remembering the swimming pool was not too far away, he now exerted himself in that direction; but it was as though the twin brothers read his mind, for they strove their utmost to prevent him from attaining his objective.

Now slowly, but determinedly, Hulo and Humo were forcing him along the side of the castle in the direction of the main doorway. Suspecting their intentions, the bronzed giant did everything in his power to prevent this. He dug his heels into the turf, but his strength and resistance was no match for the two giant brothers. Slowly but surely they were forcing and half-dragging the prisoner, keeping close to him so that he had no opportunity of kicking, or be in a position to trip either of them. Bantan could hear their heavy breathing as they maintained silence while keeping him subdued. It was a question who was struggling the most, but at any rate the prisoner was surely being forced to accommodate Hulo and Humo, though he resisted each and every step of the way.

Were the twin brothers so minded, one or the other could easily have silenced Bantan, for each had a free hand; but there was the possibility The Great One had given them orders not to injure the bronzed giant in any way. There were times, however, when each of the brothers had to use the free hand, for the prisoner was stubbornly contesting each foot of the way that he was compelled to go.

At last they had forced him to the door of the main
entrance to the castle. By some prearranged signal,
Bantan's arms were quickly drawn to his back, then
one of the brothers—Humo—gripped both wrists
while Hulo pressed the button which would open the
door. As the barely audible whining of a moter was to
be heard, the door started to open.

The bronzed giant made a final, stupendous effort
to free himself. He bent forward, almost lifting his
captor from his feet, and then he lurched backward
while in this bent position. But his endeavor to win
freedom failed, for at the next moment Hulo came to
the assistance of his hard-pressed brother. Though
Bantan protested each inch of the way, he was forced
through the opened doorway; and as the door immediately closed behind him, he realized he was once
again a prisoner inside the castle.

Once again, each brother gripping an arm tightly,
the bronzed giant was forced across the hallway
through the doorway to the room with the curtained
booth. From its concealment was to be heard maniacal
laughter, and when it ceased, a metallic voice spoke.

"Bantan, you were a guest in the castle before your
escape. But this time, have no doubt, you are to be considered a prisoner, and as such you will be treated."

Bantan's eyes blazed defiance.

"You are mad!" he shouted. "Only a madman would
do as you have. What have you done to Luane? She
and I are in love. The only reason I returned to the
castle was to rescue her from your madness."

Once again there was the sound of long-drawn
laughter from behind the curtained booth.

"Luane!" the metallic voice scoffed. "What do you

and Luane know about love? If you knew her like I know her, you wouldn't even think of loving her."

Bantan strained mightily in an effort to reach the curtained booth, but the twin brothers held him back.

"What have you done to her—madman that you are?" the captive demanded. "Why has her hair turned white? Have you subjected her to some mad experiment?"

Once again The Great One laughed loud and long, mockingly.

Again the bronzed giant attempted to surge forward, but his two captors seemingly anticipated his intentions and restrained him with not a little effort.

Now the metallic voice spoke.

"Hulo, take the prisoner to the cell next to Amar's," he instructed. "Tomorrow, we'll experiment upon him."

"As you say, O Great One," was the reply.

The bronzed giant was turned about and forced from the room to the elevator, though not without considerable resistance on his part. Presently they were at the level below the ground floor. He was pushed each inch of the way along the dimly lit corridor. His efforts to retard the twin brothers was futile, for in the end he was thrust within the dark cell. The door was closed, and a sliding wooden bar upon the outside was put into place, leaving the prisoner alone in his hopelessness.

Bantan was acutely aware of the horror of his imprisonment. From his past experience he suspected what fiendish experiments were in store for him as the subject. In despair, he slumped to the floor with his back and head resting against the door, his hands hanging limply at his sides. Although his face was uplifted to the darkened ceiling his eyes were closed in utter helplessness.

Presently, however, when the shock of his despair passed, and he tried to contemplate the near future, numerous questions surged within him seeking answers. First, he was tormented by the unaccounted change in Luane. What had happened to her? What had The Great One meant when he spoke of the nurse in the manner he had? And thus he was bombarded with these questions, and others of a similar nature, that he was unable to answer.

The realization that he had lost his dagger in the scuffle with Hulo and Humo added to his hopelessness. In a vague way he wondered why either of the twin brothers hadn't stopped to pick it up. It was possible in the excitement of the moment they had not realized he had a dagger and had drawn it from his sheath. Though he had seen Loula in the window, looking outside, there was no possibility that she would have noticed it in the short grass. He did know that were the dagger in his possession at the present moment he would not feel so utterly helpless.

The passing time seemed of no account to Bantan as he sat there in the almost pitch darkness of his cell. Everything was so quiet his hearing was intensified, though there was nothing for him to hear, realizing as he did there was no hope of rescue from his present plight.

CHAPTER XXIV

A VAINLESS SACRIFICE?

When Loula recognized the prisoner the twin brothers had taken outside Luane's quarters, her heart was
overjoyed and sad at the same time. She was happy
to know, first, that Bantan still lived, for the reports
of the past four days had revealed no sign of him during the interim after diving from his window into the
water below the cliff. Second, she was sad for him for
two reasons. Now that he had been recaptured, his
fate would be in the hands of The Great One—and
she had no reason to envy him because of that. On the
other hand, to know Luane as she was now, would be a
tremendous shock to his finer sensibilities.

She remained at the window in seeming despair
even after Hulo and Humo had forced the prisoner to
accompany them to the main entrance to the castle. As
she stood there, apparently staring unseeingly outside
at the short grass, the diffused light from the window
reached Bantan's discarded dagger and arrested her
attention.

Without a word to Luane who sat at the table with
bowed head and her face buried in her arms, the servant girl silently stepped to the door, unlocked it, and
went outside, her eyes searching for the glistening
metallic object. Coming to where it lay, she picked it
up and gazed at it lovingly for a long moment. She
then quickly concealed it within her *tupa* cloth dress,
arranging it in such a way that it would not be con-

spicuous, and at the same time so that it would not inflict an injury upon herself, for she was well aware of its keenness.

Loula then sighed deeply, looking forlornly about before she re-entered Luane's quarters, locking the door after her. A sorrowful smile touched her lips as she reseated herself at the table where her mistress still sat with her face buried in her arms, having pushed the tray and dishes to one side.

Now, aware of Loula's presence—for some few minutes having forgotten that she existed, so deep her despair—Luane looked up at the servant girl and seemed annoyed.

"Where have you been, Loula?" she demanded in a croaking voice.

"Luane, Bantan has been here," was the answer in a low voice. "He must have been looking through the window when Hulo and Humo overpowered and took him prisoner."

The nurse uttered a piteous cry, and once more buried her face in her arms and wept bitterly. When she managed to control her emotions she trembled as she raised her head.

"I hope he didn't see me through the window," she moaned. "He must never see me again. I want him always to remember me—as I was."

With the utterance of her words she again buried her tearful face in her arms and wept bitterly, rolling her head from side to side despairingly.

Loula could only watch her mistress in subdued silence but with heavy heart.

Luane again presently raised her head and looked at the servant girl through blurred eyes because of the tears that had filled them.

"I loved him so, Loula," she sighed. "For the first time in my life I loved a man—and he—curse him!—would do this to me as my punishment. I don't deserve this after the many loyal years I worked with him as nurse and assistant." She raised her eyes piteously to the ceiling. "Oh, God, I know I haven't acknowledged You as I should have all these past years, but please—I don't ask anything for myself. Please don't let anything happen to Bantan. I know he won't love me now—but it is so heavenly to know that he loved me—as I was."

So inwardly impressed with her invocations, Luane now arose from the chair, and upon seemingly feeble legs with some difficulty went down upon her knees. She raised her clasped hands in supplication to the ceiling.

The servant girl could only watch her mistress as though spellbound. Now a smile, as of benediction, came upon Luane's face and her eyes seemed to shine radiantly through unshed tears.

"He *did* return at the risk of his own life for me," she murmured hoarsely. "I shall treasure that thought so long as I live—whether it be an hour, a day, a week, a month, a year—forever—" And with these words she lowered her head and her eyes closed, but a smile remained upon her lips.

Now Loula aroused herself from the seeming state of inanimation that gripped her. Moisture filled her eyes as she arose from the table and went to Luane's side. She placed a gentle arm about her and murmured comforting words as she lifted her mistress to her feet.

"Come, Luane," she begged, "please let me help you to the couch. You are becoming exhausted."

The nurse looked at the servant girl with surprised eyes.

"Bantan risked his life for me," she crooned. "He risked his life for me."

Even after Loula had helped her mistress to the couch, Luane still crooned in a monotone that Bantan had risked his life for her.

In an apparently demented state it seemed nothing else mattered now to her. For four long days and sleepless nights the one burning question had haunted her:

If Bantan had survived the leap from the window of his room, would he return for her?

Now she knew. He had returned! In her tormented mind she knew nothing else mattered. She could grasp nothing else at the present. The fact that Bantan had been recaptured, and was again at The Great One's merciless designs was apparently beyond the comprehension of the nurse.

He had returned! That was comforting to her; but knowing herself as she must be, she did not want him to see her again—ever.

Loula stood near her mistress. One hand pressed the concealed weapon hidden beneath her *tupa* cloth dress. In her mind she was trying to reason with clearness.

For four days and nights she had remained with Luane upon strict instructions from The Great One. The only occasions she had left her alone was to prepare meals for herself and her mistress. But Luane had only consumed a single glass of fruit juice in all that time. She had no desire for food in her overwhelming grief.

Loula knew Bantan had been taken captive, and she

suspected that he would be confined in a cell on the same level as the laboratory. No longer could he expect to be given the privileges of a guest as he had previous to his escape. She also knew that there would be absolutely no hope for him this time. The only person in the castle who could help him, if he were to be helped, was herself. She had retrieved his dagger, and in some way she must restore it to him.

Feeling that Luane would not miss her too greatly, she at once decided to try and locate the prisoner. First, she would go to the kitchen and learn of the whereabouts of the twin brothers. Observing that her charge was still crooning to herself in a monotone and appeared oblivious of anything else, Loula stole softly out of the room, pausing to lock the door behind her.

In a few minutes she had reached the kitchen. As she might have anticipated, Hulo and Humo had returned there after confining the prisoner to a cell. They were seated at the table and had been partaking of a lunch preparatory to retiring. The past four days and nights had been trying ones for them, for they had constantly patrolled the castle grounds under instructions from The Great One that the escaped prisoner might return; and if so, they were to recapture and not harm him in any way.

As Loula entered, she greeted them with a smile and inquired if they had apprehended the intruder within the castle grounds.

"I was in Luane's room and heard the scuffle outside," she explained; "so it is no secret that a prisoner was taken. Was it Bantan?"

The twin brothers exchanged glances, then Hulo spoke in answer, nodding his head slightly as he did so.

"It was Bantan whom we captured. Humo and I both dislike to see him a prisoner again, for we have great respect for him. It was incredible that he dived from the window of his room—and survived."

"Did you know that Bantan and Luane had acknowledged their love for each other the night he escaped?" Loula asked, looking from one to the other.

Both brothers revealed their surprise.

"It is true," and the servant girl nodded her head. "Though Luane is happy beyond words to tell that Bantan has returned, she does not wish him to see her again. It is horrible—the injustice that has been done to her. I locked her in her quarters to come here. She is lying upon the couch, and all that she can say is that Bantan has returned for her. She doesn't realize that he is a prisoner and at the merciless designs of The Great One. And you both must bear in mind, whatever The Great One has done to us, natives that we are, is bad enough; but to carry on his fiendish experiments upon a man of his own race is horrible. Both of you admit that you respect Bantan. Does locking him in a cell show your respect?"

Disdain flashed in Loula's eyes as she spoke, and both Hulo and Humo looked uncomfortable.

"I am only a native woman," the servant girl continued in a low voice. "I do not feel that I amount to very much; but Bantan has treated me with the greatest of respect and dignity. He has made me feel that I would like to live again and not be cooped up in this castle the rest of my life. He would have taken me with him and Luane to Marja Island where we might start a new life. And I would have gone!"

Hulo stared at the servant girl as though unable to believe the truth of her words.

Now Loula stamped a foot upon the floor to prove her assertions.

"What I say is true—and I mean it!" she exclaimed.

Hulo was now shaking his head hopelessly.

"It is too late, Loula," he said in a low voice. "We have been servants of The Great One so long that we would be like outcasts were we to live elsewhere. There would be no place for us in the Mandoes village."

"Look at you—both of you," the servant girl said with flashing eyes. "Why have neither of you mated in the past instead of accepting servitude to The Great One? You could have had a mate and children. You could have been happy. Have either of you been happy here?"

Hulo stared at Loula listlessly.

"What of yourself?" he asked. "Have you not been happy until Bantan came?"

"I *thought* I was happy, Hulo," she corrected him. "But after knowing Bantan, I would have gone anywhere that he went; and if I would be just a slave to him, I would have been happy. I have been told by him that he could never love me because I am a native girl. That still didn't change my feeling for him. He suggested that I take an interest in either of you, and I told him that I might."

It was evident that Loula's tirade had some effect upon the twin brothers, for they seemed uneasy and were wishing the servant girl would leave them. Since she appeared to have no intention of doing so, Hulo yawned, then, looking knowingly at his brother, arose from his chair.

"I'm sleepy," he announced. "I'm going to bed. I've lost a lot of sleep these past four nights."

Humo arose also with a yawn and indicated he would join his brother. Since they occupied the same room, secretly Loula was pleased that they were going to bed. She was positive all the other slave workers had long since retired to their quarters upon the other side of the castle. She looked with scorn upon the twin brothers as they filed out of the kitchen. She waited a few more minutes before returning to Luane's quarters.

When she presently did so, she found her mistress as she had left her, still crooning in a monotone that Bantan had returned, but not mentioning anything about his present whereabouts, nor seeming to give a thought of that. The fact that he had returned was all that mattered. Loula stood near her, shaking her head hopelessly. To think that Luane had been reduced to this miserable state seemed unbelievable. With a sad shake of her head she approached the recumbent figure.

"Listen to me, Luane," she said earnestly. "It is true that Bantan has returned. But doesn't it matter to you that he may be in danger—because of The Great One?"

The nurse ceased her crooning and looked up at the servant girl with a querulous expression.

"It was very good of him to return, Loula," she answered. "But he mustn't see me. I want him to always remember me—as I was. He will think more of me that way."

"But, Luane," Loula added, "doesn't it matter that he may be in danger?"

The nurse pursed her lips, and for a moment appeared to be in deep thought.

"Danger?" she questioned at length. "What danger could Bantan be in?"

"The Great One has made him a prisoner in the castle," the servant girl moaned. "Don't you remember The Great One?"

A sorrowful expression now overcame Luane's features, and she again appeared in deep thought. Then, as though she recollected such a personage, she covered her eyes with her hands and started weeping.

"The Great One!" she moaned. "How could he have done to me what he has?"

"You don't want any punishment to happen to Bantan, do you?" Loula then asked. "Remember, he risked his life for you. You and I were going away with him."

Luane buried her face in her arms and her shoulders shook convulsively. When she at last controlled herself, she uncovered her features and lifted piteous eyes to the servant girl. She appeared rational for the time being. She shook her head hopelessly.

"I can't go with him now, Loula," she said. "You know I can't. But there is no reason why you can't. Perhaps he may learn to love you as he loved me. As for me, nothing matters any more. But so long as I live I'll always remember that we kissed and acknowledged our love for each other. I can die happy with that sweet thought."

With the utterance of her words her brief spell of sanity left her, and bowing her head, she again crooned in a monotone how she and Bantan had been in love.

Loula's eyes became saddened and she drew a long breath, exhaling slowly. Thinking of Bantan, she also gave thought of The Great One. She wondered if he were in his quarters—or perhaps in the laboratory, making ready with plans for more fiendish experiments with the prisoner as his subject.

The thought that the bronzed giant would eventually be reduced to the gibbering mental status that Amar was made her shudder.

Looking again at the crooning Luane, she could hardly believe the past four days and nights had wrought such a horrible change in her—and the end was not in sight yet. How well she remembered the words of The Great One when he had told Luane her punishment for disloyalty would be one year for each hour that she lived. The servant girl could scarce repress the shudder that wracked her as she looked upon the changed nurse in comparison to the loveliness she had known a scant four days ago. It was hardly possible, yet the living proof was before her.

Now she leaned toward the recumbent form of her mistress.

"Listen carefully to me, Luane," she said.

The crooning ceased as the nurse looked up at the servant girl with wondering eyes.

"I'm going to leave you alone for a short while," she said. "But I will be back soon. You will be all right?"

An affrighted look came into Luane's eyes for a moment. Her strangely thin hands clutched the servant girl's in desperation.

"You won't be long, Loula?" she begged.

"I won't be any longer than necessary," was the promise. "You will be all right?"

The nurse nodded presently.

"But don't be too long," she murmured.

At the next moment, as though nothing else mattered, Luane resumed her crooning in a monotone that Bantan had returned for her and they had been in love.

Loula regarded her mistress for a long moment in silence, then she nodded. Turning, she left the room, not bothering to lock the door behind her.

Stealthily she went her way, her quest known only to herself. She was aware of her labored breathing and the rapid thumping of her heart. Presently she stepped on the elevator and operated the lever to take her down to the level of the laboratory. In a few minutes she was softly stealing along the dimly lit corridor. Her right hand pressed at her waist where beneath the *tupa* cloth dress she could feel the outline of Bantan's dagger.

After she had passed the door of the laboratory, she did not hear it softly open and a masked face appear in the opening. Piercing blue eyes glittered wildly in recognition of the servant girl. At the next moment a tall figure in white uniform and with rubber-gloved hands was following the girl.

Loula knew where the three Amo Island prisoners were confined, also the one containing the prince known as Amar. She knew there was only one other unoccupied cell on this level and it adjoined the one Amar occupied. If Bantan had been confined at this level, the unoccupied cell would be the likely place he was to be found.

Unerringly she went to it, meanwhile, withdrawing Bantan's dagger from its place of concealment. As she reached the barred window the weapon in her right hand was extended through the bars.

"Bantan!" she softly called.

There was a muffled reply from within. At the next moment the prisoner was standing just within the door. In the dim light he at once recognized the proffered dagger and he accepted it with thanks, sheathing it at his right hip.

"I saw you captured, Bantan," the servant girl murmured. "But I could do nothing to help you at the time."

"Tell me, Loula," he whispered in reply. "While I looked through the window, Luane seemed so strangely different. What has happened to her?"

A muffled gasp was uttered by the servant girl. A strong, gloved hand covered her mouth, while another clutched her arm in a merciless grip. A smothered moan escaped through her flared nostrils. Without a word the tall figure rudely forced the girl along the dimly lit corridor the way she had come. Upon reaching the laboratory door, which had been left open, she was thrust within, and with a kick of a foot, the door was closed by the tall figure with masked features. Then he removed his hand from her mouth and spun her around to face him, his piercing blue eyes filled with rage.

Loula cowered momentarily, so frightened she was.

"Traitor!" the metallic voice accused her. His gloved hand smartly slapped the side of her face. "First, Luane proved a traitor! And now—you!" Again he slapped her face and tears came to Loula's eyes. "You know what is happening to Luane because of her disloyalty. But your fate shall be different.

There is no place in this castle for any one who would interfere with my life work. You shall be destroyed— immediately!"

With his words he again slapped the girl's face with such force that her senses reeled, and she collapsed to the floor with a moan and lay still.

With a muttered imprecation The Great One stepped to the wall and threw a switch. Nearby was a latched door made of iron, four feet in length by three in width. He opened it wide. Already warmth was emanating from the darkened chamber within. He returned to the servant girl's unconscious form. Stooping, he gathered its laxness into his arms. Approaching the door of the crematory, he thrust her feet through the opening, then quickly pushed the rest of the body within.

Recovering consciousness in these last moments, and aware that something horrible was going to happen to her, Loula's shrieks were drowned out as The Great One slammed the door shut, then he turned and departed from the laboratory.

CHAPTER XXV

LUANE'S SECRET

Drawing himself close to the barred opening, Bantan watched The Great One hustle Loula along the dimly lit corridor, and he saw the mad scientist enter the laboratory with his victim. In desperation, feeling The Great One would subject the servant girl to some unthinkable form of punishment, the bronzed giant reached out a hand through the bars then followed with his entire arm, with finger tips seeking to reach the sliding bar below. Unable to reach it, he did not give up hope, however.

Quickly he withdrew his arm and grasped the handle of his dagger. Once again he inserted his hand through the bars, and with the handle of his dagger tightly clasped, he extended his arm full length as before, and this time he felt the point of the weapon just reach the wooden bar.

Now came the question—would he be able to slide it backward by pricking it and moving his hand as much as his wrist would permit? He was grateful the point was exceptionally sharp, for it did not slip. He strained his wrist a trifle and he had the satisfaction in feeling the bar move a little. A grim smile touched his lips as repeated operations of this nature slowly moved the bar backward. While beads of perspiration gathered upon his forehead, and he felt the palm of the dagger hand become moist as well, he continued with this operation. Thinking of Loula made him hurry as much as possible. Each second seemed like a long while. His ears were listening carefully for the moment the slight drag of the wooden bar would inform him when it cleared the bracket that barred his way to freedom.

Now, it did so, and at that same moment Bantan saw The Great One leave the laboratory, slamming the door behind him. The fact that Loula had been forced to enter and that he came out alone resulted in all sorts of suggestive thoughts relative to some fiendish punishment being inflicted upon the servant girl.

Withdrawing his arm from between the bars, Bantan sheathed his dagger, then pushed the cell door open just as the mad scientist boarded the elevator and it started upward to the level above. The bronzed giant thoughtfully turned as he stepped out of the cell, and closing the door replaced the bar.

He speedily raced the length of the dimly lit corridor to the laboratory door and flung it open, his keen eyes darting all about the interior for sign of Loula. Not seeing her, he entered and closed the door behind him. He knew the girl must be somewhere within, since she had not accompanied The Great One when he had left.

As he stood there in silence, to his keen ears came a dimly muffled cry for help. An ordinary pair of ears would not have heard the faint cries, but Bantan's were of the keenest. He glanced about for a brief moment to ascertain from which direction the sounds issued. He noticed the latched iron door across the room. That seemed to be from where the barely audible cries for succor issued. In an instant he dashed to the wall and flung open the latched door. Warm air fanned his face. Then he saw a hand upraised. More faint cries were to be heard which alternated to choking sobs. Conscious, the innocent victim within raised herself so that Bantan could see her face. It was Loula!

The bronzed giant reached within for her extended hand and speedily, yet gently, drew her out of the crematory. She was sobbing quietly as he stood her upon her feet; but so great the shock she had been subjected to, she would have collapsed had she not realized the identity of her rescuer. She threw her arms about his neck with a happy cry and he felt her limbs trembling as she clung to him.

"Oh, Bantan!" she moaned. "The devil would have burned me to death!"

Upon the instant Bantan relatched the crematory door, then turned to the girl in his arms who was still sobbing.

"Loula, you are all right now," he comforted her.

"How—how did you get out of your cell?" she then asked, controlling her weeping, and her body did not shudder so convulsively.

"With the dagger you risked your life to bring me," he replied. "Without it I wouldn't have been able to free myself so that I could come to your rescue. I saw The Great One force you to enter the laboratory, and when he came out I noticed you were not with him. Now that we are both free, we must make our escape from the castle. Come, let's get out of here before the mad scientist should return and find us."

With an arm about the still weakened girl, Bantan opened the door cautiously and looked outside in the dimly lit corridor. No one was to be seen. Stepping out of the laboratory, the door was closed behind them.

They then approached the elevator shaft, suspecting the conveyance was upon the ground floor level above them.

"Can you bring the elevator down, Loula?" he asked.

The servant girl nodded. She reached for the button that would lower it and pressed it. While they waited for the elevator to come down to this level, Bantan was aware that the girl's eyes were riveted upon him with devoted gratefulness.

"Now you have saved my life, Bantan," she murmured, smiling wistfully and drawing a deep breath.

"And I owe you my liberty, Loula," he said with a smile. "Tell me, what has happened to Luane?"

The servant's girl's smile faded and her eyes became saddened.

"It's horrible!" she murmured. "She doesn't want you to see her as she is now. She wants you to remember her as she was." She shook her head hopelessly at his questioning eyes. "Nothing can help her now," she added. "Must I tell you more?"

"Couldn't I see her just once more—if it is possible?" he asked. "I cannot forget that we acknowledged our love for each other only five suns ago."

The elevator now had come to a stop at their level. They stepped aboard and Loula operated the lever.

"You really want to see Luane?" she asked, shaking her head. "She may not recognize you and then again she may."

He did not voice the silent plea that she read in his dark eyes in the dimly lit elevator. With a deep sigh and a resolute shake of her head, Loula nodded.

"As you wish, Bantan," she murmured resignedly.

Presently the elevator came to a stop and the door

was opened. Before stepping out, the servant girl looked into the corridor. It was clear. Perhaps The Great One had retired to his quarters for the night.

"Come, Bantan," she said, placing a hand upon his arm.

They went along the corridor stealthily until presently they came to Luane's quarters. Loula opened the door softly and peered within.

Luane was still lying upon the couch. She was alone in the room. Apparently she hadn't stirred since the servant girl had left her a short while before.

"Do you still want to see and talk with her, Bantan?" Loula asked with concern. "You may regret it."

He nodded, a faint, yet brave, smile touching his lips.

The servant girl stepped into the room, and her companion followed. Loula paused to lock the door, then turned to Bantan. They crossed the room noiselessly until they stood at the side of the couch, Loula standing near the head of her mistress, while the young man was near her side. He was peering down at the recumbent woman lying upon her left side so that her features were not to be readily seen.

"Luane," the servant girl whispered. "I've brought Bantan to see you."

A shudder wracked the wasted form, and she seemed to breathe stertorously.

Bantan, meanwhile, was aware of a chill fastening upon his spine, and he hardly breathed because of the horror he felt coursing through him. His keen eyes studied the snow-white hair, and something about the way Luane was lying upon the couch made him realize that he was looking at an extremely *old* woman. He tried to assure himself that could not be, for only five

suns before he had known her to be in the full bloom
of youth, with sparkling eyes, glowing skin, and the
agility of a girl his age.

Now he saw that Luane was stirring. With great
effort she seemed to be trying to turn over, but for
some reason lacked the strength to do so.

"Is that you, Loula?" the croaking voice asked. "I
don't seem to be able to move."

A shudder wracked Bantan's giant form as he heard
the voice that spoke, and as the servant girl looked
at him, she could see the painful wonder in his eyes
as he stared helplessly at the now quivering form upon
the couch.

Loula bent and put an arm about her mistress and
turned her over upon her back. As she did so, Bantan
muffled the gasp of horror that otherwise would have
escaped his lips, for he looked upon a wrinkled, mummified face that retained only a very slight resemblance
to the dear one that he had known so recently. The
features had shriveled, the cheeks were tautily drawn
and had the ashy pallor of death. The once sweet, red,
full lips were reduced to thin lines and were colorless.
Her eyes were sunken deeply in dark-rimmed sockets.

At that very moment Luane's closed lids fluttered
open, but seemed unable to remain so. Her mouth appeared to work feverishly, but at last she managed to
speak in a low, croaking tone.

"Where are you, Loula?" she muttered. "My eyes
are open, but I can't see anything."

The bronzed giant's eyes sought Loula's and he
shook his head hopelessly. Tears appeared in the servant girl's eyes, realizing as she did what a shock it
was for Bantan to see the once beautiful Luane reduced to this pitiful state of senility. He forced a brave

Bantan Looks Upon the Aged Luane

smile to his face and nodded indicatingly, then as Loula moved to one side, he went down upon his knees at Luane's side. He reached for one of her wasted hands and held it in his, meanwhile wondering why hers was so icy cold.

"Luane," he murmured chokingly. "I have come."

The nurse's features registered surprise at hearing a voice that her fading mentality must have recognized in the seemingly long-ago past.

"Who are you?" she asked in quivering tones. She tried to raise herself but lacked the strength. Her thin colorless lips moved feverishly. "The voice is familiar, but I can't see you. I must be blind."

"I am Bantan," he said in gentle tones. "Bantan."

The lusterless eyes seemed to stare up at him and her groping mentality tried to grasp the full meaning of the name.

"Bantan?" she muttered questionably. And then again: "Bantan?"

And then it seemed in her jumbled mentality there surged recognition of the identity of a man named Bantan, and what he meant to her. Her sightless eyes closed and the wasted hand at her side lifted with some effort as she tried to cover her wrinkled, mummified face. A tremor seemed to pulse through her.

"No, Bantan," she begged in a weak voice. "You— mustn't look at me as I am now. Try to remember me —as I was. I told Loula I wanted you to never see me again—as I am now."

"Listen, Luane," he said in a low voice. "Do not blame Loula. I wanted to see you."

Luane seemed to marshal her failing strength in a final effort to explain to him what had happened and that he forgive her for her deception. Her faculties became clear in her supreme endeavor. Once again her sightless eyes opened.

"Bantan, I know I should never have fallen in love with you," she confessed in quivering tones that were clear because she spoke slowly and enunciated her syllables distinctly. "And you should not have fallen in love with me. Listen to me carefully. I am over *two hundred years old*. I never told you, but The Great One is my father.

"He learned after extensive studying and experiments, the long-sought secret of longevity, and he endowed me thusly when I was very young. Together, we have kept this secret from the world. Because my father was much older than I at the time he naturally doesn't look as youthful as he might. Because of a mistake I made in those early days in a laboratory with him, his face is horribly scarred, and for that reason he wears a mask.

"When I told him that I had fallen in love with you and we were to escape, he became enraged because of my disloyalty; for, when he first endowed me with longevity, he made me promise that I would always remain with him. In a blind rage he injected a serum into my veins which would counteract the effects of longevity, and that would make me age a year for each hour that passed at the present until I looked my actual age. I must look at least a hundred years old now, and I am losing my strength fast. Already I am blind. I have forgiven my father for what he has done to me, for I realize he isn't responsible for anything he does now. Say that you will forgive me for deceiving you, Bantan. Please—forgive me—please—" Her voice trailed into nothingness.

And then it seemed her strength was spent. Her

eyes closed and she appeared lifeless. The ashy pallor
of her wasted face darkened. Her thin lips were working feverishly again as though her fading mentality
must still obtain his forgiveness. Her lips parted again
and he heard her plea.

"Please—forgive me, Bantan."

The bronzed giant's eyes were filled with unshed
tears as he stared down at the mummified face of the
Luane that he had known when she had been in the
full bloom of apparent youth and was the vibrant
picture of abounding health.

"Of course, Luane," he murmured. "To prove my
forgiveness to you—"

He bent and pressed his lips to the center of her
cold forehead. The semblance of a smile touched the
thin lips, and she sighed deeply, happily.

"Thank you, Bantan," she whispered. "Now—go
with Loula—away from this accursed island. I have
the feeling I am going to die very soon. Thank you
again."

A deep, long-drawn sigh was emitted from her
lips and then she became still. The hand that Bantan
held in his seemed to stiffen for a moment, then became lax. His eyes rested for a moment upon her
flattened chest, and he was aware there seemed no
movement.

"Luane!" he murmured. "Luane!"

Drawing back he looked upon the aged features of
what only so few days ago had been of a young woman in vibrant health and youth. An icy chill raced
the length of his spine as he placed the cold hand upon
her flat bosom. The semblance of a smile still touched
Luane's thin lips. With eyes blurred from moisture the
bronzed giant then arose to his feet, but still staring

down at the silent features as though mesmerized. He seemed unaware of time and place until he felt a warm hand close upon one of his, and he looked down into the servant girl's understanding eyes which were overflowing with tears.

"Come, Bantan," she murmured, "if we are to escape, as Luane urged, let us be on our way."

The bronzed giant's frame seemed to tremble. Once more, before he could leave, he bent and pressed his lips upon the center of Luane's cold forehead, then he straightened and drew a deep breath.

"Come, Loula," he said in a low voice, "let us be on our way."

They went to the door leading outside. Unlocking it, the servant girl pushed it open then stepped outside. Upon the threshold Bantan paused a long moment to look once more at the silent form in death. Closing his eyes briefly, he shook his head sadly. He then joined Loula, closing the door after him with the realization Luane's secret was no more.

Chapter XXVI

IN HIDING

In the dense darkness Bantan reached for Loula's hand.

"We'll go along the wall until we come to the door," he said.

The servant girl offered no comment. As the minutes passed, and their eyes became more accustomed to the night they found their way easier. The myriad stars offered scant illumination to help them. In due time they reached the massive door in the wall. The bronzed giant's groping fingers presently found the button. Pressing it, the barely audible whining sound of a motor was to be heard and the door moved inward. The young man and the girl stepped outside. Another button was located and pressed, and the door swung shut.

"At last," Loula murmured, "I'm outside the castle walls!" With her words she drew a deep breath and exhaled slowly.

"Poor Luane!" her companion murmured.

The girl's hand pressed his gently.

"It was horrible the way she changed during the past four suns," she added. "For each hour that she lived she became a year older—and would have continued so until she reached her true age."

"Over two hundred years old," he said reflectively. "One would never have guessed five suns ago."

Loula agreeingly murmured something to that effect.

"From where we are now," he said, changing the subject, "it is not too far from the cove where I have a canoe waiting. You are sure, Loula, that you want to go with me?"

The girl's hand tightened a trifle in his.

"I have nowhere else to go, Bantan," she replied in a faraway voice. "I can't return to the village, for should The Great One know that I had—and doubtless he would soon learn—he would have me brought back to the castle. Another time I might not be so fortunate as I was this last time."

"That is right," he agreed. "You have no choice but to accompany me. Come, let us be on our way."

Bantan was grateful that the foliage was sparse, for the travelling was that much easier. Naturally, owing to the darkness, it required longer to reach the edge of the cliff than when he had come this way earlier in the declining daylight hours; but at last he and the girl reached their objective. Standing at its edge and looking down into the darkness, the young man spoke to the girl at his side.

"Down below is the cove where I have a canoe provisioned and ready for launching, Loula," he said. "All we have to do now is go down the face of the cliff."

The girl looked down into the pitch darkness and a shiver pulsed through her, for she could see nothing but impenetrable blackness.

"There is no other way, Bantan?" she asked plaintively, and he could detect a tremor of fear in her voice.

"There's no other way," he admitted.

Loula heaved a deep sigh.

"If we must go down, we must," she said with a trace of bravado in her tones.

He silently admired her for words.

"You don't think I'd let you go down in the darkness alone?" he asked.

"But—but you can't carry me down," she protested mildly.

"It would be safest for you that I did," he advised. "I've been up and down a number of times and I'm more sure of the way than you would be. Come, when I'm over the edge, you get on my back and put your arms about my shoulders. Try not to have your feet touch the face of the cliff, for it might unbalance me."

"As you say, then," she acquiesced meekly.

In another moment he was backing over the edge of the cliff upon hands and knees, his toes finding a firm hold in one of the many crevices in the face of the rock.

"Now, Loula," he said.

In the darkness the girl managed to attain the position he suggested. She clung to him as he had instructed.

"Having saved your life," he said, "I'll now try to preserve it. I owe you my liberty and will be forever grateful to you for risking your life for me. Now, I'm ready to descend, so trust me."

Moisture appeared in the girl's eyes as she pressed her cheek to his shoulder.

"I'd trust you forever, Bantan," she murmured softly.

The bronzed giant started to descend the face of the cliff with the girl clinging to his back. She was careful

to obey whatever instructions he gave her while slowly
lowering himself; but that the girl was nearly frightened to death he could easily determine, for where her
bosom pressed his back he could feel the wild thumping
of her heart; and upon the occasions when he momentarily appeared to lose a handhold but almost immediately grasped another, he could hear her gasping
breath, and then she would sigh easily.

Down to the side of the cavern's opening Bantan
moved slowly. He informed Loula that was where he
had been in hiding while the villagers had been searching for him. As they passed beyond the cavern's mouth
the muffled sounds of birds roosting there was to be
heard. The bronzed giant told the girl how he had
driven the birds away that first night when he sought
refuge there, but now they had returned to their
former home.

Several times in the perilous descent thereafter Bantan's finger tips would slip a trifle, and the poor girl
clinging to him would hold her breath and her heart
would hammer still greater, but he was thankful that
she didn't panic.

After what seemed a long while to Loula, they
reached the sandy beach of the cove beneath. Bantan
heaved a sigh of relief, and the girl reluctantly released her arms from his shoulders. She leaned against
the side of the cliff, drawing deep breaths.

"I can tell you now, Bantan," she said, "how really
frightened I was."

A smile touched his lips.

"I knew all the time, Loula," he answered. "Your
thumping heart and the way you breathed told me bet-

ter than words. But, it was very brave of you to trust me as you did."

Although the girl had no words to speak in answer, she was very grateful for his praise.

With eyes accustomed to the darkness, Bantan was looking for the canoe he had left here shortly before sundown. The soft swishing of the waves laving the shore and the further booming of the surf dashing against the rocky shore to either side of the cove were the only sounds to be heard. Search as he did, there was no sight of his canoe.

"It's gone, Loula!" he exclaimed.

The girl drew near him.

"What could have happened to it?" she asked dismayingly.

"That is what I would like to know," he answered. "But wait—there is another that I cached between the rocks. The only difference is, my canoe was provisioned and the other is not. Wait here and I'll get it."

In another moment, recollecting upon which side of the cove he had hidden it, Bantan was scrambling up the rocks and with no difficulty located Bora's canoe. In the darkness he tugged upon it and finally drew it free of its hiding place. Presently he had lowered it to the sandy cove. Searching within, he ascertained its paddle was in the bottom.

"We have a canoe now, but no provisions," he said to the girl. "We can't set out for Marja without any. I have a plan. I'll paddle with you to where I first landed upon the Island. Fruit grows there in an abundance. We'll stay there and get some rest until daylight, then we'll gather the fruit we need and be on our way without further delay."

"Do whatever you think is best," Loula agreed.

Bantan dragged the canoe to the water's edge and told the girl to enter. When she was settled near the bow he pushed it into deeper water. Leaping within he picked up the paddle and plied it expertly. When the canoe was paddled out beyond the breaking waves, he then maintained a course parallel with the shore until in due time he reached that part of the island where he had first landed. He then turned the prow shoreward. When the canoe was beached both occupants leaped out, and the bronzed giant drew the water craft up on the shore and a short distance within the foliage.

"Now, Loula, we'll gather some grasses," he said. "You may sleep within the canoe and I'll sleep on the ground at its side."

With a little difficulty because of the darkness they gathered grasses, palm fronds, and ferns and arranged them in suitable pallets.

"Sleep well," he bade her, as she stepped into the canoe, and he lay upon the crude pallet he had arranged for himself at its side.

A smile of gratitude touched the girl's lips as she leaned over the edge of the canoe. She could hardly discern him in the darkness.

"Thank you, Bantan," she murmured. "I'll be ever grateful to you."

"And I'll be ever grateful to you as well," he answered.

Bantan composed himself for sleep. So quiet it was his keen ears presently were aware of the girl's even breathing, indicating that she had already fallen asleep. Constantly in his thoughts was the recollection of Luane's wrinkled, mummified features, and an irrepressible chill would race the length of his spine.

Time and again he would dispel this vision of senility, but always it returned. He then concentrated on the features of the Luane he had loved and in this was successful. Then at last weary Nature overwhelmed his subconsciousness, and in this more favorable state of mind he slept in peace.

Shortly after the lower rim of the sun cleared the eastern horizon, Bantan awoke. Feeling refreshed, he at once arose to his feet, stretching. Looking down into the canoe he saw that Loula was still sleeping soundly. She lay upon her right side, her features partly covered with her lustrous hair, and her hands were folded at her bosom. He reached down and slightly rocked the canoe. At once the girl's eyes opened and she arose to a seated position. Aware of the bronzed giant smiling down at her, she, too, smiled.

"Pleasant morning, Loula," he greeted her.

"Pleasant morning to you, Bantan," she returned the greeting.

"Ready to gather fruits so that we might sooner be on our way?" he asked. "We have a long trip ahead— four suns' paddling."

She nodded eagerly.

Presently they were gathering fruit and storing it in the canoe. When they returned to the beach with the last armful, it was then that Bantan's ears strained— Loula, too, heard what he did. The talking drum from the castle sounded. The young giant turned to the girl.

"Evidently The Great One has found me missing," he remarked. "He must be enraged to know I've escaped him again."

A wry smile touched the girl's face.

"He must wonder how it happened this time," she added. "If he were to know you rescued me from the horrible death he intended for me, he would have greater reason to be angry."

"Madman and brilliant scientist that he is," he declared with a shake of his head, "he is Luane's father. She forgave him for the horrible thing he did to her, so we cannot do less. Come, let's be on our way before warriors from the village in canoes are searching for us."

As he spoke, Bantan heard the talking drum of the village answering the one from the distant castle.

"Now the villagers will know about me," he added.

Without further loss of time the young giant, with the girl's assistance, dragged the laden canoe to the water's edge.

"Wait here," he bade her. "There is something I must do before we leave."

Bantan quickly ran to the foliage and procured a leafy branch suitable for the purpose intended. Backing down the beach he swept the branch back and forth, erasing their footprints and the mark of the canoe's bottom from the sand.

The girl had been watching him with a wondering look on her face until he reached her. He turned to her with a smile.

"That may mean the difference between being followed," he explained. "Now, let's prepare to leave."

"You think of everything," she commended.

At his indication she stepped into the canoe. He handed her the leafy branch.

"Keep this until we have reached some little distance from shore," he said.

The girl accepted the branch without comment. Bantan lost no further time launching the canoe into the surf, and in another moment had leaped within and was plying the paddle with powerful strokes. Because the canoe rode lower with the added weight of the fruit some water washed over the gunwale, but presently they were beyond the surf and the water craft rode easier.

"At last, Loula!" he said with a sigh. "We are on our way."

The girl smiled with relief. She looked to her right and then her eyes strayed to the left. Bantan was aware of the startled expression that instantly sprang on her face and she uttered a cry of disappointment.

"Look, Bantan!" she cried, pointing to her left.

As the paddler's eyes looked in that direction, he saw two canoes rounding the shoreline, approaching in their direction. Each canoe contained four paddlers, and now, having seen the canoe with the escaping fugitives, each warrior plied his paddle with greater effort.

In an instant Bantan weighed his chances of making good his escape with Loula. He shook his head. Quickly he turned the canoe about and headed for shore with powerful strokes.

The girl was silent, but her cheeks were pale. She dropped the branch into the water, knowing it was useless to hold it further.

"We can't outdistance them," Bantan said quietly, but with flashing eyes. "Our only choice is to return ashore and hope we can elude search parties until night. If so, then I'll try and steal a canoe from the village and we'll start for Marja then. The stars will be my guide."

Moisture appeared in the girl's eyes.

"Do whatever you think is best," was all she said.

Bantan's features were grim, but whenever his eyes met Loula's he managed a brief smile. Within minutes the canoe was beached, and both leaped out, and in another moment had disappeared into the foliage out of sight from the paddlers who were now nearing the surf.

"Come, Loula," the bronzed giant said. "I don't dare try to reach the cavern, for I have the feeling our pursuers will think that is where we are headed. Instead, we'll go in the opposite direction."

Bantan led the way some twenty to thirty feet from the foliage outlining the beach with the girl close upon his heels. He traversed the easiest routes so she would not become exhausted too soon. They heard the warriors when they beached their canoes give shouts, and one, apparently the leader of the expedition, then gave instructions. In the subsequent minutes their voices were fading. Pausing, while the girl reached his side, her bosom heaving from her exertion, they listened intently.

"It is as I have said, Loula." He nodded and smiled as he spoke. "The searchers are headed for the cavern. Someone in a canoe must have passed the cove just before sundown when I was on my way to the castle. My canoe was seen and towed away to the village. Knowing in the dark I would not be found they waited until morning. Those canoes had left the village before the drum from the castle announced my escape."

The girl nodded, for what he had said was quite evident.

"Have no fear," he assured her. "We'll outwit the searchers until night."

"I'll hope everything will be as you say, Bantan," the girl answered wistfully.

His smile was encouraging.

"Let's continue our way," he suggested. "We can take our time now."

They were travelling southward, and since the village was located upon the southwest shore, in a little while they could hear the sounds of children yelling and shrieking while at play. The two fugitives concealed themselves behind a clump of dense ferns and rested.

"Do you think we will be safe here, so near the village?" Loula asked her companion with a worried look upon her face.

"The villagers won't think we would dare to approach so close," he said assuringly.

The hours passed without incident while they remained in their place of hiding. Intermittently they heard shouts from the village, and in the distance they heard the crackling of underbrush. With ears straining, they ascertained the sounds did not come closer. Upon these occasions Bantan would nod assuringly to the girl, and she would smile and shake her head in silent wonder because of her inability to understand his strategy.

"How are you so sure?" she asked once.

In a low voice he told of his adventures in hiding from a vicious enemy known as Japanese.

"They had weapons that spoke death from a distance," he added. "I escaped them so now I feel I can escape from warriors armed only with spears and daggers."

"But I'm with you now," she demurred.

"My foster sister Wanya was with me then," he added.

The girl reached out a hand and rested it upon one of his.

"Just to touch you, Bantan," she said smilingly, "is all the confidence I need."

At noonday the drum from the castle and the one in the village exchanged messages for some little while. Bantan and Loula listened, more through curiosity than anything else since they could not interpret the messages that were being sent and received.

When the drums were no longer to be heard, the bronzed giant arose from where he had been squatting, and with a smile extended a hand to the girl. She reached out a hand and he clasped it and drew her to her feet. A slightly wondering expression was upon her face.

"I think it will be safe for us to return to where we beached the canoe," he said. "The searchers have been there and in all probability have taken our canoe away. We shall see."

They returned from whence they had come, keeping close to the beach but sufficiently sheltered by foliage in the event a canoe might be patrolling beyond the surf. Looking through the fronds of a magnificent fern, Bantan saw no canoes upon the shimmering water, but he did not intend to take unnecessary chances. They ate of fruit which they gathered on the way.

In due time without interference, and not once hearing any sounds of searchers nearby, the bronzed giant and the girl reached that part of the shore where they had beached their canoe. Peering through the screening foliage, as might have been expected, the laden canoe had been taken away. He nodded to the girl.

"Just as I expected," he commented.

"Do you think it will be safe to remain here until night?" she then asked.

"I don't believe the searchers will come here again," he said, nodding. "They would not feel we would return, so we will be safe."

They awaited the passing time, keeping their ears alert for any sounds which would indicate searchers were nearby. While they were thus, Loula asked Bantan to tell her more of the Japanese. In a low voice he related the experiences that she wished to know; all the while she listend in awe, but rapture shone in her dark eyes. As he was speaking, the bronzed giant's eyes were looking hither and yon, and his keen ears were always alert.

It was about an hour from sundown when they heard the drum from the castle sounding, and presently the one in the village answered. An exchange of messages followed.

"Now, Loula," Bantan suggested, "we should gather more fruit and store it here for later when I steal a canoe from the village."

Without a demur the girl joined him, and in a little while they had a variety of fruit in readiness. The sun was a short distance from the horizon by this time.

"Now," he said, "you are to remain here while I go to the village." He noticed the hurt look in her eyes as he spoke. He shook his head with a smile. "Have no fear for me."

"It isn't that I fear for you, Bantan," she said in a

low voice. "I don't like to be separated from you."

He smiled kindly as he drew near her. He placed a gentle hand upon her shoulder and observed the moisture in her eyes affected by the thought of being separated from him, even if only for a short time. With compassion he kissed her gently upon the forehead.

With a muffled, gasping cry the girl moved her head and her lips pressed the back of his hand as it rested upon her shoulder. Then she quickly drew back with a shy smile.

"Hurry, Bantan," she said, fighting back her tears. "I'll be watching and waiting for your return. The sooner you go the sooner you should return."

He nodded, and with a parting smile, was on his way. Before disappearing behind a luxuriant fern, he paused and waved to the tearful girl. She waved in return, and then the tears came as he disappeared from her view.

CHAPTER XXVII

CONCLUSION

With grimness now clear upon his face and determination in his dark eyes, Bantan stealthily crept through the foliage, pausing at frequent intervals to ascertain there was no nearby sound of searchers. Minutes passed swiftly, as they often do, especially when one was racing against the swift coming of night. Already the sun was half beyond the horizon and shadows were lengthening. It was his hope to reach the outskirts of the village, so that he might possibly reach a vantage position to survey the beach, and hope he might distinguish his own canoe among the others that must be beached from the possible reach of a high, incoming tide.

He was within a quarter-mile from his objective when he paused, hearing sounds of crackling undergrowth not far from his right. He concealed himself in a clump of gorgeous ferns surrounded by exotic flowers, the scent of which almost caused his senses to reel. He waited patiently while a small group of wearied warriors appeared with spears in hand and daggers sheathed at their hips. As he watched them pass within a dozen feet from where he was concealed, he could easily determine they appeared disgusted with their failure to locate the escaped fugitives.

A few minutes after they had passed, the bronzed giant ventured forth from his hiding place and followed surreptitiously in their wake. Presently, from the

sounds to be heard ahead, he realized he was nearing
the Mandoes village. He circled about until he was
upon the outskirts of the village, just concealed from
open view of the beach. Though the swishing water
laving the beach could be heard, beyond he observed a
half dozen nearly naked boys running along the shore
in a game of seeing how close they could come to the
washing waves without getting wet.

Vagrant emanations from cooking pots mingling
with the acrid odor of wood fires were wafted to Bantan's delicate nostrils, and he knew very shortly the
villagers would be partaking of their evening meal.

Closer he drew toward the landing, keeping concealed as much as possible, but all the while his eyes
were alert. By this time the sun had completely disappeared behind the waterline. A few warriors still
lingered in seemingly endless inspection of their canoes.
The bronzed giant had now come to the last possible
place of advance, for no further foliage grew than
that behind which he stood.

Quickly his eyes were darting from one canoe to another. Some of the warriors were leaving the inspection of their canoes, and sauntered to their respective
huts where their mates and daughters were preparing
the evening meal. The boys dashing back and forth
on the beach discontinued their game, and went running to the village, they, too, perhaps anxious to partake of their evening meal.

Now Bantan's searching eyes lit up brightly. He
espied his canoe—the one which was different from the
others! It was near the middle of the score and more
that were beached high up on the sand—almost at the
very edge of the village.

Already dusk was descending upon the water and the beach. A single warrior now remained in clear view. The silent watcher was becoming a trifle impatient when fortunately a little boy came to the warrior and spoke to him. With some reluctance he left his canoe, and followed the boy into the village.

The time had come! Crouched low, Bantan emerged from his hiding place. His canoe was some forty feet away. Like a fleet shadow he dashed toward it and flung himself at its side. Looking about, he ascertained no one had observed him, for there had been no alarming cry of discovery. Looking within his canoe he saw that all of the fruit had been removed, as would be expected, but fortunately his paddle was still within.

Looking apprehensively toward the village he could see warriors and women passing back and forth, also some children were playing near the outskirts. Crouched, he laid a hand upon the stern of the canoe, and in this manner moved it gradually toward the edge of the washing waves a good thirty feet away.

In the western sky the fast fading sun's golden light penetrated the varying cloud formations, presenting a beautiful display, but in the passing seconds the glamorous aspect changed rapidly. The darkness in the east was advancing rapidly over the countless miles of water, and the Mandoes Island was directly in its path, waiting to be absorbed by its gentle mantle.

Bantan would pause every few yards to look apprehensively toward the village. Everything still appeared in his favor. Only a few feet now remained to be covered. He seemingly froze as the drum from the distant castle was to be heard. While it was sending its message, he straightened and dragged the canoe into the surf. As he leaped into it, it was then that the village drum answered the distant one from the castle.

With powerful strokes the bronzed giant sent his canoe through the surf to presently gain the calmer water beyond. The drums were exchanging messages as he maintained a course beyond the breaking waves, and within minutes, so speedily did the canoe forge onward before the sturdy strokes of the occupant's paddle, the village landing was presently beyond sight in the quickly descending darkness.

Shortly the mantle of swiftly advancing darkness of night overswept the island. Around the southwest shore the canoe raced, and presently was coursing along the southerly side. The foliage was becoming somewhat of a blur with passing minutes and the beach was very dark.

With eyes that strained, Bantan was carefully studying the blurred formation of tree growth until at last he had reached the place where he was sure he had first landed upon the island.

Loula had been hopefully awaiting him, and when her sharp eyes discerned the movement beyond the surf, she ran out upon the beach and waved her arms frantically, though she doubted that the paddler could see her.

Bantan now turned the prow of the canoe shoreward and within a few minutes it touched the sandy beach. He immediately turned the water craft end for end. Almost at the same instant the girl reached him. She heaved a deep sigh.

"I thought you'd never come, Bantan," she murmured with relief.

"But I have, Loula," he assured her. "Come, let's get the provisions and load them in the canoe so we can be on our way."

In the darkness they made several trips with arms laden with fruits, and when the last had been brought, both sighed with relief.

"And now, Loula, we are ready," Bantan said. "Take your place."

The girl quickly scrambled into the canoe and announced she was ready.

Bantan launched the canoe into the surf and leaped within. Quickly he snatched up his paddle and plied it with mighty strokes. Some water washed over the gunwale, but not in alarming quantities. Soon the calmer water was reached. Now the bronzed giant spoke to the girl.

"When I came to Mandoes Island," he said, "my heart was filled with bitterness and a vow to avenge a great wrong. The Great One avenged the wrong for me. For some reason I cannot explain I am glad that it was so. There was happiness in knowing Luane as she was, and a sadness now that I saw her at the time of her death. But I had to see her—had I not, I would have regretted so long as I may live even though your life and mine were in peril. And now, Loula, we are going to Marja, and I hope very much you will never regret your choice."

"I had no other choice, Bantan," the girl reminded him. She laughed softly then before adding in a low voice: "I wonder how Wanya and Lori will greet me?"

"When I tell them I owe my life to you," he answered, "they will understand. You will find, Loula, that the Beneiro and the Marja are very understanding people."

The girl sighed deeply.

"I hope so," she murmured.

Bantan's eyes studied the eastern horizon. A brightly twinkling star appearing above the waterline was to be his guide for the present. He plied his paddle with rhythmic strokes.

"Perhaps you would like to sleep, Loula," he suggested. "Tomorrow, while I sleep a short while, you may relieve me paddling."

The girl lay back and moved about until she had attained a comfortable position. Then she sighed deeply.

"Thank you, Bantan," she murmured, "for making my freedom possible."

"Pleasant dreams, Loula," he answered.

While he paddled, in his mind he was wondering about the future after reaching Marja. Strangely now, he was aware of a slight twinge of regret at leaving Mandoes Island. The Great One's retrovider was a fascinating machine, and as he now recollected the incredible events it was capable of resurrecting he began to wonder if everything had been a dream that he had experienced. The presence of the native girl in the canoe with him was assurance enough that the past events had been true.

The fact that Luane had been endowed with longevity brought a quaint smile to his lips, and he began to question himself if he wouldn't like to be endowed similarly—that he might live far beyond the natural expectancy of life's normal span. All during the night while he paddled this thought was with him.

Deep within him, though at the present he was paddling his canoe *away* from Mandoes Island, he entertained the feeling that many moons would not come to pass before he would *return*.

www.ingramcontent.com/pod-product-compliance
Lightning Source LLC
Chambersburg PA
CBHW032229010726
47494CB00002B/418